THE BEST OF
SHOLOM
ALEICHEM

THE BEST OF
SHOLOM ALEICHEM

EDITED BY
Irving Howe and Ruth R. Wisse

WASHINGTON SQUARE PRESS
PUBLISHED BY POCKET BOOKS NEW YORK

WSP A Washington Square Press Publication of
POCKET BOOKS, a Simon & Schuster division of
GULF & WESTERN CORPORATION
1230 Avenue of the Americas, New York, N.Y. 10020

Published by arrangement with New Republic Books
Library of Congress Catalog Card Number: 80-12492

ISBN: 0-671-43798-4

First Washington Square Press printing March, 1982

10 9 8 7 6 5 4 3 2 1

WASHINGTON SQUARE PRESS, WSP and colophon are
trademarks of Simon & Schuster.

Printed in the U.S.A.

ACKNOWLEDGMENTS

The publishers wish to acknowledge the following copyright holders:

"Yom Kippur Scandal," "The Clock That Struck Thirteen," "Home for Passover," and "Dreyfus in Kasrilevke," are taken from *The Old Country* by Sholom Aleichem, translated by Julius and Frances Butwin. © Copyright 1946, 1974 by Crown Publishers, Inc. Used by permission of Crown Publishers, Inc.

"The Bubble Bursts," "Chava," "Get Thee Out," and "If I Were Rothschild" are taken from *Tevye's Daughters* by Sholom Aleichem, translated by Frances Butwin. © Copyright 1949, 1977 by The Children of Sholom Aleichem and Crown Publishers, Inc. Used by permission of Crown Publishers, Inc.

"On Account of a Hat," and "Eternal Life," are from *Treasury of Yiddish Stories,* edited by Irving Howe and Eliezer Greenberg. © Copyright 1953, 1954 by The Viking Press, Inc. Reprinted by permission of Viking Penguin, Inc.

All the stories in this book are translated and reprinted with the permission of the Family of Sholom Aleichem, and their cooperation is gratefully acknowledged.

CONTENTS

PART TWO

PART THREE

PART FOUR

INTRODUCTION

How do two editors write an essay together when one lives in New York City and the other in Montreal? They follow the epistolary tradition of Yiddish literature and send one another letters. That is what we did, sent real letters that we soon began to look forward to receiving. It could have gone on almost forever, but we stopped because Sholom Aleichem said, "Enough, children, enough."

IH to RW

Reading through the Sholom Aleichem stories we have brought together, I have an uneasy feeling that this is a Sholom Aleichem seldom before encountered. Or at least, seldom before recognized. Yet the stories, apart from the few translated here for the first time, are familiar enough, part of the Sholom Aleichem canon.

The writer universally adored as a humorist, the writer who could make both Jews and Gentiles laugh, and most remarkable of all, the writer who could please *every kind of Jew,* something probably never done before or since—this writer turns out to be imagining, beneath the scrim of his playfulness and at the center of his humor, a world of uncertainty, shifting perception, anxiety, even terror.

Let no innocent reader be alarmed: the stories are just as funny as everyone has said. But they now seem to me funny in a way that almost no one has said. Certainly if you look at the essay on Sholom Aleichem by the preeminent Yiddish critic S. Niger, which

Eliezer Greenberg and I anthologized in our *Voices from the Yiddish,* you will find described there a writer of tenderness and cleverness, with a profound grasp of Jewish life (all true, of course)—but not the Sholom Aleichem I now see.

Is my view a distortion, the kind induced by modernist bias and training? I'm aware of that danger and try to check myself, but still. . . . As I read story after story, I find that as the Yiddish proverb has it, "a Jew's joy is not without fright," even that great Jew who has in his stories brought us more joy than anyone else. True, there are moments of playfulness, of innocent humor, as in the portions of the adventures of Mottel the orphan that we've excerpted here—he, so to say, is Sholom Aleichem's Tom Sawyer. But the rest: a clock strikes thirteen, a hapless young man drags a corpse from place to place, a tailor is driven mad by the treachery of his perceptions, the order of *shtetl* life is undone even on Yom Kippur, Jewish children torment their teacher unto sickness. And on and on.

Perhaps the ferocious undercurrent in Sholom Aleichem's humor has never been fully seen, or perhaps Jewish readers have been intent on domesticating him in order to distract attention from the fact that, like all great writers, he can be very disturbing.

No, he isn't Kafka, and I don't at all want him to be. (The world doesn't need more than one Kafka.) Still, aren't there some strands of connecting sensibility? When Kafka read his stories aloud, he roared with laughter. And now, in reading Sholom Aleichem, I find myself growing nervous, anxious, even as I keep laughing. Like all great humorists, he attaches himself to the disorder which lies beneath the apparent order of the universe, to the madness beneath the apparent sanity. In many of the stories one hears the timbre of the problematic.

Of course, I'm exaggerating a little—but not much. And what I'm not trying to say is merely that we now see Sholom Aleichem as a self-conscious, disciplined artist rather than merely a folk-voice (or worse yet, the "folksy" tickler of Jewish vanities). For while it is true that Sholom Aleichem is tremendously close to the oral tradition of Yiddish folklore (you once remarked that a number of his stories are elaborations, or complications, of folk anecdotes), still, that folk material is itself not nearly so comforting or soft as later generations of Jews have liked to suppose.

Given the nature of Jewish life in Europe these past several centuries, how could the folk tradition have been as comforting or soft as it has come down to us through both the popularizers and the sentimentality of people who have broken from the Jewish tradition even as they have felt drawn to it? The Chelm stories, the Hershel Ostropolier stories, the Hasidic tales, even sometimes the folk songs: all have their undercurrents of darkness. Life may have been with people, but the people often lived in fright. Sholom Aleichem, then, seems to me a great writer who, like all the Yiddish writers of his moment, was close to folk sources yet employed them for a complicated and individual vision of human existence. That means terror and joy, dark and bright, fear and play. Or terror in joy, dark in bright, fear in play.

Am I wrong?

RW to IH

Your concluding words remind me of the description by Ba'al Makhshoves (the Yiddish critic and one of Sholom Aleichem's earliest admirers), of the feeling we have when we think we've committed a terrible sin, or experienced catastrophe, and wish it were all just a dream. This, according to him, is Sholom Aleichem's incomparable achievement: he conjures up the collective anxiety and then dispels it magically, laughing the danger away.

I guess Sholom Aleichem's contemporaries took the nightmarish uncertainties for granted and enjoyed the relief he alone provided. But you're right. Nowadays his name has become such a byword for folksy good humor, innocent "laughter through tears," that we're surprised to rediscover the undertone of threat in his work. It may be, as you say, our "modernist bias" that attracts us to the darker side, but there it *is,* menacing and grotesque. There is fear, not just confusion, and guilt, a nastier emotion than sorrow. That recurring image of the sick father, once powerful but now coughing fitfully between sentences, or the humiliated teacher, never able to recover his authority, suggests the fatal weakness in the culture and—more to the point—the narrator's sense of his own shared culpability in having brought it low.

And actually, how could it be otherwise? For the author of these works is a sophisticated literary man, living at some remove from the insular and cohesive society he delights in depicting. Remember I told you how startled I was to find that all the correspondence between the author and his family, his wife and children, was in Russian, obviously the language of the home. Unlike Tevye, Sholom Aleichem encouraged his children's Russification, realizing that the centrifugal force of change would leave little of the old way of life intact. Oh, to be sure, he was still the product of "tradition," and confined to a Jewish fate. Raised in a Ukrainian *shtetl,* he later suffered the indignities of living in Kiev without a residence permit, scrambled like a thousand other Menachem-Mendels to provide for his family, fled the pogroms, joined the great migration to America. In some ways it's the very typical Jewish story. But he was also the consummate artist, working the full range of modern literary genres; the shrewd journalist, attuned to every nuance of socialist, Zionist, or assimilationist politics and polemics; the exacting editor, forging a new cultural idiom and enjoying a cosmopolitan milieu. Small wonder that there is so much masking and unmasking in his stories, so many instances of dislocation and social ambiguity. Everyone was remaking himself, with varying degrees of success. And among them was Sholom Rabinowitz, experiencing all the personal and social upheavals that as "Sholom Aleichem" he would reorder with amusing grace.

Far from distorting, your comments begin to set the record straight. And if you're particularly struck by the generally overlooked "ferocity" of the work, I'm amazed by the ingenious and *self-conscious* artist behind the widely accepted notion of the folk-voice. Take "Station Baranovich," one of the train stories we decided to include. Early Yiddish readers were likely to know that their author, the man you once called "the only modern writer who may truly be said to be a culture hero," had suffered a complete collapse at that fateful stop during a grueling speaking tour, an attack of "acute pulmonary tuberculosis" that was followed by years of convalescence. At Baranovich the great entertainer, the spellbinding story teller, had almost left the train for good.

So much for fact. What about the fiction? The story is narrated by a traveling salesman. The passengers' conversation runs appropriately grim—to pogroms, murders, anti-Jewish decrees. The interior story of a certain Kivke, alternately a victim of the czarist regime and a blackmailer of his own community, might have been used by many another Jewish writer (God save us!) to demonstrate the demoralizing effects of persecution. But Sholom Aleichem, who at Baranovich was warned of his own mortality, makes this a writer's story: the fate of Kivke and of the Jewish community are ultimately in the hands of the gifted *story teller* whose untimely departure at Baranovich constitutes the story's only really fatal event. The artist can transform reality at will—a potent charm in desperate times—but his magic is subject to temporal claims. Hilarious the story is. But doesn't it also comment bitingly on the relation of the artist to his audience and to his material, of the audience to its artists and environment, of reality to art? It even manages a stroke of revenge in its parting shot: "May Station Baranovich burn to the ground!" Our colleagues analyzing "self-reflexiveness in art" should have a field day here!

It must be some fifty years since Van Wyck Brooks drew attention to Samuel Clemens lurking behind the sprightlier Mark Twain. If anything, we're a little late in exposing the negative, the harsher "World of Sholom Aleichem" and the canny Mr. Sholom Rabinowitz behind the man with the avuncular smile. Or should we stick to the compulsively naive and cheerful? As in his, "What's new with the cholera epidemic in Odessa?"

IH to RW

We've been stressing, so far, the "modern" Sholom Aleichem, a comic writer whose view of Jewish, and perhaps any other, life tends to be problematic, rather nervous, and streaked with those elements of guilt and anxiety that we usually associate with writers of the twentieth century. To see Sholom Aleichem in this way seems a necessary corrective to the view, now prevalent in Jewish life, that softens him into a toothless entertainer, a jolly gleeman of the *shtetl,* a fiddler cozy on his roof. And insofar as we reject or at least complicate this prevailing view, it's especially important to remark that Sholom Aleichem is not a "folk writer," whatever that might mean. No, he is a self-conscious artist, canny in his use of literary techniques, especially clever in his use of the monologue, which in his stories may seem to be meandering as pointlessly as an unemployed Jew on market day in the *shtetl* but which actually keeps moving toward a stringent and disciplined conclusion.

Still we should not go too far in trying to revise the common view of Sholom Aleichem. He came out of a culture in which the ferment of folk creation was still very lively, and in which the relationship between writer and audience was bracingly intimate, certainly different from what we have come to accept in Western cultures. A good many of Sholom Aleichem's stories are drawn from familiar or once-familiar folktales and anecdotes. One of his best stories, "The Haunted Tailor," is based on such materials, though as Sholom Aleichem retells it, the story emerges intellectually sharpened and complicated. It moves in its tone toward both the grotesque and the satiric, and in characterization it progresses from folk figure to individual. Tevye the dairyman, probably Sholom Aleichem's greatest character, emerges from the depths of Jewish folk experience in Eastern Europe, yet he is far more than a representative type. Tevye is a particularized Jew with his own nuances and idiosyncrasies, even as we also recognize in him a *shtetl* Everyman.

In Sholom Aleichem, then, the balance between collectivity and individual, between Jewish tradition and personal sensibility, is very fine. Coming at the point in the history of the Eastern European Jews where the coherence of traditional life has been shattered, only to let loose an enormous, fresh cultural energy, Sholom Aleichem stands as both firm guardian of the Jewish past and a quizzical, skeptical Jew prepared (as the unfolding of the Tevye stories makes clear) to encounter and maybe accept the novelty and surprise of modern Jewish life. It's just this balance, so delicate and precarious, that I find enchanting in his work. And this may be one reason that I think of him as a "culture hero," in the sense that Dickens and Mark Twain were culture heroes in their time and place. For Sholom Aleichem embodies the culture of the Eastern European Jews at a high point of consciousness, at the tremor of awareness that comes a minute before dissolution starts.

He embodies the essential values of Eastern European Jewish culture in the very accents and rhythms of his language, in the pauses and suggestions, the inside jokes and sly references. This relationship between the writer as culture hero and the culture itself is something so intimate and elusive we hardly have a way to describe it—except to say that every Jew who could read Yiddish, whether he was orthodox or secular, conservative or radical, loved Sholom Aleichem, for he heard in his stories, the charm and melody of a common *shprakh,* the language that bound all together. The deepest assumptions of a people, those tacit gestures of bias which undercut opinion and rest on such intangibles as the inflection of a phrase, the movement of shoulders, the keening of despair, the melody of a laugh—all these form the inner substance of Sholom Aleichem's work.

Take as an example the brilliant little story, "A Yom Kippur Scandal." Wit and cleverness turn upon one another; the bare anecdote on which the story is based becomes an occasion for revealing the deepest feelings of a culture. Yet Sholom Aleichem's own quizzical voice is also heard at the end. There are at least two scandals: one that a stranger, a guest of the synagogue on the holiest of days, Yom Kippur, is robbed of a substantial sum of money (or pretends that he has been robbed); the other that a youth is a violator of the fast, discovered at the service with chicken bones hidden away. Both scandals are serious, but in the eyes of the rabbi, one of Sholom Aleichem's innocents, the first seems a sin against man, the second a sin against God, and thereby the second is the greater. Sholom Aleichem doesn't stop there, for he leaves the story up in the air—it is a characteristic narrative strategy of his—so that we don't know whether the stranger really was robbed, who did it, or how the problem was solved. As if that matters in the light of the greater scandal of the chicken bones, wildly funny as it struck many of the congregants! The story follows the Jewish habit of answering a question with another question: all life is a question, and if you ask me why, I can only answer, how should I know?

The dominant quality of Sholom Aleichem's work, then, seems to me not his wit or verbal brilliance or playfulness, remarkable as all these are; it is his sense of moral poise, his assurance as both Jew and human being, his ease in a world of excess. The image of the human, drawing upon traditional Jewish past and touching upon the problematic Jewish future, has seldom received so profound a realization as in these stories. His controlling voice tells us of madness, to be sure; but so long as we can hear *that* voice, we know the world is not yet entirely mad.

So I'd like to keep in balance the two Sholom Aleichems, the traditional and the modern, who, as we read him, are of course really one.

RW to IH

I've been thinking about your emphasis on the cultural balance and "moral poise" of Sholom Aleichem, wondering how much of what you describe derives from the historical moment, and just what is specific to him. The end of the nineteenth century, that very critical period for East European Jews, when they were still thickly rooted in their traditions but freshly vulnerable to social and political changes, provided great artists with a unique literary opportunity. Yiddish, the common language, was ripe for the kind of harvest yielded during the Renaissance, when Western European writers in an analogous period of secularization and rising national awareness, plowed their vernaculars with heady expectations of gain. There are periods when the culture and its language seem to be at just the right point of tension between maturity and untried possibilities. No accident that all three of the Yiddish classical masters—Mendele Mocher Sforim (Abramovitch), I. L. Peretz, and Sholom Aleichem (Rabinowitz)—flourished almost together.

But of the three, Sholom Aleichem alone really struck the note of balance. Mendele and Peretz were both embattled writers, fiercely critical of their society, and only gradually softened by pity, doubt, and age. As underpaid employees of the Jewish community—Mendele was a school principal and Peretz a bureaucratic official—they spent most of their adult years torn between the daily routine of duty and the personal drive for literary self-expression. The strain of this divided existence, and the resentment, shows in their work. Their writing has a strong dialectic tendency, pitting the old and new, the impulses and ideas against one another in sharp confrontations. Peretz's favorite literary arena is the law court. As for Abramovitch-Mendele, his fictional autobiography literally splits his personality in two and has the critical, crotchety intellectual facing the kindly philosophic book peddler with no middle ground between them.

Sholom Aleichem is different. Though he too felt the impending break in the "golden chain" of Jewish tradition, and felt the cracks in his own life, he makes it his artistic business to *close* the gap. In fact, wherever the danger of dissolution is greatest, the stories work their magic in simulating or creating a *terra firma*. Maybe this, in part, is what the Yiddish critic, Borukh Rivkin, had in mind when he wrote that Sholom Aleichem provided the East European Jews with a fictional territory to compensate for their lack of a national soil.

The Tevye stories, of which we include a few, provide the most striking instance of stability where one would least expect it. If you follow the line of the plot, it traces nothing less than the breakup of an entire culture. At the beginning Tevye "makes a fortune," becomes a dairyman, and begins to provide for his large family. By the end he is a widower, supporting a destitute widowed daughter. A second daughter is in Siberia, a third is a convert, a fourth has committed suicide, the fifth—who married for money—has fled with her bankrupt husband to America. Tevye is attacked (albeit mildly) by his peasant neighbors and forced to flee from the land to which he feels he has as good a claim as anyone. He says, "What portion of the Bible are they reading this week? *Vayikro?* The first portion of Leviticus? Well, I'm on quite another chapter. *Leykh lekho:* get thee out. Get going, Tevye, they said to me, *get out of thy country and from thy father's house,* leave the village where you were born and spent all the years of your life and go—*unto the land that I will show thee*—wherever your two eyes lead you!" Pretty bitter stuff! God's mighty prophecy to Abraham of a promised land is applied by Tevye to himself with the caustic inversion of all the terms. This is Lear on the heath, but as his own jester. Tevye, who is actually defenseless against the barrage of challenges and attacks that lay him low, should have been a tragic victim. Instead, balancing his losses on the sharp edge of his tongue, he maintains the precarious posture of a comic hero.

All Tevye's misquotations, puns, and freewheeling interpretations that cause such hardship to even our best translators have been offered as proof of his simplicity and ignorance. Ridiculous! Tevye may not be the Vilna Gaon, but he is the original stand-up comic, playing to an appreciative audience of one: his impresario, Sholom Aleichem, who then passes on this discovered talent to us readers. Tevye has been endowed with such substantiality, so much adaptive vigor of speech and vision, that the dire events he recounts almost cease to matter. He gives proof of his creative survival even as he describes the destruction of its source. (I thought it was very fine when the Broadway production of *Fiddler on the Roof* placed Tevye, in the finale, on a revolving stage, as though he were taking his world along with him wherever he went.)

This character worked so well for Sholom Aleichem

it's not surprising that he created other versions of Tevye, including the narrator of "A Thousand and One Nights" whom we're introducing here. Yankel Yonever of Krushnik is another sturdy father, telling Sholom Aleichem the sorry tales of his children—only here the events are uglier and deadlier. The Jews are trapped between the anti-Semitic Cossacks and the invading Germans in the murderous chaos of World War I. The survivors, Yankel the narrator and Sholom Aleichem his listener, are in flight from Russia, suspended aboard ship in midocean with no ground at all underfoot. Yet even here the effect is one of moral and psychological balance, though the author has gone as far as he can go in achieving it. Yankel describes how the venerable rabbi was murdered by the Cossacks and left hanging for three days in the public square. This is the kind of brutal reality Sholom Aleichem had always avoided, and, in fact, Yankel says that at first he refused to pass the square, unwilling to witness the shame with his own eyes. When he finally goes, though, what does he see? Not the terrifying symbol of Cossack might, but the rabbi *"hanging shimenesre,"* the eighteen benedictions. Whereas ordinary Jews stand in their daily recitation of these blessings, the rabbi sways back and forth in an ultimate act of devotion. The image is so comfortingly homey; it domesticates the violence and shows us the rabbi as we can bear to look at him. Without inflated rhetoric, it also transforms a vile humiliation into triumphant martyrdom. It's just the turn of the phrase that does it, the simple substitution of "hanging" for "standing" *shimenesre* in one of the commonest Yiddish terms for praying. The English, because of the need for explanation, has to work almost too hard for the required effect, pressing on consciousness as a deliberate interpretive act. In Yiddish the redemption seems effortless.

Reading the last chapters of Tevye and this ironic version of Sheherezade, the tales of "A Thousand and

One Nights," all written during Sholom Aleichem's final years, I wonder whether he could have kept the "comedy" going much longer. It is almost impossible to avoid sentimentalizing on the one hand or falling into cynicism on the other when attempting a balanced humanism in the face of this kind of barbarity.

IH to RW

I know we have to be moving along to the literary aspects of Sholom Aleichem's work: his inventiveness with language, his fondness for the monologue as a narrative form, his curious habit of seeming to end a story before it comes to climax. But I can't resist a few more words on the matter of "moral poise"—by which, of course, we mean not some abstract doctrine but a vibrant quality of the stories themselves, communicated through details of language. It's when you come to Sholom Aleichem's stories about children that you see how balanced, at once stringent and tender, severe and loving, is his sense of life.

Some of the children's stories, like "Bandits" and "The Guest," are not at all carefree. Their dominant tone is nervousness and fright, their dominant theme, the enforced discovery, at too early an age, of the bitterness of the world. Sholom Aleichem does not hesitate to register the psychic costs of traditional Jewish life, costs in denial, repression, narrowness. But there are other stories, happier in voice, where the life-force, the child's sheer pleasure in breathing and running, breaks through. In the group translated as "Mottel the Cantor's Son," from which we've taken a few self-contained portions, the tone is lighthearted and playful. If Tom Sawyer could speak Yiddish, he'd be at home here. It's as if Sholom Aleichem were intent upon reminding his Jewish readers that we too deserve a little of the world's innocence.

Mottel represents the sadly abbreviated childhood of

the traditional *shtetl,* where life does not flow evenly
from one phase of experience to another, but all of
them, childhood, adolescence, and manhood, are com-
pressed into one. But Mottel does not yet know this, or
pretends not to know it—who can be sure which? He is
a wonderful little boy, celebrating his friendship with a
neighbor's calf and stealing apples from the gardens of
the rich. He is full of that spontaneous nature which
Jewish upbringing has not yet suppressed ("Upon one
leg I hop outside and—naturally straight to our neighbor's calf"). But he has an eye for the life about him; he
is beginning to seep up that quiet Jewish sorrow which
is part of his life's heritage ("That's an old story: a
mother's got to cry. What I'd like to know is whether all
mothers cry all the time, like mine"). Perhaps in a kind
of tacit rebellion against the heaviness, the weighted
ethicism, of Jewish life, Sholom Aleichem makes Mottel into something of a scamp, especially in the breezy
chapters we've excerpted here, where Mottel, after the
death of his father the cantor, becomes a little business-
man, selling the cider and ink that his overimaginative
brother manufactures ("Jews, here's a drink:/ Cider
from heaven / If you order just one / You'll ask for
eleven").

The Mottel stories are notable because the note they
strike is heard infrequently in Yiddish literature. The
hijinks of an adventurous boy, so favored in American
and English writing, is something (I would guess) that
Sholom Aleichem chose to write about only after con-
scious deliberation, as if to show his fellow Jews in
Eastern Europe and in the American slums what life
might be, or in their long-lost youth might once have
been. In his autobiography Sholom Aleichem writes
about childhood pleasures: ". . . this is not meant for
you, Jewish children! Yellow sunflowers, sweet-smelling grass, fresh air, fragrant earth, the clear sun—forgive me, these are not meant for you. . . . " Mottel
shows us what has been lost.

Still, even in the saddest and most burdened Yiddish writing, there is something else shown about the life of Jewish children, and now, in retrospect, this seems to form an overwhelming positive contrast to the literatures of our century. In Yiddish literature the family is still a cohesive unit; fathers may be strict, mothers tearful, brothers annoying, but love breaks through and under the barriers of ritual. If there are few carefree children in Yiddish literature, there are few unloved or brutalized children.

Perhaps all that I'm saying is that in the world of Sholom Aleichem there are still some remnants of community. And this gives him strength and security as a writer; simply because he is so much at home with his materials, he can move from one tone to another. The Mottel stories can be casual, offhand, charming, even mischievous, but then suddenly Sholom Aleichem will drop to a fierce irony, a harrowing sadness. At the end Mottel and his family are aboard ship for America. All is fun, pranks, jokes, and then comes a brief lyrical description of a Yom Kippur service in the hold of the ship, "a Yom Kippur," says this Jewish little boy, "that neither God nor man would ever forget." And it is a token of Sholom Aleichem's genius, his "moral poise," that we are entirely prepared to accept the claim that these words come from the same boy who sells cider and ink and hops on one leg toward the neighbor's calf.

RW to IH

The other day I came across a 1941 essay by Max Weinreich that runs oddly parallel to some of our main concerns. I say "oddly" because as a linguist Weinreich was dealing strictly with Sholom Aleichem's language and linguistic influence: yet he too concludes that the folksiness of Sholom Aleichem received undue attention and had a deleterious effect on its imitators, while the hard precision and richness of his language have gone almost unnoticed. Weinreich argues that the compulsive association of Yiddish with joking—an unfortunate tendency among modern Jews—has prevented a deeper appreciation of the master's verbal craftsmanship and artistic range.

It does seem that in its literary imitations of the voices and mannerisms of ordinary Jews, Sholom Aleichem's oral styles were almost *too* effective. Even sophisticated readers were so amused and dazzled by the natural flow of the language that they considered the writer to be a ventriloquist, his art a superior form of realism. As if Sholom Aleichem had anticipated the tape recorder!

This may be a compliment in its way, but in fact, the "artless garrulousness" of the characters is under surprisingly tight control, and in ways that translation may sometimes have to sacrifice. What, for example, can we do with the opening sentence of *"Dos tepl"* ("The Pot")—that famous Sholom Aleichem monologue: *"Rebbe! Ikh vil aykh fregn a shayle vil ikh aykh!"* Natural English can't attempt much more than "Rabbi, I've come to ask you a question." But the original circles back on itself, rather like this: "Rabbi, I want to ask you a question is what I want to do." The woman's circular style is the most accurate literary expression of the closed circle of her thoughts and her life. She labors within the same rounds of work and obligation set out for her by her mother; her son is dying of the very illness that claimed her husband; her poverty traps her in such narrow constraints of time and space that she cannot grasp those very possibilities that might mitigate her poverty. Above all, her mind is imprisoned in its own obsessive circularity, unable to come to the point even long enough to pose her question. Though her speech may be generally "true to life," it is actually used to give truth to her particular embattled consciousness, self-protecting and self-defeating in equal measure, and preoccupied with impending death.

At some point we would also have to admit that Sholom Aleichem's success as a stylist has frustrated our editorial choices, at least in part. The sly mockery of American Jewish assimilation, rendered through the crude, overeager borrowings of Yiddish immigrants fresh off the boat, falls flat in English, the host language. It's also difficult to distinguish in translation, as Sholom Aleichem does in the original, the many degrees of social climbers who oil their Yiddish with Russian phrases to ease the way up, and then slip comically on their malapropisms and mistakes. Sholom Aleichem's speakers are characterized as much by the quality of their language as by its apprehended meaning. I doubt that any translation can get this across.

In addition to being a marvelous tool, Yiddish is also Sholom Aleichem's metaphor for the culture. While many of his contemporaries and even some of his successors were hampered by the novelty of Yiddish as a modern literary language, Sholom Aleichem turned the fluidity and newness of Yiddish prose style to penetrating advantage. What better medium for conveying the critical changes of East European Jewish life than a "language of fusion"—to use Max Weinreich's term—in which the sources of fusion are still identifiable and in active flux? Sholom Aleichem uses the nuances of Yiddish to communicate the degree to which a speaker is integrated into the traditional culture or deviates from it in any direction—toward the "German" enlightenment, the Slavic identification with the folk, or the higher pretensions of St. Petersburg society. From the speaker's tendency to use certain aspects of the German or Slavic components of the language, one can determine his origins and aspirations, his relation to the values of his home, and the lure of the environment.

Yet too extreme an emphasis on the Hebraic element, the most indigenous component of Yiddish, is not a good sign either. Characters who affect too traditional a language are either sanctimonious hypocrites, like the members of the Burial Society in the story "Eternal Life," or con-artists of whom Sholom Aleichem provides a peerless variety. The positive characters are those who tend neither inward nor outward but speak a perfectly balanced tongue.

For Tevye, the most trustworthy of Sholom Aleichem's speakers, the fused elements of Yiddish are an eternal delight. Like a true musician, he enjoys showing the speed and grace with which he can skip from one note or one tone to another. His best jokes and quotations are polyglot, drawing attention to their mixture of high and low, old and new, indigenous and imported. He can use these combinations to achieve both comic and sentimental effects.

Even this technique of linguistic crosscutting, however, does not automatically guarantee a reliable character. Shimon-Eli, the haunted tailor, is like Tevye, a man who loves to speak in quotations which he translates, or mistranslates, or occasionally invents. His level of speech, like Tevye's, reveals his limited *cheder* education, his easy familiarity with the tradition, and an intellectual reach that exceeds its grasp. But Shimon-Eli uses quotations and linguistic jokes as clichés, the same stock phrases reappearing whoever the listener and whatever the situation. He moves instinctively back and forth through his repertoire, just as he passes through the same phases of his journey over and over again without reflection or insight. At the end, his failure to adapt, his application of tried explanations instead of fresh, deductive questions, dooms him to madness. Tevye's movement through levels of speech is the manifestation of his adaptive intelligence. Shimon-Eli's automatic movement through a similar set of paces is the surest sign of his stultification.

By the end of the nineteenth century, I. L. Peretz, who was quickly becoming the dominant influence in Yiddish literature, tried to stabilize a literary language for the purposes of normal narration. He drew attention away from the specificities of Yiddish, away from its folk expressions, the interplay of its source languages, the different dialects and levels of its various speakers. In Peretz's stories a Lithuanian rabbi and a Polish Hasid speak the same Yiddish.

But for Sholom Aleichem the unfixed nature of Yiddish was its greatest attraction, and its infinite range of dialects and oral styles the best literary means of capturing the dynamic changes—or the resistance to change—in the culture. There are times, reading Sholom Aleichem in the pulsating original, when I think we ought to have put out a Yiddish reader for the fortunate few who can use it, leaving translation to the gods.*

---

*The difficulties of translating Sholom Aleichem are almost beyond recounting. They go far deeper than the problem of rendering Yiddish idiom into English, a problem sometimes solved by finding enough English equivalents, and more often acknowledged as beyond solution because the Yiddish idiom is so deeply planted in Jewish tradition it is virtually untranslatable. A more serious problem is that of rendering the Hebraic component, which in some stories like "The Haunted Tailor" and "Tevye Strikes It Rich," is crucial to the development of both narrative and meaning.

Previous translators have simply evaded this problem by omitting the Hebrew, either in translation or transliteration, and the result has been a serious impoverishment of the work. In the present volume such gifted translators as Leonard Wolf and Hillel Halkin struggle heroically with this difficulty, each employing a different approach. What compounds the difficulty here is that the relationship between the two languages, Hebrew and Yiddish, is so complex: at some points they are two separate languages, though historically linked, but at other points they form a linguistic continuum. Yet we may also be certain that for some of Sholom Aleichem's Yiddish readers these Hebrew passages, many of them taken from the Bible and some cleverly distorted for comic effect, were almost as inaccessible as they are for most English readers. The jokes, then, are not only on one or another character, but also on us, readers who have lost or abandoned the tradition.

IH to RW

In talking about Sholom Aleichem's stories, we both remarked on the seeming oddity that many of them do not really end. Especially in those told by an internal narrator (a character who is seen and heard telling a story either to other characters or to "Mr. Sholom Aleichem"), there is roughly the following sequence: the stories move toward climax, they arouse suspense, they bring together the elements of conflict, and then, just when you expect the writer to drive toward resolution, they seem deliberately to remain hanging in the air. They stop rather than end. And this happens often enough to make us suspect that it cannot be a mere accident or idiosyncrasy. Sholom Aleichem is a self-conscious artist and he must have had something in mind. Thus, in "A Yom Kippur Scandal" we never really find out who stole the money; in "The Haunted Tailor" we are spared following the central figure to his fate; and in "Station Baranovich" the story teller provocatively refuses to complete his story. What is this all about? I have a few speculations:

1. Sholom Aleichem is persisting in the old tradition of oral story telling (though, in fact, he is a literary artist and not an oral story teller) which takes pleasure in leading the listener on, teasing him further and further. Then, as if to demonstrate the emotional power of the narrator or the moral perplexities of existence, there is a sudden, abrupt blockage—as if to say, figure out the rest for yourself, make up whatever denouement you can, it's all equally puzzling. . . .

2. Sholom Aleichem is suggesting rather slyly that, really, there are far more important things in the world than the resolution of an external action, suspenseful and exciting though it may be; indeed, what one learns along a narrative journey matters more than the final destination. Thus in "A Yom Kippur Scandal" the

question of the visitor's money—was it ever really there? did someone steal it? is he a confidence man?—counts for very little in comparison with the scandal, the shocked laughter, when it is discovered that one of the *shtetl's* pious young favorites has been secretly nibbling on chicken bones during the fast day of Yom Kippur. And the reasoning is obvious once you ponder it: the money is merely a worldly matter, while the behavior of the youth raises an issue of faith.

3. Sholom Aleichem often uses in these stories a narrating figure that might be called "the clever Jew," one who is rather worldly though still tied to some of the old ways of piety. This narrator has "been around," as merchant or traveler. In his ambiguous person he seems to straddle old world and new. Almost always there is a duel between the narrator and his audience of gullible and/or skeptical listeners within the story; or between the narrator and the readers of the story, who are in effect challenged to figure out what to make of him; or sometimes, one ventures to say, between the narrator and Sholom Aleichem himself, who stands somewhat bemused by his own creation. The puzzlement this narrator spins out in a story like "A Yom Kippur Scandal" becomes a trail toward evident laughter and possible wisdom. In "Eternal Life" the narrator is now an experienced man, one of those solid but still reasonably pious merchants that Yiddish writers liked to use as the center of their fictions. He recalls the foolishness but also the charming innocence of his youth; and if he now flees from the prospect of seeking "eternal life," is that, within the bounds of the world view by which he purports to live, so entirely a gain in maturity and rightness? In "Dreyfus in Kasrilevke" the narrator is placed within the action; he tells his "stories" (the reports he reads in the paper about the Dreyfus case) to other Jews in the little *shtetl* of Kasrilevke. At the end they refuse to believe him; they cannot credit so gross an injustice. In their "rejection" of this narrator figure, Sholom Alei-

chem has created an overpowering moment, a deeply poignant image of the Jewish refusal to believe in the full evil of the world. The "clever Jew" is thus shown in many aspects—complicated, quizzical, problematic.

4. Sholom Aleichem uses, as I've said, traditional devices of oral story telling, but he is also a sophisticated writer very much aware of his departures from that tradition. He can no longer regard a story as something that is always fixed, secure, knowable (e.g., the rebellious clock in "The Clock That Struck Thirteen," a wonderfully appropriate and homey image for the sense of collapsing order). Sholom Aleichem lived at a time when stories could be begun but not always brought to an end. Before him stories could be brought to an end; after him they could hardly be begun. What, then, one wonders, would he have made of Cocteau's remark that "Literature is a force of memory that we have not yet understood"? Perhaps he would have amended the last clause to "that we can no longer understand."

5. Sholom Aleichem knew intuitively that the boundary between comedy and tragedy is always a thin and wavering line—and for Jews, often nonexistent. Almost all of his best comic stories hover on the edge of disaster. All exemplify the truth of Saul Bellow's remark that in Jewish writing "laughter and trembling are so curiously intermingled that it is not easy to determine the relations of the two." Reading Sholom Aleichem is like wandering through a lovely meadow of laughter and suddenly coming to a precipice of doom. At the end of "The Haunted Tailor" we have a vista of madness, at the end of "A Passover Expropriation" a prospect of social violence, at the end of "A Yom Kippur Scandal" the shame of Jewish disintegration. Sholom Aleichem takes us by the hand, we are both shaking with laughter, and he leads us. . . . "And would you like to hear the rest of the story?" asks one of his narrators. "The rest isn't so nice." Assuredly not.

RW to IH

I appreciated your speculations on Sholom Aleichem's endings and narrative art. As a mundane footnote, one could also note the influence in this—as in every conceivable linguistic, stylistic, and narrative aspect of Sholom Aleichem's work—of Mendele Mocher Sforim, the man he dubbed the grandfather of modern Yiddish literature, the man who was really his own artistic progenitor. Indeed some of Mendele's finest work, also in the oral tradition, does not seem to end; but Sholom Aleichem draws attention to the inconclusiveness of his conclusions in a way his forerunner did not. It's as you say: he actively challenges our notion of the denouement or solution and avoids the verdict, the finality, of what would usually be an unhappy fate.

In general, Sholom Aleichem did not do very well with a direct approach to the great, climactic, and decisive moments of plot. When he did attempt a big love scene, or a tough social confrontation, he could be surprisingly inept. You have only to look at one of his earliest efforts, the thinly disguised autobiographical novella where the wealthy young heroine, who has been playing fantasias by moonlight, rushes through the garden and into the arms of her indigent tutor to the following momentous dialogue:

He: Polinka!
She: Rabovsky!

Impossible to read the scene without laughing—at the author's expense.

Lest this seem just the failure of a novice, one could turn to a ripe novel, like *The Storm* (1905), where Sholom Aleichem depicts the ideological clashes among the Jews in pre-Revolutionary Russia. At the moment of intended climax, when the Zionist hero is to win over the uncommitted heroine to both his politics and himself, he can do no better than to stop in the middle of the street, whip from his pocket a famous poem by Chaim Nachman Bialik, and *read* her its text for the better part of the chapter! It is not that Sholom Aleichem avoided the romantic subject, the heroic possibility, the grand style of the novel: he was simply unconvincing and demonstrably *uncomfortable* in this mode, especially at the high points of resolution, and of course, conclusion.

No, his mastery is of quite the opposite order. Beginning with no more than an anecdote, sometimes an item that his adoring readers sent him, sometimes a joke that already had whiskers on it, he would invent a speaker, give him a story to tell and the merest pretext for a tale—the amusement of a fellow passenger, the enlightenment of a stranger to town, etc. The story would be either about himself, or more often, about a third party, someone from his *shtetl* perhaps, more of a character type than a differentiated personality. And if that were not layered and indirect enough, the speaker would tell the story not to the readers, but to an intermediary who was often the author's invented self, this all-embracing soul called "Sholom Aleichem." Veiled, then, like Salome, the anecdote begins its tantalizing, captivating play, a dance of words that is meant to leave you, as the author boasts, laughing your head off!

The kernel "story" of "On Account of a Hat," one of your favorites, I know, was once told to me as a regional Jewish joke, in about ten seconds. Out of this insubstantial matter, Sholom Aleichem has woven a masterpiece with a dozen interpretations: it is the plight of the Diaspora Jew, an exposure of rootlessness, a mockery of tyranny, the comic quest for identity, a Marxist critique of capitalism, and, of course, an ironic self-referential study of literary sleight of hand. . . . It's easy to mock the highfalutin readings this story has received, but those who catch its serious import are not wrong either. Magically witty and unpretentious as it is, the story leaves you with an eerie, troubling sense of reality that begs attention. (Isaac Bashevis Singer, whose anecdotal style owes much to Sholom Aleichem, occasionally forces the serious micn of his stories with sermonettes on good, evil, and the meaning of existence. In Sholom Aleichem, you get no such prompting.)

What we have is an author who works best by indirection, in the smaller modes of fiction, from the worm's angle of vision, and with apparently flimsy materials. Even the main, archetypal figures of Sholom Aleichem are not full-blown heroes of novels, but characters or speakers in short story sequences, written over a period of years and later assembled in book form. The stature and personalities of Tevye, Menachem-Mendel, Mottel the Cantor's Son, as well as the town of Kasrilevke (Sholom Aleichem's fourth, collective "hero"), emerge from a run of episodes, each only slightly different from the one before it, that cumulatively establish their dimensions. As distinct from the normal novel, which develops a single architectonic structure, growing from introduction to a central point of resolution, Sholom Aleichem's major works beat like waves against a shore, one chapter resembling and reinforcing the last in variations of a theme. The normal novel lays human destiny out as a one-way trip, with important encounters, intersections, and moments of decision that determine one's rise or fall, success or failure, happiness or misery. The major works of Sholom Aleichem have no such suspenseful vision. A man is what he is to begin with—even Mottel, the child. He confronts all the things that happen to him and forces himself upon life again and again, and the sum of these trials shape the rhythm, constitute the meaning, of his existence.

It's the old literary knot of form and content. Sholom

Aleichem's admiration for the stubborn ruggedness of Jewish faith and the surprising vitality of the people comes to expression not just thematically, in story after story, but in the resilient, recuperative *shape* of all his major works.

Before ending, I should tell you that this serious correspondence of ours about Sholom Aleichem appeared to me the other day in a comical light. I was lecturing about Sholom Aleichem to a nice synagogue audience, and every time I illustrated a point with a quotation or the plot of a story, the audience broke into happy, appreciative laughter. After a while I must admit I found myself adding quotations and dramatizing more stories to elicit that laughter, and when the lecture was over, people came over to tell me what a good story teller I was!

You see the point. Expostulate on Kafka or Dostoevsky and people are fairly begging for your explanations and interpretations. Lecture on any other Yiddish writer—Mendele, Peretz, Asch, Grade, the brothers Singer—and your words will illumine, clarify, edify. But set out to discuss the "narrative structure" or "comic techniques" of Sholom Aleichem, and he undercuts your very best attempt. I have the uncomfortable feeling that readers may look through these letters not for any insights, but for their illustrative examples. And Sholom Aleichem would be right behind, egging them on. Consider the deliberate irreverence of his literary memoir, *Once There Were Four,* and contrast this mountaineering saga of Jewish writers with all the high, serious climbs of other European literati. He gives us no disquisitions on literature, no pen portraits of his contemporaries, no contemplative philosophy from the heights. Just four "anecdotes" on the subject of forgetting, in which three of the greatest Jewish writers of the age, and one choleric literary companion, are revealed as ordinary, anxious Jews, faltering and trembling in ordinary, if not humiliating circumstances. He deflates intellectual and artistic pretentiousness, and even undercuts the grandeur of the Alps!

We set out—I think justifiably—to take a serious new look at a well-known but not well-appreciated author. What confronts us, finally, is the quizzical smile of the author, compulsively skeptical about everything but the story.

PART
ONE

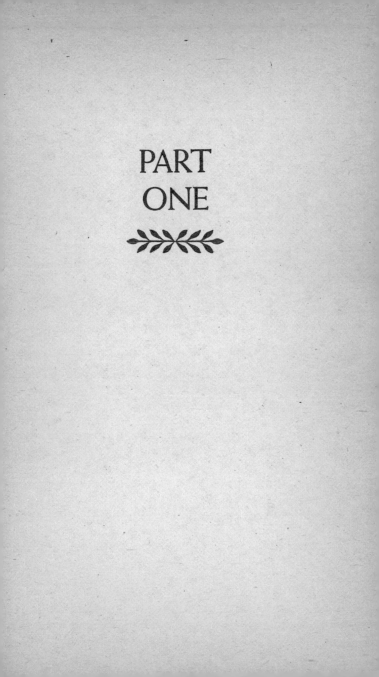

THE HAUNTED TAILOR

Ish Hoyo Be-Zolodievka, there was a man in Zolodievka, a village near Mazapevke, not far from Hapla-
povitch and Kozodoievka, between Yampoli and
Stristch, just on the way from Pistchi-Yavadeh to
Petschi-Khvost to Tetreve and from there to Yehupetz.
U'shmo Shimon-Eliyohu, and his name was Shimon-
Eli, but he was called "Shimon-Eli *Shma-Koleynu*"
because when he said his prayers in the synagogue he
had a way of working himself up, putting a trill into his
prayers and singing them at the top of his voice. *Vehoyo
hoish khayet,* and the man was a tailor—not, God forbid, one of those "ascended" tailors who sew according to the latest fashions. Rather, he was a genius patch
tailor who could make a hole or a patch invisible. He
could, for example, take an old caftan and turn it into a
cloak; then the cloak into a pair of trousers; of the
trousers he could make a shirt; and of the shirt something else again. Don't think that's such easy work—

"Untranslatable" is the translator's constant complaint, after which
he goes back to work. What I have not been able to retain in this
English version of "The Haunted Tailor" is the especially corrosive
quality which Shimon-Eli's frequent—and frequently mistaken—
quotations in Hebrew give to the story. It pleases me to believe that
Sholom Aleichem's genius has overleaped my limitations.

—*Translator's Note.*

3

and it was on this account that Shimon-Eli *Shma-Ko-leynu* was a somebody in his world, since Zolodievka was a very poor village where the making of a new suit was not so frequent a matter. In Zolodievka, therefore, they thought the world of him.

However, he had one fault—he could not get along with the well-to-do and the authorities. He liked to meddle in communal business, taking always the side of the village poor. He spoke openly against the philanthropists who busied themselves with the public welfare; and he publicly maligned the tax gatherer, calling him a money-leech, a bloodsucker, a cannibal. As for the rabbis and the ritual slaughterers, the tax gatherer's accomplices, he called them a gang of thieves and liars, deceivers, killers, gangsters, highwaymen—may the devil take them and their fathers' fathers to the generation of grandfather Terah and Uncle Ishmael into the bargain.

Among the laborers and guildsmen, Shimon-Eli *Shma-Koleynu* was thought of as a scholar. For them this meant that he was someone who understood the small print of Torah explication, because Shimon-Eli liked to sprinkle his speech with passages—sometimes whole chapters—of *Gemara,* of *Midrash* made out of whole cloth: "The people . . ." . . . "I am small . . ." . . . "Today the world was created . . ." . . . "Here you are, creator of all light . . ." . . . and other such words which he always had ready at hand. On top of all this he had a tolerably good, if somewhat loud, voice, tending toward a treble. He understood all the styles of prayer and knew all the melodies and variations by heart.

He was madly eager to get at the podium.

He was also the president of the tailor's synagogue, which cost him blows from time to time, particularly on Simkhas-Torah during the *Ato Horeyso* prayer when those who did not get to carry a Torah vented their anger at him.

All his life Shimon-Eli had been poor, but the fact had

never disheartened him. On the contrary, he liked to say, "Where there is poverty, there is life;" "Where there is hunger, there is song." As the *Gemara* says: "Poverty fits a Jew like a red handkerchief on a pretty girl." In short, Shimon-Eli was one of those of whom it is said that he was poor but happy.

He was short and ugly and his clothes were always stuck around with needles and pins. There were bits of cotton clinging to his curly black hair. He had a little goatee, a flattened nose, and there was a groove down his lower lip. His eyes were large, black, and constantly smiling. He moved with a little dance step and with a melody under his breath: *"Ha'yom haras oylem,* the world was created today—nothing to worry about."

Vayhi lo bonim u'vonoys, and he had sons and daughters. He was burdened with children of all sizes, most of them female, some of them already grown.

Sheym ishto, his wife's name was Tsippa-Beila-Reiza. She was altogether his opposite, a Cossack of a woman. From the day of their wedding she took Shimon-Eli in hand and never let go. She wore the pants, not he. He had tremendous respect for her. When, as she could do, she opened her mouth at him, he simply shivered. But more. When there was no one to see, she did not hesitate to give him a slap or two. Shimon-Eli tucked the slap into his pocket, saying *"Ha'yom haras oylem,* the world was created today— nothing to worry about." "It is written in the holy Torah, 'And he, that is to say, the husband . . . he will reign over you. . . .' Well . . . well . . . never mind. If all the kings from West to East came, it wouldn't help matters."

It happened one day that Tsippa-Beila-Reiza came home from the market. She threw her basket with her few purchases—a bit of garlic, some parsley, a few potatoes—to one side and cried angrily, "To hell with it. Racking one's brain every day thinking what to cook. You need to be smart as a prime minister. Beans and

dumplings, dumplings and beans, and again beans and
dumplings. May God not punish me for these words.
And all the while Nekhama Brukha—a poverty-
stricken, penniless, indigent, needy pauper of a
woman—*she* has a goat. Why does *she* have a goat?
Because she has a husband, Lazer Shloimo—also a
tailor—but he's a man!

"No small matter, a goat. Nothing trivial about it.
When there's a goat in the house, the children can have
a glass of milk. One can cook up some groats and milk,
and a meal becomes an easy matter. You can manage
the evening meal. And you can have a pitcher of sour
cream, some cheese now and then, some butter. One
can live."

"You're right, no doubt," Shimon-Eli said gently.
"There is a saying, 'Every Jew should have a goat.' As
it is written."

Tsippa-Beila-Reiza shrieked, "I say a goat and he
gives me a quotation. I'll give you quotations . . . I'll
quotation your eyes! He feeds me quotations. My fine
breadwinner, my *schlimazel*. I'll give you the entire
Torah for a cream borscht."

And the like. And so on. She gave him such lectures
several times a day until Shimon-Eli gave her his word
that, with God's help, she should have a goat. She could
sleep soundly on it.

From that time Shimon-Eli saved groschen upon groschen. He denied himself necessary things. He pawned
his sabbath caftan, on which he paid weekly interest.
Finally he had only to take the money he had saved and
go to Kozodoievka to buy a goat.

Why especially to Kozodoievka? There were two
reasons: first, the name of the town itself translated into
Yiddish means "milkgoats"; the second, Tsippa-Beila-
Reiza had overheard a neighbor to whom she had not
spoken in several years. She, the neighbor, had heard
from her Kozodoievka sister, who had come for a visit,
that there, in Kozodoievka, there was a primary school

teacher who was sardonically called "Chaim-Chono the Wise" because he was so stupid. This man had a wife, Thema Gittel, who was called "Thema Gittel the Silent," because, as it is said about women, she had nine measures of speech. And this quiet Thema Gittel had two goats, both of them milk-givers. It is natural to ask, "Why does she deserve two goats, milk-givers to boot? What would be the catastrophe should she not have so much as one? There are people who do not have so much as half a goat. Well . . . do they die of it?"

"You're very right," Shimon-Eli said to his wife. "You know . . . it's an old complaint. As it is written, 'To own is to bemoan.' "

"Just listen to him. Here he is again with his quotations," his wife interrupted. "One talks of a goat, and he quotes. You'd better go to the Kozodoievka teacher and say to him: 'We've heard that you own two goats, and both of them give milk. Why do you need two milk-giving goats? For scapegoats? No doubt, then, you must want to sell one of them. Sell it to me.' That's how to talk with him, do you understand?"

"Of course I understand. What do you mean?" said Shimon-Eli. "With money, will I have to beg? With money one can buy anything. Silver and gold will clean bastards and pigs. What's bad is when there is no money, as Rashi says, 'Daddy's not there, go to sleep.' Or as it is said, 'Without fingers you can't thumb your nose.' "

"Again a quotation, and once more a quotation. My head's quotationing. May you sink . . . ," said his wife, Tsippa-Beila-Reiza, burying him under nine ells of earth as she rehearsed him over and over in how to talk with Chaim-Chono the teacher in case he was willing to sell. Well, and what if he was unwilling? Why should he be unwilling? Why should he be entitled to two goats, and milkers to boot? There are Jews in the world, God be praised, who do not have so much as half a goat. If so, do they die of it?

And so on and so on, always the same theme.

Two

Ha'boyker or, it was dawn. Our tailor rose eagerly, said his prayers, took his stick and a leading rope, and peacefully started off on foot. It was Sunday, a bright, lovely summer's day. It had been a long time since Shimon-Eli could remember such a delightful day, and long since Shimon-Eli had been out in the countryside in the open air—since his eyes had seen such green traceries of branches in the wood, such a lovely blanket of green fields strewn with every kind of color. It had been long since his ears had heard such a piping of birds and the flutter of tiny wings, long since his nose had smelled such fine odors of grass and freshly turned earth.

Shimon-Eli *Shma-Koleynu* spent his days in quite another world. He looked at quite different pictures: a dark cellar . . . an oven near the door . . . next to the door, shovels and spades and a slop pail filled to the brim. Next to the slop pail, a bed made of three boards on which there were many children, God be praised, each child smaller than the next, half-naked, entirely barefoot, unkempt, and always hungry. He usually heard quite other sounds: "Mama, bread. . . . Mama, a roll. . . . Mama, something to eat." And above the clamor the voice of Tsippa-Beila-Reiza, "Eat? May the worms not eat you, dear God, together with your father, that *schlimazel.* You and him together."

And other such cries. His nose was used to other smells: the dank walls which in winter were humid and in summer bred mold . . . the smells of yeast and bran, onions and cabbage, scraped fish and tripe . . . the smell of old clothes making themselves known under the steam iron—thick steam and strange odors.

Having torn himself away for a little while from that

poverty-stricken, bare, dark world to this new, bright, fragrant light, our Shimon-Eli felt like someone who, on a hot day, has plunged naked into the sea. And the sea takes him. . . . The waves move him. . . . He bobs and he dips and he drifts. . . . He takes deep breaths glorious to the soul. For all practical purposes he is in Eden.

He thinks, "Let us consider, for example . . . how would it have hurt . . . how would it have done God any harm if every working man, for instance, came out every day . . . or let's say, just once a week . . . into something like this, into the open . . . to enjoy God's little world. *Oy,* what a little world!"

And Shimon-Eli sang a little song in the Talmudic fashion: *Ato yotsarto,* Thou has created; *Oylamkho,* your world; *mikedem,* long ago; *bokharto bonu,* and Thou hast chosen us, that we might live there in Zolodievka, jammed together head to head, hardly able to breathe. *Vatiten lonu,* and Thou hast given us . . . ah, hast Thou given us, sorrows and pain, and griefs . . . and fevers and chills . . . in your great mercy . . . cy . . . cy."

Thus sang Shimon-Eli under his breath, and he was tempted to throw himself down where he stood in a field of grass to enjoy for a while God's little world. Then he remembered his mission and said, "Enough singing, Shimon-Eli, get a move on, brother. You'll have time to rest at Dodi the Rendar's Oak Tavern. There, with God's help, one can get a little whiskey—as it is written: 'The study of Torah is the culmination of all things.' " And Shimon-Eli *Shma-Koleynu* walked on.

Three

Halfway between the two towns, Zolodievka and Kozodoievka, stood the Oak Tavern. The tavern had something like magnetic power and drew to it wagon drivers and passengers. Whether they were traveling

from Zolodievka to Kozodoievka or from Kozodoievka
to Zolodievka, they all had to stop at the Oak for at least
a few moments. No one knew the secret, not to this day.
Some say that it was because the host of the inn, Dodi
Rendar, was a genial fellow—which is to say that one
could buy a good little glass of whiskey and something
good to snack on along with it. Others said that it was
because Dodi was one of those people called "finders"
or "prophets" who, though they are not themselves
thieves, are, just the same, pals of well-known crooks
such as the famous Reb Schmelke. But since no one
knew this for certain, it's better not to mention it. . . .

Dodi was one of those hairy, thickset Jews with a big
belly and a potato nose and the voice of a wild ox. A
prosperous fellow who owned cattle, he had no troubles
to plague him. In his later years he had become a
widower and was now without ties. He was a coarse
fellow who could not tell the difference between a
prayer book and a Passover manual. For this reason
Shimon-Eli was ashamed of him. He didn't like the
notion that he, Shimon-Eli, a learned man and chairman of his synagogue, was related to a toll keeper, a
common fellow. And Dodi, for his part, was just as
ashamed that he was related to a real tailor. Each was
ashamed of the other. Just the same, when Dodi saw
Shimon-Eli *Shma Koleynu,* he welcomed him warmly
because he was afraid, not so much of Shimon-Eli
himself, but of his big mouth.

"Oh, a guest, a guest. What are you up to, Shimon-
Eli? And how is your Tsippa-Beila-Reiza? And how are
the children?"

" 'Now what are we, and what is our life? How
should we be?' " the tailor replied with a citation, as
was his wont. " 'Sometimes up, sometimes down.' As
long as we're healthy, as it is written: 'Wisdom is
smoke; smoke is wisdom.' How are you, dear kinsman?
What's going on in your village? I still remember your
dumplings and the bit of liquor from last year. That's the
main thing for you, isn't it? Your kind are not fond of

looking into books. What do you care about a Yiddish word? Ah, Reb Dodi, Reb Dodi, if your father, my Uncle Gedaliah-Wolf, were to rise from his grave and see what has become of his little Dodi, lost among village Gentiles, he would die a second death. Ah, your father, your father, Reb Dodi. A devout Jew. May he forgive me, but he used to drink from a bitter cask. In short, 'There is no man without his burden.' Give us some whiskey. As the Reb Bimbon says, 'Pawn your caftan and take a little whiskey.' "

"There you go again with your hash of quotations," Dodi said, and brought him some whiskey. "You'd do better just to tell me where you're traveling."

"I'm not traveling," Shimon-Eli said, lifting his glass, "I'm walking. As we say in the Hallel prayers, 'If you have feet, are you too sick to walk?' "

"In that case, dear cousin, where are you walking?"

"I'm walking . . ." Shimon-Eli said, drinking another glass, "to Kozodoievka to buy a goat. As it is written, 'Thou shalt buy goats.' "

"Goats?" the astonished Dodi said. "How does a tailor happen to be buying goats?"

" 'Goats' is a way of speaking," Shimon-Eli said. "What I mean is 'a goat.' May God send me the proper goat—cheap, that is. I myself would not be buying a goat. But my wife, may she live long, Tsippa-Beila-Reiza, that is . . . you know her . . . when she makes up her mind she's set for all time. She wants a goat. And a wife, you will agree, must be obeyed. It is specified in the *Talmud,* of course. You remember, eh?"

"You know that as regards *Midrash,* you and I are . . . distant cousins. But there's something I don't understand. How is it that you're an expert on goats?"

"How does a Rendar come to be an authority on prayer passages?" said Shimon-Eli, irritably. "Just the same, at Passover, with God's help, you keep time to a true Yom Kippur's 'Who shall live and who shall die?' Isn't that so?"

Dodi the Rendar well understood the insult, but he bit

his lip, thinking, "Wait, wait, my tailornik, you. You're a bit too greedy today, showing off just a little too much with your Torah. Wait, I'll give you a goat . . . that will give you the itch."

And Shimon-Eli ordered another glass of that bitter drop which is the remedy for all sorrows. There's no way to avoid the truth: Shimon-Eli liked his little drop now and then—though he was no drunkard, God forbid. When could he afford a glass of whiskey? His problem was that no sooner did he have one little drop, than he immediately had to have another. Two such drops made him tipsy, and his cheeks flamed and his eyes glittered and his tongue was set to tolling without end.

"Speaking of guilds," Shimon-Eli said, "To my guild—Shears and Press-iron: the people. There's a quality to our people that makes us all want 'honor,' no matter how little. A nothing of a shoemaker yearns to be a chairman, never mind of what—even of only his garbage can. So I say to them: 'Brothers, I need it like a hole in the head. Choose some shoemaker for your chairman. Spare me the honor. I'd rather avoid the blows.' They say, 'To hell with it. If the guild decides, that's it. Take the chairmanship and take the blows.' Shhh . . . I'm wandering a bit . . . I forgot that I have a goat to buy. *'Od hayom godol,'* time does not stand still. Good-bye, Reb Dodi. 'Mighty, mighty! We will be strong!' Good-bye, be well. And remember, make dumplings."

"Don't forget," Dodi said to him, "If the Blessed Name permits on your way back—if the Lord spares us—don't forget, blessed be his name, and stop in on your way back."

"If God wills, if God wills," Shimon-Eli said. *'Bosser v'dom,'* that is, 'One is no more than flesh and blood: *Odem,* a person; *Tsipor,* a bird'—it's simple. Just you have something proper to drink and a little bite to go with it. As our motto is: 'Steam-iron and shears: the people.' "

Four

And Shimon-Eli left the Oak Tavern in high spirits. *Vayovoy,* and he arrived in peace and health in Kozodoievka. Once in Kozodoievka, he asked around for the home of Reb Chaim-Chono the Wise, who had a wife Thema Gittel the Silent, who owned two milkgoats. He did not need to ask for long, because the village of Kozodoievka was not one of those "towns of the seacoast towns," in which one could, God forbid, get lost. The whole town was spread out before one's eyes as on a plate: there were the butcher shops, the butchers with their cleavers and the inevitable dogs; there was the marketplace where stockinged women moved from one peasant woman to another, squeezing various fowl:

> *Tshuish, tshuish. A scho tobi za kurkuh?*
> *Yaka kurkuh? Tseh piven, a ne kurkuh.*
> *Nekhai budeh piven.**

Two paces beyond was the synagogue courtyard where old women with basins sat selling pears, sunflower seeds, and beans; teachers conducted their classes while children yelled; and goats, goats without end, leaped about pulling wisps of hay from thatched roofs, while other silk-bearded goats warmed themselves in the sun and chewed their cud.

Not far away was the bathhouse with its sooty walls. After that, the lake, covered with a green scum that crawled with leeches and frogs that croaked away. The lake gleamed in the sun, glistening like diamonds and stinking to high heaven. Farther on, on the other side of the lake, there was nothing but earth and sky—no more Kozodoievka.

---

*Listen, what do you want for this hen? What hen? It's not a hen, it's a rooster. All right, a rooster. How much do you want for this hen?

When the tailor entered the house of Reb Chaim-Chono the Wise, he found him at work, wearing his large fringed prayer undergarment and a pointed *yarmulke*. He was bent over the *Gemara*, leading his pupils at the tops of their voices through the *Talmud* passage "On Damages": "Now that goat, when it saw that there was food on the top of the barrel, that same goat leaped toward that same food . . ."

"Tsifra teva l'mariah dakhita dakufa d'mata," Shimon-Eli called out in Aramaic, translating at once into ordinary Yiddish: "Good morning to you, Rebbe, to you and to your students. You are studying, I see, just such a case as has brought me here. To wit, a goat. Enough. . . . I myself would not have thought of buying a goat, but my wife, Tsippa-Beila-Reiza, that is to say, has gotten it into her head once and for all that she wants a goat. And a wife, you will agree, needs to be obeyed. It is specified in the *Gemara*.

"Why do you stare at me? Because I know *Gemara*? Though I am a working man? 'You can't tell a book by its cover.' It may be you've heard of me. I am Shimon-Eli of the blessed town of Zolodievka, member of the guild and president of the tailor's synagogue, though I need the honor like a hole in the head. 'Thanks a lot,' I told them. 'You keep the honor and spare me the blows.' They answer, 'Too bad.' If the guild says so, it's done. 'Take the honor along with the blows.' I've wandered a little from my subject and almost forgot to say, '*Sholem.*' *Sholem aleichem* to you, teacher. *Sholem aleichem* to you, pupils—holy sheep, snot-nosed troublemakers, unruly mice—may you yearn to dance the way you yearn to study. Ah, ha, did I hit it right?"

Hearing these words, the pupils pinched each other under the table and made snorting noises. Actually, they were well pleased with their guest and would have been delighted had the good Lord often sent them such visitors. But Chaim-Chono the Wise was not as happy as they were. He did not like to be interrupted in the midst of things. Calling in his wife Thema Gittel, he turned his attention to his pupils and to the goat that had been nibbling at the fodder. Once more they sang at the tops of their voices: "Rabah said, 'Guilty,' and set it down that she must pay for the fodder and the barrel that was damaged."

Shimon-Eli *Shma-Koleynu,* seeing that there was no more to be had from the teacher, turned his attention to the teacher's wife, and while the goat of the *Gemara* was being interpreted on the one hand, Shimon-Eli kept up a conversation with the teacher's wife about her goats.

"I am, as you see me, a Jew—a working man," Shimon-Eli said. "It may be you've heard of me, I am Shimon-Eli, tailor of Zolodievka, member of the guild, and president of the tailor's synagogue—an honor I need like a hole in the head. 'Thanks a lot,' I told them. 'You keep the honor and spare me the blows.'

"I've come, let me say, about one of your goats. That is, I would not myself buy a goat, but since my wife, Tsippa-Beila-Reiza, that is, is set on having a goat once and for all, and since a wife, you would agree, needs to be obeyed—it is specified in the *Talmud.*"

Thema Gittel, a small woman with a nose like a bean—a nose which she continually wipes with her fingers—listened to him a while. Then, interrupting, "So you've come, I take it, to bargain with me for one of my goats. In which case, let me tell you this, my dear man: in the first place, I'm not about to sell one of my goats. Why not? Let's not deceive ourselves. For money? What is money? Money is round and disappears, while a goat . . . is a goat. Especially a goat like this. A goat? Who says it's a goat? She's a mother, I tell you, not a goat. May the Lord avert the evil eye from her. What an easy milker, and gives so much, not to speak of how little she eats. Eats! Does she eat anything? A measure of bran and some wisps of straw from the House of Study roof.

"But never mind . . . if I were to get the right price, I might consider it. Money is . . . how would you say? . . . a temptation. For money I could buy another goat, though a goat such as my goat is hard to find. A goat? She's a mother, not a goat. Never mind. No use talking. I'll bring her in and you can see for yourself."

Thema Gittel went off and brought the goat in along with a full pitcher of milk which she said the goat had given that very morning.

Seeing the milk, the tailor's mouth watered. He said, "Tell me, dear woman. *Ma yokor,* what is the price? Because if the price isn't right, I won't buy. Do you know why? Because, in the first place, I need a goat like a hole in the head. But since my wife, may she live long, Tsippa-Beila-Reiza, that is, has got it into her head once and for all. . . ."

"What difference does it make, how much?" Thema Gittel said, interrupting. Taking a wipe at her nose, she said, "Let's hear *your* price. I'll tell you something: no matter what you pay, it will still be a bargain. Do you know why? Because if you buy this goat, you'll really have a goat."

"Listen to you," the tailor interrupted. "That's just why I want to buy her, because she's a goat—not a dragon. What I mean . . . actually, I myself don't want to buy a goat. I need a goat like a hole in the head. But since my wife, may she live long, Tsippa-Beila-Reiza, that is, has taken it into her head once and for all. . . ."

"Listen to you, that's just what I've been saying," interrupted Thema Gittel, and began once more to add up the virtues of her goat. But the tailor interrupted in his turn. They went on in this fashion until their interrupting litanies merged into a hash and a mishmash: "A goat . . . a mother, not a goat . . . I myself wouldn't buy a goat . . . a measure of bran . . . she's got it in her head, once and for all . . . money is round . . . may the Lord keep her . . . what an easy milker . . . Tsippa-Beila-Reiza, that is . . . does she eat anything? . . . once and for all . . . as for the rest . . . a wisp of straw from the House of Study roof . . . a wife needs to be obeyed . . . a goat . . . a mother . . . not a goat."

"That's enough goating between you," interrupted Chaim-Chono the Wise, turning to face his wife. "Have you ever heard the like? We are right in the midst of 'On Damages,' while they 'Goat, goat, goat, goat,' One or the other of you make up your mind. Sell the goat or don't sell the goat. My head is aching with goats."

"He's right," agreed Shimon-Eli, 'Where there is Torah, there is wisdom.' Make up your mind. Who needs more speech? *'V'li hakessef, v'li hazohov.'* My money, your wares. Just say three words: one word plus two, without garbling them . . . as it is written in the prayer book for the High Holy Days."

"Who needs your explanation? Just say what you'll give for the goat," Thema Gittel said quietly, crouched like a kitten as she licked her lips.

"What I'll give . . ." said Shimon-Eli, also quietly. "What do you mean, 'Say what you'll give'? Am I some kind of a 'sayer'? I see that it is all wasted effort. I see that there's going to be no goat bought from you today. I'm very sorry to have disturbed you." And Shimon-Eli turned and made his way to the door, as if he were leaving.

"Just look at him," said Thema Gittel, taking him by the sleeve. "What's your hurry? Is the lake burning? Make up your mind. After all, it was you who started to say something about a goat. . . ."

To be brief, the woman named her price, and the tailor named his. She came down a bit; he went up a bit. One coin up, another down, until they agreed. Shimon-Eli counted out the money and tied the goat to his rope. Thema Gittel spat on the money and wished the tailor the best of luck, her eyes moving from the money to the goat and back again. Meanwhile, keeping up a constant patter, she led the tailor out of the house, where she wished him many blessings.

"Go well and be well, and use her in good health. May she be to you as she has been to me and no worse. Better there is no equal. May she last long, may she give milk and never cease to give milk."

"Amen, and the same to you," the tailor said and started toward the door. But the goat wouldn't budge. She twisted her horns about, planted her hind feet, and made a resounding bleat like a young cantor going to the podium for the first time. She sang, "Mehhh . . . what is my crime?" and "Mehhh . . . what is my sin?" as one might say, "Where are you dragging me?"

Reb Chaim-Chono the Wise, in all his dignity, using his switch, helped drive the goat from the house. The gang of students urged her on: *"Hai Kozeh! Kozeh! Pashol Kozeh,* move it."

And the tailor went on his way.

Five

Vatima'en, and she would not. The goat, that is to say, would by no means go with the tailor toward Zolo-dievka, but tore herself in the direction of home with all her force. It did her no good. Shimon-Eli yanked at her rope and gave her to understand that she was wasting her time with her turnings and bleatings. He talked to her as follows: "It is written—you have been driven into exile by necessity. Whether you like it or not, no one wants your opinion. I, too—not now, God forbid—was once a free bird, a proper bachelor, wearing a vest and boots that creaked splendidly. What did I lack? Headaches! So God said unto me: 'Shimon-Eli, crawl into your sack. Marry Tsippa-Beila-Reiza. Beget children. Darken the days of your life.' "

In this fashion Shimon-Eli discoursed to the goat as he moved along quickly, all but running. A warm breeze tugged at the lappets of his patched caftan and stole under his earlocks and caressed his beard, bringing to him the sweet fragrance of mint and rosemary, of wildflowers and herbs that had the odor of the heavens in them and to which he was anything but accustomed. In sheer ecstasy, he began his early evening prayers, reciting the *Pitum haktoyres,* in which are enumerated all good things, rattling them off nicely in a fine cantorial melody but in a different mode. All at once . . . out of no place, Satan, the tempter, whispered into his ear: "Listen to me, Shimon-Eli, you fool. Why are you standing here, singing away on an empty stomach? It's nearly night and you've had nothing in your mouth but a couple of glasses of whiskey. Also you gave your cousin your holy word that, God willing, on your way back with the goat, you'd stop in to have a bite with him. A word given is a word given. A mouth is not a boot top." And Shimon-Eli cut short "the eighteen prayers," whizzed through the *takhnun* prayer, and made his joyful way to Dodi Rendar's.

"Good evening to you, my dear cousin, Reb Dodi. I have news for you. Congratulate me—I have bought a goat. But a goat from goatland, a goat which not even our fathers goated. Look at her and judge for yourself— you are in some fashion a learned man. Well then, guess. How much do you think I paid?"

Dodi put his hand to the visor of his cap, shielding his eyes from the setting sun that was making a golden line in the sky. He studied the goat in the manner of an expert, then guessed her value at just twice what Shimon-Eli had paid for her. This made Shimon-Eli so cheerful that he slapped the Rendar across the shoulders. "Dear Reb Dodi. This time may we both live long and well—you've guessed wrong."

Dodi Rendar pursed his lips, nodded, then spat as if to say, "A bargain, a steal."

Shimon-Eli cocked his head and crooked a finger into his vest as if he were plucking a needle from it to thread. "Well, Reb Dodi. What do you say to that? Do we know our business, eh? And if you saw how much milk she gave, God keep her, you'd die on the spot."

"Rather you than me," Reb Dodi replied.

"Amen, and the same to you," said Shimon-Eli. "Now, since my welcome is so warm, kindly put the goat into your barn so no one will steal her while I finish up the evening prayer. Then we'll have a little drink and a snack. Is it not written in the *Megillah:* 'No dancing before meals'?"

"Who knows?" said Dodi. "If you say it's written, no doubt it's written. After all, you're the Torah Jew."

Having rattled off his prayers, the tailor said, "Pour a bit of liquor from that green bottle for our health's sake. 'Health is the first wisdom,' as we say in our prayers."

With a bite to eat and a little whiskey inside him, our tailor's tongue was soon unleashed. He ticked off Zolodievka, the congregation, the affairs of the synagogue, guilds, tailoring—"Shears and steam-irons: the people." He denounced the civic leaders and the rich and the way they gave orders, saying they deserved to be sent to Siberia, "or his name wasn't Shimon-Eli."

"Do you hear," he said, tangling his speech with snatches of Torah, as was his habit: "May the devil take their parents . . . our philanthropists, I mean. All they know is how to suck blood, how to flay the poor. They get a quarter of a ruble a week out of my measly three rubles. Never mind. Their time will come. They haven't paid God's reckoning. Tsippa-Beila-Reiza, my wife, tells me I'm a *schlimazel* because, if I wanted to, I could put the squeeze on them. I've had such notions myself. But who listens to a wife? In our holy Torah it is written, 'And he shall rule over you.' You know where the passage is. The words are sweet to the tongue. Listen closely: 'He, the husband that is, shall rule. . . .' Well, never mind. As it is written, 'If you are pouring, pour some more.' "

More and more, Shimon-Eli's speech wandered. His eyelids grew heavy until, to make a long story short, he leaned against the wall and dozed off with his head tipped to one side, his hands folded over his chest—

though three fingers still clung to his goatee, like a man engrossed in thought. Except that he was wheezing and snorting and whistling through his teeth—"ts . . . ts . . . ts . . . ts . . . "—nobody in the world would have said that he was sleeping.

And though he slept his mind worked on delightedly. And he dreamed that he was at home beside his work-bench, that soon there would be a touch of prosperity in his home, and the idea pleased him. Never in his life had he seen so many little pitchers of milk, so many sacks of cheese. And butter! Whole mixing bowls of butter! One day, buttermilk; one day sour cream or sour milk with whole lumps of clabber. And buttercakes without end. Milk pancakes baked in butter and sprinkled with granulated sugar and cinnamon. And the smell, the smell. . . .

Some kind of familiar smell—ugh. He felt something crawling along his neck between his collar and his ear, across his face. The something that stank tickling his nose. . . . He felt about and touched—a bedbug. He opened an eye, then another eye, and looked toward the window. Oh, oh. Trouble, damn it. It was dawn.

"That was a good nap," Shimon-Eli said, stretching. He woke the Rendar, then hurried to the courtyard, opened the barn, took the goat's rope and shot off like an arrow toward home, racing like a man pursued. Pursued by what? The devil only knows.

Six

V'hoisho, and the woman, Tsippa-Beila-Reiza, when she saw that her husband was long in coming home, could not understand it. She began to imagine, God forbid, some disaster. Highwaymen had captured her husband, taken away his few rubles, killed him and thrown his body into a ditch, while she, Heaven help her, was left an eternal *aguna*. With so many children,

God bless them, one might as well—may it happen to the enemies of Zion—drown them and oneself along with them. Such were poor Tsippa-Beila-Reiza's thoughts that night, during which she never closed an eye. When the first rooster crowed in the morning, she dressed quickly and went out. Seating herself on the porch sill, she scanned the horizon to see whether a pitying God would let her catch a glimpse of her husband. "A *schlimazel* doesn't get lost," she thought and set herself to give him the dreadful scolding he deserved. But when she saw him and saw that he was trailing a goat behind him by a rope, her anger evaporated and she called to him, "What took you so long, my little canary? My little almond cake? I was sure that by now you were six feet under, my jewel, or that some similar misfortune had overtaken you, God forbid."

Shimon-Eli led the goat into the house, untied its rope, and started on the tale of his adventures, talking a blue streak.

"Do you hear, my wife? Have I bought a goat? From goatland. Is this a goat? A goat such as our ancestors have not goated. Let them do their best, our rich folk. Still in their wildest dreams they will not see a goat like this one. As for its food, it eats nothing except once a day a measure of bran; as for the rest, a little straw from the roof of the House of Study. And does it give milk, God save her? Like a cow—and twice a day. I saw for myself a full milk basin, as I hope to live and breathe. Is it a goat? 'It's a mother, not a goat,' that's what Thema Gittel said. I tell you, the goat is a steal, but what a deal of haggling. It took all night to get her to come down, and it was like pulling teeth. Not to mention that at the beginning she simply did not want to sell a goat. I got her down to six and a half rubles."

As he spoke, Tsippa-Beila-Reiza was thinking, "*Nekhama Brukha* . . . damn the woman. Thinks she's the only one who knows how to run a proper household. Only Eli's wife also has a goat. And wait till Blumeh-

Zalteh and Khayah-Maiteh and the rest of the sister-hood . . . Oh, Lord, Lord, may they get only half the evil they wish me. Wait till they hear." Meanwhile, she fired up the stove and got buckwheat noodles cooking for breakfast. Shimon-Eli put on his *tefillin* and said heartfelt prayers with great fervor. It had been a long time since he prayed this way. He sang the hallelujahs, made cantorial trills, snapped his fingers, and woke all the children with his singing. The children, hearing from their mother that their father had bought a goat and that noodles and milk were cooking (instant "joy and happiness"), jumped from their beds, held hands, and danced about in their shirts, accompanying them-selves with a little song which, that minute, they in-vented:

> "A goat, a goat, a little goat—
> Daddy brought a little goat;
> The little goat will give mi . . . lk,
> And mama will cook noo . . . dles . . ."

Watching the children's joy, Shimon-Eli expanded. He thought, "Poor children, to yearn so for milk. Never mind. From now on they will have God's plenty. Each day a little glass of milk, and boiled groats with milk, and milk with tea. A goat is truly a comfort to one's bones. What do I care about Fishel? I can just hear the tomcat, 'No meat for you. Just bones.' Let him choke on his bones. I don't need his meat now that, God be thanked, I have milk. And what about the Sabbath? For the Sabbath one buys fish. Where is it written that a Jew has to eat meat? I've never seen such a law. If all Jews were of my mind, they'd buy goats. Then what would our little potbellied Fishel look like? The devil take his grandfather."

Thus Shimon-Eli *Shma-Koleynu* folded his *tefillin*, washed his hands, blessed the bread, and prepared himself for a feast. Suddenly the door opened and in came Tsippa-Beila-Reiza with an empty basin, her face as red as fire, angry to the bursting point, and cursing a blue streak, all of it directed at Shimon-Eli. They weren't just curses, but more like stones falling from the sky. Pitch and sulphur spewed from Tsippa-Beila-Reiza's mouth. "May the devil take your father, the drunkard, and you, too. May you turn to stone, to bone. May you land in purgatory. May a musket shoot you. May you be hanged, drowned, and burned and roasted, and be flayed and quartered! Go, you bandit, you highwayman. Go see . . . you, you . . . apostate. What kind of goat did you bring me? A black nightmare on your head, your hands, and your feet. Good God in Heaven, dear compassionate father . . ."

The rest Shimon-Eli did not hear. He pulled down his hat and left the house to discover what the catastrophe was. Outside he looked at the goat, his beautiful jewel, and the goat stood tied to the doorpost of the house, chewing his cud. Shimon-Eli stood, stupefied, thinking what to do, where to go. He thought and thought, then said, "May he be damned to his grandfather's generation, that teacher and his wife. They've found someone to make a fool of, have they? I'll give them a fool. They'll see. Oh, that teacher. One would think from looking at him that butter wouldn't melt in his mouth. A helpless fellow—so innocent. And just see what's come of it. What a story. No wonder his pupils giggled when I was sent off with the goat while the teacher's wife was wishing me milk into eternity. I'll give them a milking. I'll milk the blood of those holy worthies."

Brooding thus, Shimon-Eli *Shma-Koleynu* started back toward Kozodoievka, with the idea of giving them the comeuppance they deserved.

Passing by the Oak Tavern, he saw the Rendar at the door with his pipe between his teeth. The tailor, though he was still some distance away, burst into laughter.

"What are you celebrating?" Dodi asked him. "What's so funny?"

"Take a look if you please. Maybe you'll laugh, too," the tailor said, laughing eerily, like a man tickled by ghosts. 'Wherever there's trouble, it comes my way.' If you know what I mean. Have I had a scolding from my wife, Tsippa-Beila-Reiza, may she live long. She gave me a belly full, and on an empty stomach, too. May the teacher and his wife get some of it. You can be sure I'm not going to hold still. There will be 'an eye for an eye.' I don't like to be played for a fool. In the meanwhile, Reb Dodi, give me a glass of whiskey to ease my heart, to rinse my throat so I may have the strength to speak, and to give my soul some consolation.

"To your health, Reb Dodi, let's be Jews, that's the main thing. As it is written: *'Ha'yom haras oylem,'* 'today the world was created, nothing to worry about.' I'll show them how to play tricks. Shears and steam-irons: the people."

Dodi, innocently sucking at his pipe, asked, "Who told you it was a trick? Maybe you misunderstood each other."

Shimon-Eli fairly leaped for anger. "What are you talking about? Do you know what you're talking about? I went to them specifically to buy a goat and made it as clear as when Jacob asked for the naked Rachel: a goat, just a goat."

Dodi pulled on his pipe, shrugged his shoulders, threw up his hands as if to say, "What have I done, in God's name? Is it my fault?"

And Shimon-Eli grabbed up the rope and started off toward Kozodoievka, seething with anger.

Seven

V'hamlamed, and the teacher was at his work. That is, he sat teaching his pupils, leading them through every case in the Talmud section "On Damages." The boys' chanting could be heard all over the courtyard:

"She flicked her tail—the cow, that is—and she broke the pitcher."

"Good morning, Rebbe, to you and to your pupils," Shimon-Eli said. "Stop for a minute. It doesn't matter. The cow won't go anywhere and the pitcher won't mend itself. . . .

"Why am I standing on ceremony? You've played me a dirty trick. Never mind. I don't like such tricks. Of course, you know the story of the two Jews in the bathhouse on Friday afternoon. They were on the highest bench. One says to the other, 'Here, take my bunch of twigs and switch me.' The other took him at his word and laid on till the blood came. The injured man said, 'What are you trying to prove? If you wanted to get even with me for something while I lay naked here on the highest bench, and you had the twigs in your hand, that I can understand: but if you meant it as a practical joke, let me tell you—I don't like such jokes.' "

"What point are you making?" the teacher asked, taking his glasses off and scratching his ear with them.

"The point has to do with you and the beautiful goat you passed off on me so innocently by way of a joke. A joke like that can end by making you laugh out of the other side of your mouth. Don't think you're dealing with some kind of a simpleton. My name is Shimon-Eli, tailor of the holy community of Zolodievka, member of the guild, and president of the tailor's synagogue— Shears and steam-irons: the people."

By this time Shimon-Eli was in a frenzy. The teacher put his glasses back on and studied the tailor as if Shimon-Eli were in a fever of hallucination. The pupils, for their part, nearly choked with suppressed laughter.

"Why are you looking at me like that, as if I were a clown?" the tailor asked. "I come to buy a goat and you palm off the devil only knows what on me."

"You don't like the goat?" the teacher asked, innocently.

"The *goat!*" he said. "If it's a goat, then you're the governor."

The class exploded with laughter and Thema Gittel the Silent came in. Now the party really began. Shimon-Eli spoke; Thema Gittel interrupted. The teacher watched; the pupils roared. Shimon-Eli and Thema Gittel kept interrupting each other until Thema Gittel, in a burst of anger, grabbed the tailor by the arm. "Come," she cried. "Come to the rabbi," she said, dragging him. "Let all Jews know how a Zolodievka tailor can make trouble. How he frames innocent people."

"Yes," Shimon-Eli said. "Very well. We'll let the world know what so-called devout, *honest* people there are here, who take a stranger for all he's worth. Come along then, come on."

The teacher put on his plush hat over his *yarmulke* and all four of them went off—the tailor, the teacher, his wife, and the goat.

When the group arrived at the rabbi's house, they found him in his robe, washing his hands, just finishing the prayer one makes after using the bathroom, the *"Asher yotsar* as thou wishest. . . ." He spoke slowly, with deliberation, squeezing his words out, *"Ne'kuvim,* holes . . . *khalulim . . . kha . . . lu . . . lim,* orifices." The prayer finished, he gathered up the skirts of his robe and seated himself on a chair without a seat—an old chair, with nothing left but legs and arm-rests and rails that were as shiny and shaky as teeth still miraculously in place long after they ought to have fallen out.

Having heard the two contenders who would not let each other talk, the rabbi sent for the deputy rabbi and the ritual slaughterer, as well as various other worthies of the town. To the tailor he said, "Be good enough to tell *your* story from beginning to end. Then we can get *her* story."

Shimon-Eli was not at all reluctant to tell his story, and to tell it again and once more. To wit: that he, Shimon-Eli the tailor, of the blessed community of Zolodievka, member of the guild and chairman of the synagogue—though much against his will: "I need it like a hole in the head. But they say, 'Take the blows and be the chairman. . . .' In brief, I came to Kozodoievka to find a goat. That is, myself I didn't want a goat. I needed a goat like a hole in the head, but since I have a wife, may she live long, Tsippa-Beila-Reiza, clamoring at me, what was there to do? She wanted a goat, and a wife, don't you agree, needs to be obeyed. So I came to Reb Chaim-Chono, the Talmud teacher, and bargained with him for a goat. 'The naked Rachel was specified.' A goat, that is to say. Well, they took my rubles and passed off the devil only knows what. For fun! Fun! He, Shimon-Eli that is, hates such tricks. Perhaps you've heard the story of the two Jews who were in the bathhouse on Friday. . . ."

Here Shimon-Eli the tailor repeated the tale of the two Jews in the bathhouse, while the rabbi, the assistant rabbis, and other dignitaries laughed.

The rabbi said, "We've heard one side of the argument. Now let's hear the other."

Chaim-Chono the Wise got up, pulled his hat down over his *yarmulke* and said, "Hear me, oh assembly. The story is as follows: I was sitting teaching my pupils the tractate 'On Damages' . . . Then this Jew from Zolodievka . . . yes, this one . . . says he's from Zolodievka . . . from Zolodievka, he says . . . bids me *sholem* . . . *sholem* he bids me . . . and tells a story . . . a story he tells me . . . that he's from Zolodievka . . . from Zolodievka, that is . . . and that he has a wife . . . he has a wife, that is. Tsippa-Beila-Reiza. Yes, I think so. Tsippa-Beila-Reiza." The teacher nodded toward the tailor who, all this while, stood clasping his beard, his eyes closed and his head tilted a little to one side. He rocked back and forth, murmuring a response in his fashion, "True, certain and sure. She has all three names: Tsippa and Beila and Reiza. That's how she was named, and it's the name I've known her by for thirty long years. But . . . what else were you going to say, old friend? But you'd do better to get things straight: 'What I said and what you said.' As King Solomon puts it: 'There is nothing new under the sun.' No tricks please.''

"I don't know anything," the teacher said, frightened, pointing to his wife. "*She* talked to him. She dealt with him. She. Me, I don't know anything."

"Very well then," the rabbi said. "Let's hear what she says." Here the rabbi pointed a finger at Thema Gittel the Silent. Thema Gittel, her face suffused with red, leaned on an elbow and, gesticulating with her other hand, began an endless rapid-fire monologue.

"Listen to me, my fellow Jews. The story is as follows: This Jew, this tailor from Zolodievka, that is either—you'll pardon the expression—crazy or drunk, I don't know which. Did you ever hear such a story? A man comes to me from Zolodievka, that fellow over there. He grabs on to me like a leech and begs me to sell him a goat—God be praised, I had two. He gives me a song and dance about how he, personally, would not buy a goat; he needs it like a hole in the head. But he has a wife, Tsippa-Beila-Reiza, that is, who has taken it into her head once and for all that she wants a goat. And a wife, he says—do you see what I mean?—needs to be obeyed. So I said, 'What's that to me? If you want to buy one of my goats, I'm willing to sell it. That is, I personally would not sell a goat because what is money after all? Money is round and rolls away; but a goat is always a goat. And especially this goat. Is it a goat? It's a mother, not a goat. God bless her, how easily she milks. And talk about eating? Does she eat anything at all? Once a day a measure of bran, and after that a wisp of straw from the roof of the House of Study.' But thinking it over, it occurred to me that, after all, I had two goats, and money *is* a temptation. . . . To make a long story short, my husband, may he live long, mixed in at this point and we agreed with the tailor on a price. How much? You will want to know. May my enemies be paid as little, so help me God. And I gave him the goat. May those I love best have such a goat. She's a mother, not a goat.

"Then he comes back, the tailor, with his libel. 'It's not a goat,' he says. Enough talk. You know what? Here stands the goat. If you'll kindly lend me a milking bucket, I'll milk her right before your eyes." And Thema Gittel borrowed a bucket from the rabbi's wife and milked the goat before them all, then passed the bucket around, first of course, to the rabbi, then to the assistant rabbis, dignitaries, and other folk.

What a tumult and shouting followed—as if the heavens had split open. Some said that the Zolodievka tailor should be required to buy drinks all around; others said that wasn't a sufficient fine—the goat should be taken from him. "No," said someone else, "the goat is a goat. May they live in prosperity and honor together." "Honor," said still another. "Let's beat some honor into him, him and his cursed goat."

Shimon-Eli, seeing how matters were going, slowly edged his way out of the rabbi's house and made off.

Eight

Va-iso hakhayat es raglaim, and the tailor took to his heels and ran off with the goat, like a man pursued by wildfire, looking back from time to time to see if he was being chased. And he thanked God that he got away, free and clear.

Approaching the Oak Tavern, Shimon-Eli thought, "I'll be damned if I'll tell him what happened." And he hid the matter from Dodi.

"Well, how did it go?" Dodi asked eagerly.

"How should it have gone?" Shimon-Eli said. "They treated me with respect. Because I'm not just anybody. I really let them have it. As for the teacher, we talked a little Torah together, and it's clear that I know a little more about the fine print than he does. In short, everyone begged my pardon, and they gave me the first goat I had bought. 'Here she is. Take her for a while,' as it is written, 'Take thou this creature and give me a drink.' "

"Not only is he a boaster, he's a liar, too," thought Dodi the Rendar. "One has to play the trick again and see what he'll say then." To the tailor, Dodi said, "I've got a little really fine old cherry wine, if you're interested."

"Ah, the Messiah wine," Shimon-Eli said, licking his lips. "Let's have a bit, and I'll test its quality. Not everyone is a connoisseur of such things."

After the first glass our tailor's tongue was unleashed, and he said to the Rendar, "Tell me, my dear cousin. After all, you are a man of some experience and certainly no fool. Tell me, do you believe in magic? In delusions?"

"For instance?" Dodi said, astonished.

"For instance," replied Shimon-Eli, "in possession, in goblins, wraiths, in reincarnated creatures."

"Why do you ask?" Dodi said, affecting a simpleton's look.

"Just because," Shimon-Eli *Shma-Koleynu* said, and started off on an endless monologue about *gilguls*, warlocks, witches, devils, gnomes, wraiths, ghosts, and spirits.

Dodi appeared to be amazed. He puffed on his pipe, then spat to avert the evil eye. "I'll tell you what, Shimon-Eli, I'm going to be afraid to sleep tonight. It's true. I've always been afraid of the dead, and now you've got me believing in *gilguls* and gnomes as well."

"How can you help it?" the tailor said. "Just try not believing. Just let one of those goblins come, overturning your kneading trough, drinking your water, sucking your pitchers dry, breaking your pots, tying the fringes of your prayer garment into knots, throwing your cat into your bed so it sits on your chest like a ten-ton weight and you can't move, and when you do get up you find the cat staring into your eyes like a soul in hell."

"Enough, enough," said the Rendar, spitting and waving his hands. "I don't want to hear any more of that. Night's coming on."

"Good-bye, then. I'm sorry if I've upset you. It's not really my fault. Goodnight."

Nine

Khshebo hakhayat, arrived at home. The tailor went into his house, intending to give Tsippa-Beila-Reiza the sound scolding she deserved, but he resisted the impulse, thinking, "A woman, after all, is only a woman. Let it pass." And for the sake of peace he told his wife a handsome lie: "I'll tell you, Tsippa-Beila-Reiza, my dear, those people have tremendous respect for me. Let me not talk about the scolding I gave the teacher and his wife. I'll spare you that, though I gave them plenty. But then I dragged them off to the rabbi and his judgment was that they should pay a fine, because when a Jew like Shimon-Eli comes to buy their goat, he should be given the greatest respect. 'Because Shimon-Eli,' said the rabbi, 'is a Jew who is a somebody.'"

Tsippa-Beila-Reiza, however, had no interest in hearing how her husband had been praised. Eagerly, she went into the house to milk the *real* goat, but it was not long before she came running out, speechless. Grabbing Shimon-Eli by the collar, she gave three great thrusts that landed him outside the house, damning him and his lovely goat together.

Immediately a crowd of men, women, and children gathered around the tailor and his fine goat and learned that this goat, whose leading rope he now held, was in Kozodoievka a goat that gave milk, but no sooner did she come to Zolodievka than she stopped being a goat. Shimon-Eli swore up and down, with oaths even an apostate would have believed, that with his own eyes he had seen the goat milked in the rabbi's house and that she had given a full bucket of milk.

People in the crowd studied the goat earnestly, asked for more details, and were told the story over and over again to their amazement. Some laughed, others cracked jokes or poked fun at the tailor. Still others shook their heads, spat against the evil eye, and said, "Some goat. If it's a goat, I'm the rabbi's wife."

"Then what is it?"

"A *gilgul,* that's what it is."

The word *gilgul* was taken up by the crowd and *gilgul* tales were soon bandied about: some that had happened here in Zolodievka, in Kozodoievka, in Yampoli, in Pistchi-Yavadeh, in Khaplapovitsch, in Petschi-Khvost—all over. Who, for example, didn't know the story of Lazer Wolf's horse and how it had to be taken out of the town, killed, and buried in shrouds? And who had not heard the story of the quarter of a chicken which, when it was being served at a Sabbath meal, moved its single wing—and other such true tales?

Finally Shimon-Eli started off toward Kozo-doievka, followed by an honor guard of pupils shouting, "Hurrah *Shma-Koleynu!* Hurrah the Milking Tailor!" and holding their sides for laughter.

This wounded Shimon-Eli to the quick. Bad enough the ill luck that had come his way—now, to be ridiculed as well. He led his goat through the town and complained to his guild, demanding to know why its members were silent on the matter. He told them the story of his adventures in Kozodoievka and showed them the goat.

Whiskey was immediately sent for, a meeting was held, and it was concluded to send a delegation to the rabbi, to the assistant rabbis, and to the other town dignitaries, to stir things up. "Who ever heard of such scoundrels? To take a poor Jew and cheat him out of his last few rubles; to sell him a so-called goat, then to pass off on him the devil only knows what. Not only that, but to play the same trick twice. Such a thing was unheard of, not even in Sodom."

And so it was. The delegation went to the rabbi, to the assistant rabbis, and to the town dignitaries and lodged their complaint as follows: "Who ever heard of such scoundrels? To take a poor Jew and cheat him out of his last few rubles; to sell him a so-called goat, then to pass off on him the devil only knows what, and to play the same trick on him twice. Such a thing was unheard of, even in Sodom."

The rabbi, the assistant rabbis, and the town dignitaries listened to the complaint and called a meeting for that evening at the rabbi's house. There it was decided, on the spot, to send a letter to the rabbi, the assistant rabbis, and the town dignitaries of Kozodoievka. And so it was. They sat themselves down and wrote a letter in Hebrew, all very fine and florid. This is the letter they sent—every jot and tittle:

> To the rabbis, assistant rabbis, town dignitaries, and renowned learned men, pillars of the world against which the entire house of Israel leans: peace and honor. First unto you, and peace unto the entire and sanctified community of Zolodievka, and may all excellence descend upon it, amen.
>
> Whereas it has come to our ears that a great wrong has been done to a man of our town, Shimon-Eli, son of the Reb Bendit Leib of blessed memory—who is known as Shimon-Eli *Shma-Koleynu*—to wit: that two of your people, the teacher Chaim-Chono and his wife, now and in the world to come, with cunning extracted from the tailor six and a half rubles of silver which they conveyed into their own vessels, then wiped their lips as if to say, "We have done no injustice."
>
> We, the undersigned, therefore, since such a thing is not done among Jews, bear witness that the above-mentioned tailor is an honest

and poor workingman who is burdened with children, that he supports himself by the sweat of his brow—and did not King David say long ago in his Psalms, "When thou eatest of the weariness of thy hands it shall be well with thee." As our sages say, the meaning of it is: Well in this world and well in the world to come . . .

Therefore, we implore you to scrutinize the matter closely and set down a judgment sentence that shall shine like the sun on one of the parties. Either let the tailor have his money repaid to him or the goat that he bought shall be returned to him, since the goat with which he arrived in Zolodievka is not a goat—on that the whole town is willing to take a solemn oath.

And let there be peace among Jews, as our sages have said: "For Jews, there is no vessel holier than peace."

Peace, then, unto you. Peace, near and far. Peace unto all. Amen. From us, your servants, to you, whose littlest finger has more girth than our thighs.

These are the words of the Rabbi ————, son of the Rabbi ———— of blessed memory . . . and the words of the Rabbi ———— ————, son of the Rabbi ———— of blessed memory . . . and the words of Baruch Caftan, Zerah Bellybutton, Fishel Tavernbouncer, Chaim Squeak, Nissel Wallow, Mottel Peeling, Yehoshuah Heshel Kiss-kiss.

Ten

Balayla ha-hu, that night, the moon gazed down at Zolodievka's gloomy half-ruined houses that stood squeezed together without courtyards or fences or trees, looking for all the world like a cemetery—an old cemetery whose gravestones looked like penitents; they were bowed so perilously that they would long ago have toppled over if they had not been propped up.

Despite the foul evening air and the unsavory smells that came from the market and the synagogue courtyard—despite the dust, dense as a wall, people, like cockroaches, were out of their holes for the evening. Men and women, old folks and children, were taking the air after a broiling day. Some sat on their stoops, chatting, exchanging nonsense, or just sitting around, or looking at the sky, at the face of the moon, or at the billions of stars which if you had eighteen heads you could not count them.

That night Shimon-Eli, the tailor, roamed the town's back streets, trailing the precious goat he had bought in Kozodoievka, trying to avoid as best he could the urchins of the town. His plan was to wait for daylight when he would make his way back to Kozodoievka.

To pass the time, he dropped in at the tavern run by Hodel, "the excise tax man's wife," to have a little drink to ease his heart, to talk with Hodel and get her advice about his trouble.

Hodel, the excise tax man's wife, was a widow with "a man's brains," who was familiar with all the leading citizens of the town and was friendly with laborers as well. How does it happen that she was called the excise tax man's wife?

The story goes that when she was young, she was a *Yefas toyar,* a very great beauty. One day the excise tax collector, a very rich man, was passing through Zolodievka and came upon her carrying a couple of geese to the *shochet.* He stopped her and asked, "Whose daughter are you?"

This man made Hodel so shy that she laughed and ran off.

Since that time, she was known as the excise tax

man's wife. There were those who said that the excise tax man later went to her home and talked with her father, Nekhamiah Vinokur, offering to marry Hodel just as she was, without a dowry. More than that, the tax man promised to put some money into Nekhamiah's pocket as well. It almost came to an engagement contract, but the town gossips made so much fuss that nothing came of it. Later she was quietly married off to some poor fellow, an epileptic. She wept bitterly and refused to go to the wedding ceremony. It was a scandal that rocked the whole town.

It was said that she was still madly in love with the excise tax man, and there was a song made up about her that women and girls in Zolodievka sing to this day. The song begins:

> The moon shone—
> It was midnight
> And Hodel sat by the door.

The song ends:

> I love you, oh my soul,
> Love without end,
> I can't live without you.

This then was the story of Hodel the excise tax man's wife, and it was to her that our tailor poured out his anguished heart. He told her everything and asked for her advice.

"What's to be done?" he said. "You are, after all—as King David says in the Song of Songs—'Black and comely.' Wise is not comely, but you are both . . . so give me some advice. What's to be done?"

"What's to be done?" Hodel said, spitting against the evil eye. "Can't you see that the thing is a *gilgul?* It's like a bomb that's going to explode. Get rid of the damn thing. Or, God forbid, the same thing will happen to you as happened to my Aunt Pearl, may she rest in peace. She's in a better world now."

"What happened to her?" a frightened Shimon-Eli asked.

"What happened?" Hodel sighed. "My Aunt Pearl, may she rest in peace, was a devout, honorable woman—my family are all honorable folk—though in this Godforsaken Zolodievka, may it burn in hell, you might not know that for the catty gossip that goes on—behind one's back, of course. To one's face it's all flattery and sweet talk. Anyway, my Aunt Pearl, may she rest in peace, went to do her shopping one day and saw a spool of thread on the ground. 'A spool of thread,' she thought. 'One can always use a spool of thread.' So she bent down and picked it up and went on her way, but the spool leaped up into her face, then fell to the ground. So she bent down and picked it up again; and again, it leaped up into her face. So she spat on it to keep away the evil eye and threw the damn thing away and started on home, but looking back, she saw it following her. She tried running, but the spool of thread followed after. In short, by the time she got home, the poor thing was half-dead. She fell into a faint. After that, she pined away for more than a year. Well, what do you make of that? Just take a guess."

"Ah," said Shimon-Eli. "All women are alike. It's all old wives' tales. Stuff and nonsense. If you pay attention to the prattling of women, you end by jumping at your own shadow. As it is written, 'Women are geese.' But never mind. 'Today the world was created—nothing to worry about.' "

And Shimon-Eli the tailor went on his way.

It was a star-filled night. The moon strolled through drifting clouds that looked like high dark mountains touched with silver. The half-moon looked down on Zolodievka that was now deep in sleep. A few householders, dreading bedbugs, had dragged their yellow bedclothes outside and were snoring away, dreaming sweet dreams: dreams of good profits at the fair, of large incomes, of profitable little shops, dreams of a bit of bed, of honorable income, or of honor itself. All sorts of dreams.

The streets were empty; not a sound to be heard anywhere. Even the butchers' dogs, now tired of their daytime strife and weary with barking, squeezed themselves under the butchers' blocks, put their muzzles between their paws, and—hush! From time to time, half a bark escaped a dog dreaming of a bone for which other dogs were already baring their teeth; or when it dreamed of a fly hovering above its nose, hummmming like the string of a bass fiddle, until the fly landed somewhere and was still. Even the nightwatchman, whose job it was to tap at shop doors—tap, tap, tap— was in keeping with the evening, drunk tonight, and stood leaning against a wall, fast asleep.

It was on this hushed night that Shimon-Eli the tailor roamed alone through the town, not knowing whether to go or stand or sit. He moved about muttering lines from the Passover song about the cat that ate the kid. "*Khad gadyah*—an only kid. A . . . a . . . a . . . an . . . on . . . on . . . only kid. 'May destruction take the damned goat.' "

He burst into laughter that immediately frightened him. Just then he passed the "Cold Synagogue"—a synagogue in which, it was said, the dead came to say their prayers on Saturday nights, wearing white garments under their prayer shawls. Shimon-Eli thought he heard singing, "*U . . . U . . . U . . .* ," like a wind blowing down the chimney on a winter night. He hurried by the "Cold Synagogue" and into one of the Gentile streets where suddenly he heard "*Psssssssss.*" It was a bird that had flown to the tip of the church steeple. And Shimon-Eli was overwhelmed by a mixture of fear and despair, against which he struggled to give himself courage as best he could, trying to find a *Talmud* passage that could be said at night to keep fear away. But he was assailed by the image of throngs of people he had known who had died long ago, and through his mind rushed all the terror tales he had ever heard: tales of ghosts and devils, of demons in the form of calves, and tales of elves that scurried about on wheels, of werewolves that crawled on all fours, of all sorts of one-eyed creatures, of tales of the living dead, inhabitants of chaos who moved about dressed in shrouds.

Finally Shimon-Eli persuaded himself that the goat trailing after him was not a goat at all, but a *gilgul* or a demon that would, any minute now, stick out a tongue ten yards long, or flap its wings, or cry *ku . . . ku . . . ri . . . ku . . .* for the whole town to hear. Shimon-Eli's brain began to whirl. He paused and untied the rope—at least he could get rid of the "bomb" trailing him. But . . . nothing doing. The creature would not go. Not for a minute. It kept right on following him. Shimon-Eli tried moving away a few paces; the creature followed. He turned to the right; so did the beast. He turned to the left; so did the goat.

" '*Shma Yisroel,*' Hear O Israel," cried Shimon-Eli, his voice no longer his own, and dashed off every which way. As he ran it seemed to him that something pursued him, and though it bleated like a goat it spoke with a human voice, with the intonation of a cantor.

"*Mehhh . . . lehkh,* King over life and of death, and the resurrection."

Eleven

Baboyker—in the morning, when Jews rose to say their prayers and women to go to market and girls to tend their flocks, Shimon-Eli the tailor was discovered sitting on the ground, with the goat, its feet tucked under, sitting beside him, chewing his cud, his beard bobbing up and down. When people spoke to the tailor he replied not a word, but stared ahead like a *golem* made of clay.

Immediately a crowd gathered, making a racket as if the sky were falling down: "Eli . . . goat . . . *Shma-Koleynu* . . . *gilgul* . . . ghost . . . werewolf . . . demon . . . *gilgul* . . . made to ride all night . . . tormented . . . exhausted." Meanwhile, rumors circulated. Everyone claimed to have seen somebody riding something.

"Who rode on what?" asked a Jew, sticking his head among the crowd. "Shimon-Eli the goat; or the goat, Shimon-Eli?"

The crowd roared with laughter.

"Damn you and your laughter," said one of the Jews, a laborer. "You should be ashamed of yourselves. Jews. Grown men. Husbands, fathers of children. What are you laughing at? Can't you see the poor tailor is in a stupor? Sick. You'd do better to get him home and send for the doctor, the devil take your grandfather." The man spoke with authority, his words as if fired from a gun, and the crowd stopped laughing. Somebody ran to get water. Somebody else to get Yudel, the healer.

They took Shimon-Eli under the arms, if you'll pardon the expression, and led him home where he was put to bed. Yudel the healer, with all his instruments, arrived shortly and gave him his "serious" treatment. He cupped him, set leeches on him, and bled him endlessly.

"The more blood we take, the better," Yudel said, "because all illness comes from bad blood." Thus Yudel explained his medical theory and promised to come back that night.

When Tsippa-Beila-Reiza saw her poor husband, the *schlimazel,* lying on the collapsed cot, covered with rags, his eyes turned up to the ceiling, speaking deliriously through parched lips, she wrung her hands, beat her head against the wall, and mourned as if she were mourning for the dead. "Oh, woe is me! What a disaster! What will become of me and of our little children?" And the children, naked and barefoot, ran in and gathered about their poor mother, helping her to mourn. The older ones wept silently, swallowed their tears, and hid their faces. The little ones, who did not understand what was going on, cried as loudly as they could. Even the smallest one, a worn, sallow-faced boy with a swollen belly, crept up to his mother's side to wail, "Mama, I'm hungry." All of them together made such a terrible music that no one seeing them could stand it for long. Those who came to the tailor's house left at once, overwhelmed and sick at heart. Asked how Shimon-Eli was, he was likely to gesture with his hand as if to say, "Bad. Too bad."

Several housewives, near neighbors, stood around, their faces tear-stained, their noses red. Before Tsippa-Beila-Reiza's very eyes, they pointed to their temples and shook their heads or nodded, as if to say, "Too bad, Tsippa-Beila-Reiza. Too bad."

Then the wonder began. Shimon-Eli *Shma-Koleynu* had lived in poverty for fifty years in Zolodievka, as unobserved as a worm in the dark. No one had talked of him; nobody knew what sort of man he was. Now that he was sick, suddenly all of his good deeds were visible, and it turned out that Shimon-Eli was a unique, pure, good soul. A saintly fellow. It was said of him that he would take from the rich to give to the poor; that, though it cost him blows, he would take the part of the poor against the whole town. Or that he would share his last bite with a hungry man. And more such virtues and praises were told about him—the way at a funeral, one speaks only good of the departed.

Suddenly nearly the entire town came to visit the sick man, and every possible effort was made to save him from dying, God forbid, an untimely death.

Twelve

V'hapoalim, and the working people of Zolodievka met together in Hodel, the excise tax man's wife's, tavern. Whiskey was put on the table. There was a tremendous shouting and racket. Tales were told, the rich were splattered with curses—behind their back, as usual.

"Zolodievka—may it burn in hell. What keeps them quiet, our big shots? All of them ready to bathe in our blood, and no one to take our part. Who is it that pays the community's expenses? We do. When troubles come, who helps? We do. Who pays the *shochet?* We do. Who supports the ritual bath? We do. Whom do they flay? Us. Jews, why are you silent? Let's go to the rabbi, to the assistant rabbis, and to the dignitaries and beat their guts out. What kind of anarchy is this—to let them kill a whole family?

And the workers went off to the rabbi, where they made an outcry to which the rabbi replied by letting them see the letter that had just been handed to him by a wagon driver. The letter came from the rabbis, the assistant rabbis, and the dignitaries of Kozodoievka.

Here is that letter:

> All honor to the rabbis, the assistant rabbis, the famous scholars (may they shine in heaven as they shine on earth), of the blessed city of Zolodievka, amen.
>
> As soon as we received your words, which were as honey to our mouths, we all met together to inquire accurately into the matter; and we have concluded that our people have been innocently maligned. Not only is your tailor a wicked fellow, he has invented a frame-up and created enmity between two communities. He is worthy to be fined. We, the undersigned, take oath and swear that with our own eyes we saw that the goat gave milk, may God grant that all Jewish goats should give so much! Pay no attention to him, that tailor, who tells lies, whatever tales he

tells. Do not believe the inventions of scoundrels, may their mouths be stopped. Peace be unto you, and to all Jews from now and into eternity.

These are the words of your younger brothers who are not worthy to kiss the dust of your feet:

The words of the Rabbi, son of the Rabbi ——————— of blessed memory; and the words of the Rabbi, son of the Rabbi ——————— of blessed memory; and the words of Henikh Gullet, Yekutiel Lumpenclod, Shepsel Potato, Fishel Wallower, Berel Whiskey, Leib Growler.

When the rabbi had read this letter to the workers, they were more furious still. "Ah, Kozodoievka scoundrels! They're making fun of us. We'll teach them respect. 'Shears and steam-irons: the people.' "

And a new meeting was called at once, whiskey was sent for, and it was concluded to take that fine goat and march to Kozodoievka and tear the place apart—the school and the whole town together.

Oymer v'oyseh, no sooner said than done. Some sixty of the workers quickly formed a mob. Tailors, shoemakers, carpenters, butchers, blacksmiths—rough, tough-looking fellows all, and all of them armed; some with tailors' yardsticks, others with steam-irons, still others with bootlasts, some with cleavers or hammers or whatever other household implements they could grab—a rolling pin or a cheese grater.

And the cry was "On to Kozodoievka—war! To destroy and to kill without quarter, once and for all. Death to the Philistines, and an end to the matter!"

"Hold on, fellows," one of the guild members called out. "You're ready for anything, but where's the goat?"

"Just look at us. Where the damn hell is the *gilgul?*"

"That *gilgul* is no dummy. Where the hell could it be?"

"Probably ran home to the teacher."

"You're crazy. You're talking like a cow."

"Then you're a horse. Where else could he be?"

But what good were these guesses? If one searched for a month of Sundays, they would not have found the goat.

Thirteen

Ka'eys, now, let us leave the haunted tailor in his wrestling with the angel of death, and the guild members readying themselves for war, and let us follow the *gilgul*—that is, the goat.

The *gilgul,* seeing the commotion in the town, considered the matter and concluded that it was none of his business. What good did it do him, dying of hunger, to be dragged about here and there after the *schlimazel* of a tailor? How much better to follow his nose into the wide world.

And the goat took off crazily, his hooves not touching the earth—taking no care for anything at all, leaping over men and women, creating destruction in the marketplace—a real terror, knocking over tables of pancakes and bread, bowls of cherries and berries, springing over pots and glassware, leaping, breaking, jumping, clatterty-bang-bang. The market women panicked, screeching, "What is it . . . what kind of *schlimazel?* . . . *a goat* . . . *a creature* . . . *a gilgul* . . . woe is me . . . a disaster . . . where is it? . . . what is it? . . . catch him . . . catch him. Catch." And the mob of men with their sleeves rolled up and women with their skirts tucked up, if you'll forgive the expression, milled about, searching. It was useless. Our goat had discovered the meaning of freedom and took off wherever his feet would take him.

And the tailor, poor fellow! "What is the moral of this

tale?" the reader will ask. Don't press me, friends. It was not a good ending. The tale began cheerfully enough, and it ended as most such happy stories do—badly. And since you know the author of the story—that he is not naturally a gloomy fellow and hates to complain and prefers cheerful stories—and you know that he hates insisting on a story's "moral," and that moralizing is not his manner. . . . Then let the maker of the tale take his leave of you smiling, and let him wish you, Jews—and all mankind—more laughter than tears. Laughter is good for you. Doctors prescribe laughter.

Translated by Leonard Wolf

A YOM KIPPUR SCANDAL

"That's nothing!" called out the man with round eyes, like an ox, who had been sitting all this time in a corner by the window, smoking and listening to our stories of thefts, robberies, and expropriations. "I'll tell you a story of a theft that took place in our town, in the synagogue itself, and on Yom Kippur at that! It is worth listening to.

"Our town, Kasrilevke—that's where I'm from, you know—is a small town, and a poor one. There is no thievery there. No one steals anything for the simple reason that there is nobody to steal from and nothing worth stealing. And besides, a Jew is not a thief by nature. That is, he may be a thief, but not the sort who will climb through a window or attack you with a knife. He will divert, pervert, subvert, and contravert as a matter of course; but he won't pull anything out of your pocket. He won't be caught like a common thief and led through the streets with a yellow placard on his back. Imagine, then, a theft taking place in Kasrilevke, and such a theft at that. Eighteen hundred rubles at one crack.

"Here is how it happened. One Yom Kippur eve, just before the evening services, a stranger arrived in our town, a salesman of some sort from Lithuania. He left his bag at an inn and went forth immediately to look for

47

a place of worship, and he came upon the old synagogue. Coming in just before the service began, he found the trustees around the collection plates. '*Sholem aleichem,*' said he. '*Aleichem sholem,*' they answered. 'Where does our guest hail from?' 'From Lithuania.' 'And your name?' 'Even your grandmother wouldn't know if I told her.' 'But you have come to our synagogue!' 'Where else should I go?' 'Then you want to pray here?' 'Can I help myself? What else can I do?' 'Then put something into the plate.' 'What did you think? That I was not going to pay?'

"To make a long story short, our guest took out three silver rubles and put them in the plate. Then he put a ruble into the cantor's plate, one into the rabbi's, gave one for the *cheder,* threw a half into the charity box, and then began to divide money among the poor who flocked to the door. And in our town we have so many poor people that if you really wanted to start giving, you could divide Rothschild's fortune among them.

"Impressed by his generosity, the men quickly found a place for him along the east wall. Where did they find room for him when all the places along the wall are occupied? Don't ask. Have you ever been at a celebration—a wedding or circumcision—when all the guests are already seated at the table, and suddenly there is a commotion outside—the rich uncle has arrived? What do you do? You push and shove and squeeze until a place is made for the rich relative. Squeezing is a Jewish custom. If no one squeezes us, we squeeze each other."

The man with the eyes that bulged like an ox's paused, looked at the crowd to see what effect his wit had on us, and went on.

"So our guest went up to his place of honor and called to the *shammes* to bring him a praying stand. He put on his *tallis* and started to pray. He prayed and he prayed, standing on his feet all the time. He never sat down or left his place all evening long or all the next day. To fast all day standing on one's feet, without ever sitting down—that only a Litvak can do!

"But when it was all over, when the final blast of the *shofar* had died down, the Day of Atonement had ended, and Chaim the *melamed,* who had led the evening prayers after Yom Kippur from time immemorial, had cleared his throat, and in his tremulous voice had already begun—'*Ma-a-riv a-ro-vim . . .*' suddenly screams were heard. 'Help! Help! Help!' We looked around: the stranger was stretched out on the floor in a dead faint. We poured water on him, revived him, but he fainted again. What was the trouble? Plenty! This Litvak tells us that he had brought with him to Kasrilevke eighteen hundred rubles. To leave that much at the inn—think of it, eighteen hundred rubles—he had been afraid. Whom could he trust with such a sum of money in a strange town? And yet, to keep it in his pocket on Yom Kippur was not exactly proper either. So at last this plan had occurred to him: he had taken the money to the synagogue and slipped it into the praying stand. Only a Litvak could do a thing like that! . . . Now do you see why he had not stepped away from the praying stand for a single minute? And yet during one of the many prayers when we all turn our face to the wall, someone must have stolen the money . . .

"Well, the poor man wept, tore his hair, wrung his hands. What would he do with the money gone? It was not his own money, he said. He was only a clerk. The money was his employer's. He himself was a poor man, with a houseful of children. There was nothing for him to do now but go out and drown himself, or hang himself right here in front of everybody.

"Hearing these words, the crowd stood petrified, forgetting that they had all been fasting since the night before and it was time to go home and eat. It was a disgrace before a stranger, a shame and a scandal in our own eyes. A theft like that—eighteen hundred rubles! And where? In the Holy of Holies, in the old synagogue of Kasrilevke. And on what day? On the holiest day of the year, on Yom Kippur! Such a thing had never been heard of before.

" '*Shammes,* lock the door!' ordered our rabbi. We have our own rabbi in Kasrilevke, Reb Yozifel, a true man of God, a holy man. Not too sharpwitted, perhaps, but a good man, a man with no bitterness in him. Sometimes he gets ideas that you would not hit upon if you had eighteen heads on your shoulders. . . . When the door was locked, Reb Yozifel turned to the congregation, his face pale as death and his hands trembling, his eyes burning with a strange fire.

"He said, 'Listen to me, my friends. This is an ugly thing, a thing unheard of since the world was created—that here in Kasrilevke there should be a sinner, a renegade to his people, who would have the audacity to take from a stranger, a poor man with a family, a fortune like this. And on what day? On the holiest day of the year, on Yom Kippur, and perhaps at the last, most solemn moment—just before the *shofar* was blown! Such a thing has never happened anywhere. I cannot believe it is possible. It simply cannot be. But perhaps—who knows? Man is greedy, and the temptation—especially with a sum like this, eighteen hundred rubles, God forbid—is great enough. So if one of us was tempted, if he were fated to commit this evil on a day like this, we must probe the matter thoroughly, strike at the root of this whole affair. Heaven and earth have sworn that the truth must always rise as oil upon the waters. Therefore, my friends, let us search each other now, go through each other's garments, shake out our pockets—all of us from the oldest householder to the *shammes,* not leaving anyone out. Start with me. Search my pockets first.'

"Thus spoke Reb Yozifel, and he was the first to unbind his gabardine and turn his pockets inside out. And following his example all the men loosened their girdles and showed the linings of their pockets, too. They searched each other, they felt and shook one another, until they came to Lazer Yossel, who turned all colors and began to argue that, in the first place, the stranger was a swindler, that his story was the pure fabrication of a Litvak. No one had stolen any money from him. Couldn't they see that it was all a falsehood and a lie?

"The congregation began to clamor and shout. What did he mean by this? All the important men had allowed themselves to be searched, so why should Lazar Yossel escape? There are no privileged characters here. 'Search him! Search him!' the crowd roared.

"Lazer Yossel saw that it was hopeless, and began to plead for mercy with tears in his eyes. He begged them not to search him. He swore by all that was holy that he was as innocent in this as he would want to be of any wrongdoing as long as he lived. Then why didn't he want to be searched? It was a disgrace to him, he said. He begged them to have pity on his youth, not to bring this disgrace down on him. 'Do anything you wish with me,' he said, 'but don't touch my pockets.' How do you like that? Do you suppose we listened to him?

"But wait . . . I forgot to tell you who this Lazer Yossel was. He was not a Kasrilevkite himself. He came from the devil knows where, at the time of his marriage, to live with his wife's parents. The rich man of our town had dug him up somewhere for his daughter, boasted that he had found a rare nugget, a fitting match for a daughter like his. He knew a thousand pages of *Talmud* by heart, and all of the Bible. He was a master of Hebrew, arithmetic, bookkeeping, algebra, penmanship—in short, everything you could think of. When he arrived in Kasrilevke—this jewel of a young man—everyone came out to gaze at him. What sort of bargain had the rich man picked out? Well, to look at him you could tell nothing. He was a young man, something in trousers. Not bad looking, but with a nose a trifle too long, eyes that burned like two coals, and a sharp tongue. Our leading citizens began to work on him: tried him out on a page of *Gemara*, a chapter from the Scriptures, a bit of Rambam, this, that, and the other. He was perfect in everything, the dog! Whenever you went after him, he was at home. Reb Yozifel himself said that he could have been a rabbi in any Jewish congregation. As for world affairs, there is nothing to talk about. We have an authority on such things in our town, Zaidel Reb Shaye's, but he could not hold a candle to Lazer Yossel. And when it came to chess—there was no one like him in all the world! Talk about versatile people . . . Naturally the whole town envied the rich man his find, but some of them felt he was a little too good to be true. He was too clever (and too much of anything is bad!). For a man of his station he was too free and easy, a hail-fellow-well-met, too familiar with all the young folk—boys, girls, and maybe even loose women. There were rumors.. . . At the same time he went around alone too much, deep in thought. At the synagogue he came in last, put on his *tallis,* and with his skullcap on askew, thumbed aimlessly through his prayerbook without ever following the services. No one ever saw him doing anything exactly wrong, and yet people murmured that he was not a God-fearing man. Apparently a man cannot be perfect . . .

"And so, when his turn came to be searched and he refused to let them do it, that was all the proof most of the men needed that he was the one who had taken the money. He begged them to let him swear any oath they wished, begged them to chop him, roast him, cut him up—do anything but shake his pockets out. At this point even our rabbi, Reb Yozifel, although he was a man we had never seen angry, lost his temper and started to shout.

" 'You!' he cried. 'You thus and thus! Do you know what you deserve? You see what all these men have endured. They were able to forget the disgrace and allowed themselves to be searched; but you want to be the only exception! God in heaven! Either confess and hand over the money, or let us see for ourselves what is in your pockets. You are trifling now with the entire

Jewish community. Do you know what they can do to you?'

"To make a long story short, the men took hold of this young upstart, threw him down on the floor with force, and began to search him all over, shake out every one of his pockets. And finally they shook out . . . Well, guess what! A couple of well-gnawed chicken bones and a few dozen plum pits still moist from chewing. You can imagine what an impression this made—to discover food in the pockets of our prodigy on this holiest of fast days. Can you imagine the look on the young man's face, and on his father-in-law's? And on that of our poor rabbi?

"Poor Reb Yozifel! He turned away in shame. He could look no one in the face. On Yom Kippur, and in his synagogue . . . As for the rest of us, hungry as we were, we could not stop talking about it all the way home. We rolled with laughter in the streets. Only Reb Yozifel walked home alone, his head bowed, full of grief, unable to look anyone in the eyes, as though the bones had been shaken out of his own pockets."

The story was apparently over. Unconcerned, the man with the round eyes of an ox turned back to the window and resumed smoking.

"Well," we all asked in one voice, "and what about the money?"

"What money?" asked the man innocently, watching the smoke he had exhaled.

"What do you mean—what money? The eighteen hundred rubles!"

"Oh," he drawled. "The eighteen hundred. They were gone."

"Gone?"

"Gone forever."

Translated by Julius and Frances Butwin

ETERNAL LIFE

If you like, I'll tell you a story of how I once tock a
burden upon myself and came close, perilously close,
to misfortune. And why, you may wonder, did it happen? Because I was very young, neither experienced
nor shrewd. It's possible, of course, that I'm still far
from wisdom, for if I were clever, wouldn't I be rich? If
you have money you're clever and handsome, and you
can sing, too.

In short, I was a young man, living, as the custom
was, off my in-laws, sitting at my studies, dipping into
forbidden books on the sly when my father-in-law and
mother-in-law weren't looking. My father-in-law
wasn't so bad. It was she, the mother-in-law, who made
the trouble; she wore the pants; she was boss! All by
herself she ran the business, made matches for her
daughters—everything singlehanded. She picked me,
too; it was she who examined me in the Law; it was she
who brought me to Zwihil from Radomishli. I'm from
Radomishli myself—surely you've heard of Radomishli! It was written up in the papers not so long
ago.

Well, so there I was in Zwihil, living off my in-laws,
sweating over Maimonides' *Guide for the Perplexed*,
hardly stepping across the threshold of the house, you

54

might say, until the time came to register for military service and I had to bestir myself, arrange my papers, figure out a way of getting an exemption, obtain a passport, and all the rest of it. This, you might say, was my first journey into the world. To show that I was now a man, I went to the market all by myself and hired a conveyance. God sent me a bargain, a lucky find—a peasant from Radomishli with a sleigh, a broad red sleigh with two wings on the sides, like an eagle. I never even noticed that he had a white horse, and a white horse, said my mother-in-law, means bad luck. "May I be lying," she said, "but I'm afraid this journey will end in trouble." "Bite off your tongue," exclaimed my father-in-law and regretted it immediately, for he soon got what was coming to him. But to me he said on the sly, "Women's superstitions."

I began to prepare for the trip—prayer shawl and phylacteries, cakes made with butter, a few rubles in my pocket, and three pillows: one to sit on, one to lean on, and one for my feet. But when the time came to say good-bye, the words stuck in my throat. It's always like that with me: I lose my tongue. What does one say? I don't know! To me it's always seemed rather coarse to turn your back on people and leave them, just like that. I don't know how you feel about it, but farewells for me are, to this day, a torment. But I seem to be losing the thread of my story. . . . I was on my way to Radomishli.

It was the beginning of winter; the snow was thick and made excellent going for the sleigh. White though it was, the horse ran like a song, and the peasant I had drawn was a silent one, the kind that answers "Eh-heh," meaning Yes, or "Ba-nee," meaning No. If you threatened him with the cholera you couldn't get another word out of him. Having eaten well, I departed happily, settled cozily in the sleigh, a pillow under me, a pillow at my shoulders, a pillow at my feet.

The nag leaps ahead; the peasant clucks; the sleigh glides; the wind blows. Snow whirls in the air and floats down upon the great wide highway. My heart is full of a strange, outlandish joy. For the first time I am going into God's little world, all by myself, my own master. And I lean back and stretch my legs in the sleigh, as proud and easy as a squire.

But in winter, no matter how warm your clothes may be, you want to stop, to catch your breath and warm your sides before you go on. I began to imagine a warm inn, a blazing samovar, a roast with hot gravy. These dreams pressed upon my heart—that is, they made me hungry. So I took up the matter of an inn with my peasant. "Ba-nee," he said, meaning No. "Is the inn far?" I asked. "Eh-heh," he drawled, meaning Yes. "How far?" But that I couldn't pry out of him. And then I began to think: imagine if the driver had been a Jew instead of a peasant! He'd have told me not only where the inn was, but who was the owner, what he was called, how many children he had, how much he had paid for the inn, how much he earned by it, how long he's been there, and whom he had bought it from—he'd have recited me an epic. A strange people. Our Jews, I mean. God bless them.

So I dreamed on about my inn and the hot samovar and the little delicacies to eat. Until God took pity on me. The peasant clucked to his nag, turned the sleigh off to a side, and there stood a small gray hut covered with snow, a country tavern. Standing alone on the white snowy plain, it seemed strangely solitary, like a remote and forgotten gravestone. We drove up to it as grand as you please, and my peasant took the horse and sleigh to the stable while I went right into the tavern, opened the door, and remained standing on the threshold, perplexed. Why, you wonder? It's a pretty story, and a short one. In the middle of the floor, on the ground, lay a corpse covered with black. At its head stood two brass candlesticks with tiny candles. Tattered children sat beside it, beating themselves on their heads with their tiny hands, weeping, yammering, crying, "Ma-ma!

Mama!" And a tall, long-legged man in a torn, summer-thin, loose coat paced back and forth, wringing his hands and muttering to himself, "What's to be done? What can I do?"

Seeing this, my first thought was to escape. "Noah," I said to myself, "clear out!" I began to back away. But the door closed behind me and something soldered my feet to the threshold. I couldn't move from the spot. Catching sight of me, the long-legged man rushed over to me with arms outstretched, like someone begging to be rescued. "What do you say to this misfortune!" he cried, showing me the weeping children. "Their mother has left them. What shall I do? What's to be done?"

"Blessed be God's righteousness," I said to him and wanted to console him with kind words, as the custom is among us. But he interrupted me and said, "It's an old story, you understand. She's been all but dead this past year. It was the true blessing, consumption. Poor thing, how she begged and prayed for death! But what shall we do, here in the middle of this barren field? What's to be done? If I go to a farm and hire a wagon to take her to town, how can I leave the children? And night is coming on. What's to be done!"

With these words my long-legged Jew burst into a strange tearless weeping, almost like laughter, and sounds resembling coughs came from his throat. "Oohoohoo! Oohoo!"

I forgot my hunger, my cold, I forgot everything and said to him, "I'm traveling from Zwihil to Radomishli and have a fine sleigh. If the village you speak of is not far, I can lend you the sleigh and wait here. If it won't take too long."

He threw his arms around me and almost kissed me. "Oh, long life to you for this good deed! You'll gain Eternal Life! As I am a Jew, Eternal Life! The village isn't far from here. Four or five miles, no more. It will hardly take an hour, and I'll send your sleigh right back. It'll bring you Eternal Life, I swear it, Eternal Life!

Children, get up from the ground and give thanks. Kiss this young man's hands and feet. He's given us his sleigh, and I will take your mother to the consecrated ground. Eternal Life! As I am a Jew, Eternal Life!''

You could scarcely say there was rejoicing. The children, when they heard their mother was to be taken away, fell upon her with still more tears. All the same, these were good tidings. Someone—a man, myself— had turned up to do them a mercy; God alone had sent him there. They looked at me as though I were a redeemer, a sort of Elijah the Prophet, and to tell the honest truth I began to see myself as no ordinary person. Suddenly I grew in stature before my own eyes, becoming what some people call a hero. At that moment I was ready to lift mountains, to overwhelm worlds. Nothing seemed impossible. So I blurted out, "You know what? I'll take her myself, with the help of my peasant, so you won't have to leave the children alone at such a time."

The more I talked this way, the more they all wept. They wept and they looked at me as if they were seeing an angel that had come down from heaven. In my own eyes I kept getting bigger by the minute, unbelievably great, so much so that I forgot I had always lived in terror of corpses, being afraid even to touch them. With my own hands I helped carry out the body and put it in the sleigh. I promised my peasant an extra half-ruble and a shot of brandy. He scratched his head doubtfully and mumbled under his breath, but after his third drink he grew more reasonable, and the three of us—the peasant, the corpse, and I—were off. Her name was Chava Nechama, daughter of Raphael Michael. I remember this name as if I had heard it today, because I kept repeating it to myself, Chava Nechama, daughter of Raphael Michael. Her husband had taken great pains to make sure I got it correctly, since the burial service could not be performed properly unless her full name was invoked. So I kept repeating, "Chava Nechama, daughter of Raphael Michael."

As I was doing this I forgot her husband's name! If you threatened to cut my head off, I couldn't remember what he called himself. He had told me his name and assured me that as soon as I came to the village I had only to mention it and the body would be taken from me, so I could continue my journey. He was well known in the village, he went there on the High Holidays, he was a liberal contributor to the synagogue and to such good causes as the ritual bath; to hear him tell it, he was virtually a legendary benefactor. He stuffed my head with instructions and directions, where to go and what to say. But I forgot every word of it. Nothing remained with me. Nothing! All my thoughts were centered on one thing only: I had a corpse on my hands. And this caused me so much tumult and panic that I nearly forgot *my* name. From early childhood I have dreaded the sight of the dead. It seemed to me, as we drove along, that the half-closed frosty eyes were looking at me and that the locked dead lips might soon open and some strange subterranean voice issue from them. Just to imagine such a sound would be enough to make you lose your senses. Not for nothing are stories told among us of people swooning or even losing their minds from fear of the dead!

We drove on with the corpse. I gave the dead woman one of my pillows; she lay there at my feet. To avoid weird and oppressive thoughts I looked toward the heavens and began to repeat silently, "Chava Nechama, daughter of Raphael Michael, Chava Nechama, daughter of Raphael Michael," until the names grew confused in my mind and I found myself saying, "Chava Raphael, daughter of Nechama Michael" and "Raphael Michael, daughter of Chava Nechama." I failed to notice that it had been growing darker, the wind was blowing fiercely, and the snow fell and fell until it covered the road marks. The sleigh now seemed to be gliding forward at random into a white waste. The peasant grumbled more and more loudly; I could have sworn he was heaping threefold blessings upon me.

'What's the matter?" I asked. He spat with rage—may God defend me! He opened his mouth and pelted me with words. I was leading him to ruin, he said, him and his horse, too. Because of the corpse in the sleigh the horse had lost its way, we had lost the road, night was coming on, and soon we would be utterly forsaken.

When I heard this I was ready to turn back with the corpse and undo my good deed. But the peasant said there was no going back; there were no longer any recognizable signs; we were circling about, lost in the fields. The road was snowed under, the sky was dark, it was night, the little nag was tired to death. "May a filthy end overtake the innkeeper and all the innkeepers of the world!" cursed the peasant. "If only he had broken his leg," he continued—and by "he" he meant himself— "before he decided to stop at that inn! If only the first drink had choked him before he let himself be talked into this folly of taking a calamity into his sled, for a few dirty coins, and being lost to the devils, nag and all, in these fields." About himself, he said, he didn't complain; maybe it was fated so. But the little nag, this innocent creature that knew nothing, what had it done to deserve such a fate?

I could have sworn that there were tears in his voice. I promised him another half-ruble and two more glasses of brandy to make him feel better, but this only made him furious, and he said that if I didn't keep quiet he'd throw the corpse out of the sleigh altogether. And I thought to myself, what will I do if he does throw out the corpse, and me with it, leaving the two of us there together in the snow, the corpse and me? Can anyone tell what a peasant will do when he becomes angry?

I grew dumb. I huddled into the pillows and tried to stay awake. After all, how can you fall asleep with a corpse in front of you? And besides, I had often heard that one must not sleep in the winter frost; from such sleep one may never waken. But my eyes began to droop. At that moment I would have given anything to be able to drop off, but I fought against it and held my eyes open with my fingers. Nevertheless they kept closing, again and again, while the sleigh flew across the soft white deep drifts, and a curious sweetness poured through my limbs. I experienced a strange, close pleasure, and I wished this sweetness to last forever, but some power kept waking me, cruelly rousing me, poking me in the sides and saying, "No, Noah, don't sleep. Stay awake!" And I forced my eyes and found this imagined sweetness to be a terrible chill that crept through my bones, and I began to know a deep fear—terror! May God have mercy on me! I imagined that the corpse stirred, uncovered itself, and looked at me with those frosty half-open eyes as though to say, "What are you doing to me, young man? Destroying a daughter of Israel who has died, the mother of tiny children, not bringing her to rest in consecrated ground?" The wind howled in my ears as if it were a human voice, and hideous thoughts ran through my mind. I saw us all under the snow, buried there, the horse, the peasant, the dead woman, and myself, the living frozen to death and only the corpse, the innkeeper's wife, come to life.

Suddenly I heard the peasant urge his horse on more cheerfully, thank God. He crossed himself in the dark with a sigh. It was as if he planted a new soul in me. Far off a tiny fire could be seen; it appeared, disappeared, and then we saw it again. A settlement, I thought, and I gave thanks to God with a full heart. To my peasant I said, "Apparently we've found the way. That's a town we're approaching, isn't it?"

"Eh-heh," said the peasant, without anger and in his usual laconic style. Right then and there I wanted to embrace him, to kiss him on the back for his good tidings and for his laconic "Eh-heh," which was dearer to me than the cleverest sermon.

"What's your name?" I asked, wondering why I hadn't thought to ask before.

"Mikita."

"Mikita!" I repeated, and found a rare charm in the sound.

"Eh-heh!" he said, and I wanted him to say more, at least a few words, for Mikita had become so dear to me, and his horse too, lovely little nag. I spoke to Mikita about him. "That's a fine little horse," I said.

"Eh-heh," answered Mikita.

"Fine sled, too."

"Eh-heh."

And more than that, though you broke him into a dozen pieces, Mikita wouldn't say.

"Don't like to talk, do you, Mikita my heart?"

"Eh-heh."

I laughed. I felt gay, happy. If I had found a treasure or a juicy piece of news the world had never heard of I couldn't have been happier. In short, I felt lucky—oh, so lucky! Do you know what I wanted? I wanted to raise my voice in song. That's my nature, I sing when I'm happy. My wife, who knows me inside out, will ask, "Well, what's happened now, Noah? How much money have you made that you're singing so loud?" Women, with their women's brains, seem to think that a man is happy only when he's making money. I wonder why it is that our women are so much more concerned with money than we, the men. Who works for it? We or they? But there, I've fallen off the track again.

So, with God's help, we arrived in the village, and it was still quite early. The place was still deep in slumber, there were many hours before day would come, and nowhere was a fire to be seen. I caught sight of a wide-gated house with a little broom hung on it to signify a hotel. We stopped, crawled down, and began to beat our fists upon the gate. We knocked and we knocked, and finally we saw a little light in the window; then we heard someone scuffing his feet and a voice came from within: "Who is it?"

"Open up, uncle," I shouted, "and you'll win Eternal Life."

"Eternal Life?" came the voice from behind the gate. "Who are you?" The lock began to turn.

"Open up," I said. "I've brought a corpse."

"A corpse? What do you mean, a corpse?"

"A corpse means someone who has died. The body of a Jewish woman from the country. From an inn."

Silence on the other side of the gate. I heard a lock turn and feet scuffle away into the distance. The light went out. What was I to do!

The whole thing angered me so that I called my peasant to help me, and we beat so hard that at last the lamp reappeared and we heard the voice again.

"What do you want from my life? What kind of plague are you?"

"In the name of God," I pleaded as with a bandit. "Take pity. I have a corpse here."

"What kind of a corpse?"

"The innkeeper's wife."

"What innkeeper?"

"I've forgotten how he calls himself, but her name is Chava Michael, daughter of Chana Raphael—Chana Raphael, daughter of Michael Chava—I mean, Chana Chava Chana—"

"Get away from here you *schlimazel,* or I'll pour a bucket of water over you."

That's what the innkeeper said. He clumped away from the window and put out the light. There was nothing we could do.

About an hour later, when the dawn began to show, the gate opened a bit. A black head streaked with pillow feathers looked out and said, "Was it you, pounding on the windows?"

"Of course. Who else?"

"What did you want?"

"I've brought a corpse."

"A corpse. Take it to the *shammes* of the Burial Society."

"Who is this sexton of yours? What's his name?"

"His name is Yechiel. You'll find him down the hill, not far from the bath."

"And where is your bath?"

"You mean to say you don't know where the bath is? I guess you don't live here. Where do you come from?"

"From Radomishli. I'm a Radomishler myself, but now I'm coming from Zwihil, and I've brought along the corpse from an inn not far from here. It's the innkeeper's wife—she died of consumption."

"A pity. But what's that to do with you?"

"Nothing, nothing at all. I was just passing through and he asked me—the innkeeper, that is. He's all alone out there in the fields, with little children, and no one to leave them with. So he asked me. And since it was a chance to win Eternal Life, I thought, why not?"

"There's something fishy about your story," he said to me. "You'll have to see the Burial Society. I mean the officers."

"Who are these officers? Where can they be found?"

"You mean to say you don't know? Reb Shepsel, one of them, lives on this side of the marketplace, and Reb Eliezer Moishe, another one, lives right in the middle of the marketplace, while Reb Yosi is near the old synagogue. The most important one is Reb Shepsel. He's the boss. He's a hard man, I may as well warn you. He won't be easy to get around."

"Thanks," I said. "May you live to give better tidings. When can I meet them?"

"When? What sort of a question is that? Why, in the morning of course, after prayers."

"Great," I said. "And in the meantime, let me come in to warm myself. What kind of a town is this anyway, a Sodom?"

Hearing these words, my host quickly locked his gate again, and the silence of a cemetery descended on the street. What could we do now? We remained standing by the sleigh, in the middle of the road, as Mikita murmured angrily, scratching his head, spitting and cursing. "May this innkeeper and all the innkeepers of the world meet a foul end." For himself, he said, meaning himself, personally, he won't complain. But this little nag of his—what do they have against such a sweet little nag that they try to kill it with hunger and cold? An innocent creature, a beast of the field that has never sinned.

I felt ashamed. "What," I asked myself, "must he be thinking in that head of his about us Jews? How must we look—we the merciful and sons of the merciful—to peasants like this, coarse and boorish, when one Jew shuts the door against another and won't even let him in to warm himself on a freezing night?" It seemed to me then that our fate, the fate of the Jews, made sense after all. I began to blame every one of us, as usually happens when one Jew is wronged by another. No outsider can find more withering things to say of us than we ourselves. You can hear bitter epithets among us a thousand times a day. "You want to change the character of a Jew?" "Only a Jew can play such a trick." "You can't trifle with a Jew." And other such expressions. I wonder how it is among the Gentiles. When they have a falling out, do they curse the whole tribe?

In any case, we sat in the sleigh in the middle of the marketplace and waited for daylight to bring a sign of life. By and by we heard doors creaking, the occasional groan of a windlass as a bucket was hauled from the well; smoke rose from chimneys, and the crowing of cocks grew stronger and livelier. Presently all doors opened and God's creatures appeared in a plenitude of forms: cows, calves, goats, and also Jews, women and girls wrapped in warm shawls and bundled up like dolls, bent triple and as frozen as winter apples in the cellar. In short, the town had revived from its cold sleep. The inhabitants awakened and poured the ritual water over their fingers before saying the prayers. The men were off to their labor of worship, prayers, study, and chanting of psalms; the women to their ovens, kneading troughs, and the tending of cows and goats.

I began to inquire after the officers of the Burial

Society. "Where does one find Reb Shepsel? Where does Reb Eliezer Moishe live? Reb Yosi?" Those whom I asked, asked me in turn, "Which Reb Shepsel? Which Eliezer Moishe? What Yosi?" There were several Shepsels and several Eliezer Moishes and even several Yosis in the town, they told me. And when I said that I was looking for the officers of the Burial Society, they grew frightened and wanted to know, "Why does a young man like you need the Burial Society so early in the morning?"

Well, I didn't give them time to feel me out and come at the facts gradually. I told them my story at once, straight from the heart, and revealed what a burden I had taken upon myself. You should have seen what happened. Do you think they set about helping me in my misfortune? Nothing of the sort! They all ran to the sleigh to peer into it and see for themselves whether I really had a corpse. A crowd formed around us, a changing crowd; because of the cold some spectators left, others came over, looked into the sleigh, shook their heads, shrugged their shoulders, inquired of one another whose corpse that could be and from where it had come, and who I might be and how I happened to have brought it. But of help they gave me none whatever. It was only with the greatest difficulty that I persuaded someone to show me the house of Reb Shepsel.

I found him facing the wall, standing, wrapped in his prayer shawl and phylacteries, and praying so sweetly, so melodiously, so raptly, that the very room seemed to sing with him. He snapped his fingers, bumbled harmoniously, twisted his trunk back and forth, made many queer and pious gestures. I had the double satisfaction of watching this extraordinary prayer—I love to listen to spirited praying—and of warming my frozen bones at the same time. And when at last he twisted his head around to me, his eyes were still full of tears and he had, for me, every appearance of a godly man, a man whose soul was as far from earth as his round fat body from heaven. And because he had not yet finished his prayers and didn't want to break off in the middle, he communicated with me in the holy tongue—that is, by means of winks and twirling of his fingers, shrugs, movements of the head, and twitching of the nose, with a few words of Hebrew thrown in for good measure. If you like, I can report our conversation word for word.

"Sholem aleichem, Reb Shepsel."

"Aleichem sholem. Iyo, sit. Sit down."

"Thanks. I've had enough sitting."

"Nu? Ma? What, what?"

"I've come to you on a great errand, Reb Shepsel. You'll win Eternal Life."

"Eternal Life? Good! But what? What?"

"I've brought you a corpse."

"A corpse? What corpse?"

"Not far from here there's an inn, and there lives a poor man, pitifully poor, and this poor man has lost his wife—she died of consumption—and he is left with small children. A great pity. If I hadn't taken pity on them I don't know what he would have done, this poor man, out there in the fields with an unburied corpse."

"Blessed be God's righteousness! But *nu?* Money? The Burial Society?"

"What money? He's poor as a mouse. Down to nothing. Burdened with children. Reb Shepsel, you'll gain Eternal Life."

"Eternal Life? But what? What? Poor folk, poor Jews here, too. *Iyo nu? Feh!"*

And because I hadn't quite grasped his meaning he turned angrily to the wall once again and resumed his prayer, much less ardently this time, squeaking somewhat and rocking himself swiftly in a sort of galloping courier's tempo. He then threw off his prayer shawl and phylacteries and turned to me with great heat, as though I had spoiled a sale for him at the fair.

"Look here," he said to me, "this is a poor town and

has enough of its own paupers who have no shrouds when they die. We have to hold collections for them. And still people come here from everywhere, from the very ends of the earth. Everyone has to die here!"

I defended myself as well as I could. I said I was innocent of any design against his town, that I was merely performing a good deed. "As though," said I, "one had found a corpse in the street! It's entitled to decent burial and last rites. You're an honest Jew, and a pious one. You can win Eternal Life by this deed."

He became even more furious. You might almost say he nearly drove me out—that is, he didn't literally drive me, but pummeled me with words. "Is that so! You are a young man representing Eternal Life? Go and make a little inspection of our town. See to it that people are prevented from dying of hunger and cold and *you* will win Eternal Life. Eternal Life indeed! A young man who trades in Eternal Life! Go, take your goods to the shiftless and the unbelievers, and peddle your Eternal Life to them. We have our own charities, and if we develop a craving for Eternal Life we'll know where to find it. What do we need you for?"

So spoke Reb Shepsel and angrily escorted me to the door, which he loudly slammed after me.

I swear to you that from that morning I took a rooted dislike to those people who are always worshiping and conversing with God. You will tell me that modern unbelievers are even worse than the orthodox old-fashioned communers-with-God, but I disagree. Now at least the hypocrisy is less glaring.

Well, Reb Shepsel had shouted at me and shown me the door. What should I do now? I turned to the others, his colleagues. But at this point a miracle occurred, a miracle straight from heaven. There was no need for me to seek them; they had come looking for me. We met nose to nose, at Reb Shepsel's door.

"Do you happen to be the young man with the goat?" they asked.

"What goat?"

"The young man, that is, who brought the corpse to our town? Is it you?"

"Yes, it's me. I'm the one."

"Come in with us to Reb Shepsel's and we'll talk it over."

"What's there to talk about? Take the corpse off my hands and you'll gain Eternal Life."

"No one's keeping you here," they said to me. "You can go any time you wish. You can even drive your corpse to Radomishli and gain our thanks for it."

"Many thanks for the advice," I said to them.

"You're welcome," they said to me.

So we made our way into Reb Shepsel's house, the three of us, and they began to dispute among themselves, quarreling, disagreeing, all but cursing one another. The two newcomers declared that Reb Shepsel had always been a hard man to deal with, a stickler for the letter of the law, a literalist. For his part, Reb Shepsel twisted to and fro, hitting back with quotations from Scripture. *The poor of your city have prior need.* But the others attacked him with strong arguments. "So? Does that mean that this young man should be turned away with his corpse?"

"God forbid!" said I. "Go off again with this dead woman? Why, I barely made it here alive. We were nearly lost in the storm. The blessed peasant wanted to throw me into the snow. I beg you, take pity. Free me from this burden. You will purchase Eternal Life."

"Eternal Life, that's quite a mouthful," answered one of the two, a tall, lean, long-fingered Jew, the one they called Eliezer Moishe. "We'll take the corpse from you and see that it's properly buried. But it'll cost you a little something."

"What do you mean?" I said. "Isn't it enough that I took this good deed upon myself, nearly perished in the field, was almost thrown from the sleigh by the peasant? And you still speak of money?"

"But you'll be winning Eternal Life, won't you?" said Reb Shepsel with such an ugly face that I loathed his soul. Only by a great effort did I hide my feelings—after all, I was at the mercy of these people.

"Listen to us," said the one called Reb Yosi, a little Jew with a meager beard, half plucked out. "You'd better realize young fellow, that there's another obstacle. You have no burial papers."

"What papers?"

"We don't know who this corpse is. She may not be the person you say she is," said the lean one with the long fingers, Eliezer Moishe.

I stared from one to the other, and the long-fingered Eliezer Moishe pointed at me and said, "Yes. Who knows? Maybe you killed a woman somewhere. Maybe she's your own wife, whom you brought here with a story about a poor innkeeper, the innkeeper's wife, little children, consumption, and Eternal Life."

Apparently I myself looked like a corpse when he said these things, for the little one they called Reb Yosi began to console me, explaining that they had nothing against me. Why should they have? They didn't suspect me of a crime. They knew I wasn't a murderer or a thief. Nevertheless, he said, I was a stranger, and a corpse is no mere sack of potatoes. A human being is involved, a corpse. They had a rabbi, they gave me to understand, and a police official. One had to think of protocol.

"Yes," said Eliezer Moishe, pointing to me and looking me up and down as if I had already been convicted of a crime, "there's protocol."

I was struck dumb. Sweat started forth, my forehead grew cold, and I felt ill, as if I were going to faint. I understood my situation only too well. I saw how I had been snared. Shame, sorrow, and heartbreak overcame me. But I thought, why enter into long negotiations with these three? I took out my small purse and said to them, "Listen to me. This is how matters stand. I see that I have gotten myself badly tangled. It was just my luck to have gone to that inn to warm myself right after the death of this innkeeper's wife, and to have listened to the pleas of the poor widower with children who promised me Eternal Life if I would give him a helping hand—and the upshot is that it's going to cost a pretty penny. All right, here's my purse. I have some seventy rubles in it. Take what you want. Just leave me enough to get me to Radomishli. But relieve me of the corpse and let me go."

I must have spoken with great emotion, for the three of them exchanged looks, refused to touch my money, and said that after all this town was not Sodom. True, it was poor, with more paupers than rich men, but to fall upon a stranger like robbers, no, that wasn't their way. They had no intention of abusing me. They would take whatever I felt I could offer in a spirit of good will, but not a penny more. Still, I would have to contribute something, it was such a poor town. The beadles, the pallbearers, the shrouds, the plot, brandy for the services—all cost money. Naturally they didn't expect any extravagance. You start to spend carelessly on an occasion like this and there's no telling how much money may spill between your fingers.

Well, what else can I tell you? Even if the innkeeper had been a man of great wealth his wife's funeral couldn't have been more impressive. The townspeople came out in droves for a sight of the young man who had brought a corpse. The rumor spread, increasingly detailed and complicated, that I was a wealthy young man who had brought the body of his mother-in-law, a woman of vast fortune, to be interred—where did they get the idea she was my mother-in-law? Crowds came into the streets to welcome me, the wealthy mourner with the rich mother-in-law. I was said to be flinging money to the poor by the fistful. People pointed at me from all sides. And the poor—an endless multitude! Never, never have I seen such a quantity of paupers. Not even on the eve of Yom Kippur was there ever so great a throng before the doors of the synagogue. They snatched at my coat, they nearly tore me to pieces. After all, an immensely rich young man pouring money! It was no ordinary thing. Luckily the officials of the Burial Society were there to protect me. They prevented me from giving away all of my money, especially the tall sexton who kept by my side all the while and kept admonishing me with his long finger. "Young man, don't throw your money away. There's no end to this." And the more he admonished, the more the beggars crowded me and tore at my flesh. "It's all right," they cried. "When you bury a rich mother-in-law you can afford to spend a few more pennies. She's left him plenty—plenty! Wishing him no bad luck, *we* should have as much as he's inherited."

"Young man," shrieked one of the beggars as he tugged at my coat, "give up half a ruble for two of us here! Or forty kopecks at least. We're two born cripples, one blind and the other lame. Give us fifteen kopecks at least for the two. Two cripples are always worth that much!"

"Cripples," shouted another beggar as he kicked the first one out of the way. "You call these cripples? My wife, there's a cripple for you! No hands, no feet, nearly lifeless, and with sick little ones. Give me five kopecks, will you, and I'll say *Kaddish* for your mother-in-law and brighten her Paradise."

Now it's easy to laugh, but it was no laughing matter at the time, for the poor multiplied all around me. They covered the marketplace within half an hour, like a plague of locusts. The pallbearers couldn't move forward. The officials had to beat the beggars off with sticks, and a free-for-all broke out. Peasants too began to collect around us, and at last the police took action. The inspector himself appeared, mounted and sporting a whip, and with a single glare and several lashes he scattered them all as if they were sparrows. Then he dismounted and approached the casket. He began to make inquiries. Who was it that had died? Of what illness? And why such disorder in the marketplace? It pleased him to begin with me. Who was I? What was my business here? Where was I bound to? I was terrified. I lost all power of speech. Why it is I don't know, but whenever I see a policeman I fall into a cold terror. I've never harmed a fly, and I know that a policeman is, after all, merely a mortal. I'm even acquainted with a man who is on friendly terms with a policeman; they visit each other; the policeman eats fish with him on High Holidays, and he is received as a guest in the policeman's house, where he feasts on eggs. This Jew is forever telling everyone what a gem his policeman is. But all the same, when I see a policeman my impulse is always to run. Perhaps it's hereditary, for I myself, you must remember, am a descendant of pogrom survivors from the days of Vailchikov. About those days I have heard stories and stories to tell you, but enough—I've fallen off the track again.

The inspector gave me a thorough grilling. I had to tell him who I was and what I was doing and where I was going, details about details. How could I explain that I lived with my in-laws at Zwihil and had to journey to Radomishli to obtain some papers? I was deeply thankful to the officers of the Burial Society for disentangling me. One of them, the fellow with the half-plucked beard, called the inspector aside and the two of them conferred in whispers of secrecy, while the tall one with the thin fingers coached me meantime, half in Hebrew and half in Yiddish, telling me what explanations to make. "You will say you live a short way from town. And that is your mother-in-law who just died. And you've come here to bury her. And while you slip him a few rubles, invent a name straight from the *Haggadah*. Meanwhile we'll get your driver away and give him a glass of spirits and keep him out of sight. Everything will be fine."

The inspector took me into a house and began to

examine me. I'll never be able to repeat what I told him. I don't remember what I said; whatever came to my head, that's what I babbled. He took everything down.

"Your name?"

"Moishe."

"Your father's name?"

"Itzko."

"Age?"

"Nineteen."

"Single?"

"Married."

"Children?"

"Children."

"Occupation?"

"Merchant."

"Who is the corpse?"

"My mother-in-law."

"Her name?"

"Yente."

"Her father?"

"Gershon."

"Her age?"

"Forty."

"Cause of death?"

"Fright."

"A fright?"

"Yes, a fright."

"What sort of fright?" he said, putting down his pen, smoking his cigarette and glaring at me from head to foot.

My tongue seemed to stick to my palate. I decided that, since I had begun with lies, I might as well continue with lies, and I made up a long tale about my mother-in-law sitting alone, knitting a sock, forgetting that her son Ephraim was there, a boy of thirteen, overgrown and a complete fool. He was playing with his shadow. He stole up to her, waved his hands over her head, and uttered a goat cry, *Mehh!* He was making a shadow goat on the wall. And at this sound my mother-in-law fell from her stool and died.

As I wove this tale he kept looking at me, never once dropping his gaze. I mumbled, repeated myself, lost the sense of what I was saying. He heard me out, spat, wiped his red mustachios, accompanied me to the casket, raised the black lid, looked at the face of the dead woman, and shook his head with suspicion. He said to the three officials, "Well, you can bury the woman. But I'll have to detain this fellow while I investigate his story and find out whether she really is his mother-in-law and really died of fright."

You can imagine how I felt. I turned aside and burst into tears, the tears of a very small child.

"What are you crying for, young man?" said the one called Reb Yosi. He consoled me: I had nothing to fear. If I was innocent.

"If you've eaten no garlic your breath will be clean." Reb Shepshel smiled with such a grin that I wanted to slap both his cheeks.

Why had I let myself be so misled as to tell such a tale and involve my mother-in-law? To make things worse, it would now reach her ears that I had killed her with fright and buried her alive.

"Don't be afraid. God is with you. The inspector isn't a bad sort. Just slip him something and tell him to drop the whole thing. He's a clever man. He knows you've told him a yarn." So spoke Eliezer Moishe as he pointed his long fingers at me. If I could, I would have torn him to pieces, the way one tears a herring.

I can relate no more. What happened afterward I hardly remember. The rest of my money was taken away, I was put in prison, and there was a trial. But all this was nothing compared with what happened when my in-laws discovered that I was in prison because I had somehow acquired a corpse. They came at once and declared that they were my father-in-law and mother-in-law—and things really began to boil. On one side the police kept asking, "Now that we know your mother-in-law is alive, this one who says she is Yente, tell us who the dead woman was." And on the other side my mother-in-law kept demanding, "There's only one thing I want to know. What did you have against me that you wanted to bury me while I was still alive?"

At the trial I was, naturally, found to be innocent. But it cost a lot of money. Witnesses were brought. The innkeeper and his children appeared, and I was freed. But what I had to endure from my mother-in-law—I wouldn't wish on my worst enemy.

From then on, when anyone mentions Eternal Life, I run.

Translated by Saul Bellow

STATION BARANOVICH

In third class our handful of Jews sat closely packed—
you might say grafted together. Actually not all sat,
only those who had pounced on the few seats. The
others stood, jammed against the compartment walls,
freely butting into the deliberations of the sitters. And a
lively forum it was. Everyone had something to say. At
the same time.

As usual, having slept well, prayed, eaten breakfast
(more or less) and topped it off with a smoke—we were
on the morning train, fresh and chirpy as April. Jabbering about what? Mention anything. Each in turn tossed
out something lively or shocking to hold his audience.
None succeeded. We flitted from subject to subject.
The drift to war was resolved (talk of mixing Scripture!)
by the price of wheat, which somehow led to the Revolution. After the Revolution we bore into the Constitution until we struck the pogroms—the outrages, the
martyrs, the new anti-Jewish decrees, the expulsions
from the villages, the stampede to America—with de-
tours into other afflictions and evils of this gracious age:
bankruptcy, expropriation, war, hangings, hunger,
cholera, the anti-Semite Purishkevich . . .

"A-z-e-v!"

Like a terrorist, someone lobbed the name and blew
out the compartment. Voices exploded from all sides:

"Azev's a czarist spy! . . . Azev's on our side! . . . Azev's for Azev! . . . A double agent on both sides!"

"I beg your pardon, but all of you (don't be offended) are fools. Why start a riot? Over Azev? Eh . . . who's Azev? A freak, a sneak, a squealer, a flea, a Mr. Nobody descended from Nobodies. I can tell you a story about someone from my village of Komink, who makes Azev (don't be offended) look like a saint."

This was said by one of the passengers leaning against the compartment wall. I turned and looked up at a large head squeezed into a silk hat, a face the color of glue setting, a grin shy two front teeth. Through this gap his *z*'s whistled, and "Azev" came out "Azhev."

He appealed to me. I envy breeziness in a Jew, and I was attracted to his openness, to his calling us "fools." For a moment the passengers were dumbfounded by this unexpected appraisal, but they rallied quickly, traded shrugs, and took turns urging him:

"You want us to beg? . . . We're begging, with pleasure."

"Tell us what happened in Komink."

"But why are you standing? Sit."

"Where? We'll snug up a bit. Here! Please . . ."

Packed tightly, they squirmed and jockeyed, and somehow pried open a patch of chair. The Kominker Jew sat with a flourish, as if he were the godfather at a circumcision, waiting for the infant to be handed over and cradled in his arms. Raking his silk hat over one eye and cuffing his sleeves, he took the floor.

"This is not a parable and not a fantasy from the *Thousand and One Nights*. I'm reporting to you an incident that took place (don't be offended) in my own Komink, told to me by my father, who heard it from his father. I understand that the story was recorded in one of our village chronicles, since destroyed in a fire. I tell you, the loss deprives us all. The chronicles, they say, were delightful, much more engaging than the stories printed today in books and magazines.

"To begin, it was in the time of Nicholas the First, when striping was common. Don't smile—ask. You never heard of striping? Striping means—you could be striped. What's a stripe? Again you're in the dark? Then I'll start even before the beginning. Picture this: two rows of cavalry wielding horsewhips, and you strut along between, obliged to complete (don't be offended) twenty-odd laps, as naked (forgive the expression) as you were born. The cavalry inflict on you what your *rebbe* inflicted when you got lost in the text. Have I made striping clear? Good. Then I can go on.

"So on this day there arrived from the commissioner—Vasilchikov was then commissioner—an order to stripe a Jew named Kivke. Who exactly this Kivke was, I cannot tell you. He owned a tavern and by reputation was not a rock of reliability, which may explain why at his age he was still a bachelor. Among his other qualities he counted a loose tongue, and in his bar he started to bandy words with the peasants—he had to go and pick a Sunday!—about theology. A little gabble-gibble here, a bit of my God-your God there, and the peasants called in the constable and filed (don't be offended) a complaint. Bartender, set up a round of drinks, and the whiskey will wash away the heresy! Instead he trumpets, 'No! Kivke never eats his words!' as if being headstrong is balm for burned fingers. After that, what could he expect? A light fine and a good day? On the other hand, who would suspect that for a few foolish words he would be flogged? To make a long story short, the constable collared Kivke and led him to the local bastille, to wait for absolution under twenty-five lashes.

"Well, you can imagine the commotion in Komink. And when was the sentence handed down? Naturally, at night—and just as naturally, Friday night. On Saturday morning the synagogue seethed.

" 'Flogging?'

" 'Kivke? Why? For what?'

" 'For nonsense, for a loose tongue.'

" 'A frame-up.'

" 'Who framed him? Kivke has a mouth like a gate.'

" 'A mouth like two gates, but flogging?'

" 'Who flogs Jews? . . .'

"The Jews of Komink sizzled all day. In the evening after blessing the *havdoleh* candle, they descended on my grandfather: 'Reb Nisel, why haven't you raised your voice? You can't let them get away with this, flogging a Jew, one of our own, a Kominker . . .'

"You're wondering, why did they besiege my grandfather? I have to explain. My grandfather (may he enjoy sunny days in Paradise) was—not that I want to brag—the most sympathetic, substantial, prominent, influential citizen of our community, respected by the authorities and somewhat of a thinker, too.

"When the uproar wore itself out, my grandfather measured the room, pacing off the length, then the width—a habit of his, according to my father (may he rest in peace)—for my grandfather to think, he had to measure. Eventually my grandfather beat his way to a stop and announced: 'Children! Go home. Stop working yourselves up. Everything, with God's help, will be straightened out. No one in Komink has ever, thank God, been whipped, and with God's help we'll see to it no one ever is . . .'

"They left with my grandfather's assurance, and in the village they understood for Reb Nisel Shapiro (may he rest in peace) a word is a deed. Cross-examination—how and what and when—would only upset him. A Jew of substance, who carries weight with the authorities—a thinker, too—such a citizen is entitled to good manners. And why not? My grandfather did what he said he would do. But what is it that he did? If you're interested, pay attention."

Seeing that everyone in the compartment was spellbound, straining to hear, the Jew from Komink put a bridle on his tongue. He brought out a sack of tobacco and rolled a cigarette, choosing among several eagerly struck matches. He inhaled contentedly, drawing the ash slowly to his lips, then snuffed out the stub. Refreshed, he continued.

"Now pay attention to how a manager manages. My grandfather (bless his saintly memory) arrived, after careful deliberation, at a simple solution. He persuaded the constable that his prisoner, Kivke that is, should (don't be offended) give up the ghost. Why the looks of alarm? Are you in pain because my grandfather, God forbid, poisoned Kivke? Rest easy. We're not assassins. What then? He worked it out—with finesse. The prisoner would retire for the night, fit and fine, and in the morning would wake up dead. . . . Now, is it going down, or can't you swallow without a finger in your mouth?

"Well . . . the day came. One morning a notice arrived from the prison, addressed to my grandfather: since a Jew named Kivke passed away in his cell during the night, and since Reb Nisel Shapiro is head of the community and administrator of the Burial Society, he is directed to assume responsibility for the corpse and arrange for its removal to the Jewish cemetery. . . . A clever blind, will you agree? But wait. Don't cheer yet. Words have it easier than deeds. Remember, this wasn't just another Jew who'd died. This Jew had been up to his elbows in heresy . . . flogging . . .

"To begin with, my grandfather had to avoid an autopsy. Then an affidavit was required, signed and sealed, certifying that a doctor had examined the cadaver immediately after death, and that death had been caused by a heart attack—it should never happen to us—a kind of apoplexy. Kivke's end. Kivke, dead.

"On top of that, there was the cost to the community—I wish everyone in this compartment earned as much in a month. And who stood the expense? My grandfather, may he rest in peace. The village knew that on him they could rely. He worked everything out, you understand, with finesse and ingenuity, square and round, tucked and stitched. The very same day, at nightfall, the beadles of the Burial Society washed and prepared the body. Led by an honor guard of soldiers, followed by the entire community, the corpse was escorted from the prison to the cemetery. Do I have to tell you, Kivke had never looked forward to such a funeral? At the gate to holy ground, the soldiers were dismissed with a few tumblers (don't be offended) of fine brandy. The bier was carried into the court for burial, and there, with his *droshky* and span of fired-up stallions, waited Simon the leather-puller (so my father, may he rest in peace, called him when he told me the story). Before the cock crowed, our cadaver (don't be offended) was on the far side of Rogatke. With luck and our blessings, Kivke was slipped into Rodevil, and from there—goodbye forever—over the border into Brod.

"You understand, of course, that Kominck waited impatiently for Simon to return from Rodevil. No one slept much. Least of all, my grandfather, may he rest in peace. Anything could happen. If the corpse—our Kivke—fell into their hands at the border and was brought back alive and beaming, the village would be exiled to the far side of Siberia.

"But God lent a hand, and Simon the leather-puller rolled in from Rodevil behind his fired-up stallions, bringing a handwritten note from Kivke: *'I wish to report . . . I'm in Brod!'*

"Our village went wild. Immediately, a feast was patched together—in my grandfather's house, of course—and runners were sent for the prison guard, the constable, the doctor, and other notables. The music was loud, the drinking heavy, and soon the prison guard (don't be offended) was kissing my grandfather and his family. And the constable was discovered at dawn, waltzing on my grandfather's roof without (forgive the expression) his pants.

"A trifle? A life redeemed! A Jew delivered from

striping! Splendid, no? Well, dear Jews, don't rush to conclusions. This is all preamble. The story itself hasn't even begun. If you're interested, please bear with me. I must get off at this station to ask the dispatcher how far is Baranovich. There I change trains."

Tipping back his silk hat, he left. The passengers waited, exchanging appraisals of the Kominker and his Kominker chronicle.

"How do you fancy our friend?"

"He's pleasant enough."

"Colorful."

"He'll never have to beg for words."

"Uses them well."

"But the story?"

"Entertaining."

"Too short."

Someone recalled a similar episode in his village. Not exactly similar, but a similar circumstance. Which stirred another passenger's memory. The two began to talk at once, and others took sides about who interrupted whom. The growing brawl was cut short by the entrance of the Jew from Komink. Unresolved, the dispute collapsed. Like a wall, the passengers, open-eyed and open-eared, closed around the Kominker.

"Where were we? Finished, thank God, with a Jew named Kivke? Yes . . . you would agree? Then, my dear friends, you would be mistaken. Six months passed, or a year, the time isn't important, and a letter from Kivke arrived addressed to my grandfather: *'First, I wish to report that I am well, thank God, and look forward to hearing the same from you. Secondly, I don't understand the Germans, and they don't understand me. Thirdly, I'm without a groschen and without a job, and without help. I can only lift up my heels, stretch out, and wait for the angel of death . . .'*

"Are you following this prodigy? To help means to help with money. The village had its laugh, tore the letter (don't be offended) into little pieces, and forgot

Kivke. In less than three weeks a new letter was delivered, again from our corpse, again addressed to my
grandfather, again *I wish to report,* and again *without
help* . . . Only this *without help* was bitter: '*What do
you want from me? I should have accepted my punishment. By now the wounds would have healed. I'd be
keeping body and soul together, not roaming around
idle, surrounded by Germans, swollen with hunger . . .*'

"This time, my grandfather (may he rest in peace)
called the community together: 'We have to send him
something . . .' And when Reb Nisel Shapiro opened
his hand, you couldn't have a cramp in yours. Funds
were collected (my grandfather, I don't have to spell
out, gave most), and the village (don't be offended)
forgot there ever existed a Jew named Kivke.

"Kivke, however, did not forget Komink. Six
months went by, maybe a year—the months aren't
important. Again an envelope arrived, again addressed
to my grandfather, again *I wish to report,* and once
again *without help*. . . . But this time, thank God, with a
mazel-tov: '*Since I am soon to be married, with a jewel
for a bride—the daughter of a fine family—and since,
without help, I will be forced to break my word, please
send the two hundred in gold I pledged toward the
dowry.*'

"Our problem! Kivke's wedding plans! What can I
tell you, the letter went from hand to hand, and the
village held its sides laughing. Komink took turns
snickering: 'That's a *mazel-tov?* . . . Did you hear, two
hundred in gold for a dowry? . . . A jewel of a family
. . . Cheh-cheh-cheh . . .'

"The 'cheh-cheh-cheh' was good for two weeks, until a new envelope was delivered again from Kivke,
again addressed to my grandfather. This letter left out
the *I wish to report* but not the *without help:* '*I am
puzzled by your failure to forward the two hundred in
gold that I pledged. Unless the funds are received*

promptly, the wedding will be called off, and out of shame I will face two choices: either to drown myself in the river or to return to Komink to face the whip . . .'

"These last words flew up the community's nose (don't be offended) like pepper, and the cackling stopped. That night my grandfather assembled the pillars of the village, who concluded that a delegation, led by my grandfather, would pass among the Jews of Komink to raise Kivke's dowry.

"They had no choice, but don't run out of sympathy yet for Komink.

"With the two hundred in gold they sent their best wishes and their hope that Kivke and his bride would grow old together, in health and prosperity, honored by their children and grandchildren. The village was convinced the normal complications and disappointments of marriage would overwhelm Kivke and he would forget that Komink ever existed. As it turned out—when? who? Not Kivke. In less than six months, certainly in less than a year—I don't remember exactly—my grandfather heard from him again! *'My bride was sent to me by the Almighty, may all Jewish husbands know such contentment. But . . . no one is perfect. She has a father—before you deal with him, pray for redemption. He lies, cheats, swindles—a fox with two legs. He drove us into the street, but not before he bled us of the two hundred in gold. Therefore please send another two hundred immediately. Otherwise I must either throw myself into the river or return to Komink to face the whip . . .'*

"The village was not amused. Two dowries? That seemed greedy. Komink ignored the letter. Kivke brooded two or three weeks, and then my grandfather (don't be offended) heard from him again, here and there . . . Why hadn't they sent the two hundred? What was there to think about? He would wait another ten days, and if the money hadn't come, Komink would soon, God willing, have a guest. And he closed the letter with a *together let us say amen*. The devil—you understand—asking for their prayers!

"Komink belched fire and fury. But again the leaders of the community met in my grandfather's house, and again a delegation, led by my grandfather, went through the village. Few (don't be offended) found charity in their hearts. No one wanted to send another groschen to the rascal, but it isn't easy to turn your back on Reb Nisel Shapiro. Still my grandfather had to agree to one condition: this was the last collection.

"My grandfather wrote to him—Kivke, that is—letting him know whatever the circumstances, without exception, not to dream of appealing to them again. Naturally, as you'd expect, Kivke was terrorized . . . Before the next holiday, the righteous one wrote from Brod again. Now what? *'Since I have come across a German, respected and honest, and have become his partner in crockery, a business without risk, and since from this business I expect to support my new bride . . . therefore, please send four-hundred-fifty in gold. And for God's sake, don't dillydally. My partner has many offers, ten for one. Without crockery, God forbid, I have nothing to turn to, and with nothing to turn to, I can only throw myself into the river or go home to face the whip . . .'* The old story!

"In closing, Kivke served notice that if they didn't send four-hundred-fifty in gold, it would end up costing them more, since they would have to reimburse his expense from Brod to Komink and from Komink back to Brod. The devil—they should understand—could call down not only prayers, but curses, too.

"Do I have to tell you how this soured the holiday? Most of all, my grandfather's, may he rest in peace, who was left (don't be offended) with the hot coal in his hand. At the meeting in his house, he heard only grumbling.

" 'Enough! He thinks he's tapping a mine.'

" 'There's an end to everything.'

" 'If I can get tired of eating *kreplach,* I can get tired of Kivke.'

" 'Your Kivke will make beggars of us all.'

"My grandfather asked, 'Why is he my Kivke?'

" 'When he was in prison, whose idea was it? Who sent him apoplexy?'

"My grandfather saw—he was no fool—that he was wasting words. The community had closed its purse. So he turned to the authorities, to the constable, to the prison guard . . . But who? Where? For Kivke, they wouldn't give up even a glass of kvass. A peasant isn't a Jew; he doesn't take someone else's suffering to heart. So my grandfather sent the cutthroat (may his name be erased) a number of *zhlotys* and some plain words. (My grandfather, bless his memory, knew how when he wanted to!) He called Kivke a fraud, a boor, a sinner, a leech, Satan, spiteful, degenerate, and a few other things; warned him, for the last time, not to write again; and reminded him that the Almighty saw everything and punished severely. My grandfather (his was still a Jewish heart!) closed by begging Kivke to spare the village further pain and to have pity on him as he approached his midnight years. Kivke's reward would be happiness in marriage and prosperity in business.

"So my grandfather (may he rest in peace) wrote to Kivke—and in a clear, strong hand he signed, *Nisel Shapiro.* A folly you'll agree, if you listen carefully (don't be offended) to what happened next."

Here the Kominker paused, drew out his sack of tobacco, and painstakingly rolled a cigarette. He inhaled deeply, once . . . twice . . . exhaling pleasurably, ignoring his audience who waited expectantly for the story's end. After he puffed the cigarette into smoke and ash, he coughed, blew his nose, rolled up his sleeves, and continued.

"Don't think my grandfather's letter made the scoundrel lose his courage. Not even a lick. A half-year went by, or a year, and a letter arrived (don't be offended) from the swindler, with this news: '*First, I wish to report that my partner, the German—may he be driven mad by nightmares—is a thief; he picked me clean and threw me out. I considered filing charges, but I'd lay eyes on more holding a candle to the sun than suing a German. Instead I rented a shop, right next to his, and opened my own business—also crockery. With the Almighty's help I'll bury him, and with both hands feed him dirt! However, there's one loose end—I need a thousand in gold. Therefore, please send . . .*'

"There and here . . . and he—Kivke, that is—closed his letter: '*. . . if I don't receive my thousand in gold in eight days, I'll mail your last letter, which you signed in your own hand, "Reb Nisel Shapiro," to Valchikov to the Commissioner, and tell him everything from A to Z: how I suffered my stroke, how I rose from the dead, how Simon the leather-puller smuggled me into Brod, and how you've been sending me money to keep me quiet.*'

"Well how do you like that for regards? As soon as my grandfather, may he rest in peace, finished reading Kivke's sweet message, he felt (don't be offended) dizzy and fainted. The paralysis, may it never happen to us . . . Say, have we stopped? Where are we?"

The conductor called out, "Baranovich! Station Baranovich!" and rushed past the window of our car.

As soon as he heard "Baranovich" the Jew from Komink jumped up and wrestled loose his bag, a packsack crammed with odd bulges. Straining, he dragged it behind him toward the door, toppled the bag to the platform, and plunged after it. Jostled and driven by the crush of passengers, he held tight to his bag, sweating, nosing into one face after another and asking, "Baranovich?"

"Baranovich."

The passengers of our compartment, I among them, swarmed after the Kominker, clinging to his sleeve.

"That's not fair!"

"You can't leave us like this!"

"What happened next?"

"Finish the story! We won't let you go until you tell us the end!"

The Kominker struggled to free his sleeve. "What end? It was just the beginning! Take your hands off. You want me to miss my train? Baranovich! This is Station Baranovich! Didn't you hear? Can't you see?"

See? Before we could blink, he was gone.

May Station Baranovich burn to the ground!

Translated by Reuben Bercovitch

THE POT

Rabbi! A question's what I want to ask you. I don't know if you know me or if you don't know me. Yente's who I am, Yente the dairy-vender. I deal in eggs, see, and also geese, hens, and ducks. I have my steady customers, two-three households—may God give them health and long life, because if they didn't support me, I couldn't buy the bread to make a prayer over. I manage, see—grab a groschen here, grab a groschen there, sometimes here, sometimes there, give a little, take a little—manage, if you can call it that. Of course, if my husband (may he rest in peace) was with me now, in the flesh—*well!* . . . Though to tell the truth, life with him was not what you'd call milk and honey. A wage earner (you should pardon the expression) he wasn't. He'd just sit and study, sit and study, while I slaved away. That's what I'm used to, slaving away—ever since I was a child in my mother's house (may she rest in peace). Batya was her name, see—Batya the candle-fitter. She'd buy up tallow from the butchers and braid the candles. Who'd heard then about gas? Or about lamps with glass tops, that drip all the time? Just last week a glass top of mine burst, and two weeks before that . . .

Now, what were we saying? Yes, you said, *died young.* . . . When my Moishe Ben Zion died (may he rest in peace), he was all of twenty-six years old. Huh? Twenty-six? Let's try that again. Nineteen he was at our wedding; eight years it's been since he died; that makes it, altogether, nineteen and eight . . . Seems it's as much as twenty-three! So how did I get twenty-six? Because I forgot about those seven years he was sick. Though as for being sick, he was sick much longer than that. He was always sickly. I mean, he was really *healthy,* except for that cough. It was the cough, see, that did him in. He was always coughing (may it never happen to you, Rabbi). Not *always,* of course, but at times when the cough got into him he'd start coughing, and once he'd start, he'd cough and cough and cough. The doctors said he had some kind of "spasm"—that is, the kind that if you want to cough, you cough, and if you don't want, you don't. One-two skidoo! Fiddlesticks! Goats should know as much about getting into strange gardens as they know (the doctors, I mean) about what's going on. Take Reb Aaron, the *shochet's* boy, Yockel they call him. He had a toothache, see, and they tried everything, from soup to nuts, but nothing helped. So he went and put garlic in his ear (Yockel, that is). He'd heard that garlic's a cure for toothaches. Well, there he was climbing the walls, and he kept the garlic a secret. So the doctor came and took his pulse. Why his pulse, you idiot? Anyway, if they hadn't carried him off (Yockel, that is) to Yehupetz, do you know where he'd be by now? *There,* with his sister Pearl. Poor thing, her luck left her (God forbid it should happen to you, Rabbi) in childbirth . . . .

But what were we saying? Yes, you said, *a widow* . . . I became a widow (may it never happen in this house) when I was still young, a girl you might say, with a small child, and half a house on Pauper's Street, the other half of Lazer the carpenter's place. Do you know it? It's not far from the bathhouse. But you're wondering, aren't you, why only half a house? Actually it's not mine. It belongs to my brother-in-law; Ezriel's his name. You must know him—he's from Vesselikut, some sort of town somewhere, and as for a living, he makes a living from fish, quite a good living, depending on what the river's like. If it's calm outside, fish get caught, and if fish get caught, then the price is cheap. When the wind's out, fish don't get caught, and then the price is high. But things go better if fish get caught. That's what he says, Ezriel I mean. So I asked him, "Where's the logic?" So he said, "The logic is simple logic. If it's calm outside, fish get caught, and if fish get caught, then the price is cheap. When the wind's out, fish don't get caught, and then the price is high. But things go better if fish get caught." So I said to him, "Yes, but where's the *logic?*" So he said, "Simple. If it's calm outside, fish get caught, and if fish get caught, then the price is cheap." "Phooey on you!" I said to him. Go and reason with a clod! . . .

What were we saying, now? Yes, you said, *your own house.* . . . Naturally it's better to have a little corner of your own. "What's mine is mine," as they say, "and not anyone else's." So I have my bit of what's mine, my half a house. I can't complain. But I ask you, why does a poor widow with a one-and-only child need all of half a house? A place to lay my head, that's plenty! Especially when the place needs a roof—it's been years since the house had a decent roof on it. He kept pestering me, my sweet brother-in-law (Ezriel, I mean), that the house needs to be covered by a roof! "It's time," he said, "for it to be covered!" "So cover it," I said. So he said, "Let's cover it!" "Right," I said. "Let's cover it." Cover-cover, cover-shmover—that's how things remained. Because for a roof you need straw, not to mention shingles. Where could I get the money? Well, I rented out two rooms, see. One little room to Chaim Chono, an old man, deaf and already senile. His children pay me five gulden a week for rent, and he eats at their place every second day. That is, one day he eats and one day he fasts. And on the day that he eats, he eats boils and scabs. That's what he says (Chaim Chono, I mean), and maybe it's a lie—maybe old people grumble, you know. No matter how much you give them, it's not enough; wherever you sit them down, the chair's too hard; whatever you do for them, it's the wrong thing . . .

Now, what were we saying? Yes, you said, *boarders* . . . No decent Jew should have to trouble with them! Still, Chaim Chono's deaf, a quiet boarder. As they say, "never seen, never heard." But it was my luck to rent out the other room to Gnessi. She's a flour dealer, see—has a stall for flour. Some piece of goods! But you should have seen her at the start: soft as honey-pie, all sweetness and light, couldn't do enough for me. Butter wouldn't melt in her mouth. What did *she* need, after all? A corner of the oven to heat her pot, that's all; the edge of the board once a week, maybe, to salt her scrap of meat; an inch or two of the table, once in a blue moon, for rolling her strip of noodle dough. "And the children?" I asked her. "Where will you put your children, where? Gnessi, I know you have children, they should be well." So she said, "What are you talking about, Yente darling? Do you know what kind of children they are? *Children!* They're diamonds, not children! Summer, they roam outside all day long. Winter, they climb up on a shelf over the oven, like sweet lambs. You won't hear a peep from them."

A pretty kettle of fish I got myself into—may it happen to all my enemies! Some children! God forgive me for my words, but one brat's worse than the other! A piece of bread isn't enough for them! Day and night they're at it. They scream, they tear and claw, they murder each other. It's hell! What am I saying, *hell*? Hell's paradise, I tell you, compared to them! And that's not all. In fact, that's not even the problem. Children you can deal with. A whack, a pinch, a smack—after all, they're children! But God sent her a husband. Oyzer's his name. I'm sure you know him, he's the assistant *shammes* in the lower prayer-house. A kosher Jew, poor thing, and no fool either, it seems; but you should hear how she lets him have it, Gnessi I mean. Oyzer, here! Oyzer, there! Oyzer, this! Oyzer, that! 'Oyzer-Oyzer! And him, either he makes some wisecrack (he's a smart aleck too, on top of everything else), or else he grabs his hat and goes off. I tell you, it's a great success, that marriage—a real winner and that's all! . . .

What were we saying? Yes, you said, *bad neighbors* . . . Bad isn't the word! I hope God Almighty won't think I have an evil tongue. Anyway, *I* don't have to be the one to spread rumors. What do I have against her? She's a woman who likes to give bread to the poor. But who can figure her out? When she gets into one of her moods, God help and defend us all! It's a shame to talk of it—I wouldn't say it to anyone else, but with you, I know, it'll stay a secret. . . . *Shh*. . . . She beats him up—her husband, I mean, when no one's looking! "Oy!" I said to her, "Gnessi, Gnessi! Aren't you afraid of God? Of God, Gnessi, you're not afraid?" So she said, "Go bother your grandmother." So I said, "The devil take it!" So she said, "Whoever keeps an eye on someone else's pot, let that person be the scapegoat!" So I said, "Whoever has nothing better to watch than *that* pot, should have his eyes taken out." So she said, "May every eavesdropper drop dead!" What do you say, Rabbi, to such a big mouth? . . .

But what were we saying? Yes, you said, *I like things clean*. . . . Why should I deny it? I really do like it to be clean in every nook and corner. How does that make me guilty? Maybe it's just that she can't stand it (Gnessi, I mean) that my place is clean, my place is nice and tidy, my place is bright. And by her? You should see—chaos and darkness, everything topsy-turvy, like a hurricane hit it. The chamber pot's always full—up to your neck, Rabbi. Up to your eyes! Phooh! Comes morning, it's thunder and lightning! Call those children? Demons, not children! Just like my Dovidel—as black to white! Because my Dovidel, he should be well, he's in *cheder* all day, see, and as soon as he comes home at night he gets to work: either he prays, see, or else he studies, or else he looks through some book or other. And *her* children—God shouldn't punish me for these words, but if it's not eating, it's crying, or it's banging their heads against the wall. You understand me, Rabbi? Is it my fault that God blessed her with such brats, terrors of the earth, and that me He gave such a gift, a piece of gold, a jewel, he shouldn't be taken from me (my Dovidel, I mean), because he costs me enough tears, see! Don't think it's that I'm just a woman! A man in my place couldn't bear it! Don't be insulted, Rabbi, but some men, see, are a thousand times worse than women. If they feel the pinch, they don't know if they're coming or going. Do you need examples? Here, take Yosi, Moishe-Avram's boy. As long as Frumme-Neche was alive, he managed; and when she died (may it never happen in this house), he just let go and gave up, body and soul. "Reb Yosi," I said to him, "God help you! All right, your wife died. What's there to do? That's God's business. The Lord gives and the Lord takes away—how's it written there in our Holy Scriptures? You don't have to be told, do you, Rabbi? You probably know it all. . . ."

Now, what were we saying? Yes, you said, *an only son* . . . He's my one and only, as they say—the apple of my eye, Dovidel I mean. You don't know him? He's named after my father-in-law, see, Dovid Hirsch. You should see him, my Dovidel (may he live a long life)— the image of his father, exactly Moishe Ben Zion, even the same height. And that face! Just like *his* (may he rest in peace)—yellowish, exhausted, skin-and-bones, and *weak,* weak and worn out, poor thing, from studying, from the *Gemara.* "Enough is enough," I said to him; "my sweet son, rest a little. Just look at your face, will you! Here, take something to eat, drink something.

Have this glass of chicory. Here, take it!" "The chic-ory," he said, *"you'd* better drink, mother. You work beyond your strength," he said. "I'd do better to help you carry the parcels from market." What an idea! "Do you know what you're talking about?" I said. "What do you mean, you'll carry parcels? My enemies won't live to see the day, and I have plenty of enemies! You have to study," I said, "so study already! Sit and study."

And meanwhile I can't keep my eyes off him, Dovidel I mean. Just like *him* (may he rest in peace). Even the cough's the same, woe is me. Woe and desolation! Every time he coughs it tears my heart out. Because, you know, it almost did me in just to get him to grow up. To begin with, no one believed the child would live (may he live a long life): Whatever the sickness, the plague, the disease, him it hit. If it's measles you want, *he's* got it. You'd like chicken pox? He's got chicken pox. Diph-theria or the measles? He has it. Scarlet fever, the mumps, whooping cough? Why not? *What* not? How many nights I spent at his bedside only God can count. It seems, though, that my tears did the trick (and maybe also his father's spirit, a bit), because I did live to see his *bar mitzvah,* after all. You think that's that, don't you? Well, listen to this gem. One night, wouldn't you know, he was coming home from *cheder,* it was winter, and he met something, someone, dressed all in white and beat-ing the air with both hands. Naturally the child was scared to death. Poor thing, he fell in a faint on the snow, and they brought him to me half-dead, see, just barely alive. And when he came to, then he really collapsed. Lay there burning with fever for no more or less than six weeks! How I survived is a miracle from heaven. What didn't I do? I made deals with all the angels! I bargained for him a hundred times over, and pulled him back out of the jaws of death! I even tagged another name on him: Chaim, for *life*—Chaim Dovid Hirsch. And tears . . . *tears!* What's the point of talking about tears? "Dear God," I said, arguing my case with the Almighty. "You want to punish me? Punish! Any way you like, but my child, see, you mustn't take from me!"

After God granted me the gift, made my son well again, Dovidel said to me, "Know what, mother? I've got regards for you from Father. Father came to visit me." Well, I felt the life go out of me and my heart pounding, *bam, bam, bam!* "Let him intercede for us," I said; "it's a sure sign you'll live long, God willing, and be well." That's what I said, with my heart going *bam, bam, bam!* It was only much later, quite a while afterwards, that I found out about the one dressed in white. He was, do you know who? . . . Well, guess, Rabbi. After all, you're a wise man! . . . Reb Lippa, that's who it was, Lippa the water-carrier! Just that day, see, he had to go and buy himself a new fur pelt, a white one yet. And since there was a burning frost outside, he decided he'd like to warm himself, so he stood there clapping one hand against the other. May my troubles come to rest on his head! Did you ever hear of such nerve? That a Jew should suddenly put on a white fur pelt, without rhyme or reason!

Now, what were we saying? Yes, you said, *health.* . . . Health, that's the main thing. That's what our doctor says. He told me I should give him pills (my Dovidel, that is), and cook broths, see, every day a broth, made from at least a quarter chicken. And if I can manage it, he said, I should also feed him with milk and butter, and with chocolate, too, he said, if I can manage *that.* A fine story—*if* I can manage it! Think, is there anything in the world I couldn't manage for my Dovidel? Just suppose, for some reason, they'd tell me, "Go Yente, dig the earth, chop wood, carry water, knead clay, rob a church, just for Dovidel." Would I find some excuse not to? I'd do it in a split second, even in the middle of the night, in the biggest frost! Look, he took a notion this summer (my Dovidel I mean) that he wanted certain books, prayer books probably. And since I go into the best houses, see, he asked me could I get him these books, or prayer books, and he wrote me down the books on paper. So I came and showed them the paper and asked for the books, or prayer books . . . once, twice, three times. They laughed at me. "Yente," they said, "why do you need such books? Do you feed the hens with them, or maybe the geese and ducks?" "Laugh, laugh," I thought to myself, "as long as my Dovidel has what to read." All night long, night after night, he looked through those books, or prayer books, and asked me to bring him more and more. Should I begrudge him? I brought those back and took others. And here that doctor came, the wise-guy—"Can you manage, for Dovidel's sake, to make a broth every day, from at least a quarter chicken?" Rabbi, if he'd said three quarters of a chicken, would I have tried to find a way out? Where in the world, I ask you, do such doctors come from? Where do they grow? What sort of yeast do they use to cook them up? What kind of ovens? . . .

What were we saying? Yes, you said *broth* . . . Every day I've made a broth for him (my Dovidel, I mean) from a quarter chicken, and in the evening, when he comes home from his studies, he eats and I sit opposite him with some work in my hands, and I feel just ready to burst with joy. And I pray to God, God should help me so that tomorrow, God willing, I'll be able to prepare another broth from a quarter chicken. Sometimes he'll say to me, "Mother, why don't you eat with me?" So I say, "Eat and be healthy. I ate already." So he says, "What did you eat?" "What I ate, I ate," I say, "so long as I ate. Eat well." And when he's done with studying the books, or prayer books, it's only then, see, that I'll take a couple of baked potatoes from the oven, or else I'll rub a piece of bread with onion, and make myself a feast. And I swear to you by all that's holy—I should only live so long and see my Dovidel happy—that I get more pleasure from that piece of onion than I'd get from the most delicious meal, because I remember that Dovidel (God preserve him) just ate a broth made from a quarter chicken, and tomorrow, God willing, there'll be another broth made from a quarter chicken.

Still, there's one little problem—that cough he coughs all the time, poor thing. I begged the doctor, see, to get him something for the cough. So he said (the doctor I mean), "How old was your husband when he died, and what did he die of?" So I said, "He died of death. His years ran out, see, and he died. What kind of comparison is that to this?" So he said, "I need to know it. I've examined your son," he said. "You have a fine son, a fine upstanding boy." "Thank you very much," I said, "that much I know myself. What you'd better give me, see, is a remedy for his cough so he'll stop coughing and coughing." So he said, "That can't be done. You just have to watch that he doesn't study so much." "What else should he do?" I said. So he said, "He should eat a lot, and go for a walk every day. And the main thing," he said, "he mustn't sit at night studying his books. If it's his fate to be a doctor someday, it won't do him any harm to wait a few years longer."

"What I dreamed last night," I thought to myself, "and tonight and every night of the year—may all my worst dreams! . . . But there's something fishy here. He's not talking straight. How come my Dovidel's to be a doctor, of all things? Why shouldn't he become something better, a governor, why not?"

So I went home, see, and told it all to my Dovidel. His face got red as a flame. "Do you know what, mother?" he said to me. "Don't go to the doctor any more, and don't talk to him." So I said, "I can't stand him already. Can't I tell he's a lunatic?" Imagine, a doctor with such habits—prying into a patient's life! "How do you live? From what do you live? Where do you get your living?" What's *his* business? Doesn't he get his half a ruble? Why can't he just take it and write the prescription? . . .

What were we saying? Yes, you said, *a chicken with-*

out a head . . . Of course I run around like a chicken without a head! What else would you expect, with all I've got to worry about—eggs and hens and geese and ducks, and those rich ladies always on my back, each of them wanting to have first pick, each one trembling that maybe the others got the best eggs and fattest hens. I sleep in my street clothes! So when do I have time, tell me yourself, Rabbi, to cook a broth? I'm never at home! But as they say, if you set your mind on it you find a way. Very early, see, before I get off to market, I heat the oven. Then I rush back from the market for a minute to salt the quarter chicken, and then I'm off again to work. And rush back again, to rinse the meat and put on the cooking pot. Then I ask her, that lodger of mine (Gnéssi, I mean), to watch my pot. That is, when the pot boils, she should cover it and rake over the ashes. Some big job! How often does it happen that I'll cook a whole supper for her? After all, we're Jews, God help us. We're among people, aren't we, not wandering in the desert! Then in the evening, when I come home from work, I blow up the fire, and warm up the pot, see, and a fresh broth is what he gets to eat (my Dovidel, I mean). So it seems everything's fine, right? But there's the lodger of mine, that big . . . No, I won't say it. Let not the word be spoken! This morning, of all mornings, she had to go and cook a dairy meal for her children—*halushkas,* or *balabeshkas* with milk. What got into her that she had to make *balabeshkas* with milk? Why all of a sudden this morning out of the clear blue? I should know so much about hard times! She's a strange bird, that flour dealer. With her it's all or nothing. Three days go by and she won't light a fire in the oven. Then suddenly, she'll get in the mood—start up a casserole pot with buckwheat *kasha.* That's what *she* says, but you've got to put on your glasses to see a speck of buckwheat. Or else she'll put on a soup of beans and barley, or a pot of fish-potatoes, and you can smell the onion a mile off, not to mention the pepper she peppered it with. After that, her children can go open-mouthed and empty-bellied for the next half a week, yowling "Hoo-ah! Hoo-ah!" . . .

What were we saying? Yes, you said, *schlimazel* . . . She started in, that lodger of mine, and rolled out a dough of *balabeshkas* from buckwheat flour, and put a pot of milk to boil on the oven. And her children set up such a celebration, such cries of joy—my God! You'd think they'd never seen a drop of milk. Though mind you, all our enemies should earn as much, as there was milk in that pot! Maybe two spoonfuls, the rest water. But for such poor people, I guess, that's something too. Meanwhile, guess who the wind blew in? The *shammes!* Oyzer must have sniffed all the way out there at his prayer-house that back here a royal feast was cooking. So he came flying home, with a wisecrack as usual: "Happy holidays!" "A miserable, a dark and bitter day to you!" she said. "Why so early?" So he said, "I was afraid. God forbid I should come late for the blessing! Tell me Gnessi, what's cooking there on the oven?" "The plague," she said, "in a little pot, especially for you." So he said, "Why not a big pot? It could be for both of us!" So she said, boiling mad, "Damn you with your wisecracks!" And she reached for the potholder to get the pot. Well, the pot turned over, and the milk—splash! all over the oven! What shrieks and screams! Gnessi was cursing her husband with deadly curses—lucky for him he managed to slip out fast—and the children were yowling as if someone has just killed their father and mother. "A curse on *balabeshkas* with milk," I said. "What if the broth's spoiled? The milk, God forbid, might have made my pot *treyf!*" So she said, "The devil take you, together with your broth and your pot! Maybe my *balabeshkas* with milk," she said, "are just as precious to me as all your pots and all the broths you cook for that precious son of yours!" "I'll tell you what," I said. "May you all be sacrificed for the smallest fingernail from the smallest finger of my Dovidel!" So she said, "I'll tell *you* what. Your Dovidel should be sacrificed for all of us—he's only one!" What do you say to a slut like that? Shouldn't she have her mouth slapped shut with a wet towel? . . .

What were we saying? Yes, you said, *from dairy and meat on the same oven, no good can come*. . . . So there was the pot, see, upside-down, and the milk spilled all over the oven. Rabbi, I'm afraid that (God forbid) it may *just* have touched my pot, and then I'm a lost soul! Come to think of it, though, how could the milk have reached it? My pot was standing there in a far corner, shoved away somewhere at the opposite end of the oven. But it's the old story—the chicken or the egg? Anything's possible; how can I be sure? Just my rotten luck! What if . . . ? Rabbi, I'll tell you the honest truth, see. Never mind the broth. A broth is a broth. Of course, it breaks my heart—what will Dovidel eat, poor thing? But I'll probably think up something, probably. Yesterday, I bought some geese at the market, made some roasts to sell, so there are a few giblets left for Saturday—heads, innards, this, that. You can make *something* from it! But woe is me, Rabbi, how *can* I, if I don't have a pot? I'm afraid if you say the pot is *treyf,* I'm left without a pot, see; and without a pot, it's like I'm without a hand, because I've only got one pot. That is, as for pots, I used to have three meat pots. But then Gnessi (may she sink into the earth) once borrowed a pot from me, a brand new pot, and then she goes and gives me back a crippled pot. So I said to her, "What kind of pot is this?" So she said, "It's your pot." So I said, "How come I get back a crippled pot when I gave you a brand new pot?" So she said, "Shut it. Don't yell like that, who needs your things? First of all, I gave you back a brand new pot. Second, the pot I took from you was a crippled pot. And third, I never even took a pot from you. I have my own pot, so get off my back!" There's a slut for you! . . .

Now, what were we saying? Yes, you said, *no such thing as having too many pots*. . . . There I was, see, left with two pots, two good pots I mean, and one crippled pot. Two pots. But how can a poor person dare to have two pots? It must have been decreed in heaven that when I came home today from the market with two hens, one hen should get loose and be scared by the cat. I bet you're wondering how a cat got into this. It's *her,* Gnessi and her brats! They got their grimy hands on a cat somewhere, so day and night they torture it to death. "It's a pity," my Dovidel keeps telling them, "a shame and a pity! That's a living thing!" But try and argue with such rotten, no-good do-nothings. To make a long story short, they tied something to the cat's tail, and she started jumping (the cat I mean), doing cartwheels, standing on her head. So the hen got scared and flew right to the top shelf, and crash, a pot gone to hell! Do you think it was the crippled pot? Of course, what else! If something's got to break, count on it, it'll be the good pot! That's the way it's been since the world began. What I'd like to know, see, is why that is. For example, two people go along, this one goes along and that one goes along. One is an only son, a one-and-only, his mother trembles over him. And the other. . . Rabbi, God be with you! What's the matter with you? . . . *Rebbetsen!* What are you hiding for? Quick, get over here! Hurry up! The Rabbi looks sick! Looks like he's going to faint! . . . Water! *Water!* . . .

Translated by Sacvan Bercovitch

THE CLOCK THAT STRUCK
THIRTEEN

The clock struck thirteen.

That's the truth. I wasn't joking. I am telling you a true story of what happened in Kasrilevke, in our own house. I was there.

We had a hanging clock. It was an ancient clock that my grandfather had inherited from his father and his father's father straight back to the days of Count Chmielnitzki.

What a pity that a clock is a lifeless thing, mute and without speech. Otherwise what stories it could have told and told. It had a name throughout the town—Reb Nochem's clock—so unfaltering and true in its course that men came from all directions to set their own clocks and watches by it. Only Reb Leibesh Akoron, a man of learning and philosophy, who could tell time by the sun and knew the almanac by heart, said that our clock was—next to his little watch—just so much tin and hardware, not worth a pinch of snuff. But even he had to admit that it was still a clock. And you must remember that Reb Leibesh was the man who, every Wednesday night, climbed to the roof of the synagogue or to the hilltop nearby, before the evening prayers, to catch the exact moment when the sun went down—in one hand his watch, and in the other—his almanac. And just as the sun sank below the housetops he muttered to himself: "On the dot!"

He was always comparing the two timepieces. Walking in without so much as a "good evening," he would glance up at our hanging clock, then down at his little watch, then over to his almanac, again at our clock, down to his watch, over to the almanac, several times, and away he went.

Only one day when he came in to compare the two timepieces with his almanac, he let out a yell, "Nochem! Quick! Where are you?"

My father, more dead than alive, came running. "What—what's happened, Reb Leibesh?"

"You are asking me?" shouted Reb Leibesh, raising his little watch right up to my father's face, and pointing with his other hand up to our clock: "Nochem, why don't you say something? Can't you see? It's a minute and a half fast! A minute and a half! Cast out the thing!" He hurled the words like an angered prophet with a base image before him.

My father did not like this at all. What did he mean, telling him to cast the clock out? "Where is it written, Reb Leibesh, that my clock is a minute and a half *fast?* Maybe we can read the same sentence backward—that your watch is a minute and a half *slow*. How do you like that?"

Reb Leibesh looked at my father as at a man who has just said that Sabbath comes twice a week or that the Day of Atonement falls on Passover. Reb Leibesh didn't say a word. He sighed deeply, turned around, slammed the door, and away he went.

But we didn't care. The whole town knew that Reb Leibesh was a man whom nothing could please. The best cantor you ever heard sounded like a crow; the wisest man was—an ass; the best marriage—a failure; the cleverest epigram—a dull commonplace.

But let us return to our clock. What a clock that was! Its chimes could be heard three doors away. Boom . . .

boom . . . boom . . . Almost half of the town ordered its life according to it. And what is Jewish life without a clock? How many things there are that must be timed to the minute—the lighting of the Sabbath candles, the end of the Sabbath, the daily prayers, the salting and the soaking of the meat, the intervals between meals . . .

In short, our clock was the town clock. It was always faithful to us and to itself. In all its existence it never knew a repairman. My father, himself, was its only master. He had "an intuitive understanding of how it worked." Every year before Passover he carefully removed it from the wall, cleaned the insides with a feather duster, took out from within a mass of spiderwebs, mutilated flies which the spiders had lured inside, along with dead cockroaches that had lost their way and had met their sad fate there. Then, cleaned and sparkling, he hung the clock on the wall again and it glowed. That is, they both glowed, the clock because it had been polished and cleaned, and my father—because the clock did.

But there came a day when a strange thing happened. It was on a beautiful cloudless day when we were sitting at the noonday meal. Whenever the clock struck I liked to count the strokes, and I did it out loud.

"One, two, three . . . seven . . . eleven, twelve, thirteen . . ."

What . . . thirteen!

"Thirteen!" cried my father, and burst out laughing. "A fine mathematician you are—may the evil eye spare you. Whoever heard of a clock striking thirteen?"

"Thirteen," I said. "On my word of honor. Thirteen."

"I'll give you thirteen smacks," cried my father, aroused. "Don't ever repeat such nonsense. Fool! A clock can't strike thirteen."

"Do you know what," my mother broke in, "I'm afraid that the child is right. It seems to me that I counted thirteen, too."

"Wonderful," said my father. "Another village heard from."

But at the same time he too began to suspect something. After dinner he went to the clock, climbed on a stool, and prodded around inside until the clock began to strike. All three of us counted, nodding our heads at each stroke: "One, two, three . . . seven . . . nine . . . eleven, twelve, thirteen."

"Thirteen," repeated my father, with a look in his eye of a man who had just beheld the wall itself come to life and start talking. He prodded once more at the wheels. Once more the clock struck thirteen. My father climbed down from the stool pale as a sheet and remained standing in the middle of the room, looking down at the floor, chewing his beard and muttering to himself, "It struck thirteen . . . How is that? What does it mean? If it was out of order it would have stopped. What then?"

"What then?" said my mother. "Take down the clock and fix it. After all, you're the expert."

"Well," agreed my father, "maybe you're right." And taking down the clock he busied himself with it. He sweated over it, he worked all day over it, and at last hung it back in its place. Thank the Lord, the clock ran as it should, and when midnight came we stood around it and counted each stroke till twelve. My father beamed at us.

"Well," he said, "no more thirteen."

"I've always said you were an expert," my mother said. "But there is one thing I don't understand. Why does it wheeze? It never used to wheeze like this before."

"You're imagining it," my father said. But listening carefully, we heard the clock wheeze when it got ready to ring, like an old man catching his breath before he coughs—"wh-wh-wh"—and then the boom . . . boom . . . boom. But even the boom itself was not the boom of olden days. The old boom had been a happy one, a joyous one, and now something sad had crept in, a sadness like that in the song of an old, worn-out cantor toward the end of the Day of Atonement . . .

As time went on the wheezing became louder and the ringing more subdued and mournful, and my father became melancholy. We could see him suffering as though he watched a live thing in agony and could do nothing to help it. It seemed as though at any moment the clock would stop altogether. The pendulum began to act strangely. Something shivered inside, something got caught and dragged, like an old man dragging a bad leg. We could see the clock getting ready to stop forever. But just in time, my father came to the decision that there was nothing wrong with the clock itself. What was wrong was the weight. Not enough weight. And so he fastened to the weight the pestle of my mother's mortar—a matter of several pounds. The clock began to run like a charm, and my father was happy again, a new man.

But it didn't last long. Again the clock began to fail. Again the pendulum began to act strangely, swinging sometimes fast and sometimes slow. It was heartrending, it tore you apart, to see the clock languish before your eyes. And my father, watching it, drooped also, lost interest in life, suffered anguish.

Like a good doctor devoted to his patient, considering every known treatment or possible remedy, my father tried every way imaginable to save the clock.

"Not enough weight, not enough life," said my father, and attached to the weight more and more objects. First an iron frying pan, and then a copper pitcher, then a flatiron, a bag of sand, a couple of bricks . . . Each time the clock drew fresh life and began to run. Painfully, with convulsions, but it worked. Till one night when a catastrophe took place.

It was a Friday night in winter. We had just eaten the Sabbath meal of delicious spicy fish with horseradish, fat chicken soup with noodles, pot roast with prunes and potatoes, and had said the grace that such a meal deserved. The candles were still flickering. The servant girl had just brought in the freshly roasted sunflower seeds, when in came Muma Yente, a toothless, dark-skinned little woman whose husband had abandoned her years ago and gone off to America.

"Good Sabbath," said Muma Yente, breathless as usual. "I just knew you'd have sunflower seeds. The only trouble is—what can I crack them with? May my old man have as few years to live as I have teeth in my mouth . . .

"M-m-m," she went on, faster and faster, "I can still smell your fish, Malka . . . What a time *I* had getting fish this morning, with that Sarah-Pearl—the million-airess—standing next to me at the market. I was just saying to Menasha the fishman, 'Why is everything so high today?' when Sarah-Pearl jumps up with, 'Quick, I'm in a hurry. How much does this pickerel weigh?' 'What's your rush?' I say to her. 'The town isn't on fire. Menasha won't throw the fish back into the river. Among the rich,' I let them know, 'there is plenty of money but not much sense.' Then she goes and opens her mouth at me. 'Paupers,' says she, 'shouldn't come around here. If you have no money you shouldn't hanker after things.' What do you think of her nerve? What was she before she married—a peddler herself—standing in her mother's stall at the market?"

She caught her breath and went on: "These people and their marriages! Just like Abraham's Pessel-Peiseh who is so delighted with her daughter just because she married a rich man from Stristch, who took her just as she stood, without dowry. Wonderful luck she has. They say she is getting to look a sight. The life those children lead her . . . What do you think—it's so easy to be a stepmother? God forbid! Look at that Chava for instance. A good, well-meaning soul like that. But you should see the trouble she has with her stepchildren. The screaming you hear day and night, the way they

talk back to her. And what's worse—pitch-patch—
three smacks for a penny . . ."

The candles begin to gutter. The shadows tremble on
the walls, they mount higher and higher. The sunflower
seeds crackle. All of us are talking, telling stories to the
company at large, with no one really listening. But
Muma Yente talks more than anybody.

"Listen to this," she lets out, "there is something
even worse than all the rest. Not far from Yampola, a
couple of miles, some robbers attacked a Jewish tavern
the other night, killed everyone in the family, even an
infant in a cradle. The only one left was a servant girl
asleep on top of the oven in the kitchen. She heard the
shrieks, jumped down from the oven, and looking
through a crack in the door, saw the master and mistress lying murdered on the floor in a pool of blood. She
took a chance—this servant girl—and jumped out the
window, running all the way to town yelling, 'Children
of Israel, save us! Help! Help! Help!' "

Suddenly, in the midst of Muma Yente's yelling, "Help!
Help!"—we hear a crash—bang—smash—boom—
bam! Immersed in the story, all we could think was that
robbers were attacking our own home and were shooting at us from all sides—or that the room had fallen
in—or a hurricane had hit us. We couldn't move from
our seats. We stared at each other speechless—waiting.
Then all of us began to yell, "Help! Help! Help!"

In a frenzy my mother caught me in her arms, pressed
me to her heart, and cried, "My child, if it's going to
happen, let it happen to me! Oh . . ."

"What is it?" cries my father, "What happened to
him?"

"It's nothing. Nothing," yells Muma Yente, waving
her arms. "Be quiet."

And the girl runs in from the kitchen, wild-eyed.
"What's the matter? What's happened? Is there a fire?
Where is it?"

"Fire? What fire?" shouts Muma Yente at the girl.

"Go burn, if you want to. Get scorched, if you like."
She keeps scolding the girl as if it's all her fault, then
turns to us.

"What are you making this racket for? What are you
frightened of? What do you think it is? Can't you see?
It's just the clock. The clock fell down. Now do you
know? Everything you could imagine was hung on it—a
half a ton at least. So it fell down. What's strange about
that? You wouldn't have been any better yourself . . . "

At last we come to our senses. We get up from the
table one by one, go up to the clock and inspect it from
all sides. There it lies, face down, broken, shattered,
smashed, ruined forever.

"It is all over," says my father in a dull voice, his
head bent as if standing before the dead. He wrings his
hands and tears appear in his eyes. I look at him and I
want to cry, too.

"Hush, be quiet," says my mother, "why do you
grieve? Perhaps it was destined. Maybe it was written
in heaven that today, at this minute, the end should
come. Let it be an atonement for our sins—though I
should not mention it on the Sabbath—for you, for me,
for our children, for our loved ones, for all of Israel.
Amen. *Selah.*"

All that night I dreamed of clocks. I imagined that I
saw our old clock lying on the ground, clothed in a white
shroud. I imagined that I saw the clock still alive, but
instead of a pendulum there swung back and forth a
long tongue, a human tongue, and the clock did not ring,
but groaned. And each groan tore something out of me.
And on its face, where I used to see the twelve, I saw
suddenly number thirteen. Yes, thirteen. You may believe me—on my word of honor.

Translated by Julius and Frances Butwin

HOME FOR PASSOVER

Two times a year, as punctually as a clock, in April and again in September, Fishel the *melamed* goes home from Balta to Hashtchavata to his wife and children, for Passover and for the New Year. Almost all his life it has been his destiny to be a guest in his own home, a most welcome guest, it is true, but for a very short time, only over the holidays. And as soon as the holidays are over he packs his things and goes back to Balta, back to his teaching, back to the rod, to the *Gemara* that he studies with the unwilling small boys of Balta, back to his exile among strangers and to his secret yearning for home.

However, when Fishel does come home, he is a King! Bath-Sheba, his wife, comes out to meet him, adjusts her kerchief, becomes red as fire, asks him quickly without looking him in the eye, "How are you, Fishel?" And he answers, "How are *you?*" And Froike, his boy, now almost thirteen, holds out his hand, and the father asks him, "Where are you now, Ephraim, in your studies?" And Reizel, his daughter, a bright-faced little girl with her hair in braids, runs up and kisses him.

"Papa, what did you bring me for the holidays?"

"Material for a dress, and for your mother a silk shawl. Here, give Mother the shawl."

And Fishel takes a new silk (or maybe half-silk) shawl out of his *tallis*-sack, and Bath-Sheba becomes redder than ever, pulls here kerchief low over her eyes, pretends to get busy around the house, bustles here and there, and gets nothing done.

"Come, Ephraim, show me how far you've got in the *Gemara*. I want to see how you're getting along."

And Froike shows his father what a good boy he has been, how well he has applied himself, the understanding he has of his work, and how good his memory is. And Fishel listens to him, corrects him once or twice, and his soul expands with pride. He glows with happiness. What a fine boy Froike is! What a jewel!

"If you want to go to the baths, here is a shirt ready for you," says Bath-Sheba, without looking him in the eye, and Fishel feels strangely happy, like a man who has escaped from prison into the bright, free world among his own people, his loved and faithful ones. And he pictures himself in the room thick with steam, lying on the top ledge together with a few of his cronies, all of them sweating, rubbing each other and beating each other with birch rods and calling for more, more . . .

"Harder! Rub harder! Can't you make it harder!"

And coming home from the bath, refreshed, invigorated, almost a new man, he dresses for the holiday. He puts on his best gabardine with the new cord, steals a glance at Bath-Sheba in her new dress with the new silk shawl, and finds her still a presentable woman, a good, generous, pious woman . . . And then with Froike he goes to the synagogue. There greetings fly at him from all sides. "Well, well! Reb Fishel! How are you? How's the *melamed?*" "The *melamed* is still teaching." "What's happening in the world?" "What should happen? It's still the same old world." "What's doing in Balta?" "Balta is still Balta." Always, every six months, the same formula, exactly the same, word for word. And Nissel the cantor steps up to the lectern to start the evening services. He lets go with his good, strong voice that grows louder and stronger as he goes along. Fishel is pleased with the performance. He is also pleased with Froike's. The lad stands near him and prays, prays with feeling, and Fishel's soul expands with pride. He glows with happiness. A fine boy, Froike! A good Jewish boy!

"Good *yontif!* Good *yontif!*"

"Good *yontif* to you!"

They are home already and the *seder* is waiting. The wine in the glasses, the horseradish, the eggs, the *haroses,* and all the other ritual foods. His "throne" is ready—two stools with a large pillow spread over them. Any minute now Fishel will become the king, any minute he will seat himself on his royal throne in a white robe, and Bath-Sheba, his queen with her new silk shawl, will sit at his side. Ephraim, the prince, in his new cap and Princess Reizel with her braids will sit facing them.

Make way, fellow Israelites! Show your respect! Fishel the *melamed* has mounted his throne! Long live Fishel!

The wits of Hashtchavata, who are always up to some prank and love to make fun of the whole world (and especially of a humble teacher) once made up a story about Fishel. They said that one year, just before Passover, Fishel sent a telegram to Bath-Sheba reading like this: *"Rabiata sobrani. Dengi vezu. Prigotov puli. Yedu tzarstvovat."* In ordinary language this is what it meant: "Classes dismissed. Purse full. Prepare *kneydlach.* I come to rule." This telegram, the story goes on, was immediately turned over to the authorities in Balta, Bath-Sheba was searched but nothing was found, and Fishel himself was brought home under police escort. But I can tell you on my word of honor that this is a falsehood and a lie. Fishel had never in his life sent a telegram to anyone. Bath-Sheba was never searched. And Fishel was never arrested. That is, he was arrested once, but not for sending a telegram. He was arrested because of a passport. And that not in Balta but in Yehupetz, and it was not before Passover but in the middle of summer. This is what happened.

Fishel had suddenly decided that he would like to teach in Yehupetz that year and had gone there without a passport to look for work. He thought it was the same as Balta where he needed no passport, but he was sadly mistaken. And before he was through with that experience he swore that not only he but even his children and grandchildren would never go to Yehupetz again to look for work . . .

And ever since that time he goes directly to Balta every season and in the spring he ends his classes a week or two before Passover and dashes off for home. What do you mean—dashes off? He goes as fast as he can—that is, assuming that the roads are clear and he can find a wagon to take him and he can cross the Bug either over the ice or by ferry. But what happens if the snows have melted and the mud is deep, there is no wagon to be gotten, the Bug has just opened and the ferry hasn't started yet because of the ice, and if you try to cross by boat you risk your very life—and Passover is right in front of your nose? What can you do? Take it the way a man does if he's on his way from Machnivka to Berdichev for the Sabbath, or from Sohatchov to Warsaw—it's late Friday afternoon, the wagon is going up a hill, it's getting dark fast, suddenly they're caught in a cloudburst, he's dead hungry—and just then the axle snaps! It's a real problem, I can assure you . . .

Well, Fishel the *melamed* knows what that problem is. As long as he has been a teacher and has taken the trip from Hashtchavata to Balta and from Balta to Hashtchavata, he has experienced every inconvenience that a journey can offer. He has known what it is to go more than halfway on foot, and to help push the wagon, too. He has known what it is to lie together with a priest in a muddy ditch, with himself on bottom and the priest on top. He has known how it feels to run away from a pack of wolves that followed his wagon from

Hashtchavata as far as Petschani—although later, it is true, he found out that it was not wolves but dogs. . . . But all these calamities were nothing compared with what he had to go through this year when he was on his way to spend the Passover with his family.

It was all the fault of the Bug. This one year it opened up a little later than usual, and became a torrent just at the time when Fishel was hurrying home—and he had reason to hurry! Because this year Passover started on Friday night—the beginning of Sabbath—and it was doubly important for him to be home on time.

Two

Fishel reached the Bug—traveling in a rickety wagon with a peasant—Thursday night. According to his reckoning he should have come there Tuesday morning, because he had left Balta Sunday noon. If he had only gone with Yankel-Sheigetz, the Balta coachman, on his regular weekly trip—even if he had to sit at the rear with his back to the other passengers and his feet dangling—he would have been home a long time ago and would have forgotten all about the whole journey. But the devil possessed him to go into the marketplace to see if he could find a cheaper conveyance; and it is an old story that the less you pay for something, the more it costs. Jonah the Drunkard had warned him, "Take my advice, Uncle, let it cost you two rubles but you'll sit like a lord in Yankel's coach—right in the very back row! Remember, you're playing with fire. There is not much time to lose!" But it was just his luck that the devil had to drag an old peasant from Hashtchavata across his path.

"Hello, Rabbi! Going to Hashtchavata?"

"Good! Can you take me? How much will it cost?"

How much it would cost—that he found it necessary to ask; but whether or not he would get home in time for

Passover—that didn't even occur to Fishel. After all, even if he went on foot and took only tiny steps like a shackled person, he should have been able to reach Hashtchavata in less than a week . . .

But they had hardly started out before Fishel was sorry that he had hired this wagon, even though he had all the room in the world to stretch out in. It became apparent very soon that at the rate at which they were creeping they would never be able to get anywhere in time. All day long they rode and they rode, and at the end of the day they had barely got started. And no matter how much he kept bothering the old peasant, no matter how many times he asked how far they still had to go, the man did not answer. He only shrugged his shoulders and said, "Who can tell?"

It was much later, toward evening, that Yankel-Sheigetz overtook them, with a shout and whistle and a crack of the whip—overtook them and passed them with his four prancing horses bedecked with tiny bells, and with his coach packed with passengers inside, on the driver's seat, and some hanging onto the rear. Seeing the teacher sitting alone in the wagon with the peasant, Yankel-Sheigetz cracked his whip in the air again and cursed them both, the driver and the passenger, as only he could curse, laughed at them and at the horse, and after he had passed them he turned back and pointed at one of the wheels: "Hey, *schlimazel!* Look! One of your wheels is turning!"

"Whoa!" the peasant yelled, and together the driver and passenger climbed down, looked at every wheel, at every spoke, crawled under the wagon, searched everywhere, and found nothing wrong.

Realizing that Yankel had played a trick on them, the peasant began to scratch the back of his neck, and at the same time he cursed Yankel and every other Jew on earth with fresh new curses that Fishel had never heard in all his life. He shouted louder and louder and with every word grew angrier and angrier.

"Ah, shob tubi dobra ne bulo!" he cried. "Bad luck to you, Jew! I hope you die! I hope you never arrive! Every one of you die! You and your horse and your wife and your daughter and your aunts and your uncles and your cousins and your second-cousins and—and—and all the rest of your cursed Jews!"

It was a long time before the peasant climbed into his wagon again and was ready to start. But even then he was still angry; he couldn't stop yelling. He continued to heap curses at the head of Yankel-Sheigetz and all the Jews until, with God's help, they came to a village where they could spend the night.

The next morning Fishel got up very early, before dawn, said his morning prayers, read through the greater part of the *Book of Psalms,* had a bagel for breakfast, and was ready to go on. But Feodor was not ready. Feodor had found an old crony of his in the village and had spent the night with him, drinking and carousing. Then he slept the greater part of the day and was not ready to start till evening.

"Now, look here, Feodor," Fishel complained to him when they were in the wagon again, "the devil take you and your mother! After all, Feodor, I hired you to get me home for the holidays! I depended on you. I trusted you." And that wasn't all he said. He went on in the same vein, half pleading, half cursing, in a mixture of Russian and Hebrew, and when words failed him he used his hands. Feodor understood well enough what Fishel meant, but he did not answer a word, not a sound, as though he knew that Fishel was right. He was as quiet and coy as a little kitten until, on the fourth day, near Petschani, they met Yankel-Sheigetz on his way back from Hashtchavata with a shout and a crack of the whip and this good piece of news: "You might just as well turn back to Balta! The Bug has opened up!"

When Fishel heard this his heart sank, but Feodor thought that Yankel was making fun of him again and began to curse once more with even greater vigor and originality than before. He cursed Yankel from head to foot, he cursed every limb and every bone of his body. And his mouth did not shut until Thursday evening when they came to the Bug. They drove right up to Prokop Baraniuk, the ferryman, to find out when he would start running the ferry again.

And while Feodor and Prokop took a drink and talked things over, Fishel went off into a corner to say his evening prayers.

Three

The sun was beginning to set. It cast its fiery rays over the steep hills on both sides of the river, in spots still covered with snow and in spots already green, cut through with rivulets and torrents that bounded downhill and poured into the river itself with a roar where they met with the running waters from the melting ice. On the other side of the river, as if on a table, lay Hashtchavata, its church steeple gleaming in the sun like a lighted candle.

Standing there and saying his prayers with his face toward Hashtchavata, Fishel covered his eyes with his hand and tried to drive from his mind the tempting thoughts that tormented him: Bath-Sheba with her new silk shawl, Froike with his *Gemara,* Reizel with her braids, and the steaming bath. And fresh *matzo* with strongly seasoned fish and fresh horseradish that tore your nostrils apart, and Passover borscht that tasted like something in Paradise, and other good things that man's evil spirit can summon . . . And no matter how much Fishel drove these thoughts from his mind, they kept coming back like summer flies, like mosquitoes, and they did not let him pray as a man should.

And when he had finished his prayers Fishel went back to Prokop and got into a discussion with him about the ferry and the approaching holiday, explaining to him half in Russian, half in Hebrew, and the rest with his hands, how important a holiday Passover was to the Jews, and what it meant when Passover started on Friday evening! And he made it clear to him that if he did not cross the Bug by that time tomorrow—all was lost: in addition to the fact that at home everybody was waiting for him—his wife and children (and here Fishel gave a heartrending sigh)—if he did not cross the river before sunset, then for eight whole days he would not be able to eat or drink a thing. He might as well throw himself into the river right now! (At this point Fishel turned his face aside so that no one could see that there were tears in his eyes.)

Prokop Baraniuk understood the plight that poor Fishel was in, and he answered that he knew that the next day was a holiday; he even knew what the holiday was called, and he knew that it was a holiday when people drank wine and brandy. He knew of another Jewish holiday when people drank brandy too, and there was a third when they drank still more—in fact they were supposed to become drunk, but what they called that day he had forgotten . . .

"Good, that's very good!" Fishel interrupted with tears in his voice, "But what are we going to do now? What if tomorrow—God spare the thought . . ." Beyond that, poor Fishel could not say another word.

For this Prokop had no answer. All he did was to point to the river with his hand, as, though to say, "Well—see for yourself . . ."

And Fishel lifted his eyes and beheld what his eyes had never before seen in all his life, and he heard what his ears had never heard. For it can truthfully be said that never before had Fishel actually seen what the out-of-doors was like. Whatever he had seen before had been seen at a glance while he was on his way somewhere, a glimpse snatched while hurrying from *cheder* to the synagogue or from synagogue to *cheder*. And now the sight of the majestic blue Bug between its two steep banks, the rush of the spring freshets tumbling down the hills, the roar of the river itself, the dazzling splendor of the setting sun, the flaming church steeple, the fresh, exhilarating odor of the spring earth and the air, and above all the simple fact of being so close to home and not being able to get there—all these things together worked on Fishel strangely. They picked him up and lifted him as though on wings and carried him off into a new world, a world of fantasy, and he imagined that to cross the Bug was the simplest thing in the world—like taking a pinch of snuff—if only the Eternal One cared to perform a tiny miracle and rescue him from his plight.

These thoughts and others like them sped through Fishel's head and carried him aloft and bore him so far from the riverbank that before he was aware of it, night had fallen, the stars were out, a cool wind had sprung up and had stolen in under his gabardine and ruffled his undershirt. And Fishel went on thinking of things he had never thought of before—of time and eternity, of the unlimited expanse of space, of the vastness of the universe, of the creation of heaven and earth itself . . .

Four

It was a troubled night that Fishel the *melamed* spent in the hut of Prokop the ferryman. But even that night finally came to an end and the new day dawned with a smile of warmth and friendliness. It was a rare and balmy morning. The last patches of snow became soft, like *kasha,* and the *kasha* turned to water, and the water poured into the Bug from all directions . . . Only here and there could be seen huge blocks of ice that looked like strange animals, like polar bears that hurried and chased each other, as if they were afraid that they would be too late in arriving where they were going . . .

And once again Fishel the *melamed* finished his

prayers, ate the last crust of bread that was left in his sack, and went out to look at the river and to see what could be done about getting across it. But when he heard from Prokop that they would be lucky if the ferry could start Sunday afternoon, he became terrified. He clutched his head with both hands and shook all over. He fumed at Prokop, and scolded him in his own mixture of Russian and Hebrew. Why had Prokop given him hope the night before; why had he said that they might be able to get across today? To this Prokop answered coldly that he had not said a word about crossing by ferry, he had only said that they might be able to get across, and this they could still do. He could take him over any way he wanted to—in a rowboat or on a raft, and it would cost him another half ruble—not a kopek more.

"Have it your own way!" sobbed Fishel. "Let it be a rowboat. Let it be a raft. Only don't make me spend the holiday here on the bank!"

That was Fishel's answer. And at the moment he would have been willing to pay two rubles, or even dive in and swim across—if he could only swim. He was willing to risk his life for the holy Passover. And he went after Prokop heatedly, urged him to get out the boat at once and take him across the Bug to Hashtchavata, where Bath-Sheba, Froike, and Reizel were waiting for him. They might even be standing on the other side now, there on the hilltop, calling to him, beckoning, waving to him . . . But he could not see them or hear their voices, for the river was wide, so fearfully wide, wider than it had ever been before.

The sun was more than halfway across the clear, deep-blue sky before Prokop called Fishel and told him to jump into the boat. And when Fishel heard these words his arms and legs went limp. He did not know what to do. In all his life he had never been in a boat like that. Since he was born he had never been in a boat of any kind. And looking at the boat he thought that any minute it would tip to one side—and Fishel would be a martyr!

"Jump in and let's go!" Prokop called to him again, and reaching up he snatched the pack from Fishel's hand.

Fishel the *melamed* carefully pulled the skirt of his gabardine high up around him and began to turn this way and that. Should he jump—or shouldn't he? On the one hand—Sabbath and Passover in one, Bath-Sheba, Froike, Reizel, the scalding bath, the *seder* and all its ceremonial, the royal throne. On the other hand—the terrible risk, almost certain death. You might call it suicide. Because after all, if the boat tipped only once, Fishel was no more. His children were orphans. And he stood with his coat pulled up so long that Prokop lost his patience and began to shout at him. He warned him that if Fishel did not jump in at once he would spit at him and go across by himself to Hashtchavata. Hearing the beloved word Hash-tcha-va-ta, Fishel remembered his dear and true ones again, summoned up all his courage—and fell into the boat. I say "fell into" because with his first step the boat tipped ever so slightly, and Fishel, thinking he would fall, drew suddenly back, and this time he really did fall, right on his face . . . Several minutes passed before he came to. His face felt clammy, his arms and legs trembled, and his heart pounded like an alarm clock: tick-tock, tick-tock, tick-tock!

As though he were sitting on a stool in his own home, Prokop sat perched in the prow of the boat and coolly pulled at his oars. The boat slid through the sparkling waters, and Fishel's head whirled. He could barely sit upright. No, he didn't even try to sit. He was hanging on, clutching the boat with both hands. Any second, he felt, he would make the wrong move, any second now he would lose his grip, fall back or tumble forward into the deep—and that would be the end of Fishel! And at this thought the words of Moses' song in *Exodus* came back to him: "They sank as lead in the mighty waters." His hair stood straight up. He would not even be buried in consecrated ground! And he made a vow . . .

But what could Fishel promise? Charity? He had nothing to give. He was such a poor, poor man. So he vowed that if the Lord brought him back home in safety he would spend the rest of his nights studying the Holy Writ. By the end of the year he would go, page by page, through the entire Six Orders of the *Talmud*. If only he came through alive . . .

Fishel would have liked to know if it was still far to the other shore, but it was just his luck to have sat down with his face to Prokop and his back to Hashtchavata. And to ask Prokop he was afraid. He was afraid even to open his mouth. He was so sure that if he so much as moved his jaws the boat would tip again, and if it did, where would Fishel be then? And to make it worse, Prokop became suddenly talkative. He said that the worst time to cross the river was during the spring floods. You couldn't even go in a straight direction. You had to use your head, turn this way and that. Sometimes you even had to go back a little and then go forward again.

"There goes one as big as an iceberg!" Prokop warned. "It's coming straight at us!" And he swung the boat back just in time to let a huge mass of ice go past with a strange roar. And then Fishel began to understand what kind of trip this was going to be!

"Ho! Look at that!" Prokop shouted again, and pointed upstream.

Fishel lifted his eyes slowly, afraid to move too fast, and looked—looked and saw nothing. All he could see anywhere was water—water and more water.

"There comes another! We'll have to get past—it's too late to back up!"

And this time Prokop worked like mad. He hurled the boat forward through the foaming waves, and Fishel became cold with fear. He wanted to say something but was afraid. And once more Prokop spoke up: "If we don't make it in time, it's just too bad."

"What do you mean—too bad?"

"What do you think it means? We're lost—that's what."

"Lost?"

"Sure! Lost."

"What do you mean—lost?"

"You know what I mean. Rubbed out."

"Rubbed out?"

"Rubbed out."

Fishel did not understand exactly what these words meant. He did not even like the sound—lost—rubbed out. He had a feeling that it had to do with eternity, with that endless existence on a distant shore. And a cold sweat broke out all over his body, and once again the verse came to him, "They sank as lead in the mighty waters."

To calm him down Prokop started to tell a story that had happened a year before at this same time. The ice of the Bug had torn loose and the ferry could not be used. And just his luck one day an important-looking man drove up and wanted to go across. He turned out to be a tax officer from Ouman, and he was ready to pay no less than a ruble for the trip. Halfway across, two huge chunks of ice bore down upon them. There was only one thing for Prokop to do and he did it: he slid in between the two chunks, cut right through between them. Only in the excitement he must have rocked the boat a trifle too much, because they both went overboard into the icy water. It was lucky that he could swim. The tax collector apparently couldn't, and they never found him again. Too bad . . . A ruble lost like that . . . he should have collected in advance . . .

Prokop finished the story and sighed deeply, and Fishel felt an icy chill go through him and his mouth went dry. He could not say a word. He could not make a sound, not even a squeak.

Five

When they were halfway over, right in the middle of the current, Prokop paused and looked upstream. Satisfied with what he saw, he put the oars down, dug a hand deep into his pocket and pulled out a bottle from which he proceeded to take a long, long pull. Then he took out a few black cloves and while he was chewing them he apologized to Fishel for his drinking. He did not care for the whiskey itself, he said, but he had to take it, at least a few drops, or he got sick every time he tried to cross the river. He wiped his mouth, picked up his oars, glanced upstream, and exclaimed, "Now we're in for it!"

In for what? Where? Fishel did not know and he was afraid to ask, but instinctively he felt that if Prokop had been more specific he would have added something about death or drowning. That it was serious was apparent from the way Prokop was acting. He was bent double and was thrashing like mad. Without even looking at Fishel he ordered, "Quick, Uncle! Lie down!"

Fishel did not have to be told twice. He saw close by a towering block of ice bearing down upon them. Shutting his eyes, he threw himself face down on the bottom of the boat, and trembling all over began, in a hoarse whisper, to recite *Shma Yisroel*. He saw himself already sinking through the waters. He saw the wide-open mouth of a gigantic fish; he pictured himself being swallowed like the prophet Jonah when he was escaping to Tarshish. And he remembered Jonah's prayer, and quietly, in tears, he repeated the words: "The waters compassed me about, even to the soul; the deep was round about me. The weeds were wrapped about my head."

Thus sang Fishel the *melamed* and he wept, wept bitterly, at the thought of Bath-Sheba, who was as good as a widow already, and the children, who were as good as orphans. And all this time Prokop was working with all his might, and as he worked he sang this song:

Oh, you waterfowl!
You black-winged waterfowl—
You black-winged bird!

And Prokop was as cool and cheerful as if he were on dry land, sitting in his own cottage. And Fishel's "encompassed me about" and Prokop's "waterfowl," and Fishel's "the weeds were wrapped" and Prokop's "black-winged bird" merged into one, and on the surface of the Bug was heard a strange singing, a duet such as had never been heard on its broad surface before, not ever since the river had been known as the Bug . . .

"Why is he so afraid of death, that little man?" Prokop Baraniuk sat wondering, after he had got away from the ice floe and pulled his bottle out of his pocket again for another drink. "Look at him, a little fellow like that—poor, in tatters . . . I wouldn't trade this old boat for him. And he's afraid to die!"

And Prokop dug his boot into Fishel's side, and Fishel trembled. Prokop began to laugh, but Fishel did not hear. He was still praying, he was saying *Kaddish* for his own soul, as if he were dead. . . .

But if he were dead would he be hearing what Prokop was saying now?

"Get up, Uncle. We're there already. In Hashtchavata."

Fishel lifted his head up slowly, cautiously, looked around on all sides with his red, swollen eyes.

"Hash-tcha-va-ta?"

"Hashtchavata! And now you can give me that half-ruble!"

And Fishel crawled out of the boat and saw that he was really home at last. He didn't know what to do first. Run home to his wife and children? Dance and sing on the bank? Or should he praise and thank the Lord who had preserved him from such a tragic end? He paid the boatman his half-ruble, picked up his pack, and started to run as fast as he could. But after a few steps he stopped, turned back to the ferryman: "Listen, Prokop, my good friend! Come over tomorrow for a glass of Passover brandy and some holiday fish. Remember the name—Fishel the *melamed!* You hear? Don't forget now!"

"Why should I forget? Do you think I'm a fool?"

And he licked his lips at the thought of the Passover brandy and the strongly seasoned Jewish fish.

"That's wonderful, Uncle! That's wonderful!"

Six

When Fishel the *melamed* came into the house, Bath-Sheba, red as fire, with her kerchief low over her eyes, asked shyly, "How are you?" And he answered, "How are *you?*" And she asked, "Why are you so late?" And he answered, "We can thank God. It was a miracle." And not another word, because it was so late.

He did not even have time to ask Froike how he was getting along in the *Talmud,* or give Reizel the gift he had brought her, or Bath-Sheba the new silk shawl. Those things would have to wait. All he could think of now was the bath. And he just barely made it.

And when he came home from the bath he did not say anything either. Again he put it off till later. All he said was, "A miracle from heaven. We can thank the Lord. He takes care of us . . ."

And taking Froike by the hand, he hurried off to the synagogue.

Translated by Julius and Frances Butwin

ON ACCOUNT OF A HAT

"Did I hear you say absentminded? Now, in our town, that is, in Kasrilevke, we've really got someone for you—do you hear what I say? His name is Sholem Shachnah, but we call him Sholem Shachnah Rattle-brain, and is he absentminded, is this a distracted creature, Lord have mercy on us! The stories they tell about him, about this Sholem Shachnah—bushels and baskets of stories—I tell you, whole crates full of stories and anecdotes! It's too bad you're in such a hurry on account of the Passover, because what I could tell you, Mr. Sholom Aleichem—do you hear what I say?—you could go on writing it down forever. But if you can spare a moment I'll tell you a story about what happened to Sholem Shachnah on a Passover eve—a story about a hat, a true story, I should live so, even if it does sound like someone made it up."

These were the words of a Kasrilevke merchant, a dealer in stationery, that is to say, snips of paper. He smoothed out his beard, folded it down over his neck, and went on smoking his thin little cigarettes, one after the other.

I must confess that this true story, which he related to me, does indeed sound like a concocted one, and for a long time I couldn't make up my mind whether or not I should pass it on to you. But I thought it over and decided that if a respectable merchant and dignitary of Kasrilevke, who deals in stationery and is surely no *litterateur*—if he vouches for a story, it must be true. What would he be doing with fiction? Here it is in his own words. I had nothing to do with it.

This Sholem Shachnah I'm telling you about, whom we call Sholem Shachnah Rattlebrain, is a real-estate broker—you hear what I say? He's always with land-owners, negotiating transactions. Transactions? Well, at least he hangs around the landowners. So what's the point? I'll tell you. Since he hangs around the landed gentry, naturally some of their manner has rubbed off on him, and he always has a mouth full of farms, home-steads, plots, acreage soil, threshing machines, renova-tions, woods, timber, and other such terms having to do with estates.

One day God took pity on Sholem Shachnah, and for the first time in his career as a real-estate broker—are you listening?—he actually worked out a deal. That is to say, the work itself, as you can imagine, was done by others, and when the time came to collect the fee, the big rattler turned out to be not Sholem Shachnah Rat-tlebrain, but Drobkin, a Jew from Minsk province, a great big fearsome rattler, a real-estate broker from way back—he and his two brothers, also brokers and also big rattlers. So you can take my word for it, there was quite a to-do. A Jew has contrived and connived and has finally, with God's help, managed to cut himself in—so what do they do but come along and cut him out! Where's justice? Sholem Shachnah wouldn't stand for it—are you listening to me? He set up such a holler and an outcry—"Look what they've done to me!"—that at last they gave in to shut him up, and good riddance it was, too.

When he got his few cents Sholem Shachnah sent the greater part of it home to his wife, so she could pay off some debts, shoo the wolf from the door, fix up new outfits for the children, and make ready for the Pass-over holidays. And as for himself, he also needed a few things, and besides he had to buy presents for his fam-ily, as was the custom.

Meanwhile the time flew by, and before he knew it, it was almost Passover. So Sholem Shachnah—now lis-ten to this—ran to the telegraph office and sent home a wire: *"Arriving home Passover without fail."* It's easy to say "arriving" and "without fail" at that. But you just try it! Just try riding out our way on the new train and see how fast you'll arrive. Ah, what a pleasure! Did they do us a favor! I tell you, Mr. Sholom Aleichem, for a taste of Paradise such as this you'd gladly forsake your own grandchildren! You see how it is: until you get to Zolodievka there isn't much you can do about it, so you just lean back and ride. But at Zolodievka the fun begins, because that's where you have to change, to get onto the new train, which they did us such a favor by running out to Kasrilevke. But not so fast. First there's the little matter of several hours' wait, exactly as an-nounced in the schedule—provided, of course, you don't pull in after the Kasrilevke train has left. And at what time of night may you look forward to this treat? The very middle, thank you, when you're dead tired and disgusted, without a friend in the world except sleep—and there's not one single place in the whole station where you can lay your head, not one. When the wise men of Kasrilevke quote the passage from the Holy Book, *"Tov shem meshemen tov,"* they know what they're doing. I'll translate it for you: We were better off without the train.

To make a long story short, when our Sholem Shach-nah arrived in Zolodievka with his carpetbag he was half dead; he had already spent two nights without sleep. But that was nothing at all to what was facing him—he still had to spend a whole night waiting in the station. What shall he do? Naturally he looked around for a place to sit down. Whoever heard of such a thing? Nowhere. Nothing. No place to sit. The walls of the station were covered with soot, the floor was covered with spit. It was dark, it was terrible. He finally discovered one miserable spot on a bench where he had just room enough to squeeze in, and no more than that, because the bench was occupied by an official of some sort in a uniform full of buttons, who was lying there all stretched out and snoring away to beat the band. Who this Buttons was, whether he was coming or going, he hadn't the vaguest idea—Sholem Shachnah, that is. But he could tell that Buttons was no dime-a-dozen official. This was plain by his cap, a military cap with a red band and a visor. He could have been an officer or a police official. Who knows? But surely he had drawn up to the station with a ringing of bells, had staggered in, full to the ears with meat and drink, laid himself out on the bench as in his father's vineyard, and worked up a glorious snoring.

It's not such a bad life to be a Gentile, and an official one at that, with buttons, thinks he—Sholem Shachnah, that is—and he wonders, dare he sit next to this Buttons, or hadn't he better keep his distance? Nowadays you never can tell whom you're sitting next to. If he's no more than a plain inspector, that's still all right. But what if he turns out to be a district inspector? Or a provincial commander? Or even higher than that? And supposing this is even Purishkevitch himself, the famous anti-Semite (may his name perish)? Let someone else deal with him, and Sholem Shachnah turns cold at the mere thought of falling into such a fellow's hands. But then he says to himself—now listen to this—Buttons, he says, who the hell is Buttons? And who gives a hang for Purishkevitch? Don't I pay my fare the same as Purishkevitch? So why should he have all the comforts of life and I none? If Buttons is entitled to a delicious night's sleep, then doesn't he—Sholem Shachnah, that is—at least have a nap coming? After all, he's human too, and besides, he's already gone two nights without a wink. And so he sits down on a corner of the bench and leans his head back, not, God forbid, to sleep, but just like that, to snooze. But all of a sudden he remembers he's supposed to be home for Passover, and tomorrow is Passover eve! What if, God have mercy, he should fall asleep and miss the train? But that's why he's got a Jewish head on his shoulders—are you listening to me or not? So he figures out the answer to that one, too—Sholem Shachnah, that is—and goes looking for a porter, a certain Yeremei (he knows him well), to make a deal with him. Whereas he, Sholem Shachnah, is already on his third sleepless night and is afraid, God forbid, that he may miss his train, therefore let him—Yeremei, that is—in God's name, be sure to wake him, Sholem Shachnah, because tomorrow night is a holiday, Passover. "Easter," he says to him in Russian and lays a coin in Yeremei's mitt. "Easter, Yeremei, do you understand, *goyisher kop?* Our Easter." The peasant pockets the coin, no doubt about that, and promises to wake him at the first sign of the train—he can sleep soundly and put his mind at rest. So Sholem Shachnah sits down in his corner of the bench, gingerly, pressed up against the wall, with his carpetbag curled around him so that no one should steal it. Little by little he sinks back, makes himself comfortable, and half shuts his eyes—no more than forty winks, you understand. But before long he's got one foot propped up on the bench and then the other; he stretches out and drifts off to sleep. Sleep? I'll say sleep, like God commanded us: with his head thrown back and his hat rolling away on the floor. Sholem Shachnah is snoring like an eight-day wonder. After all, a human being, up two nights in a row—what would you have him do?

He had a strange dream. He tells this himself—that is, Sholem Shachnah does. He dreamed that he was riding home for Passover—are you listening to me?—but not on the train, in a wagon, driven by a thievish peasant, Ivan Zlodi we call him. The horses were terribly slow, they barely dragged along. Sholem Shachnah was impatient, and he poked the peasant between the shoulders and cried, "May you only drop dead, Ivan darling! Hurry up, you lout! Passover is coming, our Jewish Easter!" Once he called out to him, twice, three times. The thief paid him no mind. But all of a sudden he whipped his horses to a gallop and they went whirling away, up hill and down, like demons. Sholem Shachnah lost his hat. Another minute of this and he would have lost God knows what. "Whoa, there, Ivan old boy! Where's the fire? Not so fast!" cried Sholem Shachnah. He covered his head with his hands—he was worried, you see, over his lost hat. How can he drive into town bareheaded? But for all the good it did him, he could have been hollering at a post. Ivan the Thief was racing the horses as if forty devils were after him. All of a sudden—tppprrru!—they came to a dead stop. What's the matter? Nothing. "Get up," said Ivan, "time to get up."

Time? What time? Sholem Shachnah is all confused. He wakes up, rubs his eyes, and is all set to step out of the wagon when he realizes he has lost his hat. Is he dreaming or not? And what's he doing here? Sholem Shachnah finally comes to his senses and recognizes the peasant. This isn't Ivan Zlodi at all, but Yeremei the porter. So he concludes that he isn't on a high road after all, but in the station at Zolodievka, on the way home for Passover, and that if he means to get there he'd better run to the window for a ticket, but fast. Now what? No hat. The carpetbag is right where he left it, but his hat? He pokes around under the bench, reaching all over, until he comes up with a hat—not his own, to be sure, but the official's, with the red band and the visor. But Sholem Shachnah has no time for details and he rushes off to buy a ticket. The ticket window is jammed; everybody and his cousins are crowding in. Sholem Shachnah thinks he won't get to the window in time, perish the thought, and he starts pushing forward, carpetbag and all. The people see the red band and the visor and they make way for him. "Where to, Your Excellency?" asks the ticket agent. What's this Excellency, all of a sudden? wonders Sholem Shachnah, and he rather resents it. Some joke, a Gentile poking fun at a Jew. All the same he says—Sholem Shachnah, that is—"Kasrilevke." "Which class, Your Excellency?" The ticket agent is looking straight at the red band and the visor. Sholem Shachnah is angrier than ever. I'll give him an Excellency so he'll know how to make fun of a poor Jew! But then he thinks: Oh well, we Jews are in Diaspora—do you hear what I say?—let it pass. And he asks for a ticket third class. "Which class?" the agent blinks at him, very surprised. This time Sholem Shachnah gets good and sore and he really tells him off. "Third!" he says. All right, thinks the agent, third is third.

In short, Sholem Shachnah buys his ticket, takes up his carpetbag, runs out onto the platform, plunges into the crowd of Jews and Gentiles, no comparison intended, and goes looking for the third-class carriage. Again the red band and visor work like a charm; everyone makes way for the official. Sholem Shachnah is wondering, what goes on here? But he runs along the platform till he meets a conductor carrying a lantern. "Is this third class?" asks Sholem Shachnah, putting one foot on the stairs and shoving his bag into the door of the compartment. "Yes, Your Excellency," says the conductor, but he holds him back. "If you please, sir, it's packed full, as tight as your fist. You couldn't squeeze a needle into that crowd." And he takes Sholem Shachnah's carpetbag—you hear what I'm saying?—and sings out, "Right this way, Your Excellency, I'll find you a seat." "What the devil!" cries Sholem Shachnah. "Your Excellency and Your Excellency!" But he hasn't much time for the fine points; he's worried about his carpetbag. He's afraid, you see, that with all these Excellencies he'll be swindled out of his belongings. So he runs after the conductor with the lantern, who leads him into a second-class carriage. This is also packed to the rafters, no room even to yawn in there. "This way please, Your Excellency!" And again the conductor grabs the bag and Sholem Shachnah lights out after him. "Where in blazes is he taking me?" Sholem Shachnah is racking his brains over this Excellency business, but meanwhile he keeps his eye on the main thing—the carpetbag. They enter the first-class carriage, the conductor sets down the bag, salutes, and backs away, bowing. Sholem Shachnah bows right back. And there he is, alone at last.

Left alone in the carriage, Sholem Shachnah looks around to get his bearings—you hear what I say? He has no idea why all these honors have suddenly been heaped on him—first class, salutes, Your Excellency. Can it be on account of the real-estate deal he just closed? That's it! But wait a minute. If his own people, Jews, that is, honored him for this, it would be understandable. But Gentiles! The conductor! The ticket agent! What's it to them? Maybe he's dreaming. Sholem Shachnah rubs his forehead and while passing down the corridor glances in the mirror on the wall. It nearly knocks him over! He sees not himself but the official with the red band. That's who it is! "All my bad dreams on Yeremei's head and on his hands and feet, that lug! Twenty times I tell him to wake me and I even give him a tip, and what does he do, that dumb ox, may he catch cholera in his face, but wake the official instead! And me he leaves asleep on the bench! Tough luck, Sholem Shachnah old boy, but this year you'll spend Passover in Zolodievka, not at home."

Now get a load of this. Sholem Shachnah scoops up his carpetbag and rushes off once more, right back to the station where he is sleeping on the bench. He's going to wake himself up before the locomotive, God forbid, lets out a blast and blasts his Passover to pieces.

And so it was. No sooner had Sholem Shachnah leaped out of the carriage with his carpetbag than the locomotive did let go with a blast—do you hear me?—one followed by another, and then, good night!

The paper dealer smiled as he lit a fresh cigarette, thin as a straw. "And would you like to hear the rest of the story? The rest isn't so nice. On account of being such a rattlebrain, our dizzy Sholem Shachnah had a miserable Passover, spending both *seders* among strangers in the house of a Jew in Zolodievka. But this was nothing—listen to what happened afterward. First of all, he has a wife—Sholem Shachnah, that is—and his wife—how shall I describe her to you? *I* have a wife, *you* have a wife, we all have wives, we've had a taste of Paradise, we know what it means to be married. All I can say about Sholem Shachnah's wife is that she's A Number One. And did she give him a royal welcome! Did she lay into him! Mind you, she didn't complain about his spending the holiday away from home, and she said nothing about the red band and the visor. She let that stand for the time being; she'd take it up with him later. The only thing she complained about was the telegram! And not so much the telegram—you hear what I say?—as the one short phrase, *without fail*. What possessed him to put that into the wire: *Arriving home Passover without fail*. Was he trying to make the telegraph company rich? And besides, how dare a human being say "without fail" in the first place? It did him no good to answer and explain. She buried him alive. Oh, well, that's what wives are for. And not that she was altogether wrong—after all, she had been waiting so anxiously. But this was nothing compared with what he caught from the town—Kasrilevke, that is. Even before he returned, the whole town—you hear what I say?—knew all about Yeremei and the official and the red band and the visor and the conductor's Your Excellency—the whole show. He himself—Sholem Shachnah, that is—denied everything and swore up and down that the Kasrilevke smart alecks had invented the entire story for lack of anything better to do. It was all very simple: the reason he came home late, after the holidays, was that he had made a special trip to inspect a wooded estate. Woods? Estate? Not a chance—no one bought *that!* They pointed him out in the streets and held their sides, laughing. And everybody asked him, 'How does it feel, Reb Sholem Shachnah, to wear a cap with a red band and a visor?' 'And tell us,' said others, 'what's it like to travel first class?' As for the children, this was made to order for them—you hear what I say? Wherever he went they trooped after him, shouting, 'Your Excellency! Your excellent Excellency! Your most excellent Excellency!' "

"You think it's so easy to put one over on Kasrilevke?"

Translated by Isaac Rosenfeld

DREYFUS IN KASRILEVKE

I doubt if the Dreyfus case made such a stir anywhere as it did in Kasrilevke.

Paris, they say, seethed like a boiling vat. The papers carried streamers, generals shot themselves, and small boys ran like mad in the streets, threw their caps in the air, and shouted wildly, "Long live Dreyfus!" or "Long live Esterhazy!" Meanwhile the Jews were insulted and beaten, as always. But the anguish and pain that Kasrilevke underwent, Paris will not experience till Judgment Day.

How did Kasrilevke get wind of the Dreyfus case? Well, how did it find out about the war between the English and the Boers or what went on in China? What do they have to do with China? Tea they got from Wisotzky in Moscow. In Kasrilevke they do not wear the light summer material that comes from China and is called pongee. That is not for their purses. They are lucky if they have a pair of trousers and an undershirt, and they sweat just as well, especially if the summer is a hot one.

So how did Kasrilevke learn about the Dreyfus case? From Zeidel.

Zeidel, Reb Shaye's son, was the only person in town who subscribed to a newspaper, and all the news of the world they learned from him, or rather through him. He read and they interpreted. He spoke and they supplied the commentary. He told what he read in the paper, but they turned it around to suit themselves, because they understood better than he did.

One day Zeidel came to the synagogue and told how in Paris a certain Jewish captain named Dreyfus had been imprisoned for turning over certain government papers to the enemy. This went into one ear and out of the other. Someone remarked in passing, "What won't a Jew do to make a living?"

And another added spitefully, "A Jew has no business climbing so high, interfering with kings and their affairs."

Later when Zeidel came to them and told them a fresh tale, that the whole thing was a plot, that the Jewish Captain Dreyfus was innocent and that it was an intrigue of certain officers who were themselves involved, then the town became interested in the case. At once Dreyfus became a Kasrilevkite. When two people came together, he was the third.

"Have you heard?"

"I've heard."

"Sent away for good."

"A life sentence."

"For nothing at all."

"A false accusation."

Later when Zeidel came to them and told them that there was a possibility that the case might be tried again, that there were some good people who undertook to show the world that the whole thing had been a plot, Kasrilevke began to rock indeed. First of all, Dreyfus was one of *ours*. Secondly, how could such an ugly thing happen in Paris? It didn't do any credit to the French. Arguments broke out everywhere; bets were made. Some said the case would be tried again, others said it would not. Once the decision had been made, it was final. All was lost.

As the case went on, they got tired of waiting for

Zeidel to appear in the synagogue with the news; they began to go to his house. Then they could not wait that long, and they began to go along with him to the post office for his paper. There they read, digested the news, discussed, shouted, gesticulated, all together and in their loudest voices. More than once the postmaster had to let them know in gentle terms that the post office was not the synagogue. "This is not your synagogue, you Jews. This is not your community hall."

They heard him the way Haman hears the *grager* on Purim. He shouted, and they continued to read the paper and discuss Dreyfus.

They talked not only of Dreyfus. New people were always coming into the case. First Esterhazy, then Picquart, then General Mercies, Pellieux Gonse. . . .

There were two people whom Kasrilevke came to love and revere. These were Emile Zola and Labori. For Zola each one would gladly have died. If Zola had come to Kasrilevke the whole town would have come out to greet him; they would have borne him aloft on their shoulders.

"What do you think of his letters?"

"Pearls. Diamonds. Rubies."

They also thought highly of Labori. The crowd delighted in him, praised him to the skies, and, as we say, licked their fingers over his speeches. Although no one in Kasrilevke had ever heard him, they were sure he must know how to make a fine speech.

I doubt if Dreyfus's relatives in Paris awaited his return from the Island as anxiously as the Jews of Kasrilevke. They traveled with him over the sea, felt themselves rocking on the waves. A gale arose and tossed the ship up and down, up and down, like a stick of wood. "Lord of Eternity," they prayed in their hearts, "be merciful and bring him safely to the place of the trial. Open the eyes of the judges, clear their brains, so they may find the guilty one and the whole world may know of our innocence. Amen. *Selah.*"

The day when the good news came that Dreyfus had arrived was celebrated like a holiday in Kasrilevke. If they had not been ashamed to do so, they would have closed their shops.

"Have you heard?"

"Thank the Lord."

"Ah, I would have liked to have been there when he met his wife."

"And I would have liked to see the children when they were told, 'Your father has arrived.' "

And the women, when they heard the news, hid their faces in their aprons and pretended to blow their noses so no one could see they were crying. Poor as Kasrilevke was, there was not a person there who would not have given his very last penny to take one look at the arrival.

As the trial began, a great excitement took hold of the town. They tore not only the paper to pieces, but Zeidel himself. They choked on their food, they did not sleep nights. They waited for the next day, the next and the next.

Suddenly there arose a hubbub, a tumult. That was when the lawyer, Labori, was shot. All Kasrilevke was beside itself.

"Why? For what? Such an outrage! Without cause! Worse than in Sodom!"

That shot was fired at their heads. The bullet was lodged in their breasts, just as if the assassin had shot at Kasrilevke itself.

"God in heaven," they prayed, "reveal thy wonders. Thou knowest how if thou wishest. Perform a miracle, that Labori might live."

And God performed the miracle. Labori lived.

When the last day of the trial came, the Kasrilevkites shook as with a fever. They wished they could fall asleep for twenty-four hours and not wake up till Dreyfus was declared a free man.

But as if in spite, not a single one of them slept a wink

that night. They rolled all night from side to side, waged war with the bedbugs, and waited for day to come.

At the first sign of dawn they rushed to the post office. The outer gates were still closed. Little by little a crowd gathered outside and the street was filled with people. Men walked up and down, yawning, stretching, pulling their earlocks and praying under their breath.

When Yadama the janitor opened the gates they poured in after him. Yadama grew furious. He would show them who was master here, and pushed and shoved till they were all out in the street again. There they waited for Zeidel to come. And at last he came.

When Zeidel opened the paper and read the news aloud, there arose such an outcry, such a clamor, such a roar that the heavens could have split open. Their outcry was not against the judges who gave the wrong verdict, not at the generals who swore falsely, not at the French who showed themselves up so badly. The outcry was against Zeidel.

"It cannot be!" Kasrilevke shouted with one voice. "Such a verdict is impossible! Heaven and earth swore that the truth must prevail. What kind of lies are you telling us!"

"Fools!" shouted Zeidel, and thrust the paper into their faces. "Look! See what the paper says!"

"Paper! Paper!" shouted Kasrilevke. "And if you stood with one foot in heaven and the other on earth, would we believe you?"

"Such a thing must not be. It must never be! Never! Never!"

And—who was right?

Translated by Julius and Frances Butwin

TWO ANTI-SEMITES

Max Berlliant is a lost cause. He travels from Lodz to Moscow and from Moscow to Lodz several times a year. He knows all the buffets, all the stations along the way, is hand in glove with all the conductors, and has visited all the remote provinces—even the ones where Jews are only allowed to stay twenty-four hours. He has sweated at all the border crossings, put up with all kinds of humiliations, and more than once has been aggravated—has eaten his heart out, in fact—and all because of the Jews. Not because the Jews as a people exist, but because he himself—don't shout, whisper it—is also a Jew. And not even so much because he's a Jew, as because—if you'll forgive me for saying so—he looks so Jewish. That's what comes of creating man in God's image! And what an image! Max's eyes are dark and shining, his hair the same. It's real Semitic hair. He speaks Russian like a cripple, and, God help us, with a Yiddish singsong. And on top of everything he's got a nose! A nose to end all noses.

As if that weren't enough, our hero is unlucky in his occupation. He's a traveling salesman and it's part of his job to be friendly. He has to talk a lot, and in his business it's important that he should not just talk, but that he should be heard, and not just be heard, but above all be seen. In short, he's a sorry creature.

144

True, our hero did avenge himself on his beard. Beardless now, and decked out like a bride, he curls his whiskers, files his nails, wears a tie as glorious as what the Lord God himself might have worn had he ever worn a tie. Max has accustomed himself to the food in railway restaurants, but he continually vents his bitterness on the pigs of the world. If even half the curses he heaps on the species were to come true, I would be happy. But what's the use of being fussy? Might as well be hung for a sheep as for a lamb, so Max took his life in his hands and began to eat lobster.

Why do I say he took his life in his hands? May our worst enemies know as much about their noses as Max Berlliant knows about eating lobsters. Should he cut them with a knife or stab them with a fork? Or should he eat them whole, just as they come?

Despite all these glorious achievements Max Berlliant can't hide his Jewishness; not from us, the Jews, nor from them, the Gentiles. You can pick him out like a counterfeit coin in a handful of change, and in a crowd of Abels he stands out like a Cain. At every twist and turn he is reminded who he is and what he is. In short, he's a sorry creature.

If Max Berlliant was unhappy up to the time of Kishinev, after Kishinev no one could touch him for misery. To harbor deep in your heart a great sorrow, and what's worse to be ashamed of it, is a special kind of hell. Max was as ashamed of what had happened in Kishinev as if he was personally responsible for it, almost as if Kishinev was part of himself. And as luck would have it, right after the incidents in Kishinev, his firm sent him into the very districts where it had all happened: Bessarabia.

That's when a new hell opened up under his feet. He had heard a thousand horror stories about Kishinev in his home town. Wasn't it enough that his heart had flooded with grief and filled with blood when he was told about the atrocities in Kishinev, atrocities such as never had been known or heard before? Will he ever forget the day they offered up special prayers in the synagogues for the slaughtered of Kishinev? Or how, on that day, the old men wept and the women fainted?

It must surely have happened to you while sitting on a train that you passed the place where some great catastrophe has occurred. You know in your heart that you are safe because lightning doesn't strike twice in the same spot. Yet you can't help remembering that not so long ago trains were derailed at this very point, and carloads of people spilled over the embankment. You can't help knowing that here people were thrown out head first, over there bones were crushed, blood flowed, brains were splattered. You can't help feeling glad that you're alive; it's only human to take secret pleasure in it.

Max knew he was bound to meet people in these parts eager to talk about the pogroms. He would have to listen to the wails and groans of those who had lost their near and dear, and he would also be forced to endure the righteous exhortations and malicious remarks of the Gentiles. So the closer they came to Bessarabia, the more he tried to find some way of escape, some way to hide from his own soul.

As they approached the region Max thought of staying behind when the other passengers got off. Then he changed his mind and jumped down onto the platform with the others when the train stopped. He made his way to the buffet as if he hadn't a care in the world. He ordered a drink, followed it up with some tasty tidbits forbidden to Jews, washed it all down with a beer, lit a cigar, and went up to the counter where they sell books and newspapers. There his glance fell on a certain ugly anti-Semitic newspaper called *The Bessarabian*, published by a certain ugly anti-Semite called Krushevan. And here in the very region where this fine newspaper was conceived, hatched, and born, it lay innocently— almost anonymously—all by itself on the counter. Not a soul was buying it, nobody even gave it a second look.

The local Jews don't buy it because it's so scurrilous, and the Gentiles don't buy it because they are sick and tired of it. So there it lies, nice and neat on the counter, put there to remind the world that somewhere on the face of this earth lives a certain Krushevan, a man who neither rests nor sleeps in his tireless search for new ways to warn the world against that dread disease: Judaism.

Max Berlliant is the only one to buy a copy of *The Bessarabian*. And why is that? Maybe because of the same urge that drives him to eat lobster. Or maybe he wants to see for himself what that dog of dogs has to say about Jews? It's a proven fact that the readers of anti-Semitic newspapers are mostly Jews. That means us, little brothers, with all due respect . . . And though the publishers of such newspapers know it, they act on the principle that even if the Jew is *treyf,* his money is *kosher.* . . .

Accordingly our Max buys himself a copy of *The Bessarabian,* brings it back to the train, stretches out on the seat, and covers himself with the newspaper the way you cover yourself with a blanket. And while he is thus busying himself, a thought flies through his head: "What, for instance, would a Jew think if he came across a man stretched out on the seat covered with a copy of *The Bessarabian?* Surely it would never occur to him that the man under the newspaper might be a Jew . . . What an idea, what a great way to get rid of Jews and at the same time keep a seat all to myself."

So reasoned our hero. And in order to make sure that no mother's son should find out who was lying there, he covered his face with the newspaper; he hid his nose, also his eyes and hair, and indeed the whole physiognomy—the one made in God's own image. He pictured to himself how in the middle of the night an old Jew, weighed down with packs and bundles, creeps onto the train, looks around for a seat, sees someone lying there covered with *The Bessarabian,* figures that he must be a squire at least, but a bad lot in any case, and probably an anti-Semite—possibly even Krushevan himself. So the old Jew with his packs and bundles spits three times and goes away, while he, Max, remains lying there in lonely splendor, lording it over the whole seat. "Oh, oh, as I live and breathe, what a great joke!"

So much did this plan please our Max as he lay under his *Bessarabian,* that he burst into laughter. After all, when you have eaten, washed it down with beer, smoked a cigar, and toward evening stretch out on a seat all to yourself—you have something to crow about. . . .

Hush now, let's have quiet. Our hero, Max Berlliant, the traveling salesman whose route stretches from Lodz to Moscow and from Moscow to Lodz, is lying on a seat covered with the latest issue of *The Bessarabian.* He has just dozed off, so let's not disturb him.

Let's admit it, Berlliant is smart. But this time fate outsmarted him. Everything happened almost as he imagined. Someone did come onto the train—a burly fellow with two suitcases, and someone did notice him as he lay there covered with his *Bessarabian.* But instead of spitting three times and going away, the newcomer stood there studying him, this queer anti-Semite with the Semitic nose (for, during his sleep the newspaper had slipped off Max's face to reveal his nose, his stigma).

Our new arrival stands there, smiling. After placing his suitcase on the seat opposite Max, he steps out on the platform and returns with a fresh issue of *The Bessarabian.* Out of his suitcase he takes a pillow, a blanket, a pair of slippers, a bottle of eau de cologne, and makes himself comfortable. Then, stretching out on the seat opposite, he covers himself with the newspaper in exactly the same way as our Max Berlliant. He lies there smoking, looking at Max and smiling. He closes first one eye, then the other, and finally dozes off.

So let's leave our two *Bessarabians* sound asleep,

seat to seat. In the meantime we'll introduce the reader to our new character: who he is and what he is.

He is a general. Not a general in the army and not a governor-general, but a general inspector, an agent for a company. His real name is Chaim Nyemchick, but he signs himself Albert, and everybody calls him Patti.

I admit it sounds a bit crazy. How from a Chaim you get an Albert is understandable. After all, among us Jews doesn't a Velvel become a Vladimir, an Israel an Isadore, and an Avrom an Avukem? But how does a Chaim get to be a Patti? To answer this we'll have to employ logic, study linguistics, and use common sense.

Our first move is to get rid of the "ch" in Chaim. Then we say goodbye to the "i" and the "m," leaving only the "a" by itself. So all we have to do now is add on an "l" and a "b" and an "e" and an "r" and a "t." Now doesn't that add up to Albert? And from Albert it's just a step to Alberti, and from Alberti we get first Berti, then Betti, and finally—how could we miss?—Patti! *Sic transit gloria mundi.* In other words, this is how to make a turkey out of a duck.

Our character is called Patti Nyemchick and he's a general inspector who travels the world the same as Max Berlliant. But his nature is entirely different. He's lively, active, and expressive. And in spite of the fact that his name is Patti and he's a general inspector, he's a Jew like other Jews, and he loves Jews. He also enjoys entertaining people with stories and telling Jewish jokes.

Patti Nyemchick is known far and wide as a raconteur, but he has one fault: whatever the anecdote, he'll swear by all that's holy that his story is true and that it actually happened. The trouble is he keeps changing the locale of his stories and forgetting what he said last time. It's also rumored that Patti, this inspector general, skims over prayers, bluffs his way through difficult Hebrew passages, exaggerates—or as they say in our parts, he's a liar.

So, having come into the train and having noted how our Max Berlliant is stretched out on the seat under an issue of the notorious *Bessarabian,* and having recognized from his nose that Max could in no way be a relation, either close or distant, to Krushevan and his fancy anti-Semitic rag, Patti's first thought is: "This'll make a great story; this'll have them rolling in the aisles."

That's the reason why Patti slipped out, provided himself with a copy of *The Bessarabian,* and lay down opposite our Max. Wondering what would come of it, he dozed off.

Now let's leave Patti the general inspector under *The Bessarabian* copy two, and return to Max the traveling salesman under *The Bessarabian* copy one.

Two

Max Berlliant had a bad night. It must have been the things he ate at the station, because his sleep was troubled. He dreamed that he wasn't Max Berlliant at all, but Krushevan, the editor of *The Bessarabian*—and that he was riding, not on a train, but bareback on a wild boar, while a lobster, boiled and red, kept waving its claws at him, and all the while cries and echoes of *"Ki-shi-nev"* sounded from afar.

Now a little breeze seems to whistle in Max's ears. He hears the sound of rustling leaves and women's dresses and wants to open his eyes and can't. When he tries to touch his nose he finds he hasn't got one; his nose is gone—disappeared without a trace. And in the place where his nose used to be is a copy of *The Bessarabian,* and he can't remember where he is. He tries to move and can't. He knows he's dreaming but he can't wake up, he can't get hold of himself. He simply cannot.

He lies there stunned and suffering, in utter confusion. He feels his strength leaving and summons up his last bit of willpower. Finally he manages to squeeze out a groan, so low that he's the only one who hears it. He opens one eye a little, just a tiny little bit, and sees a ray of light. In the light he sees the figure of a man lying stretched out on the seat opposite him, also alone, and like him, taking up the whole seat. And that man is also covered with a copy of the same issue of *The Bessarabian*.

Our Max is amazed and bewildered. It seems to him that it's himself who is stretched out on the seat opposite, and he can't understand the logic of how he, Max, can possibly be lying there. How can a man see his own reflection without a mirror? Every single hair on his head stands on end, one at a time.

Gradually our Max begins to collect his thoughts and understand that the man on the seat opposite is not himself, Max, but someone else altogether. He wonders: "Where did the fellow come from and why is he lying on the seat opposite? And why is he covered with a copy of *The Bessarabian*?"

Max doesn't have the patience to wait for morning. He's in a hurry to answer the riddle, and right away. So he starts stirring, rattling his newspaper until he hears that the person on the seat opposite is also stirring and rattling his newspaper. He keeps still for a minute, then takes a quick look and sees the other fellow regarding him with a half-smile. Our two *Bessarabian* customers are lying there across from each other, staring but not talking. Although each anti-Semite is dying to know who the other one is, they hide their curiosity and keep mum.

Then Patti has an idea and starts to whistle the tune of that well-known Yiddish folk song:

> A little fire
> burns cosily
> in the old wood stove . . .

Our Max takes up the tune and whistles out the next line:

> And the room is hot . . .

Then slowly, slowly both anti-Semites sit up, throw off the *Bessarabians,* and together they burst into the familiar refrain. This time they don't whistle it, but sing the words with loud abandon:

> The rebbe sits
> with little children
> and recites with them
> the Hebrew alphabet . . .

Translated by Miriam Waddington

A PASSOVER EXPROPRIATION

Kasrilevke has always danced to the tune of Odessa. Since the disturbances began, the two towns do not differ by a hair. A strike in Odessa—a strike in Kasrilevke. In Odessa, agitation for a constitution—in Kasrilevke, agitation for a constitution. Odessa, a pogrom—Kasrilevke, a pogrom. A joker started a rumor that people in Odessa are cutting off their noses, and people in Kasrilevke began to sharpen their knives. It's a good thing that in Kasrilevke each likes to look at what the other is doing; everyone waited for someone elsc to cut off his nose. They're still waiting.

After such a preface, it's no wonder that scarcely a day passes that you don't read in the papers of a new misfortune in Kasrilevke: a "gang" invaded a baker's and expropriated all he had baked; a cobbler had almost finished a pair of boots—all that remained was to add the soles and heels—when they attacked him in broad daylight, intoning the well-known verse, "Lift your hands in the sanctuary and bless you the Lord," and took away the boots. Or a poor man went begging house to house—it happened on a Thursday—when he was trapped somewhere in an alley; they pushed a pistol in his face and shook out everything he had. Or listen to a story that a woman tells . . . But what a woman tells is something not to be repeated. A female is nervous, the times are disturbing; she may mistake a milk cow for a pear tree . . . I don't want to be held responsible.

In short, the town has experienced a series of expropriations, each more frightful than the next. It is dangerous to be alive! One began to long for the good old days when a police inspector (you only had to slip him a ruble) knew how to keep a whole city in his hand. We began to turn to God and pray: "Lord of the universe! Help us—bring 'em back. 'Renew our days of old!' "

This is still no more than an introduction. Now the story really begins.

Benjamin Lastetchke is the richest man in Kasrilevke. There is no end to his greatness! For one thing, he has rich in-laws in all parts of the world. True, they're not as rich as they used to be. What with today's conditions and business failures, this is not surprising. It's only a wonder that Jews manage as well as they do. But Kasrilevke Jews—they're stronger than iron! They are packed together like herring in a barrel, and there they feed on one another. It's a bit of luck that each year America draws almost twice as many as die here from hunger, pogroms, or other calamities. But since God has willed it, there is still a rich man in Kasrilevke, one called Benjamin Lastetchke, the envy of all because he doesn't have to depend on anyone—except his rich in-laws. You may think that having to depend on a rich in-law is not exactly such a tasty piece of bread, since most rich in-laws (not to be repeated) are stingy by nature. Still, Benjamin Lastetchke is the rich man of Kasrilevke. If you need a favor, where do you go? To Benjamin Lastetchke. He listens. Sometimes he helps with a bit of advice or a wise saying, sometimes with a sigh. These don't hurt. Without them, would it be better? It's all down the drain anyway.

What is the difference between a rich man in Kasrilevke and one in Yehupetz? Rich men in Yehupetz have a soft heart. The cannot bear the misery of poor people. So they close the door, stand a butler at the threshold, and admit no son of Adam who is not well-dressed. Comes the dear summer, they rise like swallows and off to foreign parts—just try to find them! But let a rich man in Kasrilevke try to do it—they will tear him apart! Benjamin Lastetchke (he has no choice) is head and front of the community. In all matters pertaining to charity, he is the first among us not only to make a donation but to take his walking stick in hand and go house to house asking for contributions from paupers—for other paupers.

Especially before Passover, when it comes to collecting money for wheat—ah!—that is when you can take delight in watching Benjamin Lastetchke, even if only from afar. I doubt that the most zealous civic leader in the entire world, while engaged in the hottest campaign, has ever sweated as much as our Benjamin Lastetchke in the four weeks before the holidays! He swears that between Purim and Passover he sleeps in his clothing! Might as well believe him, because how does he stand to gain? He does not ask to be paid for his work. Ah, you may say he does it for the honor? Maybe. . . . But why should this disturb you? A man wants honor. Even princes don't disdain it. We won't change human nature—it is too late.

Two

The custom of wheat for the poor is an old one. It's a very old-fashioned method of philanthropy. Nonetheless, I do not think it is as distasteful as our modern thinkers would like to persuade us. They say, "philanthropy is an offense against society." I don't want to join them in debate. I merely want to answer that, in my opinion, there is a custom which is even more offensive: that the wealthy do not give and you have to pluck it out of their teeth. What is even a thousand times worse is that the nice people who don't want to give will try, so to speak, to talk a child into your belly: they don't give because of a principle. These are the sort of people you ought to run away from. They are dry like a dried fish and gloomy like a cat. Thank God, in Kasrilevke this "principle" is not yet in fashion. Those who do not give do not because they have nothing to give. However, when it comes to contributions for wheat, even this will not serve as an excuse. There is a saying in Kasrilevke: everyone must either give money or take it.

Strange are the people of Kasrilevke! Thousands of years have passed since their great-grandfathers broke the chains of Egyptian exile—and they still can't lose the habit of eating unleavened bread eight days each year. I'm afraid this dry morsel won't be out of style for a long time. Other days of the year, a Jew in Kasrilevke may swell up with hunger; but as soon as Passover arrives, let the world stand on its head, he must be supplied with *matzos*. It has never happened yet that at this time a Jew should die of hunger. If such a thing occurs, it should be charged to the account of the whole year; that is, he died not because (God forbid) he had no *matzos* during the eight days, but because he had no leavened bread in 357 other days. As you understand, there is a big difference.

Three

There is no rule without an exception. This year, the one we are describing, was one whose like we had never heard of. It seemed there were more takers than givers. If they hadn't been ashamed, very few of the inhabitants would have refused money for wheat. Oh, a pity to look at our rich Benjamin Lastetchke, how he sits in "committee" this last day and keeps turning the applicants away: "There is no money . . . it has run out . . . do not take offense."

"Maybe next year," answered the people who had been refused, adding under their nose, "May *you* come to us for charity."

One after another, the poor people came out of the committee office, hands empty and faces red as if from a steam bath, cursing from one end of the world to the other—may it fall into the sea!

Among the last of those who were rejected was a pack of young fellows, workers who'd been idle, without a stitch of work, the entire winter. They'd already sold all of their belongings. One had pawned a silver watch and for what he got he bought cigarettes which they all smoked to quiet their hunger—it was a sort of communal affair.

When they came to the committee office, they put forward as their spokesman a ladies' tailor called Shmuel-Abba Fingerhut. Although he was the speaker-in-command, he was helped out by the entire group, all arguing and complaining they are dying of hunger, that they are falling face forward to the ground. The chairman of the committee, Benjamin Lastetchke, let them speak, and when they stopped he began in this fashion: "Do not take offense, but your words are wasted. In the first place, you are not married and we give only to those who are. In the second (no evil eye attend you), you are young fellows who can get a job and earn what is needed. In the third place, this year has brought a good crop of poor people—more takers than givers. Fourthly, I'm ashamed to say it, but since early morning we haven't even got a broken penny in the cash box. If you don't believe me—look!"

And the chairman of the committee turned his pockets inside out so they might see, with their own eyes, that he had no money. He was pure as gold. They were left speechless—except for their leader Shmuel-Abba Fingerhut. No one has to prime his tongue. He turned to the chairman with a full-length sermon, half Yiddish, half Russian, to the following effect: "A pity you didn't start at the very end—you would not have had to waste so much of your powder. But I'll give you an answer to each of your arguments. One, if we are bachelors, that is good for you: fewer poor in town. Two, you spoke of work. Do us a favor: give us work and we'll turn the wide world upside down. Three, when you use the phrase 'poor people'—capitalism is to blame for exploitation of the proletariat. And four, if you turn your pockets inside out, that proves nothing at all. We're sure that in your home your own cupboards are full of *matzos*, eggs, onions and potatoes, and goose fat and other such items, as well as wine for the 'four cups.' . . . You're all bourgeois, exploiters without conscience—*Bolsheh nitchevo:* You are nothing else. *Tovarishtchi*—comrades, let's go!"

We must admit that Kasrilevke, which dances to the tune of Odessa and other big cities, is not—as yet—so far advanced that an exploiter such as Benjamin Lastetchke should open his cupboards and give the poor his *matzos,* his eggs, onions and potatoes, and goose fat, as well as wine for his 'four cups,' while he himself, his wife and children are left just so. . . . But I am convinced, sure as twice two is four, that my Kasrilevke exploiters certainly will get to do it. Just let Odessa or Yehupetz or other big cities set an example. Kasrilevke, my friends, has no obligation to be the first one at the fair.

Four

With a clear conscience, bathed and festive, Benjamin Lastetchke sat with his wife and children at the first *seder,* calm and well-disposed, like a true king at ease in his kingdom. To his right, the queen, his wife Sarah-Leah, dressed in best regalia, with a new silken shawl near which hung two long earrings of genuine 84-karat silver. Around the board his children, princes and princesses—a bouquet of washed hair, red cheeks, gleaming tiny eyes. Even Zlotke the maid—who on other days is in yoke and harness, toiling like a donkey—has shampooed her hair with a scented soap and got herself into a new calico dress and new half-boots and put a wide red ribbon on her shiny, swarthy forehead. All feel so good, delighted, and free, as if they themselves just got out of Egypt.

Starting with a boom, the youngest of the princes rattled off the Four Questions. The king—his father Benjamin Lastetchke—began slowly, in a loud voice with a lovely tune, to give him the explanation, the old explanation, *"Avodim hayinu*—we were slaves, *lefaro bemitzrayim*—of Pharaoh in Egypt. And God delivered us with a mighty hand. He paid off Pharaoh with ten nice afflictions. . . ." In a loud voice, to a special tune, they began to count the nice afflictions. When suddenly . . .

Five

Suddenly a knock on the door; then another knock. Then two more. . . . Who could this be? Should they open or not? It was decided that yes, they would, because the knocking, as it went on, grew louder. King, queen, and princes were silent. Zlotke, the maid, opened the door. Into the house there rushed the whole pack of young fellows, the leader Shmuel-Abba Fingerhut, in front with a broad "Good *yontif!*" . . .

Our rich Benjamin Lastetchke, though his heart was in his boots, summoned up his courage to face them: "A good *yontif!* Look who's here. What is the good word?"

Shmuel-Abba Fingerhut, the official spokesman, came forward with a sermon in his own manner, Yiddish mixed with Russian, which might be translated:

"You are in a well-lit room, sitting with a glass of wine, celebrating the holy feast. And we—poor proletarians—are perishing. from hunger. I find this *"n'yesprovedle"*: it is unjust. I *"prikozeve,"* command, that you surrender your holiday dinner to us, and don't dare utter a peep. Don't open any window, don't call any police, or it will be too bad. We will smash you. . . . Comrade Moishe, where's the bomb?"

Six

The last few words were enough to paralyze the whole household; they sat riveted to their places. When this "Comrade Moishe," a young cobbler with a dark complexion, a black forelock, and grimy fingers, went to the table and with a flourish set down some sort of a long cylindrical object covered by a rag, the household became like Lot's wife when she turned around wanting to see what had happened to Sodom and Gomorrah.

Zlotke the servant, her teeth chattering, brought them first of all the hot peppered fish, then the broth with fat dumplings, pancakes, puddings, and other good things which the fellows put away with such appetite as if it really had been a long time since they had eaten. And they drank each morsel down with wine, as if they had promised themselves not to leave a drop. Even the symbolic shank bone, egg, greens, bitters, and sweet paste received the proper treatment. They didn't leave a trace or memory of the *seder*—only the *Haggadah*. While this was going on, the speaker-in-chief, Shmuel-Abba Fingerhut, continued to jeer at our rich man, the exploiter Benjamin Lastetchke, using these words: "As a rule, we read the *Haggadah* while you eat the dumplings. But this time *you* read the *Haggadah* while we eat the dumplings. . . . Your health, bourgeois. God grant—you'll become a proletarian like us. Next year, may we celebrate a constitution!"

The Epilogue of the Tragedy

It was midnight. The poor rich man, Benjamin Lastetchke, and his houschold still sat around the table,
still in a fright. On the table still stood the "calamity"—
the tall, cylindrical object covered with a rag. Before
they left, members of the pack had warned them they'd
better sit in place for the next two hours; otherwise it
would be bad. . . . That night, no one fell asleep. They
thanked God they had come out of it alive.

But what happened to the tall, cylindrical "calamity"
that stood on the table? If you wonder, we will reassure
you: a tin of shoe polish—filled with matzo meal—isn't
dangerous at all. It may stand a thousand years and it
won't blow up anything, unless, God forbid. . . . "a
good *yontif!*"

Translated by Nathan Halper

IF I WERE ROTHSCHILD

If I were Rothschild, ah, if I were only Rothschild—a Kasrilevke *melamed* let himself go once upon a Thursday while his wife was demanding money for the Sabbath and he had none to give her. If I were only Rothschild, guess what I would do. First of all I would pass a law that a wife must always have a three-ruble piece on her so that she wouldn't have to start nagging me when the good Thursday comes and there is nothing in the house for the Sabbath. In the second place I would take my Sabbath gabardine out of pawn—or better still, my wife's squirrel-skin coat. Let her stop whining that she's cold. Then I would buy the whole house outright, from foundation to chimney, all three rooms, with the alcove and the pantry, the cellar and the attic. Let her stop grumbling that she hasn't enough room. "Here," I would say to her, "take two whole rooms for yourself—cook, bake, wash, chop, make, and leave me in peace so that I can teach my pupils with a free mind."

This is the life! No more worries about making a living. No more headaches about where the money for the Sabbath is coming from. My daughters are all married off—a load gone from my shoulders. What more do I need for myself? Now I can begin to look around the town a little. First of all I am going to provide a new roof for the old synagogue so the rain won't drip on the heads of the men who come to pray. After that I shall build a new bathhouse, for if not today, then tomorrow—but surely soon—there is bound to be a catastrophe—the roof is going to cave in while the women are inside bathing. And while we are putting up a new bathhouse we might as well throw down the old poorhouse, too, and put up a hospital in its place, a real hospital such as they have in big towns, with beds and bedding, with a doctor and attendants, with hot broths for the sick every day. . . . And I shall build a home for the aged so that old men, scholars who have fallen upon hard times, shouldn't have to spend their last days on the hearth in the synagogue. And I shall establish a Society for Clothing the Poor so that poor children won't have to run around in rags with—I beg your pardon for mentioning it—their navels showing. Then I shall institute a Loan Society so that anyone at all— whether teacher or workman, or even merchant— could get money without having to pay interest and without pawning the shirt off his back. And a Society for Outfitting Brides so that any girl old enough to marry and without means should be outfitted properly and married off as befits a Jewish girl. I would organize all these and many other such societies in Kasrilevke.

But why only here in Kasrilevke? I would organize such societies everywhere, all over the world, wherever our brethren the Sons of Israel are to be found. And in order that they should all be run properly, with a system, guess what I would do. I would appoint a Society to head them all, a Board of Charity that would watch over all the societies under it. This Board of Charity would keep watch over all of Israel and see to it that Jews everywhere had enough to live on and that they lived together in unity. It would see to it that all Jews sit in *yeshivas* and study the Bible, the *Talmud*, the *Gemara*, and the various commentaries and learn all the seven wisdoms and the seventy-seven languages. And over all these *yeshivas* there would be one great *yeshiva* or Jewish Academy which would naturally be located in Vilno. And from there would come the greatest scholars and wise men in the world. And all of this education would be free to everyone, all paid for out of my pocket. And I would see to it that it was all run in orderly fashion, according to plan, so that there should be none of this grab-and-run, hit-and-miss, catch-as-catch-can business. Instead, everything would be run with a view to the common welfare.

But in order to have everyone think only of the common welfare, you have to provide one thing. And what is that? Naturally, security. For, take it from me, security from want is the most important thing in the world. Without it there can be no harmony anywhere. For alas, one man will impoverish another over a piece of bread; he will kill, poison, hang his fellow man. Even the enemies of Israel, the Hamans of the world—what do you think they have against us? Nothing at all. They don't persecute us out of plain meanness but because of their lack of security. It's lack of money, I tell you, that brings envy, and envy brings hatred, and out of hatred come all the troubles in the world, all the sorrows, persecutions, killings, all the horrors and all the wars. . . .

Ah, the wars, the wars. The terrible slaughters. If I were Rothschild I would do away with war altogether. I would wipe it off completely from the face of the earth.

You will ask how? With money, of course. Let me explain it to you. For instance, two countries are having a disagreement over some foolishness, a piece of land that's worth a pinch of snuff. "Territory" they call it. One country says this "territory" is hers and the other one says, "No, this territory is mine." You might think that on the First Day, God created this piece of land in her honor. . . . Then a third country enters and says, "You are both asses. This is everybody's 'territory'; in other words, it's a public domain." Meanwhile the argument goes on. "Territory" here, "territory" there.

They "territory" each other so long that they begin shooting with guns and cannons and people start dying like sheep and blood runs everywhere like water. . . .

But if I come to them at the very beginning and say, "Listen to me, little brothers. Actually, what is your whole argument about? Do you think that I don't understand? I understand perfectly. At this feast you are concerned less with the ceremonial than with the dumplings. 'Territory' is only a pretext. What you are after is something else—something you can get your hands on—money, levies. And while we are on the subject of money, to whom does one come for a loan if not to me, that is, to Rothschild? I'll tell you what. Here, you Englishmen with the long legs and checkered trousers, take a billion. Here, you stupid Turks with the scarlet caps, take a billion also. And you, Aunt Reisel—Russia, that is—take another billion. With God's help you will pay me back with interest, not a large rate of interest, God forbid, four or five percent at the most—I don't want to get rich off you."

Do you understand what I've done? I have not only put over a business deal, but people have stopped killing each other in vain, like oxen. And since there will be no more war, what do we need weapons for? For what do we need armies and cannons and military bands, and all the other trappings of war? The answer is that we don't. And if there are no more weapons and armies and bands and other trappings of war, there will be no more envy, no more hatred, no Turks, no Englishmen, no Frenchmen, no Gypsies, and no Jews. The face of the earth will be changed. As it is written: "Deliverance will come—" The Messiah will have arrived.

And perhaps, even—if I were Rothschild—I might do away with money altogether. For let us not deceive ourselves, what is money anyway? It is nothing but a delusion, a made-up thing. Men have taken a piece of paper, decorated it with a pretty picture and written on it, *Three Silver Rubles*. Money, I tell you, is nothing but a temptation, a piece of lust, one of the greatest lusts. It is something that everyone wants and nobody has. But if there were no more money in the world there would be no more temptation, no more lust. Do you understand me or not? But then the problem is, without money how would we Jews be able to provide for the Sabbath? The answer to that is—How will I provide for the Sabbath now?

Translated by Frances Butwin

PART
TWO

TEVYE STRIKES IT RICH

If you're meant to strike it rich, Pani Sholom Aleichem, you may as well stay home with your slippers on, because good luck will find you there, too. The more it blows the better it goes, as King David says in his Psalms—and believe me, neither brains nor brawn has anything to do with it. And vice versa: if it's not in the cards you can run back and forth till you're blue in the face, it will do as much good as last winter's snow. How does the saying go? Flogging a dead horse won't make it run any faster. A man slaves, works himself to the bone, is ready to lie down and die—it shouldn't happen to the worst enemy of the Jews. Suddenly, don't ask me how or why, it rains gold on him from all sides. In a word, *revakh ve'hatsoleh ya'amoyd la'yehudim,* just like it says in the Bible! That's too many words to translate, but the general sense of it is that as long as a Jew lives and breathes in this world and hasn't more than one leg in the grave, he mustn't lose faith. Take it from my own experience—that is, from how the good Lord helped set me up in my present line of business. After all, if I sell butter and cheese and such stuff, do you think that's because my grandmother's grandmother was a milkman? But if I'm going to tell you the whole story, it's worth hearing from beginning to end. If you don't mind, then, I'll sit myself down here beside you and let my horse chew on some grass. He's only human too, don't you think, or why else would God have made him a horse?

Well, to make a long story short, it happened early one summer, around Shavuos time. But why should I lie to you? It might have been a week or two before Shavuos too, unless it was several weeks after. What I'm trying to tell you is that it took place exactly a dog's age ago, nine or ten years to the day, if not a bit more or less. I was the same man then that I am now, only not at all like me; that is, I was Tevye then too, but not the Tevye you're looking at now. How does the saying go? It's still the same lady, she's just not so shady. Meaning that in those days (it should never happen to you) I was such a miserable beggar that rags were too good for me. Believe me, I'm no millionaire today either. If from now until autumn the two of us earned what it would take to make me one, we wouldn't be doing half-bad. Still, compared to what I was then I've become a real tycoon. I've got my own horse and wagon. I've got two cows that give milk, bless them, and a third cow waiting to calf. Forgive me for boasting, but we're swimming in cheese, cream, and butter. Not that we don't work for it, mind you: you won't find any idlers at my place. My wife milks the cows. The kids carry the cans and churn butter. And I, as you see, go to market every morning and from there to all the rich summer *dachas* in Boiberik. I stop to chat with this one, with that one; there isn't a rich Jew I don't know there. When you talk with such people, you know, you begin to feel that you're someone yourself and not such a one-armed tailor any more. And I'm not even talking about the Sabbath. On the Sabbath, I tell you, I'm king. I have all the time in the world; I can even pick up a Jewish book if I want: the Bible, psalms, Rashi, Targum, Perek, you-name-it. . . . I tell you, if you could only see me then, you would say: "He's really some fine fellow, that Tevye!"

To get to the point, though . . . where were we? Oh, yes . . . in those days, with God's help, I was poor as a devil. No Jew should starve as I did. Not counting suppers, my wife and kids went hungry three times a day. I worked like a dog dragging logs by the wagonful from the forest to the train station for—I'm embarrassed even to tell you—half a ruble a day . . . and not even every day either. You try feeding a house full of little mouths on that, to say nothing of a horse who's moved in with you and can't be put off with some verse from the Bible, because he expects to eat every day and no buts! So what does the good Lord do? I tell you, it's not for nothing that they say He's a *zon u'mefarnes lakol,* that He runs this world of his with more brains than you or I could. He sees me eating my heart out for a slice of bread and says: "Now, Tevye, are you really trying to tell me that the world has come to an end? Eh, what a damn fool you are! In no time I'm going to show you what God can do when He wants. About face, march!" As we say on Yom Kippur, *mi yorum u'mi yishpoyl*—leave it to Him to decide who goes on foot and who gets to ride. The main thing is confidence. A Jew must never, never give up hope. How does he go on hoping, you ask, when he's already black in the face? But that's the whole point of being a Jew in this world! What does it say in the prayer book? *Ato b'khartonu!* We're God's chosen people; it's no wonder the whole world envies us. . . . You don't know what I'm talking about? Why, I'm talking about myself, about the miracle God helped me to. Be patient and you'll hear all about it.

Vayehi hayom, as the Bible says: one fine summer day in the middle of the night, I'm driving home through the forest after having dumped my load of logs. I feel like my head is in the ground, a black desert could grow in my heart; it's all my poor horse can do to drag his feet along behind him. "It serves you right, you *schlima-zel,*" I say to him, "for belonging to someone like me! If you're going to insist on being Tevye's horse, it's time you knew what it tastes like to fast the whole length of a summer's day." It was so quiet that you could hear every crack of the whip whistle through the woods. The sun began to set; the day was done for. The shadows of the trees were as long as the exile of the Jews. And with the darkness a terrible feeling crept into my heart. All sorts of thoughts ran in and out of my head. The faces of long-dead people passed before me. And when I thought of coming home—God help me! The little house would be pitch dark. My naked, barefoot kids would peek out to see if their *schlemiel* of a father hadn't brought them some bread, maybe even a freshly baked roll. And my old lady would grumble like a good Jewish mother: "A lot he needed children—and seven of them at that! God punish me for saying so, but my mistake was not to have taken them all and thrown them into the river." How do you think it made me feel to hear her say such things? A man is only flesh and blood, after all; you can't fill a stomach with words. No, a stomach needs herring to fill it; herring won't go down without tea; tea can't be drunk without sugar; and sugar, my friend, costs a fortune. And my wife! "My guts," says my wife, "can do without bread in the morning, but without a glass of tea I'm a stretcher case. That baby's sucked the glue from my bones all night long."

Well, one can't stop being a Jew in this world: it was time for the evening prayer. (Not that the evening was about to run away, mind you, but a Jew prays when he must, not when he wants to.) Some fine prayer it turned out to be! Right smack in the middle of the *shimenesre,* the eighteen benedictions, a devil gets into my crazy horse and he decides to go for a jaunt. I had to run after the wagon and grab the reins while shouting "God of Abraham, Issac, and Jacob" at the top of my voice— and to make matters worse, I'd really felt like praying for a change, for once in my life I was sure it would make me feel better . . .

In a word, there I was running behind the wagon and singing the *shimenesre* like a cantor in a synagogue. *M'khalkel khayim b'khesed,* who provideth life with His bounty . . . it better be all of life, do you hear me? *U'm'kayem emunoso lisheyney ofor,* Who keepeth faith with they who slumber in earth . . . who slumber in earth? With my troubles I was six feet underground already. And to think of those rich Yehupetz Jews sitting all summer long in their *dachas* in Boiberik, eating and drinking and swimming in luxury! Master of the Universe, what have I done to deserve all this? Am I or am I not a Jew like any other? *Gevalt! Re'eh-no b'onyenu.* See us in our affliction . . . take a good look at us poor folk slaving away and do something about it, because if you don't, who do you think will? *Refo'enu ve'nerofey,* Heal our wounds that we be whole . . . please concentrate on the healing because the wounds we already have. *Borekh oleynu,* Bless the fruits of this year . . . kindly arrange a good harvest of corn, wheat and barley—although what good it will do me is more than I can say: does it make any difference to my horse, I ask you, if the oats I can't afford to buy it are expensive or cheap?

But God doesn't tell a man what He thinks, and a Jew had better believe that He knows what He's up to. *V'lamalshinim al tehi tikvo,* May the slanderers have no hope . . . those are the big shots who say there is no God. What wouldn't I give to see the look on their faces when they line up for Judgment Day! They'll pay with back interest for everything they've done, because God has a long memory, one doesn't play around with Him. No, what he wants is for us to be good, to beseech and cry out to Him. *Ov harakhamom,* merciful, loving Father! *Shma koleynu,* You better listen to what we tell you! *Hus v'rakhem oleynu,* pay a little attention to my wife and children, the poor things are hungry! *R'tseh,* take decent care of your people again, as once you did long ago in the days of the Temple, when the Priests and the Levites sacrificed before you . . .

All of a sudden—whoaaa! My horse stopped short in its tracks. I rushed through what was left of the prayer, opened my eyes, and looked around me. Two weird figures, dressed for a masquerade, were approaching from the forest. "Robbers!" I thought at first, then caught myself. "Tevye," I said, "what an idiot you are! Do you mean to tell me that after traveling through this forest by day and by night for so many years, today is the day for robbers?" And bravely smacking my horse on the rear as though what I saw were no affair of mine, I said, "Giddap!"

"Hey, a fellow Jew!" One of the two holy terrors called out to me in a woman's voice and waved a scarf at me. "Don't run away, mister. Wait a second; we won't do you any harm."

"It's a ghost for sure!" I thought to myself. But a second later I thought, "What kind of monkey business is this, Tevye? Since when are you so afraid of ghouls and goblins?" So I pulled up my horse and took a good look at the two. They really did look like women. One was quite old and had a silk kerchief on her head, while the other was young and wore a wig. Both were beet-red and sweating buckets.

"Well, well, well, good evening!" I said to them as loudly as I could to show that I wasn't a bit put out. "How can I be of service to you? If you're looking to buy something, I'm afraid I'm out of stock, unless you're interested in some fine hunger pangs, a week's supply of heartache, or a head full of scrambled brains. Anyone for some chilblains, assorted aches and pains, worries to turn your hair gray?"

"Calm down, calm down," they said to me. "Just listen to him run on! Say a good word to a Jew, and you'll get a mouthful of bad ones in return. We don't want to buy anything. We simply wanted to ask whether you happened to know the way to Boiberik."

"The way to Boiberik?" I did my best to laugh. "You might as well ask me whether I know that my own name is Tevye."

"You say your name is Tevye? We're very pleased to meet you, Reb Tevye. We wish you'd explain to us, though, what the joke is all about. We're strangers around here; we come from Yehupetz and have a summer place in Boiberik. The two of us went out this morning for a little walk and have been going around in circles ever since without finding our way out of these woods. A little while ago we heard someone singing in the forest. At first we thought, who knows, maybe it's a highwayman. But as soon as we came closer and saw that you were, thank goodness, a Jew, you can imagine how much better we felt. Do you follow us?"

"A highwayman?" I laughed. "That's a good one! Did you ever hear the story of the Jewish highwayman who fell on somebody in the forest and begged him for a pinch of snuff? If you'd like, I'd be only too glad to tell it to you."

"The story," they said, "can wait. We'd rather you showed us the way to Boiberik first."

"The way to Boiberik? You're standing on it right now. This path will take you to Boiberik whether or not you want to go to Boiberik."

"But if this is the way to Boiberik, why didn't you say before that this is the way to Boiberik?"

"I didn't say that this is the way to Boiberik, because you didn't ask me whether this is the way to Boiberik."

"Well, if this is the way to Boiberik," they said, "would you possibly happen to know by any chance how far away to Boiberik it is?"

"To Boiberik," I said, "it's not a long way at all. Only a few miles. About two or three. Maybe four. Unless it's five."

"Five miles?" screamed both women at once, wringing their hands and all but breaking out in tears. "Do you realize what you're saying? Do you have any idea? *Only* five miles!"

"Well," I said, "what would you like me to do about it? If it were up to me, I'd make it a little shorter. But there are worse fates than yours, let me tell you. How would you like to be stuck in a wagon creeping up a muddy hill with the Sabbath only an hour away? The rain whips straight in your face, your hands are numb, your heart is too weak to beat, and suddenly . . . bang! Your front axle's gone and snapped."

"You're talking like a halfwit," said one of the two women. "I swear, there's a screw loose in your head. Why are you telling us fairytales from *The Arabian Nights?* We haven't the strength left to take another step. Except for a cup of coffee with a butter roll for breakfast, we haven't had a bite of food all day—and you expect us to stand here listening to your stories . . ."

"That," I said, "is a different story. How does the saying go? It's no fun dancing on an empty stomach. And you don't have to tell me what hunger tastes like; that's something I happen to know. It's not at all unlikely, in fact, that I haven't even seen a cup of coffee and a butter roll for over a year . . ." The words weren't out of my mouth when I saw a cup of hot coffee with cream and a fresh butter roll before my eyes, not to mention what else was on the table. "Idiot," I thought to myself, "a person might think you were raised on coffee and rolls; I suppose plain bread and herring would make you sick?" But just to spite me my imagination kept insisting on coffee and rolls. I could smell the coffee, I could taste the roll on my tongue—my God, how fresh, how delicious it was . . .

"Do you know what, Reb Tevye?" the two women said to me. "We've got a brilliant idea. As long as we're standing here chatting, why don't we hop into your wagon and give you the chance to take us back to Boiberik yourself. How about it?"

"I'm sorry," I said, "but you're spitting into the wind. You're going to Boiberik and I'm coming from Boiberik. How do you suppose I can go both ways at once?"

"That's easy," they said. "We're surprised you haven't thought of it already. If you were a scholar,

you'd have realized right away: you simply turn your
wagon around and head back in the other direction. . . .
Don't get so nervous, Reb Tevye. We should only have
to suffer the rest of our lives as much as getting us home
safely, God willing, will cost you."

"My God," I thought, "they're talking Chinese. I
can't make head or tail of any of it." And for the second
time that evening I thought of ghosts, witches, and
things that go bump in the night. "You block of wood,"
I said to myself, "what are you standing there for like a
tree stump? Jump back into your wagon, give the horse
a crack of your whip, and get away while the getting is
good!" Well, don't ask me what devil got into me, but
when I opened my mouth again I said, "Hop
aboard!"

They didn't have to be invited twice. I climbed in
after them, gave my cap a tug, let the horse have the
whip, and one, two, three—we're off! Did I say off? Off
to no place fast. My horse is stuck to the ground, a
cannonshot wouldn't budge him. "Well," I told myself,
"that's just what you get for stopping in the middle of
nowhere to chat with a pair of females. It's just your
luck that you couldn't think of anything better to
do . . ."

Just picture it if you can: the woods all around, the
eerie stillness, night coming on—and here I am with
these two apparitions pretending to be women. . . . My
blood began to whistle like a teakettle. I remembered a
story I once had heard about a coachman who was
driving by himself through the woods when he spied a
sack of oats lying on the path. Well a sack of oats is a
sack of oats, so down from the wagon he jumps, shoulders the sack, barely manages to heave it into his wagon
without breaking his back, and drives off as happy as
you please. A mile or two later he turns around to look
at his sack . . . did someone say sack? What sack?
Instead there's a billygoat with a beard. He reaches out
to touch it and it sticks out a tongue a yard long at him,
laughs like a hyena, and vanishes into thin air . . .

"Well, what are you waiting for?" the two women asked me.

"What am I waiting for? You can see for yourselves what I'm waiting for. My horse is happy where he is. He's not in a frisky mood."

"Then use your whip," they say to me. "What do you think it's for?"

"Thank you for your advice," I said to them. "It's very kind of you to remind me. The problem is that my four-legged friend is not afraid of such things. He's as used to getting whipped as I'm used to getting gypped." I tried to sound casual but I was burning with a ninety-nine year fever.

Well, why bore you? I let that poor horse have it. I whipped him as long as I whipped him hard, until he finally picked up his heels and we began to move through the woods. As we did, a new thought occurred to me. "Ah, Tevye, are you ever a numbskull! Once a beggar, always a beggar; that's the story of your life. Just imagine: here God hands you an opportunity that comes a man's way once in a hundred years—and you forget to clinch the deal in advance, so that you don't even know what's in it for you! Any way you look at it—as a favor or a duty, as a service or an obligation, as an act of human kindness or something even worse than that—it's certainly no crime to make a little profit on the side. When a soup bone is stuck in somebody's face, who doesn't give it a lick? Stop your horse right now, you imbecile, and spell it out for them in capital letters: 'Look, ladies, if it's worth such-and-such to you to get home, it's worth such-and-such to me to take you; if it isn't, I'm afraid we'll have to part ways.' " On second thought, though, I thought again: "Tevye, you're an imbecile to call yourself an imbecile! Supposing they promised you the moon, what good would it do you? Don't you know that you can skin a bear in the forest but you still can't sell its hide there?"

"Why don't you go a little faster?" the two women asked, poking me from behind.

"What's the matter," I asked, "are you in some sort of a hurry? You should know that haste makes waste." From the corner of my eye I stole a look at my passengers. They were women, all right, no doubt of it: one wearing a silk kerchief and the other a wig. They sat there looking at each other and whispering back and forth.

"Is it still a long way off?" one of them asked me.

"No longer off than we are from there," I answered. "Up ahead there's an uphill and a downhill. After that there's another uphill and a downhill. After that there's a real uphill and a downhill, and after that it's straight as the crow flies to Boiberik . . . "

"The man's a numbskull for sure!" whispered one of the women to the other.

"I told you he was bad news," said the second.

"He's all we needed," said the first.

"He's crazy as a loon," said the second.

I certainly must be crazy, I told myself, to let these two characters treat me like this.

"Excuse me," I said to them, "but where would you two ladies like to be dumped?"

"Dumped? What kind of language is that? You can go dump yourself if you like!"

"Oh, that's just coachman's talk," I said. "In ordinary parlance we would say: 'When we get to Boiberik safe and sound, with God's help, where do I drop off *mesdames?*' "

"If that's what it means," they said, "you can drop us off at the green *dacha* by the pond at the far end of the woods. Do you know where it is?"

"Do I know where it is?" I said. "I know my way around Boiberik the way you do around your own home. I wish I had a thousand rubles for every log I've carried there. Just last summer, in fact, I brought a couple of loads of wood to the very *dacha* you're talking about. There was a rich Jew from Yehupetz living there, a real millionaire. He must have been worth a hundred grand, if not twice that."

"He's still living there," said both women at once, regarding each other with a whisper and a laugh.

"Well," I said, "seeing as the ride you've taken was no short haul, and as you may have some connection with him, would it be too much of me to request of you, if you don't mind my asking, to put in a good word for me with him? Maybe he's got an opening, a position of some sort. Really anything would do . . . You never know how things will turn out. I know a young man named Yisroel, for instance, who comes from a town not far from here. He's a real nothing, believe me, a zero with a hole in it. So what happens to him? Somehow, don't ask me how or where, he lands this swell job, and today he's a bigshot clearing twenty rubles a week, or maybe it's forty, who knows . . . Some people have all the luck! Do you by any chance happen to know what happened to our slaughterer's son-in-law, all because he picked himself up one fine day and went to Yehupetz? The first few years there, I admit, he really suffered; he damn near starved to death. Today, though, I only wish I were in his shoes and could send home the money that he does. Of course, he'd like his wife and kids to join him but he can't get them a residence permit. I ask you, what kind of life is it for a man to live all alone like that? I swear, I wouldn't wish it on a dog . . .

"Well, bless my soul, will you look at what we have here: here's your pond and there's your green *dacha!*" And with that I swung my wagon right through the gate and drove like nobody's business clear up to the porch of the house. Don't ask me to describe the excitement when the people sitting there saw us drive up. What a racket! Happy days!

"Oy, grandma!"

"Oy, oy, oy, mama!"

"Oy, auntie, auntie!"

"Thank God they're back!"

"Mazel tov!"

"*Gevalt,* where have you been?"

"We've been out of our minds with worry all day long!"

"We had scouts out looking for you on all the roads!"

"The things we thought happened to you, it's too horrible for words: highwaymen or maybe a wolf! So tell us, what happened?"

"What happened? What happened shouldn't have happened to a soul. We lost our way in the woods and blundered about for miles. Suddenly along comes a Jew. What, what kind of a Jew? A Jew, a *schlimazel,* with a wagon and horse. Don't think we had an easy time with him either, but here we are!"

"Incredible! It sounds like a bad dream. How could you have gone out in the woods without a guide? What an adventure, what an adventure. Thank God you're home safe!"

In no time lamps were brought out, the table was set, and there began to appear on it hot samovars flowing with tea, bowls of sugar, jars of preserves, plates full of pastry and all kinds of baked goods, followed by the fanciest dishes, soup brimming with fat, roast meats, a whole goose, the best wines and salad greens.

I stood a ways off and thought, "So this, God bless them, is how these Yehupetz tycoons eat and drink. It's enough to make the devil jealous! I'd pawn my last pair of socks if it would help to make me a rich Jew like them." You can imagine what went through my mind. The crumbs that fell from that table alone would have been enough to feed my kids for a week, with enough left over for the Sabbath. "*Gevalt, Gottenyu,*" I thought. "They say you're a long-suffering God, a good God, a great God; they say that you're merciful and fair. Perhaps you could explain to me then why it is that some folk have everything and others have nothing twice over? Why does one Jew get to eat butter rolls while another gets to eat dirt?" . . . A minute later, though, I said to myself: "Ach, what a fool you are,

Tevye, I swear! Do you really think He needs your advice on how to run the world? If this is how things are, it's how they were meant to be; the proof is that if they were meant to be different, they would be. It may seem to you that they ought to have been meant to be different . . . but it's for that you're a Jew in this world! A Jew must have confidence and faith. He must believe, first, that there is a God, and second that if there is, and that if it's all the same to Him, and that if it isn't putting Him to too much trouble, He can make things a little better for the likes of you . . ."

"Wait a minute," I heard someone say. "What happened to the coachman? Has the *schlimazel* left already?"

"God forbid!" I called out from where I was. "Do you mean to suggest that I'd just walk off without so much as saying good-bye? Good evening, it's a pleasure to meet you all. Enjoy your meal; I can't imagine why you shouldn't."

"Come on in out of the dark," said one of them to me, "and let's have a look at your face. Perhaps you'd like a little brandy?"

"A little brandy?" I said. "Who can refuse a little brandy? God may be God but brandy is brandy." "*L'chayim!*" I emptied the glass in one gulp. "God should only help you to stay rich and happy," I said, "because since Jews can't help being Jews, somebody else had better help them."

"What name do you go by?" asked the man of the house, a fine-looking Jew with a *yarmulke*. "Where do you come from? Where do you live now? What's your work? Do you have a wife? Children? How many?"

"How many children?" I said. "Forgive me for boasting; but if each child of mine were worth a million rubles, as my Golde tries to convince me, I'd be the richest man in Yehupetz. The only trouble is that poor isn't rich and a mountain's no ditch. How does it say in the prayer book? *Hamavdil beyn koydesh l'khoyl,* some make hay while others toil. There are people who have money, and I have daughters. And you know what they say about that: better a house full of boarders than a house full of daughters. But why complain when we have God for our father? He looks after everyone; that is, He sits up there and looks at us slaving away down here. What's my work? For lack of any better suggestions, I break my back dragging logs. As it says in the *Talmud: b'makom she'eyn ish,* a herring too is a fish. Really, there'd be no problem if it weren't for having to eat. Do you know what my grandmother used to say? What a shame we have mouths, because if we didn't we'd never be hungry . . . But you'll have to excuse me for carrying on like this. You can't expect straight words from a crooked brain—and especially not when I've gone and drunk brandy on an empty stomach.''

"Bring the Jew something to eat!'' ordered the man of the house, and right away the table was laid again with food I never dreamed existed: fish, cold cuts, roasts, fowl, more gizzards and chicken livers than you could possibly count.

"What would you like to eat?'' I was asked. "Come on, wash your hands and sit down.''

"A sick man is asked,'' I answered, "a healthy one is served. Still, thank you anyway . . . a little brandy, with pleasure . . . but to sit down and make a meal of it when back home my wife and children, they should only be healthy and well . . . So you see, if you don't mind, I'll . . .''

What can I tell you? They seem to have gotten the point, because before I knew it my wagon was being loaded with goodies: here rolls, there a fish, a pot roast, a quarter of a chicken, tea, sugar, a cup of chicken fat, a jar of jam.

"Here's a gift to take home to your wife and children,'' they said. "And now please tell us how much we owe you for your trouble.''

"To tell you the truth,'' I said, "who am I to tell you

what you owe me? You pay me what you think it was worth. What's a few pennies more or less between us? I'll still be the same Tevye when we're done."

"No," they said, "we want you to tell us, Reb Tevye. You needn't be afraid. We won't chop your head off."

"Now what?" I thought to myself. I was really in a pretty pickle. It would be a crime to ask for one ruble when they might agree to two. On the other hand, if I asked for two they might think I was mad. Two rubles for one little wagon ride?

"Three rubles!" The words were out of my mouth before I could stop them. Everyone began to laugh so hard that I could have crawled into a hole in the ground.

"Please forgive me," I said, "if I've said the wrong thing. Even a horse, who has four feet, stumbles now and then, so why not a man with one tongue . . ."

The laughter grew even louder. I thought they would all split their sides.

"Stop laughing now, all of you!" ordered the man of the house. He pulled a large wallet from his pocket, and out of the wallet he fished—how much do you think? I swear you'll never guess—a ten-ruble note, all red as fire, as I hope to die! And do you know what else he says to me? "This," he says, "is from me. Now children, let's see what each of you can dig up out of his pockets."

What can I possibly tell you? Five- and three- and one-ruble notes flew onto the table. I started shaking all over until I was sure I was going to faint.

"Well, what are you waiting for?" says the man of the house to me. "Take your money from the table and have a good trip home."

"God reward you," I said, "a hundred times over; may He bring you good luck and happiness for the rest of your lives." I couldn't scrape up that money (who could even count it?) and stuff it into my pockets fast enough. "Good night," I said. "You should all be happy and well—you, and your children, and their children after them, and all their friends and relations."

I had already turned to go when the old woman with the silk kerchief stopped me and said, "One minute, Reb Tevye. There's a special present that I'd like to make you. You can come pick it up in the morning. I have the strangest cow—it was once a wonderful beast, it gave twenty-four glasses of milk every day. Someone must have put a hex on it, though, because now you can't milk it at all—that is, you can milk it all you want, you just won't get any milk . . ."

"I wish you a long life," I said, "and one you won't wish was any shorter. We'll not only milk your milk cow, we'll milk it for milk. My wife, God bless her, is such a wizard around the house that she can bake a noodle pudding from air, cook soup from a fingernail, whip up a Sabbath meal from an empty cupboard, and put hungry children to sleep with a box on the ear. . . . Well, please don't hold it against me if I've run on a little too long. And now good night to you all and be well," I said, turning to go to the yard where my wagon was. . . . Good Lord! With my luck one always has to expect a disaster, but this was an out-and-out misfortune. I looked this way, I looked that way—*ve'hayeled eynenu:* there wasn't a horse in sight.

This time, Tevye, I thought, you're really in a fix! And I remembered a charming story I had read in a book about a gang of goblins who once played a prank on a Jew, a pious *Hasid,* by luring him to a castle outside of town where they wined and dined him and suddenly disappeared, leaving a naked woman behind them. The woman turned into a tigress, the tigress turned into a cat, and the cat turned into a poisonous snake . . . "Between you and me, Tevye," I said just to myself, "how do you know that they're not pulling a fast one on you?"

"What are you mumbling and grumbling about there?" someone asked me.

"What am I mumbling about?" I replied. "Believe me, it's not for my health. In fact, I have a slight problem. My horse—"

"Your horse," someone said, "is in the stable. You only have to go there and look for it."

I went to the stable and looked for it. I swear I'm not a Jew if the old fellow wasn't standing there as proud as punch among the tycoon's horses, chewing away at his oats for all he was worth.

"I'm sorry to break up the party," I said, "but it's time to go home, old boy. Why make a hog of yourself? Before you know it you'll have taken one bite too many . . ."

In the end it was all I could do to wheedle him out of there and back into his harness. Away home we flew, on top of the world, singing Yom Kippur songs as tipsily as you please. You wouldn't have recognized my horse; he ran like the wind without my so much as mentioning the whip and looked like he'd been reupholstered. When we finally got home late at night, I joyously woke up my wife.

"*Mazel tov,* Golde," I said to her. "I've got good news!"

"A black *mazel tov* yourself," she says to me. "Tell me, my fine breadwinner, what's the happy occasion? Has my goldfingers been to a wedding or a *bris?*"

"To something better than a wedding and a *bris* combined," I said. "In a minute, my wife, I'm going to show you a treasure. But first go wake up the kids. Why shouldn't they also enjoy some Yehupetz cuisine . . ."

"Either you're delirious, or else you're temporarily deranged, or else you've taken leave of your senses, or else you're totally insane. All I can say is, you're talking just like a madman, God help us!" says my wife. When it comes to her tongue she's a pretty average Jewish housewife.

"And you're talking just like a woman!" I answered. "King Solomon wasn't joking when he said that out of a thousand females you won't find one with a head on her shoulders. It's a lucky thing that polygamy's gone out of fashion." And with that I went out to the wagon and began unpacking all the dishes I'd been given and set them out on the table. When that gang of mine saw all the rolls and smelled all the meat, they fell on it like a pack of wolves. Their hands trembled so they could hardly snatch anything up. I stood there with tears in my eyes, listening to their jaws work away like a plague of starving locusts.

"So tell me," says my woman when she's done, "who's been sharing their frugal repast with you, and since when do you have such good friends?"

"Don't worry, Golde," I said, "you'll hear it all in good time. First put the samovar on, so that we can sit down and drink a glass of tea in style. Generally speaking, one only lives once, am I right? So it's a good thing that we now have a cow of our own that gives twenty-four glasses of milk every day; in fact, I'm planning to go fetch her in the morning. And now, Golde," I said to her, pulling out my wad of bills, "be a sport and guess how much I have here!"

You should have seen my wife turn pale as a ghost. She was so flabbergasted that she couldn't say a word.

"God be with you, Golde my darling," I said to her. "You needn't look so frightened. Are you worried that I've stolen it somewhere? *Feh*, you should be ashamed of yourself! How long haven't you been married to me that you should think such thoughts of your Tevye? This is kosher money, you sillyhead, earned fairly and squarely by my own wits and hard work. The fact is that I've just saved two people from great danger. If it weren't for me, God only knows what would have become of them . . ."

In a word, I told her the whole story from beginning to end, the entire rigamarole. When I was through we counted all the money, then counted it again, then counted it once more to be sure. Whichever way we counted, it came to exactly thirty-seven rubles and no cents.

My wife began to cry.

"Why are you crying like an idiot?" I ask her.

"How can I help crying," she says, "when the tears won't stop coming? When the heart is full, it runs out at the eyes. God help me if something didn't tell me that you were about to come with good news. You know, I can't remember when I last saw my Grandma Tzeitl (may she rest in peace) in a dream—and just before you came I dreamed that I saw a big milkcan filled to the brim, and my Grandma Tzeitl was carrying it under her apron to keep the evil eye away, and all the children were shouting, 'Look, mama, look . . .' "

"Don't go smacking your lips before you've tasted the pudding, Golde, my darling," I said to her. "I'm sure that Grandma Tzeitl is enjoying her stay in Paradise, but that doesn't make her an expert on what's happening down here. Still, if God went through all the trouble of getting us a milk cow, it stands to reason that He'll see to it that the milk cow will give milk. . . . What I wanted to ask you, though, Golde, my dear, is what should we do with all the money?"

"It's funny you asked me that, Tevye," she says, "because that's just what I was going to ask you."

"Well, if you were going to ask me anyway," I say, "suppose I ask you. What do you think we should do with so much capital?"

We thought. And the harder we thought, the dizzier we became planning one business scheme after another. What didn't we deal in that night? We bought a pair of horses and quickly sold them for a windfall; with the profits we opened a grocery store in Boiberik, sold out all the stock, and opened a drygoods store; after that we invested in some woodland, found a buyer for it, and came out a few more rubles ahead; next we bought up the tax concession at Anatevka, farmed it out again, and with the income started a bank . . .

"You're completely out of your mind!" my wife suddenly shouted at me. "Do you want to throw away our hard-earned savings lending money to good-for-nothings and be left with no more than your whip again?"

"So what do you suggest," I said, "that it's better to go bankrupt trading in grain? Do you have any idea of the fortunes that are being lost right this minute on the wheat market? If you don't believe me, go to Odessa and see for yourself."

"What do I care about Odessa?" she says. "My great-grandparents didn't live there and neither will my great-grandchildren, and neither will I as long as I have legs not to take me there."

"So what do you want?" I ask her.

"What do I want?" she says. "I want you to talk sense and stop acting like a moron."

"Well, well," I said, "look who's the wise one now. Apparently there's nothing that money can't buy, even brains. I might have known this would happen."

To make a long story short, after quarreling and making up a few more times we decided to buy, in addition to the beast I was to pick up in the morning, a milk cow that gave milk. . . .

It might occur to you to ask why we decided to buy a cow when we could just as well have bought a horse. But why buy a horse, I ask you, when we could just as well have bought a cow? We live close to Boiberik, which is where all the rich Yehupetz Jews come to spend the summer in their *dachas*. And you know those Yehupetz Jews—nothing is too good for them. They expect to have everything served on a silver platter: wood, meat, eggs, poultry, onions, pepper, parsley. . . . So why shouldn't I be the man to walk into their parlor with cheese, cream, and butter? They like to eat well, they have money to burn, you can make a fat living from them as long as they think that they're getting the best—and believe me, fresh produce like mine they can't even get in Yehupetz. The two of us, my friend, should only have good luck in our lives for every time I've been stopped by the best type of people, Gentiles even, who beg to be my customers. "We've heard, Tevye," they say to me, "that you're an honest fellow, even if you are a rat-Jew. . . ." I ask you, do you ever get such a compliment from Jews? My worst enemy should have to lie sick in bed for as long as it would take me to wait for one! No, our Jews like to keep their praises to themselves, which is more than I can say about their noses. The minute they see that I've bought another cow, or that I have a new cart, they begin to rack their brains: "Where is it all coming from? Can our Tevye be passing out phony banknotes? Or perhaps he's making moonshine in some still?" Ha, ha, ha. All I can say is: keep wondering until your heads break, my friends, and enjoy it. . . .

Believe it or not, you're practically the first person to have heard my story—the whole where, what, and when of it. And now, you'll have to excuse me, because I've run on a little too long. We all have our (what is the word?) *vocations* in life. How does it say in the Bible? *Kol oyrev l'mineyhu*, it's a wise bird that feathers its own nest. So you'd better be off to your books, and I to my milk cans and jugs. . . .

There's just one request I have of you, Pani: please don't stick me in any of your books. And if that's too much to ask, at least do me a favor and leave my name out of it.

And oh, yes, by the way: don't forget to take care and be well!

Translated by Hillel Halkin

THE BUBBLE BURSTS

"There are many thoughts in a man's heart." So I believe it is written in the Torah. I don't have to translate the passage for you, Mr. Sholom Aleichem. But, speaking in plain Yiddish, there is a saying: "The most obedient horse needs a whip; the cleverest man can use advice." In regard to whom do I say this? I say it in regard to myself, for if I had once had the good sense to go to a friend and tell him such and such, thus and so, this calamity would never have taken place. But how is it said? *"Life and death issue from thine own lips.—* When God sees fit to punish a man he first takes away his good sense."

How many times have I thought to myself: Look, Tevye, you dolt, you are not supposed to be a complete fool. How could you have allowed yourself to be taken in so completely and in such a foolish way? Wouldn't it have been better for you if you had been content with your little dairy business whose fame has spread far and wide, everywhere from Boiberik to Yehupetz? How sweet and pleasant it would have been if your little hoard still lay in its box, buried deep where not a soul could see or know. For whose business is it whether Tevye has money or not? Was anyone concerned with Tevye when he lay buried nine feet deep, wrapped in his poverty like a dead man in his shroud? Did the world

191

care when he starved three times a day together with his wife and children?

But lo and behold! When God turned his countenance on Tevye and caused him to prosper all at once, so that at last he was beginning to arrive somewhere, beginning to save up a ruble now and then, the world suddenly became aware of his presence, and overnight, mind you, plain Tevye became Reb Tevye, nothing less. Suddenly out of nowhere a multitude of friends sprang up. As it is written: *"He is beloved by everyone."* Or, as we put it: "When God gives a dot, the world adds a lot."

Everyone came to me with a different suggestion. This one tells me to open a drygoods store, that one a grocery. Another one says to buy a building—property is a sound investment, it lasts forever. One tells me to invest in wheat, another in timber. Still another suggests auctioneering. "Friends!" I cry. "Brothers! Leave me alone. You've got the wrong man. You must think I'm Brodsky, but I am still very far from being a Brodsky. It is easy to estimate another's wealth. You see something that glitters like gold at a distance. You come close and it's only a brass button."

May no good come to them—I mean those friends of mine, those well-wishers—they cast an evil eye on me. God sent me a relative from somewhere, a distant kinsman of some kind whom I had never before seen. Menachem-Mendel is his name—a gadabout, a wastrel, a faker, a worthless vagabond, may he never stand still in one place. He got hold of me and filled my head with dreams and fantasies, things that had never been on land or sea. You will ask me: *"Wherefore did it come to pass?"* How did I ever get together with Menachem-Mendel? And I will answer in the words of the *Haggadah: "For we were slaves."* It was fated, that's all. Listen to my story.

I arrived in Yehupetz in early winter, with my choicest merchandise—over twenty pounds of butter fresh from butterland and several pails of cheese. I had salted away everything I had, you understand, didn't leave a smidgen for myself, not as much as a medicine spoon would hold. I didn't even have the time to visit all of my regular customers, the summer people of Boiberik, who await my coming as a good Jew waits for the coming of the Messiah. For say what you will, there isn't a merchant in Yehupetz who can produce a piece of goods that comes up to mine. I don't have to tell you this. As the prophet says: *"Let another praise thee.—* Good merchandise speaks for itself."

Well, I sold out everything to the last crumb, threw a bundle of hay to my horse and went for a walk around the town. *"Man is born of dust and to dust he returneth."* After all, I am only human. I want to see something of the world, breathe some fresh air, take a look at the wonders Yehupetz displays behind glass windows, as though to say: "Use your eyes all you want, but with your hands—away!"

Standing in front of a large window filled with seven and a half ruble gold pieces, with piles of silver rubles and stacks of paper money of all kinds, I think to myself: God in Heaven! If I had only a tenth of what all of this is worth! What more could I ask of God and who would be my equal? First of all, I would marry off my oldest daughter, give her a suitable dowry and still have enough left over for wedding expenses, gifts, and clothing for the bride. Then I would sell my horse and wagon and my cows and move into town. I would buy myself a synagogue seat by the Eastern Wall, hang strips of pearls around my wife's neck, and hand out charity like the richest householders. I would see to it that the synagogue got a new roof instead of standing as it does now, practically roofless, ready to cave in any minute. I would open a school for the children and build a hospital such as they have in other towns so that the town's poor and sick wouldn't have to lie underfoot in the synagogue. And I would get rid of Yankel Sheigetz as president of the Burial Society. There's been enough guzzling of brandy and chicken livers at public expense!

"Sholem aleichem, Reb Tevye," I hear a voice right

in back of me. I turn around and take a look. I could swear I have seen this man somewhere before.

"*Aleichem sholem,*" I answer. "And where do you hail from?"

"Where do I hail from? From Kasrilevke," he says. "I am a relative of yours. That is, your wife Golde is my second cousin once-removed."

"Hold on!" I say. "Aren't you Boruch-Hersh Leah-Dvoshe's son-in-law?"

"You've hit the nail right on the head," he says. "I am Boruch-Hersh Leah-Dvoshe's son-in-law and my wife is Sheina Sheindel, Boruch-Hersh Leah-Dvoshe's daughter. Now do you know who I am?"

"Wait," I say. "Your mother-in-law's grandmother, Sarah-Yenta, and my wife's aunt, Fruma-Zlata, were, I believe, first cousins, and if I am not mistaken you are the middle son-in-law of Boruch-Hersh Leah-Dvoshe. But I forget what they call you. Your name has flown right out of my head. Tell me, what is your name?"

"My name," he says, "is Menachem-Mendel Boruch-Hersh Leah-Dvoshe's. That's what they call me at home, in Kasrilevke."

"If that's the case," I say, "my dear Menachem-Mendel, I really owe you a *sholem aleichem* and a hearty one! Now, tell me, my friend, what are you doing here, and how is your mother-in-law and your father-in-law? How is your health, and how is business with you?"

"As far as my health," he says, "God be thanked. I am still alive. But business is not so gay."

"It will get better, with God's help," I tell him, stealing a look meanwhile at his shabby coat and the holes in his shoes. "Don't despair, God will come to your aid. Business will get better, no doubt. As the proverb says: '*All is vanity.*—Money is round, it is here today, gone tomorrow.' The main thing is to stay alive and keep hoping. A Jew must never stop hoping. Do we wear ourselves down to a shadow in the meanwhile? That's why we are Jews. How is it said? If you're a soldier you have to smell gunpowder. *'Man is likened to a broken pot.*—The world is nothing but a dream.' Tell me, Menachem-Mendel, how do you happen to be in Yehupetz all of a sudden?''

"What do you mean how do I happen to be in Yehupetz all of a sudden? I've been here no less than a year and a half.''

"Oh," said I, "then you belong here. You are living in Yehupetz.''

"Shh!" he whispers, looking all about him. "Don't talk so loud, Reb Tevye. I *am* living in Yehupetz, but that's just between you and me.''

I stare at him as though he were out of his mind. "You are a fugitive," I ask, "and you hide in the middle of the public square?''

"Don't ask, Reb Tevye. You are apparently not acquainted with the laws and customs of Yehupetz. Listen and I'll explain to you how a man can live here and still not live here." And he began telling me a long tale of woe, of all the trials and tribulations of life in the city of Yehupetz.

When he finished I said to him, "Take my advice, Menachem-Mendel. Come along with me to the country for a day and rest your tired bones. You will be a guest at our house, a very welcome guest. My wife will be overjoyed to have you.''

Well, I talked him into it. He went with me. We arrive at home. What rejoicing! A guest! And such a guest! A second cousin once-removed. After all, blood is thicker than water. My wife starts right in, "What is new in Kasrilevke? How is Uncle Boruch-Hersh? And Aunt Leah-Dvoshe? And Uncle Yossel-Menashe? And Aunt Dobrish? And how are their children! Who has died recently? Who has been married? Who is divorced? Who has given birth? And who is expecting?''

"What do you care about strange weddings and strange circumcisions?" I tell my wife. "Better see to it that we get something to eat. As it is written, *'All who are hungry enter and be fed.*—Nobody likes to dance on an empty stomach.' If you give us a *borscht,* fine. If not, I'll take *knishes* or *kreplach,* pudding or dumplings. *Blintzes* with cheese will suit me, too. Make anything you like and the more the better, but do it quickly."

Well, we washed, said grace, and had our meal. *"They ate,"* as Rashi says. "Eat, Menachem-Mendel, eat," I urged him. " *'Forget the world,'* as King David once said. It's a stupid world, and a deceitful one, and health and happiness, as my grandmother Nechama of blessed memory used to say—she was a clever woman and a wise one—health and happiness are only to be found at the table."

Our guest—his hands trembled as he reached for the food, poor fellow—couldn't find enough words in praise of my wife's cooking. He swore by everything holy that he couldn't remember when he had eaten such a dairy supper, such perfect *knishes*.

"Stuff and nonsense," I tell him. "You should taste her noodle pudding. Then you would know what heaven on earth can be."

After we had eaten and said our benedictions, we began talking, each one naturally talking of what concerned him most. I talk about my business, he of his. I babble of this, that, and the other, important and unimportant. He tells me stories of Yehupetz and Odessa, of how he had been ten times over, as they say, "on horseback and thrown off the horse." A rich man today, a beggar tomorrow, again a rich man, and once more a pauper. He dealt in something I have never heard of in my life—crazy-sounding things—stocks, bonds, shares-shmares. The devil alone knew what it was. The sums that he reeled off his tongue were fantastic—ten thousand, twenty thousand, thirty thousand—he threw money around like matches.

"I'll tell you the truth, Menachem-Mendel," I say to him. "Your business sounds very involved; you need brains to understand all of that. But what puzzles me most is this: from what I know of your better half it's a wonder to me that she lets you go traipsing around the world and doesn't come riding after you on a broomstick."

"Don't remind me of that," he says with a deep sigh. "I get enough from her as it is, both hot and cold. If you could see the letters she writes me you would admit that I am a saint to put up with it. But that's a small matter. That's what a wife is for—to bury her husband alive. There are worse things than that. I have also, as you know, a mother-in-law. I don't have to go into detail. You have met her."

"It is with you as it is written: *'The flocks were speckled and streaked and spotted.*—You have a boil on top of a boil and a blister on top of that.' "

"Yes," he says. "You put it very well, Reb Tevye. The boil is bad enough in itself, but the blister—ah, that blister is worse than the boil."

Well, we kept up this palaver until late into the night. My head whirled with his tales of fantastic transactions, of thousands that rose and fell, fabulous fortunes that were won and lost and won again. I tossed all night long dreaming in snatches of Yehupetz and Brodsky, of millions of rubles, of Menachem-Mendel and his mother-in-law.

Early the next morning he begins hemming and hawing and finally comes out with it. Here is what he says. "Since the stock market has for a long time been in such a state that money is held in high esteem and goods are held very low, you Tevye have a chance to make yourself a pretty penny. And while you are getting rich you will at the same time be saving my life, you will actually raise me from the dead."

"You talk like a child," I say to him. "You must think I have a big sum of money to invest. Fool, may we both earn before next Passover what I lack to make me a Brodsky."

"I know," he says, "without your telling me. But

what makes you think we need big money? If you give me a hundred rubles now, I can turn it in three or four days into two hundred or three hundred or six hundred or maybe even into a thousand rubles."

"It may be as it is written: *'The profit is great, but it's far from my pocket.'* Who says I have anything to invest at all? And if there is no hundred rubles, it's as Rashi says: *'You came in alone and you go out by yourself.'* Or, as I put it, 'If you plant a stone, up comes a boulder.' "

"Come now," he says to me, "you know you can dig up a hundred rubles. With all the money you are earning and with your name . . ."

"A good name is an excellent thing," I tell him. "But what comes of it? I have my name and Brodsky has the money. If you want to know the truth, my savings come all in all close to a hundred rubles. And I have two dozen uses for it. First of all, to marry off my daughter . . ."

"Just what I've been trying to tell you," he breaks in. "When will you have the opportunity to put in a hundred rubles and to take out, with God's help, enough to marry off your daughter and to do all the other things besides?"

And he went on with this chant for the next three hours, explaining how he could make three rubles out of one and ten out of three. First you bring in one hundred rubles somewhere, and you tell them to buy ten pieces of I-forget-what-you-call-it, then you wait a few days until they go up. You send a telegram somewhere else to sell the ten pieces and buy twice as many for the money. Then you wait and they rise again. You shoot off another telegram. You keep doing this until the hundred rubles become two hundred, then four hundred, then eight hundred, then sixteen hundred. It's no less than a miracle from God. There are people in Yehupetz, he tells me, who until recently went barefoot—they didn't have a pair of shoes to their names. They worked as errand boys and messengers. Now they own palatial homes, their wives have expensive stomach ailments, they go abroad for cures. They themselves fly all over Yehupetz on rubber wheels; they don't recognize old friends any more.

Well, why should I drag out the story? I caught the fever from him. Who knows, I think to myself, maybe he was sent by my good angel? He tells me that people win fortunes in Yehupetz, ordinary people with not more than five fingers to each hand. Am I any worse than they? I don't believe he is a liar; he couldn't make all these things up out of his own head. Who knows, suppose the wheel turns, and Tevye becomes a somebody in his old age? How much longer can I keep on toiling and moiling from dawn until dark? Day in and day out—the same horse and wagon, night and day the same butter and cheese? It's time, Tevye, that you took a little rest, became a man among men, went into the synagogue once in a while, turned the pages of a holy book. Why not? And on the other hand, if I lose out, if it should fall buttered side down? But better not think of that.

"What do you say?" I ask my wife. "What do you think of his proposition?"

"What do you want me to say?" she asks. "I know that Menachem-Mendel isn't a nobody who would want to swindle you. He doesn't come from a family of nobodies. He has a very respectable father, and as for his grandfather, he was a real jewel. All of his life, even after he became blind, he studied the Torah. And Grandmother Tzeitl, may she rest in peace, was no ordinary woman either."

"A fitting parable," I said. "It's like bringing Chanukah candles to a Purim feast. We talk about investments and she drags in her Grandmother Tzeitl who used to bake honeycake, and her grandfather who died of drink. That's a woman for you. No wonder King Solomon traveled the world over and didn't find a female with an ounce of brains in her head."

To make a long story short, we decided to form a

partnership. I put in my money and Menachem-Mendel, his wits. Whatever God gives, we will divide in half. "Believe me, Reb Tevye," he says, "you won't regret doing business with me. With God's help the money will come pouring in."

"Amen and the same to you," I say. "From your lips into God's ears. There is just one thing I want to know. How does the mountain come to the prophet? You are over there in Yehupetz and I am here in the country; and money, as you know, is a delicate substance. It isn't that I don't trust you, but as Father Abraham says, *'If you sow with tears you shall reap with joy.*—It's better to be safe than sorry.' "

"Oh," he says, "would you rather we drew up a paper? Most willingly."

"Listen," I say to him, "if you want to ruin me, what good will a piece of paper do me? *'The mouse is not the thief.*—It isn't the note that pays, but the man.' If I am hung by one foot I might as well be hung by both."

"Believe me, Reb Tevye," he says to me, "I swear to you on my word of honor, may God be my witness, that I have no tricks up my sleeve. I won't swindle you, but I will deal with you honestly. I will divide our earnings equally with you, share and share alike—a hundred to you, a hundred to me, two hundred to you, two hundred to me, four hundred to you, four hundred to me, a thousand to you, a thousand to me."

So I dug out my little hoard, counted the money over three times, my hands shaking the whole time, called over my wife as a witness, and explained to him again that this was blood-money I was giving him, and sewed it carefully inside his shirt so that no one would rob him of it on the way. He promised that he would write me not later than a week from Saturday and tell me everything in detail. Then we said good-bye with much feeling, embraced like close friends, and he went on his way.

When I was left alone there began to pass in front of

my eyes all sorts of visions—visions so sweet that I wished they would never end. I saw a large house with a tin roof right in the middle of town, and inside the house were big rooms and little rooms and pantries full of good things, and around it a yard full of chickens and ducks and geese. I saw the mistress of the house walking around jingling her keys. That was my wife Golde, but what a different Golde from the one I knew. This one had the face and manner of a rich man's wife, with a double chin and a neck hung with pearls. She strutted around like a peacock giving herself airs, and yelling at the servant girls. And here were my daughters dressed in their Sabbath best, lolling around, not lifting a finger for themselves. The house was full of brightness and cheer. Supper was cooking in the oven. The samovar boiled merrily on the table. And at the head of the table sat the master of the house, Tevye himself, in a robe and skullcap, and around him sat the foremost house-holders of the town, fawning on him. "If you please, Reb Tevye. Pardon me, Reb Tevye."—And so on.

"What fiendish power money has!" I exclaimed.

"Whom are you cursing?" asked Golde.

"Nobody. I was just thinking," I told her. "Day-dreams and moonshine . . . Tell me Golde, my love, do you know what sort of merchandise he deals in, that cousin of yours, Menachem-Mendel?"

"What's that?" she said. "Bad luck to my enemies! Here he has spent a day and a night talking with the man, and in the end he comes and asks me, 'What does he deal in?' For God's sake, you made up a contract with him. You are partners."

"Yes," I said. "We made up something, but I don't know what we made up. If my life depended on it, I wouldn't know. There is nothing, you see, that I can get hold of. But one thing has nothing to do with the other. Don't worry, my dear wife. My heart tells me that it is all for the best. We are going to make a lot of money. Say amen to that and go cook supper."

Well, a week goes by and two and three. There is no news from my partner. I am beside myself with worry. It can't be that he has just forgotten to write. He knows quite well how anxiously we are waiting to hear from him. A thought flits through my head. What shall I do if he skims off the cream for himself and tells me that there is no profit? But that, I tell myself, can't be. It just isn't possible. I treat the man like one of my own, so how can he turn around and play a trick like that on me? Then something worse occurs to me. Profit be hanged. Who cares about profit? *"Deliverance and protection will come from the Lord."* May God only keep the capital from harm. I feel a chill go up and down my back. "You old fool," I tell myself. "You idiot. You made your bed, now lie on it. For the hundred rubles you could have bought yourself a pair of horses such as your forefathers never had, or exchanged your old wagon for a carriage with springs."

"Tevye, why don't you think of something?" my wife pleads with me.

"What do you mean why don't I think of something? My head is splitting into little pieces from thinking and she asks why don't I think."

"Something must have happened to him on the road," says my wife. "He was attacked by robbers, or else he got sick on the way. Or he may even be dead."

"What will you dream up next, my love?" I ask. "All of a sudden she has to start pulling robbers out of thin air." But to myself I think: "No telling what can happen to a man alone on the road."

"You always imagine the worst," I tell my wife.

"He comes of such a good family," she says. "His mother, may she intercede for us in Heaven, died not long ago, she was still a young woman. He had three sisters. One died as a girl; the other one lived to get married but caught cold coming from the bath and died; and the third one lost her mind after her first child was born, ailed for a long time, and died too."

"To live until we die is our lot," I tell her. "We must

all die sometime. A man is compared to a carpenter. A carpenter lives and lives until he dies, and a man lives and lives until he dies."

Well, we decided that I should go to Yehupetz. Quite a bit of merchandise had accumulated in the meanwhile—cheese and butter and cream, all of the best. My wife harnessed the horse and wagon, and *"they journeyed from Sukos"*—as Rashi says. On to Yehupetz!

Naturally my heart was heavy and my thoughts gloomy as I rode through the woods. I began to imagine the worst. Suppose, I think to myself, I arrive and begin to inquire about my man and they tell me, "Menachem-Mendel? Oh, that one? He has done well by himself. He has feathered his own nest. He owns a mansion, rides in his own carriage, you wouldn't recognize him." But just the same I gather up courage and go to his house. "Get out!" they tell me at the door, and shove me aside with their elbows. "Don't push your way, Uncle. We don't allow that."

"I am his relative," I tell them. "He is my wife's second cousin once-removed."

"Mazel-tov," they tell me. "We are overjoyed to hear it. But just the same it won't hurt you to wait a little at the door."

It occurs to me that I should slip the doorman a bribe. As it is said: *"What goes up must come down"* or "If you don't grease the axle the wheels won't turn." And so I get in.

"Good morning to you, Reb Menachem-Mendel," I say.

Who? What? *"There is no speech. There are no words."* He looks at me as though he has never seen me before. "What do you want?" he says.

I am ready to faint. "What do you mean?" I say. "Don't you recognize your own cousin? My name is Tevye."

"Tevye . . ." he says slowly. "The name sounds familiar."

"So the name sounds familiar to you. Maybe my

wife's *blintzes* sound familiar, too? You may even remember the taste of her *knishes* and *kreplach?*"

Then I imagine exactly the opposite. I come in to see Menachem-Mendel and he meets me at the door with outstretched arms. "Welcome, Reb Tevye. Welcome. Be seated. How are you? And how is your wife? I've been waiting for you. I want to settle my account with you." And he takes my cap and pours it full of gold pieces. "This," he tells me, "is what we earned on our investment. The capital we shall leave where it is. Whatever we make we shall divide equally, share and share alike, half to me, half to you, a hundred to me, a hundred to you, two hundred to you, two hundred to me, five hundred to you, five hundred to me. . . ."

While I am lost in this dream, my horse strays from the path, the wagon gets caught against a tree, and I am jolted from behind so suddenly that sparks fly in front of my eyes. "This is all for the best," I comfort myself. "Thank God the axle didn't break."

I arrive in Yehupetz, dispose of my wares quickly and, as usual, without any trouble, and set out to look for my partner. I wander around for an hour; I wander around for two hours. It's no use. It's as Jacob said about Benjamin: *"The lad is gone."* I can't find him anywhere. I stop people in the street and ask them, "Have you seen or have you heard of a man who goes by the elegant name of Menachem-Mendel?"

"Well, well," they tell me, "if his name is Menachem-Mendel, you can look for him with a candle. But that isn't enough. There is more than one Menachem-Mendel in the world."

"I see, you want to know his family name. At home in Kasrilevke he is known by his mother-in-law's name—Menachem-Mendel Leah-Dvoshe's. What more do you want? Even his father-in-law, who is a very old man, is known by his wife's name, Boruch-Hersh Leah-Dvoshe's. Now do you understand?"

"We understand very well," they say. "But that isn't

enough. What does this Menachem-Mendel do? What
is his business?"

"His business? He deals in seven and a half ruble
gold pieces, in Putilov shares, in stocks and bonds. He
shoots telegrams here, there, and everywhere—to St.
Petersburg, Odessa, Warsaw."

They roll with laughter. "Oh, you mean Menachem-
Mendel-who-deals-in-all-and-sundry? Turn left and follow this street and you will see many hares running
around. Yours will be among them."

"Live and learn," I say to myself. "Now I am told to
look for hares." I follow the street they pointed out to
me. It's as crowded as our town square on market day. I
can barely push my way through. People are running
around like crazy—shouting, waving their hands, quarreling. It's a regular bedlam. I hear shouts of "Putilov,"
"shares," "stocks . . ." "he gave me his word . . ."
"here is a down payment . . ." "buy on margin . . ."
"he owes me a fee . . ." "you are a sucker . . ." "spit in
his face . . ." "look at that speculator." Any minute
they will start fighting in earnest, dealing out blows.
"Jacob fled," I mutter to myself. "Get out, Tevye,
before you get knocked down. God is our Father, Tevye
the Dairyman is a sinner. Yehupetz is a city, and Menachem-Mendel is a breadwinner. So this is where people
make fortunes? This is how they do their business?
May God have mercy on you, Tevye, and on such
business."

I stopped in front of a large window with a display of
clothing in it and whom should I see reflected in it but
my partner Menachem-Mendel. My heart was
squeezed with pity at the sight. . . . I became faint. . . .
May our worst enemies look the way Menachem-Mendel looked. You should have seen his coat. And his
shoes. Or what was left of them. And his face! A corpse
laid out for burial looks cheerful by comparison. "Well,
Tevye," I said to myself as Esther had once said to
Mordecai, " *'if I perish, I perish.*—I am done for.' You

may as well kiss your savings good-bye. *'There is no bear and no woods.*—No merchandise and no money.' Nothing but a pack of troubles.''

He looked pretty crestfallen on his part. We both stood there, rooted to the ground, unable to speak. There seemed to be nothing left to say, nothing left to do. We might as well pick up our sacks and go over the city begging.

"Reb Tevye," he says to me softly, barely able to utter the words, the tears are choking him so, "Reb Tevye, without luck, it's better never to have been born at all. Rather than live like this, it is better to hang from a tree or rot in the ground.''

"For such a deed," I burst out, "for what you've done to me, you deserve to be stretched out right here in the middle of Yehupetz and flogged so hard that you lose consciousness. Consider for yourself what you've done. You've taken a houseful of innocent people who never did you a speck of harm, and without a knife you slit their throats clear through. How can I face my wife and children now? Tell me, you robber, you murderer, you—''

"It is all true, Reb Tevye," he says, leaning against the wall. "All true. May God have mercy on me.''

"The fires of hell," I tell him, "the tortures of Gehenna are too good for you.''

"All true," he says. "May God have pity on me. All true. Rather than to live like this, Reb Tevye, rather than to live—" And he hangs his head.

I look at him standing there, the poor *schlimazel,* leaning against the wall, his head bent, his cap awry. He sighs and he groans and my heart turns over with pity.

"And yet," I say, "if you want to look at it another way, you may not be to blame either. When I think it over, I realize that you couldn't have done it out of plain knavery. After all, you were my partner, you had a share in the business. I put in my money and you put in your brains. Woe unto us both. I am sure you meant it for the best. It must have been fate. How is it said? *'Don't rejoice today, because tomorrow—'* Or, 'Man proposes and God disposes.'

"If you want proof, just look at my business. It seems to be completely foolproof, a guaranteed thing. And yet when it came to pass last fall that one of my cows lay down and died and right after her a young calf—was there anything I could do about it? When luck turns against you, you are lost.

"I don't even want to ask you where my money is. I understand only too well. My blood-money went up in smoke, it sank into the grave. . . . And whose fault is it if not mine? I let myself be talked into it. I went chasing after rainbows. If you want money, my friend, you have to work and slave for it, you have to wear your fingers to the bone. I deserve a good thrashing for it. But crying about it won't help. How is it written? *'If the maiden screamed*—You can shout until you burst a blood vessel.' Hindsight, as they say . . . It wasn't fated that Tevye should be a rich man. As Ivan says, 'Mikita never had anything and never will.' God willed it so. *'The Lord giveth and the Lord taketh away.'* Come, brother, let's go get a drink."

And that, Mr. Sholom Aleichem, is how my beautiful dream burst like a bubble and vanished into thin air. Do you think I took it to heart? Do you think I grieved over the loss of my money? Not at all. We know what the proverb says: *"The silver and the gold are mine.—* Money is worthless." Only man is important, that is, if he is really a man, a human being. For what did I grieve then? I grieved for the dream I had lost, the dream of wealth that was gone forever. For I had longed, how I had longed, to be a rich man, if only for a short while. But what did it avail me? The proverb says, *"Perforce you live and perforce you die.—*You live in spite of yourself and you wear out your shoes in spite of yourself."

"You, Tevye," says God, "stick to your cheese and

butter and forget your dreams." But what about hope? Naturally, the harder life is the more you must hope. The poorer you are the more cheerful you must be.

Do you want proof? But I think I have talked too long already. I have to be on my way; I have to tend to business. As it is said: *"Every man is a liar.*—Everyone has his affliction." Farewell, be healthy and happy always. . . .

Translated by Frances Butwin

CHAVA

"*Give thanks unto the Lord, for He is good.*—Whatever He ordains, His way is the best." It has to be the best, for if you had the wisdom of a Solomon could you improve on it? Look at me—I wanted to be clever, I turned and twisted this way and that, and tried everything I knew, and then when I saw it was no use, I took my hand off my chest, as the saying is, and said to myself, "Tevye, you're a fool, you won't change the world. The Lord has given us the *'pain of bringing up children,'* which means that in raising children you have to accept the bad with the good and count them as one."

Take, for instance, my oldest daughter, Tzeitl, who went and fell in love with the tailor Mottel Kamzoil. Have I got anything against him? True, he is a simple, unlettered fellow who can't read the learned footnotes at the bottom of the page, but is that anything against him? Everybody in the world can't be a scholar. At least he is an honest man and a hard-working one. She's already borne him a whole brood of young ones; they have a houseful of hungry mouths to feed, and both of them, he and she, are struggling along "*in honor and in riches,*" as the saying is. And yet if you ask her, she will tell you that she is the happiest woman in the world, no one could be happier. There is only one tiny flaw—they don't have enough to eat. "*That's the end of the first round with the Torah.*—There's Number One for you."

209

About my second daughter, about Hodel, I don't have to tell you. You know about her already. With her I played and I lost. I lost her forever. God knows if my eyes will ever behold her again, unless it should be in the next world. To this day I can't bring myself to talk about her calmly. I mention her name and the old pain returns. Forget her, you say? How can you forget a living human being? And especially a child like Hodel! If you could only see the letters she writes me. . . . They are doing very well, she tells me. He sits in prison and she works for a living. She washes clothes all day, reads books in between, and goes to see him once a week. She lives in the hope that very soon the pot will boil over, as they say, the sun will rise and everything will become bright. He will be set free along with many others like him, and then, she says, they will all roll up their sleeves and get to work to turn the world upside down. Well, what do you think of that? Sounds promising, doesn't it?

But what does the Lord do next? He is, after all, *"a gracious and merciful Lord,"* and He says to me, "Wait, Tevye, I will bring something to pass that will make you forget all your former troubles."

And so it was. It's a story worth hearing. I would not repeat it to anyone else, for while the pain is great, the disgrace is even greater. But how is it written? *"Shall I conceal it from Abraham?*—Can I keep any secrets from you?" Whatever is on my mind I shall tell you. But one thing I want to ask of you. Let it remain between you and me. For I repeat: the pain is great, but the disgrace—the disgrace is even greater.

How is it written in Perek? *"The Holy One, blessed be He, wished to grant merit to Israel—"* The Lord wanted to be good to Tevye, so He blessed him with seven female children, that is, seven daughters, each one of them a beauty, all of them good-looking and charming, clever and healthy and sweet-tempered— like young pine trees! Alas, if only they had been ill-tempered and ugly as scarecrows, it might have been better for them, and certainly healthier for me. For what use is a fine horse, I ask you, if you have to keep it locked up in a stable? What good are beautiful daughters if you are stuck away with them in a forsaken corner of the world, where you never see a live person except for Anton Poperilo, the village mayor, or the clerk Fyedka Galagan, a young fellow with a long mane of hair and tall peasant boots, or the Russian priest, may his name be blotted out?

I can't bear to hear that priest's name mentioned, not because I am a Jew and he is a priest. On the contrary, we've been on friendly terms for a number of years. By that I don't mean that we visit at each other's homes or dance at the same weddings. I only mean that when we happen to meet we greet each other civilly: "Good morning." "Good day. What's new in the world?"

I've never liked to enter into a discussion with him, for right away the talk would turn to this business of *your God* and *my God*. Before he could get started I would recite a proverb or quote him a passage from the Bible. To which he replied that he could quote me a passage from the Bible also, and perhaps better than I, and he began to recite the Scriptures to me, mimicking the sacred language like a Gentile: *"Berezhit bara alokim*—In the beginning the Lord created the Heavens. . . ."* Then I told him that we had a folktale, or a *medresh* to the effect that. . . . "A *medresh*," he interrupted me, "is the same as *Talmud*," and he didn't like *Talmud*, "for *Tal-mud* is nothing but sheer trickery." Then I would get good and angry and give him what he had coming. Do you think that bothered him? Not in the least. He would only look at me and laugh and comb his long beard with his fingers. There is nothing in the world, I tell you, so maddening as a person who doesn't answer when you abuse him. You shout and you scold, you are ready to burst a gut, and he stands there and smiles. . . . At that time I didn't understand what that smile of his meant, but now I know what was behind it. . . .

Well, to return to my story. I arrived at home one day—it was toward evening—and whom should I see but the clerk Fyedka standing outside with my Chava, that's my third daughter, the one next to Hodel. When he caught sight of me, the young fellow spun around quickly, tipped his hat to me, and was off. I asked Chava, "What was Fyedka doing here?"

"Nothing," she said.

"What do you mean nothing?"

"We were just talking."

"What business have you got talking with Fyedka?" I asked.

"We've known each other for a long time," she said.

"Congratulations!" I said. "A fine friend you've picked for yourself."

"Do you know him at all?" she asked. "Do you know who he is?"

"No," I said, "I don't know who he is. I've never seen his family tree. But I am sure he must be descended from a long and honorable line. His father," I said, "must have been either a shepherd or a janitor or else just a plain drunkard."

To this Chava answered, "Who his father was I don't know and I don't care to know. All people are the same to me. But Fyedka himself is not an ordinary person, of that I am sure."

"Tell me," I said, "what kind of person is he? I'd like to hear."

"I would tell you," she said, "but you wouldn't understand. Fyedka is a second Gorky."

"A second Gorky? And who, may I ask, was the first Gorky?"

"Gorky," she said, "is one of the greatest men living in the world today."

"Where does he live," I asked, "this sage of yours, what is his occupation and what words of wisdom has he spoken?"

"Gorky," she said, "is a famous author. He is a writer, that is, a man who writes books. He is fine and honest and true, a person to be honored. He also comes from plain people, he was not educated anywhere, he is self-taught . . . here is his portrait." Saying this, she took a small photograph from her pocket and handed it to me.

"So this is he," I said, "this sage of yours, Reb Gorky? I can swear I have seen him somewhere before, either at the baggage depot, carrying sacks, or in the woods hauling logs."

"Is it a crime then if a man works with his hands? Don't you yourself work with your hands? Don't all of us work?"

"Yes, yes," I said, "you are right. We have a certain proverb which says, *'When thou eatest the labor of thine own hands*—If you do not work, you shall not eat.' But I still don't understand what Fyedka is doing here. I would be much happier if you were friends at a distance. You mustn't forget *'Whence thou camest and whither thou goest*—Who you are and who he is.' "

"God created all men equal," she said.

"Yes, yes," I said, "God created Adam in his own image. But we mustn't forget that each man must seek his own kind, as it is written: *'From each according to his means. . . .' "*

"Marvelous!" she cried. "Unbelievable! You have a quotation for everything. Maybe you also have a quotation that explains why men have divided themselves up into Jews and Gentiles, into lords and slaves, noblemen and beggars?"

"Now, now, my daughter, it seems to me you've strayed to the *'sixth millennium.' "* And I explained to her that this had been the way of the world since the first day of Creation.

"And why," she wanted to know, "should this be the way of the world?"

"Because that's the way God created the world."

"And why did God create the world this way?"

"If we started to ask why this, and wherefore that, *'there would be no end to it*—a tale without end.' "

"But that is why God gave us intellects," she said, "that we should ask questions."

"We have an old custom," I told her, "that when a hen begins to crow like a rooster, we take her away to be slaughtered. As we say in the morning blessing, *'Who gave the rooster the ability to discern between day and night. . . .'*"

"Maybe you've done enough jabbering out there," my wife Golde called out from inside the house. "The *borscht* has been standing on the table for an hour and he is still out there singing Sabbath hymns."

"Another province heard from! No wonder our sages have said, *'The fool hath seven qualities.*—A woman talks nine times as much as a man.' We are discussing important matters and she comes barging in with her cabbage *borscht*."

"My cabbage *borscht*," said Golde, "may be just as important as those 'important matters' of yours."

"Mazel-tov! We have a new philosopher here, straight from behind the oven. It isn't enough that Tevye's daughters have become enlightened, now his wife has to start flying through the chimney right up into the sky."

"Since you mention the sky," said Golde, "I might as well tell you that I hope you rot in the earth."

Tell me, Mr. Sholom Aleichem, what do you think of such crazy goings-on on an empty stomach?

Now let us, as they say in books, leave the prince and follow the fortunes of the princess. I am speaking of the priest, may his name and memory be blotted out. Once toward nightfall I was driving home with my empty milk cans—I was nearing the village—when whom should I see but the priest in his cast-iron *britzka* or carriage, approaching from the other direction. His honor was driving the horses himself, and his long, flowing beard was whipped about by the wind.

"What a happy encounter!" I thought to myself. "May the bad luck fall on his head."

"Good evening," he said to me. "Didn't you recognize me, or what?"

"It's a sign that you will get rich soon," I said, lifted my cap and was about to drive on. But he wouldn't let me pass. "Wait a minute, Tevel, what's your hurry? I have a few words to say to you."

"Very well. If it's good news, then go ahead," I said. "But if not, leave it for some other time."

"What do you mean by some other time?" he asked.

"By some other time, I mean when the Messiah comes."

"The Messiah," said he, "has already come."

"That I have heard from you more than once," I said. "Tell me something new, little father."

"That's just what I want to tell you. I want to talk to you about yourself, that is, about your daughter."

At this my heart almost turned over. What concern could he have with my daughter? And I said to him, "My daughters are not the kind, God forbid, that need someone to do the talking for them. They can manage their own affairs."

"But this is the sort of thing she can't speak of herself. Someone else has to speak for her. It's a matter of utmost importance. Her fate is at stake."

"And who, may I ask, concerns himself with the fate of my child? It seems to me that I am still her father, am I not?"

"True," he said, "you are her father, but you are blind to her needs. Your child is reaching out for a different world, and you don't understand her, or else you don't wish to understand her."

"Whether I don't understand her, or don't wish to understand her, is beside the point. We can argue about that sometime if you like. But what has it got to do with you, little father?"

"It has quite a lot to do with me," he said, "for she is now under my protection."

"What do you mean she is under your 'protection'?"

"It means she is now in my care."

He looked me straight in the eye as he said this and stroked his long, flowing beard with his fingers.

"What!" I exclaimed. "My child is in your care? By what right?" I felt myself losing my temper.

He answered me very calmly, with a little smile. "Now don't start getting excited, Tevel. We can discuss this matter peaceably. You know that I am not, God forbid, your enemy, even though you are a Jew. As you know, I am very fond of the Jewish people, even though they are a stiff-necked race. And my heart aches for them because in their pride they refuse to admit that we mean everything for their own good."

"Don't speak to me of our own good, little father," I said, "for every word that comes from your lips is like a drop of poison to me—it's like a bullet fired straight at my heart. If you are really the friend you say you are, I ask only one thing of you—leave my daughter alone."

"You are a foolish person," he said to me. "No harm will come to your daughter. She is about to meet with a piece of great good luck. She is about to take a bridegroom—and such a bridegroom! I couldn't wish a better fate to one of my own."

"Amen," I said, forcing a laugh, though inside me burned all the fires of hell. "And who, may I ask, is this bridegroom, if I may have the honor of knowing?"

"You must be acquainted with him," he said. "He is a gallant young man, an honest fellow and quite well-educated, though he is self-taught. He is very much in love with your daughter and wants to marry her, but cannot because he is not a Jew."

"Fyedka!" I thought to myself, and the blood rushed to my head, and a cold sweat broke out all over my body, so that I could barely sit upright in my cart. But show him how I felt? Never. Without replying I picked up the reins, whipped my horse, and *"departed like Moses."* I went off without as much as a fare-thee-well.

I arrived at home. What a scene greeted me! The

children all lying with their faces buried in pillows, weeping; my Golde weaving around the house like a ghost. I looked for Chava. Where is Chava? She is nowhere to be found. I didn't ask where she was. I knew only too well. Then it was that I began to feel the tortures of a soul that is damned. I was full of rage and I didn't know against whom. I could have turned on myself with a whip. I began yelling at the children, I let out all my bitterness toward my wife. I couldn't rest in the house, so I went outside to the barn to feed my horse. I found him with one leg twisted around the block of wood. I took a stick and began laying it into him, as though I were going to strip off his skin and break his bones in half. "May you burn alive, you *schlimazel*. You can starve to death before I will give you as much as an oat. Tortures I will give you and anguish and all the ten plagues of Egypt. . . . "

But even as I shouted at him I knew that my horse did not deserve it; poor innocent creature, what did I have against him? I poured out some chopped straw for him, went back to the house and lay down. . . . My head was ready to split in two as I lay there thinking, figuring, arguing with myself back and forth. What could it all mean? What was the significance of all this? *"What was my sin and what my transgression?"* How did Tevye sin more than all the others that he should be punished thus above all the others? " *'Oh, Lord Almighty, what are we, and what is our life?'* What sort of cursed creature am I that you should constantly bear me in mind, never let any plague that comes along, any blight or affliction, pass me by?"

As I lay there torturing myself with such thoughts, I heard my wife groaning and moaning beside me. "Golde," I said, "are you sleeping?"

"No," she said. "What is it?"

"Nothing," I said. "Things are bad with us, very bad. Maybe you can think of what's to be done."

"You ask me what's to be done. Woe is me, how

should I know? A child gets up in the morning, sound and fresh, gets dressed, and falls on my neck, kissing and hugging me, and weeping all the time, and she won't tell me why. I thought that, God forbid, she had lost her mind. I asked her, 'What's the matter with you, daughter?' She didn't say a word, but ran out for a while to see to the cows, and disappeared. I waited an hour, two hours, three hours. Where is Chava? There is no Chava. Then I said to the children, 'Run over and take a look at the priest's house. . . .' "

"How did you know, Golde, that she was at the priest's house?"

"How did I know? Woe is me. Don't I have eyes in my head? Am I not her mother?"

"If you do have eyes in your head, and if you are her mother, why did you keep it all to yourself? Why didn't you tell me?"

"Tell you? When are you at home that I can tell you anything? And if I do tell you something, do you listen to me? If a person says anything to you, you answer him with a quotation. You drum my head full of quotations and you've done your duty by your children."

After she finished I could hear her weeping in the dark. "She is partly right," I thought to myself, "for what can a woman understand of such matters?" My heart ached for her; I could not bear to listen to her moaning and groaning. "Look here, Golde," I said, "you are angry because I have a quotation for everything. I have to answer you even that with a quotation. It is written: *'As a father has mercy on his children,'* This means that a father loves his child. Why isn't it written: *'As a mother has mercy on her children'?* For a mother is not the same as a father. A father can speak differently with his child. You will see—tomorrow I will go and speak to her."

"I hope you will get to see her, and him also. He is not a bad man, even if he is a priest. He has compassion in his heart. You will plead with him, get down on your knees to him, maybe he will have pity on us."

"Whom are you talking about?" I said. "That priest? You want me to bow down to the priest? Are you crazy or out of your head? *'Do not give Satan an opening,'* it is said. My enemies will never live to see that day."

"What did I tell you?" she said. "There you go again."

"Did you think," I said, "that I would let a woman tell me what to do? You want me to live by your woman-ish brains?"

In such talk the whole night passed. At last I heard the first cock crow. I got up, said my morning prayers, took my whip with me, and went straight to the priest's house. A woman is nothing but a woman. But where else could I have gone? Into the grave?

Well, I arrived at the priest's yard and his dogs gave me a royal welcome. They leaped at me and tried to tear off my coat and sink their teeth into my calves to see if they liked the taste of a Jew's flesh. It was lucky that I had taken my whip along. I gave them this quotation to chew on—*"Not a dog shall bark."* Or, as they say in Russian: *"Nehai sobaka daram nie breshe."* Which means, "Don't let a dog bark for nothing."

Aroused by the barking and the commotion in the yard, the priest came running out of his house and his wife after him. With some effort they drove off the happy throng that surrounded me and invited me to come in. They received me like an honored guest and got ready to put on the samovar for me. I told the priest it wasn't necessary to put on the samovar; I had something I wanted to say to him in private. He caught on to what I meant and motioned to his spouse to please be so kind as to shut the door on the outside.

When we were alone I came straight to the point without any preambles, and asked him first of all to tell me if he believed in God. Then I asked him to tell me if he knew what it felt like to be parted from a child he loved. And then I asked him to tell me what, according to his interpretation, was right and what was wrong. And one more thing I wanted him to make clear for me.

What did he think of a man who sneaked into another man's house, and began tearing it apart, turning beds, tables, and chairs—everything, upside down.

Naturally he was dumbfounded by all this, and he said to me, "Tevel, you are a clever man, it seems to me, and yet you put so many questions to me and you expect me to answer them all at one blow. Be patient and I shall answer them one at a time, the first question first and the last question last."

"No, dear little father," I said. "You will never answer my questions. Do you know why? Because I know all your answers beforehand. Just tell me this: is there any hope of my getting my child back, or not?"

He leaped up at this. "What do you mean getting her back? No harm will come to your daughter—just the opposite."

"I know," I said. "I know. You want to bring her a piece of great good luck. I am not speaking of that. I only want to know where my child is and if I can see her."

"Everything, yes," he said, "but that, no."

"That's the way to talk," I said. "Come to the point. No mincing of words. And now good-bye. May God repay you in equal measure for everything you have done."

I came home and found Golde lying in bed all knotted up like a ball of black yarn. She had no more tears left to weep. I said to her, "Get up, my wife, take off your shoes, and let us sit down and mourn our child as God has commanded. *'The Lord hath given and the Lord hath taken away.'* We are neither the first nor the last. Let us imagine that we never had a daughter named Chava, or that like Hodel she went off to the ends of the earth. God is All-Merciful and All-Good. He knows what He is doing."

As I said this I felt the tears choking me, standing like a bone in my throat. But Tevye is not a woman. Tevye can restrain himself. Of course, you understand, that's only a way of speaking. First of all, think of the disgrace! And second, how can I restrain myself when I've lost my child, and especially a child like Chava. A child so precious to us, so deeply embedded in our hearts, both in her mother's and mine. I don't know why she had always seemed dearer to us than any of the other children. Maybe because as a baby she had been so sickly, and we had gone through so much with her. We used to stay up whole nights nursing her, and many a time we snatched her, literally snatched her, from the jaws of death, breathed life into her as you would into a tiny crushed chick. For if God wills it, He makes the dead come to life again, as we say in Hallel: *"I shall not die, but I will live.*—If you are not fated to die, you will not die." And maybe we loved her so because she had always been such a good child, so thoughtful and devoted, both to her mother and me. Now I ask you, how could she have done this thing to us?

Here is the answer: first of all, it is fate. I don't know about you, but as for me, I believe in Providence. Second, it was witchcraft. You may laugh at me, and I want to tell you that I am not so misguided as to believe in spirits, elves, and such nonsense. But I do believe in witchcraft, in the evil eye. For what else could it have been? Wait, listen to the rest of the story, and you will agree with me.

Well, when the Holy Books say, *"Perforce you must live.*—Man does not take his own life—" they know what they are talking about. There is no wound so deep that it does not heal in time; there is no sorrow so great that you do not forget it eventually. That is, you do not forget, but what can you do about it? *"Man is likened to a beast.*—Man must work, man must till the earth in the sweat of his brow." And so we all went to work. My wife and children got busy with the pitchers of milk, and I took to my horse and wagon and *"the world continued in its course*—the world does not stand still." I told everyone at home to consider Chava as dead. There was no more Chava. Her name had been blotted out. Then I gathered up some dairy stuff—cheese and butter and such, all fresh merchandise—and set off for Boiberik to visit my customers in their *dachas*.

I arrived in Boiberik and I was met with great rejoicing. "How are you, Reb Tevye?" "Why don't we see you anymore?" "How should I be?" I told them. " '*We renew our days as of old.*—I am the same *schlimazel* as always.' One of my cows just dropped dead." They appeared surprised. "Why do so many miracles happen to you, Reb Tevye?" And they began questioning me, wanting to know what kind of cow it was that had dropped dead, how much she had cost, and if I had many cows left. They laughed and joked and made merry over me as rich people will make merry over a poor man and his troubles, when they have just eaten their fill and are in a good mood, and the weather is perfect, sunny and warm and balmy, just the weather to drowse in. But Tevye is the sort of person who can take a joke even at his own expense. I would sooner die on the spot than let them know how I felt.

When I got through with my customers, I set out for home with my empty milk cans. As I rode through the woods I slackened the horse's reins, let him nibble at will, and crop a blade of grass now and then. I let my thoughts roam at will also. I thought about life and death, this world and the next, what the world is altogether about, what man has been created for, and other such things. Anything to drive my gloom away, to keep from thinking about Chava. But just as if to spite me she kept creeping in among my thoughts.

First she appeared before me in her own image, tall, lovely, blooming, like a young tree. Then I saw her as a little baby, sick and ailing, a frail little nestling, snuggled in my arms, her head drooping over my shoulder. "What do you want, Chaveleh? Something to suck on? A piece of candy?" And for the moment I forgot what she had done to me and my heart went out to her in longing. Then I remembered and a great anger seized me. I burned with anger against her and against him and against the whole world, but mostly against myself because I wasn't able to forget her, even for a minute. Why couldn't I forget her, why couldn't I tear her out of my heart completely? Didn't she deserve to be forgotten?

For this, I thought, Tevye had to be a Jew among Jews, to suffer all his life long, to keep his nose to the grindstone, bring children into the world—in order to have them torn from him by force, to have them fall like acorns from a tree and be carried away by the wind and by smoke. I thought to myself, "It's like this: a tree grows in the forest, a mighty oak with outspread branches, and an ignorant lout comes along with an axe and chops off a branch, then another and another. What is a tree without branches, alas? Go ahead, lout, chop down the whole tree and let there be an end. . . . What good is a naked oak in the forest?"

In the midst of these thoughts I suddenly became aware that my horse had stopped. What's the matter? I lift up my eyes and look. It is she, Chava. The same as before, not changed at all; she is even wearing the same dress. My first impulse was to jump off the wagon and take her in my arms. But something held me back. "What are you, Tevye? A woman? A weakling?" I pulled in my horse's reins. "Giddap, *schlimazel.*" I tried to go to the right. I look—she is also going to the right. She beckons to me with her hand as though to say, "Stop a while, I have something to tell you."

Something tears at my insides, something tugs at my heart. I feel myself going weak all over. Any moment I will jump off the wagon. But I restrain myself, pull the horse's reins in, and turn left. She also turns left. She is looking at me wildly, her face is deathly pale. What shall I do? Should I stop or go on? And before I know what's happened, she's got the horse by the bridle and is saying to me, "Father, I will sooner die on the spot before I let you move another step. I beg you, father, listen to me."

"So," I think to myself, "you want to take me by force. No, my dear, if that's what you are trying to do, I see that you don't know your father very well." And I began whipping my horse with all my might. The horse obeys me, he leaps forward. But he keeps moving his ears and turning his back. "Giddap," I tell him. " '*Judge not the vessel but its contents.*—Don't look where you aren't supposed to.' " But do you think that I myself wouldn't like to turn my head and look back at the place where I left her standing? But Tevye is not a woman. Tevye knows how to deal with the Tempter.

Well, I don't want to drag my story out any longer. Your time is valuable. If I have been fated to suffer the punishments of the damned after death, I surely have expiated all my sins already. If you want to know about the tortures of hell that are described in our Holy Books, ask me. I can describe them all to you. All the rest of the way, as I drove, I thought I could hear her running after me, calling, "Listen, father, listen to me." A thought crossed my mind, "Tevye, you are taking too much upon yourself. Will it hurt if you stop and listen to her? Maybe she has something to say that is worth hearing. Maybe—who can tell—she is regretting what she has done and wants to come back to you. Maybe she is being badly treated and wants you to save her from a living hell." Maybe and maybe and maybe . . . And I saw her as a little child once more and I was reminded of the passage: "*As a father has mercy on his children* . . ." To a father there is no such thing as a bad child. I blamed myself and I told myself, '*I do not deserve to be pitied*—I am not worthy of the earth I walk upon.'

"What are you fuming and fretting for?" I asked myself. "Stubborn mule, turn your wagon around and go back and talk to her. She is your own child." And peculiar thoughts came into my mind. What is the meaning of Jew and non-Jew? Why did God create Jews and non-Jews? And since God did create Jews and non-Jews, why should they be kept apart from each other and hate each other, as though one were created by God and the other were not? I regretted that I wasn't as learned as some men so that I could arrive at an answer to this riddle. . . .

And in order to chase away these painful thoughts I began to chant the words of the evening prayer: *"Blessed are they who dwell in Thy house, and they shall continue to praise Thee. . . ."* But what good was this chanting when inside of me a different tune was playing? *Chava*, it went. *Cha-va*. The louder I recited the prayer, the plainer the word *Chava* sounded in my own ears. The harder I tried to forget her, the more vividly she appeared before me, and it seemed to me that I heard her voice calling, "Listen, father, listen to me." I covered my ears to keep from hearing her voice and I shut my eyes to keep from seeing her face, and I started saying *Shimenesre* and didn't know what I was saying. I beat my breast and cried aloud, *"For we have sinned,"* and I didn't know for what I was beating my breast.

I didn't know what I was saying or doing. My whole life was in a turmoil, and I myself was confused and unhappy. I didn't tell anyone of my meeting with Chava. I didn't speak about her to anyone and didn't ask anyone about her, though I knew quite well where they lived and what they were doing. But no one could tell from my actions. My enemies will never live to see the day when I complain to anyone. That's the kind of man Tevye is.

I wonder if all men are like me, or if I am the only crazy one. For instance, let us imagine—just suppose it should happen—if I tell you this, you won't laugh at me? I am afraid that you will laugh. But just let us suppose that one fine day I should put on my Sabbath gabardine and stroll over to the railway station as though I were going away on the train, going to see them. I walk up to the ticket window and ask for a ticket. The ticket seller asks me where I want to go. "To Yehupetz," I tell him. And he says, "There is no such place." And I say, "Well, it's not my fault then." And I turn myself around and go home again, take off my Sabbath clothes and go back to work, back to my cows and my horse and wagon. As it is written: *"Each man to his labor*—The tailor must stick to his shears and the shoemaker to his last."

I see that you are laughing at me. What did I tell you? I know what you're thinking. You're thinking that Tevye is a big imbecile. . . . That's why I say: *"Read to this part on the great Sabbath before Passover,"* meaning, it's enough for one day. Be well and happy and write me often. And don't forget what I asked you. Be silent as the grave concerning this. Don't put what I told you into a book. And if you should write, write about someone else, not about me. Forget about me. As it is written: *"And he was forgotten—"* No more Tevye the Dairyman!

Translated by Frances Butwin

GET THEE OUT

Greetings to you, Mr. Sholom Aleichem, heartiest greetings. I've been expecting you for a long time and wondering why I didn't see you anymore. I kept asking, *"Where are you?"* as God once asked of Adam, and I was told that you have been traveling all over the world, visiting faraway countries—*"the one hundred and twenty-seven provinces of Ahasheurus,"* as we say in the *Megillah*.

But you are looking at me strangely. You seem to be hesitating and wondering, "Is it he, or isn't it he?" It is he, Mr. Sholom Aleichem, it is he, your old friend Tevye in person. Tevye the Dairyman, the very same as before, but not a dairyman any longer. Just an ordinary, everyday Jew, and greatly aged, as you can see. And yet I am not so old in years. As we say in the *Haggadah:* *"I look like a man of seventy.—*I am still far from seventy." Then why should my hair be so white? Believe me, dear friend, it's not from joy. My own sorrows are partly to blame and partly the sorrows of all Israel. For these are difficult times for us Jews—hard, bitter times to live in.

But that isn't what's troubling you, I can see. The shoe pinches on the other foot. You must have remembered that I told you good-bye once, as I was about to leave for Palestine. Now you are thinking, "Here is

Tevye, just back from the Holy Land," and you are eager to know what's going on in Palestine—you want to hear about my visit to Mother Rachel's Tomb, to the Cave of Machpelah, and the other holy places. Wait, I will set your mind at rest; I will tell you everything, if you have the time and would like to hear a strange and curious tale. Then listen carefully, as it is written: *"Hear ye!"* And when you have heard me out, you yourself will admit that man is nothing but a fool and that we have a mighty God who rules the Universe.

Well, what portion of the Bible are *you* studying this week in the synagogue? *Vaikro?* The first portion of Leviticus? I am on a different portion entirely— on *Lech-lecho* or *Get thee out*. I have been told, *"Get thee out*—get a move on you, Tevye—*out of thy country*— leave your own land—*and from thy father's house*—the village where you were born and spent all the years of your life—*to the land which I will show thee*—wherever your two eyes lead you." That's the lesson I am on now. And when was I given this lesson to study? Now that I am old and feeble and all alone in the world, as we say on Rosh Hashanah: *"Do not cast me off in my old age."*

But I am getting ahead of my story. I haven't told you about the Holy Land yet. What should I tell you, dear friend? It is indeed a *"land flowing with milk and honey,"* as the Bible tells us. The only trouble is that the Holy Land is over there and I am still here—*outside of the Promised Land.* He who wrote the *Megillah* or Book of Esther must have had Tevye in mind when he had Esther say, *"If I perish, I perish."* I have always been a *schlimazel,* and a *schlimazel* I will die. There I stood, as you remember, with one foot practically in the Holy Land. All I had to do was to buy a ticket, get on a ship, and I'm off. But that isn't the way God deals with Tevye. He had something different in store for me. Wait and you will hear.

You may remember my oldest son-in-law, Mottel

Kamzoil the tailor from Anatevka. Well, our Mottel goes to sleep one night in the best of health, and never gets up. Though I shouldn't have said he was in the *best* of health. How could he be, a poor workingman, alas, sitting day and night *"absorbed in study and worship of God,"* meaning that he sat in a dark cellar day and night bent over a needle and thread, patching trousers. He did this so long that he got the coughing sickness, and he coughed and coughed until he coughed out his last piece of lung. Doctors couldn't help him, medicines didn't do any good, nor goats' milk, nor honey and chocolate.
. . . He was a fine boy, the salt of the earth; it's true, he had no learning, but he was an honest fellow, unassuming, and without any false pretensions. He loved my daughter with all his heart, sacrificed himself for the children—and he thought the world of me!

And so we conclude the text with: *"Moses passed away."* In other words, Mottel died, and he left me with a millstone around my neck. Who could begin to think about the Holy Land now? I had a Holy Land right here at home. How could I leave my daughter, a widow with small children and without any means of support? Though if you stop to think, what could I do for her, an old man like me, a sack full of holes? I couldn't bring her husband back to life or return the children's father to them. And besides, I am only human myself. I would like to rest my bones in my old age, take life easy, find out what it feels like to be a human being. I've done enough hustling and bustling in my lifetime. Enough striving after the things of this world. It's time to begin thinking about the next world. I had gotten rid of most of my goods and chattels, sold my cows and let my horse go quite some time ago. And all of a sudden in my old age I have to become a protector of orphans and provide for a family of small children. But that isn't all. Wait. More is coming. For when troubles descend on Tevye, they never come singly. The first one always brings others trailing after it. For instance, once when a cow of mine died, didn't another one lie down and die the very next day? That's how God created the world and that's how it will remain. There is no help for it.

Do you remember the story of my youngest daughter Beilke and her great good fortune? How she caught the biggest fish in the pond, the contractor Padhatzur who had made a fortune in the war and was looking for a beautiful young bride—how he sent Ephraim the Matchmaker to me, how he met my daughter and fell in love with her, how he begged for her on his knees, threatened to kill himself if he couldn't have her, how he was ready to take her just as she was, without any dowry, and showered her with gifts from head to foot, with gold and diamonds and jewels? It sounds like a fairy tale, doesn't it? The wealthy prince, the poor maiden, the great palace. But what was the end of this beautiful tale? The end was a sorry one. May God have pity on us all! For if God wills it, the wheel of fortune can turn backwards and then everything begins to fall buttered side down as we say in Hallel: *"Who raiseth up the poor out of the dust."* And before you can turn around—Crash! *"That looketh down low upon heaven and upon the earth*—everything is shattered into little pieces."

Thus God likes to play with us human beings. That's how he played with Tevye many times, raising him up, and casting him down, like Jacob ascending and descending the ladder. And that is what happened to Padhatzur. You remember his great riches, his airs and pretensions, the splendor of his mansion in Yehupetz with its dozen servants and thousand clocks and mirrors. What do you think was the outcome of all this? The outcome was that he not only lost everything and had to sell all his clocks and mirrors and his wife's jewels, but went bankrupt in the bargain, and made such a sorry mess of everything that he had to flee the country and become a fugitive. . . . He went to where the holy Sabbath goes. In other words, he ran off to

America. That's where all the unhappy souls go, and that's where they went.

They had a hard time of it in America at first. They used up what little cash they had brought with them, and when there was nothing more to chew on, they had to go to work, both he and she, doing all kinds of back-breaking labor, like our ancestors in Egypt. Now, she writes me, they are doing quite well, God be thanked. Both of them are working in a stocking factory, and they manage to "scrape up a living," as they say in America. Here we call it being one jump ahead of the poorhouse. It's lucky for them, she tells me, that there are just the two of them—they have neither chick nor child. *"That too is for the best."*

And now, I ask you, doesn't he deserve to be cursed with the deadliest curses, I mean Ephraim the Matchmaker, for arranging this happy match? Would she have been any worse off if she had married an honest workingman the way Tzeitl did, or a teacher, like Hodel? You might argue that their luck didn't hold out either, that one was left a young widow, and the other had to go into exile with her husband. But these things are in God's hands. Man cannot provide against everything. If you want to know the truth, the only wise one among us was my wife Golde. She looked about her in good time and decided to leave this miserable world forever. For tell me yourself, rather than to suffer the *"pain of bringing up children,"* the way I have suffered, isn't it better to lie in the earth and be eaten by worms? But how is it said: *"Perforce thou must live.*—Man doesn't take his own life, and if he does, he gets rapped on the knuckles for it." But in the meanwhile we have strayed off the path. *"Let us return to our original subject."*

Where were we? At section *Lech-lecho* or *Get thee out*. But before we go on with section *Lech-lecho* I shall ask you to stop with me for a moment at section *Balak*. It has always been a custom since the world began to study *Lech-lecho* or *Get thee out* first, and *Balak* or the lesson of revenge later, but with me the custom was reversed and I was taught the lesson of *Balak* first and *Lech-lecho* afterward. And I was drilled in *Balak* so thoroughly that I want you to hear about it. The lesson may come in handy some day.

This happened some time ago, right after the war, during the troubles over the Constitution when we were undergoing *"salvations and consolations"*—that is, when reprisals were being carried out against Jews. The pogroms began in the big cities, then spread to the small towns and villages. But they didn't reach me, and I was sure that they never would reach me. Why? Simply for this reason: that I have lived in the village for so many years and had always been on such friendly terms with the peasants. I had become a *"Friend of the Soul and Father of Mercy"* to them—"Brother Tevel" was their best friend. Did they want advice? It was, "do as brother Tevel says." Did one of them need a remedy for fever? It was, "Go to Tevel." A special favor? Also to Tevel. Tell me, why should I worry about pogroms and such nonsense when the peasants themselves had assured me many times that I had nothing to be afraid of? They would never permit such a thing, they told me. *"But it came to pass."*—Listen to my story.

I arrived home from Boiberik one evening. I was still in my prime then—how do you say it?—in high feather. I was still Tevye the Dairyman who sold milk and cheese and butter. I unhitched my horse, threw him some oats and hay, and before I had time to wash my hands and say a prayer before eating, I take a look outside and see the yard is full of peasants. The whole village has turned out to see me, from the Mayor, Ivan Poperilo, down to Trochin the Shepherd, and all of them looking stiff and strange in their holiday clothes. My heart turned over at the sight. What holiday was this? Or had they come like Balaam to curse me? But at once I thought, "Shame on you, Tevye, to be so suspicious of these people after all these years you have lived among them as a friend." And I went outside and greeted them warmly, "Welcome, friends, what have you come for? And what good news do you bring?" Then Ivan Poperilo the Mayor stepped forward and said, right out, without any apologies, "We came here, Tevel, because we want to beat you up."

What do you think of such talk? Tactful, wasn't it? It's the same as speaking of a blind man as *sagi nohor* or having too much light. You can imagine how I felt when I heard it. But to show my feelings? Never. That isn't Tevye's way. *"Mazel-tov,"* I said, "why did you get around to it at this late date? In other places they've almost forgotten all about it." Then Ivan said very earnestly, "It's like this, Tevel, all this time we've been trying to decide whether to beat you up or not. Everywhere else your people are being massacred, then why should we let you go? So the Village Council decided to punish you, too. But we haven't decided what to do to you. We don't know whether to break a few of your windowpanes and rip your featherbeds, or to set fire to your house and barn and entire homestead."

When I heard this, my spirits really sank low. I looked at my guests standing there, leaning on their sticks and whispering among themselves. They looked as though they really meant business. "If so," I said to myself, "it's as David said in the psalm, *'For the waters are come in even into the soul.'* You are in bad trouble, Tevye. *'Do not give Satan an opening.*—You cannot trifle with the Angel of Death.' Something has to be done."

Well, why should I spin out the story any longer? A miracle took place. God sent me courage and I spoke up boldly. "Listen to me, gentlemen. Hear me out, dear friends. Since the Village Council has decreed that I must be punished, so be it. You know best what you do, and perhaps Tevye has merited such treatment at your hands. But do you know, my friends, that there is a Power even higher than your Village Council? Do you know that there is a God in Heaven? I am not speaking now of *your* God or *my* God, I am speaking of the God who rules over all of us, who looks down from Heaven and sees all the vileness that goes on below. It may be that He has singled me out to be punished through you, my best friends. And it may be just the opposite, that He doesn't want Tevye to be hurt under any circumstances. Who is there among us who knows what God has decreed? Is there one among you who will undertake to find out?''

They must have seen by then that they couldn't get the best of Tevye in an argument. And so the Mayor, Ivan Poperilo, spoke up. "It's like this, Tevel, we have nothing against you yourself. It's true that you are a Jew, but you are not a bad person. But one thing has nothing to do with the other. You have to be punished. The Village Council has decided. We at least have to smash a few of your windowpanes. We don't dare not to. Suppose an official passed through the village and saw that your house hadn't been touched. We would surely have to suffer for it.''

That is just what he said, as God is my witness. Now I ask you, Mr. Sholom Aleichem, you are a man who has traveled all over the world. Is Tevye right when he says that we have a great and merciful God?

Well, that's the end of section *Balak*. They came to curse and remained to bless. Now let us turn to section *Lech-lecho* or *Get thee out*. This lesson was taught to me not so long ago and in real earnest. This time fine speeches didn't help me; orations didn't avail me. This is exactly the way it happened. Let me tell it to you in detail, the way you like to have a story told. . . .

It was in the days of Mendel Beiliss, when Mendel Beiliss became our scapegoat and was made to suffer the punishments of the damned. I was sitting on my doorstep one day sunk in thought. It was the middle of summer. The sun was blazing and my head was splitting. "Lord, Lord," I thought, "what times these are!

What is the world coming to? And where is God, the ancient God of Israel? Why is He silent? Wherefore does He permit such things to happen?" Wherefore and why and wherefore once more? And when you ask questions of God you begin to ponder about the universe and go on asking: What is this world? And the next world? And why doesn't the Messiah come? Wouldn't it be clever of him to appear at this very moment riding on his white horse? That would be a master stroke! It seems to me that he has never been so badly needed by our people as now. I don't know about the rich Jews, the Brodskys in Yehupetz for instance, or the Rothschilds in Paris. It may be that they never even give him a thought. But we poor Jews of Kasrilevke and Mazapevka and Zolodievka, and even of Yehupctz and Odessa, watch and wait and pray for him daily. Our eyes are strained from watching. He is our only hope. All we can do is hope and pray for this miracle—that the Messiah will come.

And while I am sitting there deep in such thoughts, I look up and see someone approaching, riding on a white horse. He comes riding up to my door, gets off, ties the horse to the post, and comes straight up to me. *"Zdrastoi,* Tevel," he says—"Greetings, Tevye." "Greetings to you, your honor," I answer him with a smile, though in my heart I am thinking, *"Haman approacheth.—* When you're waiting for the Messiah, the village constable comes riding." I stand up and say to him, "Welcome, your honor, what goes on in the world? And what good news do you bring?" And all this time I am quaking inside, waiting to hear what he has to say. But he takes his time. First he lights a cigarette, then he blows out the smoke, spits on the ground, and at last he speaks up. "How much time do you need, Tevel," he says, "to sell your house and all your household goods?"

I look at him in astonishment. "Why should I sell my house? In whose way is it?"

"It isn't in anybody's way," he says, "but I came to

tell you that you will have to leave the village."

"Is that all?" I asked. "And how did I come to deserve such an honor?"

"I can't tell you," he says, "I am not the one who's sending you away. It's the provincial government."

"And what has the government against me?"

"Against you? Nothing. You aren't the only one. Your people are being driven out of all the villages, out of Zolodievka and Rabilevka, and Kostolomevka, and all the others. Even Anatevka, which up to now has been a town, has become a village and your people are being driven from there too."

"Even Lazer-Wolf the Butcher?" I asked. "And Naphtali-Gershon the Lame, and the *shochet* of Anatevka? And the rabbi?"

"Everybody, everybody." And he made a motion with his hand as though he were cutting with a scythe. I felt a little easier at this. How do we say it? *"The troubles of the many are a half-consolation."* But anger at this injustice still burned inside of me. I said to him, "Is your honor aware of the fact that I have lived in this village much longer than you have? Do you know that in this corner of the world lived my father before me, and my grandfather and grandmother before him?" And I began naming all the different members of my family, telling him where each one had lived and where each one died. The constable heard me out, and when I had finished he said, "You are a clever Jew and you certainly know how to talk, but what good are these tales of your grandfather and grandmother to me? Let them enjoy their rest in Paradise. And you, Tevel, pack up your things and go, go to Berdichev."

That made me good and angry. It wasn't enough that you brought me this glad tidings, you Esau, you have to poke fun at me besides? "Pack up and go, go to Berdichev," he tells me. I couldn't let that pass. I had to tell him a thing or two. "Your honor," I said, "in all the years you have been constable here, have you ever heard the villagers complaining of Tevye? Has anyone ever accused Tevye of stealing from him, or robbing him, or cheating him in any way? Ask any of the peasants if I didn't live alongside them like the best of neighbors? How many times did I come to you yourself, your excellency, to plead in their behalf, to ask you not to ill-treat them?"

I could see that this was not to his taste. He got up, crushed his cigarette between his fingers, threw it away, and said to me, "I have no time to waste on idle chatter. I received a paper and that's all I know. Here, sign right here. They give you three days to sell your household goods and get out of the village."

When I heard this, I said, "You give me three days to get out, do you? For this may you live three years longer *'in honor and in riches.'* May the Almighty repay you many times over for the good news you brought me today." And I went on, laying it on thick, as only Tevye can do. After all, I thought to myself, what did I have to lose? If I had been twenty years younger and if my Golde had still been alive, if I were the same Tevye the Dairyman as in ancient days, I would have fought to the last drop for my rights. But *"what are we and what is our life?"* What am I today? Only half of my former self, a broken reed, a shattered vessel. "Ah, dear God, our Father," I thought, "why do you always have to pick on Tevye to do Thy will? Why don't you make sport of someone else for a change? A Brodsky, for instance, or a Rothschild? Why don't you expound to them the lesson *Lech-lecho*—Get thee out? It seems to me that it would do them more good than me. In the first place they would find out what it means to be a Jew. In the second place they would learn that we have a great and mighty God."

But this is all empty talk. You don't argue with God; you don't give Him advice on how to run the world. When He says, *"Mine is the heaven and mine is the earth,"* it means that He is the master and we have to obey Him.

I went into the house and said to my daughter,

"Tzeitl," I said, "we are going away. We are moving to town. We've lived in the country long enough. *'He who changes his place changes his luck.'* Start packing right away, get together the pillows and featherbeds, the samovar and the rest. . . . I am going out to see about selling the house. An order came for us to get out of here in three days and not leave a trace behind us."

When she heard this, my daughter burst into tears. The children took one look at her and burst out crying, too. What shall I tell you? There was weeping and wailing and lamentation, just like on Tisha-Bov, the day on which we mourn the destruction of the Temple. I lost my temper and began scolding. I let out all the bitterness that was in my heart to my daughter. "What have you got against me?" I said. "Why did you have to start blubbering all of a sudden like an old cantor at the first *Sliches?* What do you think I am—God's favorite son? Am I the only one chosen for this honor? Aren't other Jews being driven out of the villages, too? You should have heard what the constable had to say. Even your Anatevka which has been a town since the world began has, with God's help, become a village too, all for the sake of the few Jews who live there. Are we any worse off than all the others?"

That is how I tried to comfort her. But after all she is only a woman. She says to me, "Where will we turn, father? Where will we go looking for towns?" "You talk like a fool," I said to her. "When God appeared to our great-great-grandfather Abraham and said to him, 'Get thee out of this country,' did Abraham question Him? Did he ask, 'Where shall I turn?' God told him, 'Go unto the land which I will show thee.' Which means, '. . . into the four corners of the earth.' And we too will go wherever our eyes lead us, where all the other Jews are going. Whatever happens to all the children of Israel, that will happen to this son of Israel. And why should you consider yourself luckier than your sister

Beilke who was once a millionairess? If 'scraping up a living' in America with her Padhatzur is good enough for her, this is good enough for you. Thank God that we at least have the means with which to go. We have a little saved up from before, a little from the sale of the cows, and I will get something from the house. A dot and a dot make a full pot. *'That too is for the best.'* And even if we had nothing at all, we would still be better off than Mendel Beiliss."

And so I persuaded her that we had to go. I gave her to understand that when the constable brings you a notice to leave, you can't be hoggish and refuse to go. Then I went off to the village to dispose of my house. I went straight to Ivan Poperilo the Mayor because I knew that he'd had his eye on my house for a long time. I didn't give him any reasons or explanations, I am too smart for that. All I said was, "I want you to know, Ivan, my friend, that I am leaving the village." He asked me why. I told him that I was moving to town because I wanted to live among Jews. "I am not so young anymore," I said. "Who knows—I might die suddenly." Says Ivan to me, "Why can't you die right here? Who is preventing you?" I thanked him kindly and said, "You'd better do the dying here, instead of me. I will go and die among my own people. I want you to buy my house and land. I wouldn't sell it to anyone else, but to you I will."

"How much do you want for your house?" he asked me. "How much will you give me?" I said. Again he asked, "How much do you want?" And I countered with, "How much will you give?" We bargained and dickered thus until at last we agreed on a price, and I took a substantial down payment from him then and there, so that he wouldn't change his mind. I am too smart for that. And that was how in one day I sold out all my belongings, turning everything into good money, and went off to hire a wagon to move the few odds and ends that were left. And now something else happened to me, something that can happen only to Tevye. Be patient a little longer and I will tell you in a few words.

Well, I arrived at home, and found not a house, but a ruin—the walls bare, stripped of everything, almost weeping in their nakedness. The floor was piled with bundles and bundles and bundles. On the empty hearth sat the cat, looking as lonely and forsaken as an orphan. My heart was squeezed tight and tears stood in my eyes. If I weren't ashamed before my daughter, I would have wept. After all, this was my homestead. This village was the nearest thing to a fatherland that I could ever have. Here I had grown up, here I had struggled all my days, and now all of a sudden in my old age, I am told, "Get thee out." Say what you will, it's a heartache. But Tevye is not a weakling. I restrained myself and called out in a cheerful voice, "Tzeitl, where are you? Come here." And Tzeitl came out of the other room, her eyes red and her nose swollen with weeping. "Aha," I thought, "my daughter has started wailing again like an old woman on the Day of Atonement. That's women for you—crying at the least excuse. Tears must come cheap to them." "Fool," I told her, "why are you crying again? Aren't you being silly? Just stop and consider the differences between you and Mendel Beiliss." But she wouldn't listen to me. "Father," she said, "you don't know why I'm crying."

"I know very well why you're crying," I told her. "Why shouldn't I know? You are crying because you will miss your home. You were born in this house, this is where you grew up, and your heart aches at having to leave it. Believe me, if I were someone else and not Tevye, I'd be kissing these bare walls myself and embracing these empty shelves. . . . I would be down on my knees on this earth. For I shall miss every particle of it as much as you. Foolish child! Look, do you see the cat sitting there like an orphan on the hearth? She is nothing but an animal, a dumb creature, and yet she too is to be pitied, left alone and forsaken without a master."

"I want to tell you that there is someone who is more to be pitied," said Tzeitl.

"For instance?" I asked.

"For instance, we are going away and leaving a human being behind us, alone and forsaken."

"What are you talking about?" I said to her. "What's all this gibberish? Which human being? Whom are we forsaking?"

"Father," she said, "I am not talking gibberish. I am speaking of Chava."

When she uttered that name it was just as if she had thrown a red-hot poker at me, or hit me over the head with a club. I began yelling at her, "Why bring Chava up all of a sudden? How many times have I told you that she is dead?"

Do you think she was taken aback by this outburst? Not in the least. Tevye's daughters are made of sterner stuff. "Father," she said, "don't be angry with me. Remember what you yourself told me many times, that it is written that one human being must have pity on another the way a father has pity on his child."

Did you ever hear anything like this before? I grew even more furious with her. "Don't speak to me of pity," I shouted. "Where was her pity when I lay like a dog in front of the priest while she was probably in the next room and no doubt heard every word? Where was her pity when her mother lay covered with black in this very room? Where was she then? And all the sleepless nights I spent? And the heartache I suffered and that I suffer to this day when I remember what she did to me and for whom she forsook me? Where is her pity for me?" My throat went dry, my heart began to hammer, and I couldn't speak anymore.

Do you think that Tevye's daughter didn't find an answer to this too? "You yourself have said, father, that God forgives him who repents."

"You speak of repentance, do you? It's too late for that. The limb which has been torn from the tree must wither. The leaf which has fallen to the ground must rot. Don't say another word to me about it. *'Here ends the lesson for the great Sabbath before Passover.'* "

When she saw that she was getting nowhere with talk, and that Tevye was not the person to be won over with words, she fell on my neck and began kissing my hands and pleading with me, "May I suffer some evil, may I die here on the spot, if I let you cast her off as you cast her off that time in the forest when she came to plead with you and you turned your horse around and fled."

"What are you hanging around my neck for? What do you want from me? What have you got against me?" I cried.

But she wouldn't let me go. She clasped my hands in hers and went on, "May I meet with some misfortune, may I drop dead, if you don't forgive her, for she is your daughter the same as I am."

"Let me go. She is not my daughter. My daughter died long ago."

"No, father, she didn't die, and she is your daughter still. The moment she found out that we were being sent away she swore to herself that if we were driven out, she would go too. That's what she told me herself. Our fate is her fate, our exile is her exile. You have the proof right here. This bundle on the floor is hers," said Tzeitl, all in one breath the way we recite the names of the ten sons of Haman in the *Megillah,* and pointed to a bundle tied in a red kerchief. Then she opened the door to the next room and called out, "Chava."

And what shall I tell you, dear friend? There she stood in the doorway, Chava herself in the flesh, tall and beautiful, just as I remembered her, except that her face looked a little drawn and her eyes were somewhat clouded. . . . But she held her head up proudly and looked straight at me. I looked back at her, and then she

stretched out both arms to me and said one word—
"Father."

Forgive me if tears come to my eyes when I recall
these things. But don't think that Tevye weakened and
wept in front of his daughters. I have my pride to
consider. But you understand that in my heart I felt
differently. You are a father yourself and you know how
you feel, when a child of yours, no matter how it has
erred, looks into your eyes and says, "Father." But
then again I remembered the trick she had played on
me, running off with that peasant Fyedka Galagan. I
remembered the priest, may his name and memory be
blotted out, and poor Golde lying dead on the
ground. . . . How can you forget such things? How can
you forget?

And yet she was still my child. The same old saying
came to me. *"A father has mercy on his children."* How
could I be so heartless and drive her away when God
Himself has said, *"I am a long-suffering God and slow
to anger"?* And especially since she had repented and
wanted to return to her father and to her God? Tell me
yourself, Mr. Sholom Aleichem, you are a wise man
who writes books and gives advice to the whole world.
What should Tevye have done? Should he have embraced her and kissed her and said as we do on Yom
Kippur at *Kol Nidre: "I have forgiven thee in accor-
dance with thy prayers.—*Come to me, my child"? Or
should I have turned my back on her as I did once
before and said, "Get thee out. Go back where you
came from"? Try to put yourself in my place and tell me
truthfully what would you have done? And if you don't
want to tell me right away, I will give you time to think it
over. Meanwhile I must go—my grandchildren are
waiting for me. And grandchildren, you must know, are
a thousand times dearer and more precious than one's
own children. *Children and grandchildren*—that's
something to reckon with!

Farewell, my friend, and forgive me if I have talked

too much. You will have something to write about now. And if God wills it, we shall meet again. For since they taught me the lesson—*Lech-lecho,* Get thee out—I have been wandering about constantly. I have never been able to say to myself, "Here, Tevye, you shall remain." Tevye asks no questions. When he is told to go, he goes. Today you and I meet here on this train; tomorrow we might see each other in Yehupetz; next year I might be swept along to Odessa or to Warsaw or maybe even to America. Unless the Almighty, the Ancient God of Israel, should look about him suddenly and say to us, "Do you know what, my children? I shall send the Messiah down to you." Wouldn't that be a clever trick? In the meanwhile, good-bye, go in good health, and give my greetings to all our friends and tell them not to worry. Our ancient God still lives!

Translated by Frances Butwin

PART THREE

FROM MOTTEL THE CANTOR'S SON

My Brother Elye's Drink

For One Ruble A Hundred!
Earn one hundred rubles a month or more
Just by knowing what's in this book.
The cost is one ruble plus postage.
Hurry! Offer Limited!

This my brother Elye read in a newspaper somewhere just after he'd left his father-in-law's table. He left the table not because his time was up—he'd been promised three whole years' board and got not even three-quarters of one year—but because of tragedy. Yoine the baker went bankrupt and instead of a rich man was now a poor one. How bad luck fell upon him I've already told you, and I don't tell a story twice unless asked. This time even asking won't help because I'm so busy. I'm earning money. I carry about a drink my brother Elye makes with his own hands. He found out how to do this from a book that costs only a ruble. With this book you can earn a hundred rubles a month and more. My brother Elye, soon as he read that such a book existed, sent off the ruble—our last—and told our mother she had nothing more to worry about: "Mama, thank God, we're saved. We'll have," he said, pointing to his throat, "money up till here."

247

"What's this?" she asked. "You got a job?"

"Better than that," my brother answered as his eyes lit up, apparently from joy. He told her to wait a few days until a book came.

"What book?"

"Wait, you'll see," he answered and asked if she could use a hundred rubles a month. She answered that she could live on one hundred a year so long as she could count on that amount. My brother Elye told her that her reach was too small and went off to the post office. He goes there every day now to inquire about the book. Over a week has passed and still no book. In the meantime, says my mother, we still have to live. "You can't just spit out your soul," she says. How you spit out a soul I have no idea.

Two

All right, calm down—the book's here. No sooner did we unpack it than my brother Elye sat down to read it. And he found there any number of different ways to make money. You can earn a hundred rubles by making the best inks or the best black shoe polish; or by driving off mice, roaches, and other pests; or by manufacturing liqueurs, sweet brandies, lemonade, soda water, kvass, and still cheaper drinks.

My brother Elye settled for the last idea. First of all because he'd earn over one hundred rubles a month. It says so, right there in the book. Second, that way you can keep away from ink, shoe polish, mice, roaches, and other pests. The only problem is which drink to choose. For liqueurs and brandies you need Rothschild's fortune. For lemonade and soda water you need a kind of machine, some kind of stone that costs who knows how much. What's left is kvass. Kvass is the kind of drink that costs little and sells fast, especially in a summer as hot as this. From kvass, you should know, our kvass-maker, Boruch, has grown rich. He makes bottled kvass. It's known all over the world. It shoots out of the bottle like a cannon. How it shoots nobody knows. That's Boruch's secret. They say he puts something in there that makes it shoot. Some say it's a raisin, others say hops. When summer comes along he doesn't have enough hands. He makes a bundle.

The kvass that my brother Elye makes from the formula isn't bottled and doesn't shoot. Ours is a completely different kind. How it's made I can't tell you. My brother Elye doesn't let anyone near him when he makes it. He pours in water—everyone sees that; but when he mixes in the other ingredients he shuts himself off in my mother's alcove. Neither I, nor my mother, nor my sister-in-law Brokhe has the right to be near. Nevertheless, if you promise to keep a secret I'll tell you what's in the drink. I know the ingredients. There's lemon peel, loose honey, something called cream of tartar that's more sour than vinegar; the rest is water. There's more water than anything. The more water, the more kvass. This is stirred well with a plain stick— that's what the book says—and the drink is ready. After that it's poured into a big pitcher and you throw in a piece of ice. Ice is the main ingredient. Without ice the drink is nothing. This I know without the book. I once tried kvass without ice and thought I'd drop dead.

When the first barrel of kvass was ready it was decided I'd be the one to go out peddling it in the street. Who else? My brother Elye—it's beneath his dignity; he's a married man. My mother—definitely not. We'd never allow her to go around with a pitcher, yelling, "Kvass! Kvass! Everybody, kvass!" So it was decided this should be my work. I felt the same way. I was thrilled at the news. My brother Elye began showing me what to do. I'm to hold the pitcher in one hand by a rope, the glass in the other hand. In order to get people to stop I'm supposed to sing loudly:

> *Ice cold kvass*
> *a kopek a glass;*
> *cool and sweet*
> *can't be beat.*

I told you long ago that I have a nice voice, a soprano inherited from my father, he should rest in peace. I sang out heartily and turned the call upside down.

> *Cool as a beet*
> *can't be sweet;*
> *ice in a glass*
> *try some kvass.*

I don't know what was so great—my singing or the kvass, or maybe the day was so hot, but I sold the first pitcher in half an hour and came home with almost a ruble. My brother Elye handed the money over to my mother and immediately filled up another pitcher. He said if I could make five or six trips a day we'd take in exactly a hundred rubles for the month. Figure it out for yourself. Take off the four Saturdays plus expenses and you'll know the profits. The drink itself costs very little, almost nothing. The big expense is ice. This means we have to sell a pitcher very fast in order to use the ice for a second pitcher, a third, and so on. In fact, I have to run. Boys chase me, a whole gang of ruffians. They make fun of the way I sing. Who cares? I try to sell out the pitcher fast and run home for another. I don't even know how much I made the first day. I only know that my brother Elye, my sister-in-law Brokhe, and my mother all praised me to the skies. For supper I got a piece of watermelon, a slice of cantaloupe, two prunes, and, of course, kvass—we drink it like water. At bedtime, my mother prepared my mattress on the floor and asked if, Heaven forbid, my feet hurt. My brother Elye laughed at her and he said I'm the kind of boy that nothing ever hurts. "Of course," I said. "Proof is, if you want, I'll go right out in the middle of the night with the pitcher."

The three of them laughed at my ingenuity, but in my mother's eyes I saw tears. That's an old story: a mother has to cry. What I'd like to know is if all mothers cry all the time or only mine.

Three

Business keeps pouring in. One day's hotter than the next. It's roasting. People pass out from the heat; children fall like flies. If not for kvass we'd burn up. Without exaggeration, I make ten rounds a day with the pitcher. My brother Elye looked into the barrel and saw it was just about empty. He got the idea of adding a pail of water. He isn't the first to come up with the plan; I did it before him. I've played the trick several times. Almost every day I go over to our neighbor Peshe and give her a glass of our drink. Her husband, Moishe the bookbinder, I give two glasses. He's a good person. The children also get glasses; let them also know how good a drink we make. I give the blind uncle a glass to taste; poor man, he's a cripple. All my friends I give kvass, free. In order not to lose anything I add water to the pitcher. For each glass I give away free I add two of water. We do the same at home. If, for example, my brother Elye takes a glass of kvass, he immediately pours in some water. He's right: it's a sin to waste a kopek. My sister-in-law Brokhe drinks a few glasses of kvass—she's crazy about my brother Elye's kvass—she pours in water. My mother occasionally tastes some kvass—she has to be asked; by herself she won't take it—she pours in water. In other words, we never lose a drop of merchandise, and we make good money, knock on wood. My mother's paid off a lot of debts, redeemed a few big pledges, like the bedding. A table's come into the house; a chair. Friday night and Saturday we have meat, fish, and white *khale*. I've been prom-ised for the holidays, God willing, a new pair of boots. Seems no one's as well off as we.

Four

Go be a prophet and guess that a tragedy would hit us—that our drink would spoil, good only for the slop pail. As if that wasn't enough, I was almost arrested. Listen to this. One day I wandered over to our neighbor Peshe with the pitcher of kvass. Her whole bunch took kvass and so did I. I was now short some twelve-thir-teen glasses, so I went to the room where the water was. Apparently, instead of the drinking pail I found the washtub. I poured fifteen-twenty glasses into the pitcher and went to the street with a new tune I made up:

> *Drink, one and all*
> *only the best—*
> *the taste of Heaven*
> *for me and the rest.*

A man stops me, pays his kopek, and orders a glass of kvass. He drinks the whole glass and wrinkles up his face. "Hey! What kind of drink is this?" he wants to know. Let him talk to himself; I have two customers waiting for kvass. One sips half a glass, and the other a third. They pay, spit out, and walk away. Another brings the glass to his lips, tries it, and says it tastes of soap and is salty. The next one looks at the glass and gives it back with the comment, "What is this stuff?"

"A drink," I say.

"A drink? It's a stink, not a drink."

Somebody else comes over, tastes, and throws the glassful in my face. Soon I'm surrounded by a circle of men, women, and children. They talk, they gesticulate, they get excited. A Russian policeman sees the gathering and comes over to ask what's going on. They tell him. He looks into my pitcher and demands a taste. He drinks, spits, and gets ready to murder me: "Where'd you get the soapsuds?"

"From a book," I answer. "It's my brother's work; he makes the stuff himself."

"Who's your brother?" he asks.

"My brother Elye," I answer.

"Which Elye?" he asks.

"Idiot! Don't mention your brother," several men call to me half in Hebrew. Suddenly there's yelling, buzzing, and shouting. People keep coming over. The policeman holds me by the hand and wants to take us—me and the drink—to the police station. The noise grows. "An orphan! A poor orphan!" I hear from all sides. My heart tells me I'm in a tight squeeze. I look pleadingly about me: "Jews, have mercy." They want to slip the policeman a coin. He refuses. An old man with mischievous eyes calls out to me in Hebrew, "Mottel, tear your hand away from the *goy*. Lift your feet and beat it." I tear my hand away, pick up my feet, and run home. I fall into the house half-dead.

"Where's the pitcher?" my brother asks.

"In the police station," I answer and fall upon my mother in tears.

We Flood the World with Ink

What a fool I was. Just because I sold bad kvass I thought they'd chop off my head. Nothing happened. I got scared for nothing. Is it all right for Yente to sell lard as goose fat? For Gedalye the butcher to sell the town unkosher meat? That's how our neighbor Peshe comforted my mother. My mother's strange that way: she takes everything to heart.

That's what I like about my brother Elye. He didn't

get flustered when we got burned with the kvass. So long as he has the book, everything's all right. He bought a book for a ruble. It's called, *For One Ruble a Hundred*. He's learning it by heart. There are endless formulas there for making money. He knows almost all of them. He knows how to make ink, how to make shoe polish, how to drive off mice, roaches, and other pests. He figures he'll try ink; it's a good item. These days everybody's learning how to write. He's gone to Yudel the scribe to check how much ink he uses. "A fortune in ink," he answers. Yudel the scribe has some sixty girls he's teaching to write. Boys don't study with him; they're afraid. He hits—with a ruler over the hand. Girls, he's not supposed to hit; spanking, certainly not. It upsets me I wasn't born a girl. First of all, I wouldn't have to pray every day. I'm sick of it; every day the same thing. Then I could be rid of *cheder*. I'm in school half a day. I study very little but I make it up in slaps. From the teacher? No, from his wife. What does she care if I take care of the cat? You should see that poor cat. She's always hungry. She whines quietly (pardon the comparison) like a human being. It tears my heart out. They have no pity. What do they want from the cat? If she sniffs at someone they scream "Scat!" and she runs off where no one can find her. They don't let her keep her head up. Once she disappeared for a few days, and I was sure, God forbid, she'd dropped dead. Finally, she came with a litter. . . . All right, I'm coming back to my brother Elye's ink.

Two

My brother Elye says the world isn't what it used to be. There was a time, he says, when if you wanted to make ink you'd buy ink balls, crumble them, cook them over the flame—who knows how long—and throw them in copper-water. To make the ink shiny you added a bit of sugar—a complex procedure. Today, he says, it's a pleasure. You buy a powder at the druggist's and a bottle of glycerine. Mix it with water, a second over the fire—and it's ready. That's what my brother says. He went to the druggist and came home with a bunch of powders and a whole bottle of glycerine. Then he shut himself up in the alcove and did something. What, I don't know; it's a secret. To him everything's a secret. If he wants my mother to get him a bowl he calls her over quietly and says, "Mama, the bowl." He mixed the powders and the glycerine in a big pot bought for the occasion. The pot he then shoved into the oven and asked my mother quietly to bolt the house door. We couldn't imagine what was going on. Every minute my mother glanced at the oven. She was probably afraid the stove would explode. Next we rolled the kvass barrel into the room. Then we slowly took the pot out of the oven and gently poured the mixture into the barrel. After that we began adding water. When the barrel was over half full my brother Elye cried "Enough!" and sat down with the book, *For One Ruble a Hundred*. He read and then asked quietly for a new pen and a fresh sheet of white paper—"the kind you write appeals on," he whispered into my mother's ear. Then he dipped the pen into the barrel and scribbled on the white paper in curlicues and zigzags. He showed the scribble first to my mother, then to my sister-in-law Brokhe. Both stared, then called out, "It writes."

Soon he returned to the business of adding water. After a few pails he raised his hands: "Enough." He dipped the pen into the barrel, again scribbled on the white paper, and carried it to my mother, then to my sister-in-law Brokhe. Both looked at the paper: "It writes."

We did all this several times until the barrel was full; there was no more room for water. My brother Elye raised his hands: "Enough," and the four of us sat down to eat.

Three

After dinner we began pouring the ink into bottles, bottles my brother Elye had dragged together from the whole world. All kinds of bottles and flasks, large and small. Beer bottles, wine bottles, kvass bottles, whiskey bottles, plain bottles. He bought used corks to save money, a new funnel, and a tin dipper to pour ink from the barrel into the bottles. Once more he whispered to my mother to bolt the door, and the four of us threw ourselves into the work. The work was well divided. My sister-in-law Brokhe rinsed the bottles and handed them to my mother. My mother checked inside each bottle and handed it on to me. I had to put the funnel into the bottle with one hand and steady the bottle with the other. My brother Elye had only to fill the dipper from the barrel and empty it into the funnel. The work went well and was lots of fun. There was one problem— ink spots on the fingers, the hand, the nose, and whole face. Both of us, my brother Elye and I, grew black as demons. This was the first time I ever saw my mother laugh. My sister-in-law Brokhe, naturally, almost split her sides. My brother Elye hates to be laughed at. He yelled at my sister-in-law Brokhe and asked what she was laughing at. She only laughed harder. He gets angrier; she laughs harder. She falls into spasms which could kill her. This goes on until my mother pleads for a halt and tells the two of us to go wash. My brother has no time for washing; he thinks of nothing but bottles. We've used up the bottles. There aren't any more bottles. Where do you get more bottles? He calls over my sister-in-law Brokhe, gives her money, and whispers in her ear that she should go for bottles. She listens, stares at him, and bursts out laughing. He gets angry and whispers the same secret in my mother's ear. My mother goes for bottles and the rest of us pour water into the barrel. Not all at once, of course, but gradually.

After each pail my brother lifts his hands and says to himself, "Enough." Then he dips the pen in the barrel, writes on the white paper, and says to himself, "It writes."

This went on until my mother returned with a load of bottles. Then we started all over, pouring ink from barrel to bottle, until we were once more without bottles.

"How long will this go on?" my sister-in-law Brokhe called out.

"Don't give us the evil eye," my mother shot back as my brother Elye gave Brokhe an angry look as if to say, "Maybe you're my wife, but God pity us, you're still a fool."

Four

How much ink we have I can't tell you. I'm afraid there may be a thousand bottles. What's the result of all this? There's nowhere to put the bottles. My brother Elye's been everywhere; selling them retail, one by one, is hopeless. That's what my brother Elye told our neighbor's husband, Moishe the bookbinder. When Moishe came over and saw, knock on wood, all our bottles, he grew frightened and stopped short. He turned to my brother and a strange conversation took place between them.

"What are you frightened of?"

"What do you have in the bottles?"

"What do you expect? Wine?"

"What wine? It's ink."

"If you know, why do you ask?"

"What are you going to do with so much ink?"

"Drink it."

"No, seriously. You're going to sell retail, too?"

"You think I'm crazy? When I sell, it'll be ten bottles, twenty bottles, fifty bottles. That's called wholesale. Do you know what wholesale is?"

"I know what wholesale is. Who'll you sell it to?"

"To the rabbi."

My brother went around to the storekeepers. He went to one large dealer who told him to bring a sample bottle—he wants to look it over. To another he brought a sample, but the man wouldn't touch it; it had no label. A bottle has to have a pretty label with a design. My brother told him. "I don't make designs; I make ink."

"All right, go on making it."

He tried Yudel the scribe. Yudel the scribe answers with something nasty. He's already bought enough ink for the whole summer. "How many bottles?" my brother Elye asked.

"Bottles?" Yudel the scribe answered. "I bought one bottle of ink and I'll use it up till it's done. Then I'll buy another one." This is what you get from a teacher. First he says he uses a fortune in ink. Now he says he uses a bottle that doesn't run out. My brother Elye was beside himself. What is he going to do with so much ink? First he said he wouldn't sell ink retail, only in volume. Now he's changed his mind. I'd like to know what retail means.

Here's what it means. It won't hurt you to listen.

Five

My brother Elye got hold of a big sheet of paper. He sat down and wrote in large, prayer book letters:

> *Ink Sold Here*
> *Wholesale and Retail*
> *Low Cost and Good Quality*

The words "Low Cost" and "Good Quality" were written so large they occupied almost the whole sheet. When the writing dried he hung the paper outside the door. Lots of people passed by and stopped to stare. I saw them through the window. My brother Elye also looked through the window and cracked his knuckles, a sure sign he was upset. He said to me, "You know what? Stand by the door and listen to what they're saying."

He didn't have to coax me. I stood by the door and watched to see who stopped by and hear what they said. After half an hour I went back inside. My brother Elye came over and asked quietly, "Well?"

"Well, what?"

"What did they say?"

"Who?"

"The people passing by."

"They said it's written nicely."

"That's all?"

"That's all."

My brother Elye sighed. What's he sighing about? My mother asked the same question: "What are you sighing about, you silly child. Wait a bit. In one day you expect to sell the whole thing?"

"At least a beginning," he said with tears in his throat.

"Listen to me; don't be a fool. Wait, my child, with the help of God you'll have your start." That's what my mother said as she set the table. We washed and sat down to eat, the four of us squeezed among the bottles. The bottles make it horribly crowded in the house. As soon as we made the blessing over the bread a strange young man came running into the house. I know him; he's already engaged. His name's Kopel. His father is a tailor, a ladies' tailor.

"You sell ink here?"

"Yes, what do you want?"

"I want a little ink."

"How much do you need?"

"Just a kopek's worth."

My brother Elye almost went crazy. If he hadn't been ashamed in front of my mother he'd have smacked Kopel the bridegroom and thrown him out of the house.

Instead, he controlled himself and poured out a kopek's worth of ink. A quarter of an hour goes by and a girl comes in. I don't know her. She picks her nose and says to my mother, "You make ink here?"

"Yes, what do you want?"

"My sister wants to know if you'd lend her some ink. She has to send a letter to her fiancé in America."

"Who's your sister?"

"Bashe the seamstress."

"Ah, see how she's grown. Knock on wood. I didn't recognize you. Do you have an inkwell?"

"How would we have an inkwell? My sister asks maybe you have a pen. She'll write the letter to America and give you back the pen and ink."

My brother Elye is no longer at the table. He's in the alcove quietly pacing back and forth, looking down and biting his nails.

Six

"Why did you make so much ink? You want to supply the world with ink in case of a shortage?" That's what our neighbor's husband, Moishe the bookbinder, said to my brother. He has a way of throwing salt on wounds; otherwise, he's not such a bad person, just somewhat annoying. He likes to bore into your insides.

But my brother Elye gave it to him. He told him to take care of himself instead of mixing things up, like a Passover *Haggadah* together with penitential prayers. Moishe the bookbinder knows well what this dig means. Once he took on a job from a coachman. The coachman gave him a *Haggadah* to bind. A tragedy occurred: by mistake he bound a few pages of penitential prayers into the *Haggadah*. The coachman himself may not have caught his mistake, but the neighbors heard him singing, "The soul is yours; the body, your handiwork" instead of "Pour out your wrath." He confused Passover deliverance with High Holiday mournfulness.

This became a big joke. The next day the coachman came to our neighbor the binder and wanted to tear him in two. "Thief!" he cried. "What do you have against me? Why did you mix yeast with *matzo*—"The soul is yours" with Passover *Haggadah?* I'm going to tear your insides out."

That year we really had a lively holiday.

Don't be upset that I've thrown in this story. I'm coming right back to our marvelous business ventures.

Aftermath of the Ink Flood

My brother Elye goes around completely confused. What do we do with the ink?

"Ink, again?" my mother asks.

"I'm not talking about ink!" my brother Elye says. "The devil with it. I'm talking about the bottles. There's money in the bottles. We've got to empty them and make money."

From everything he has to make money. Now we're stuck with having to throw out all that ink. Where do you do this? It's ridiculous.

"The only thing we can do," says my brother Elye, "is to wait till nightfall. At night it's dark; no one will see."

We hardly get through till nightfall. Out of spite, the moon shines like a lantern. When you really need the moon it shuts itself up. Now it's here; who sent for it? That's what my brother Elye says as we carry bottle after bottle to dump outside. Dumping it in one spot makes a river, so you're not supposed to spill the whole thing in one place. That's what my brother Elye says, and I listen to him. I keep looking for new spots. Every bottle, a different place. The neighbor's wall—splash.

The neighbor's fence—splash. Two goats grazing in the moonlight—splash.

"Enough for now," my brother Elye says, and we go to bed. It's quiet and dark. Crickets chirp. The cat purrs behind the stove. A very lethargic cat; day and night she'd snuggle and nap. From outside the door comes the sound of quiet footsteps. Maybe it's a demon? My mother isn't asleep yet; she seems never to sleep. I always hear her cracking her fingers; moaning, groaning, and talking to herself. That's her nature. Every night she unburdens her heart a little, pouring out her troubles. Whom does she speak to? To God? She keeps groaning, "God, oh God."

Two

I'm still lying on my mattress on the floor and in my sleep I hear a lot of yelling. Familiar voices. Slowly I open my eyes and it's bright daylight. The sun's rays force their way in through the window. Somebody's calling me outside. I try to recall what happened yesterday. Aha! Ink. I jump out of bed and dress quickly. My mother's in tears—when isn't she? My sister-in-law Brokhe is enraged, as usual. My brother Elye is in the middle of the room with his head down; maybe I can milk something out of him.

What's the story? There's not one story, but many. Our neighbors got up in the morning and the hoopla started—they were being murdered. One had a whole wall sprayed with ink; another a new fence. The third had two white goats now unrecognizably black. All this would have been tolerable if not for the slaughterer's stockings. His wife had hung his new pair of white stockings on our neighbor's fence and now they were ruined. Who asked her to hang the stockings on a strange fence? My mother offered to buy her a new pair if she'll only keep still. What about the wall? The fence?

It's been agreed that my mother and sister-in-law Brokhe will respectfully stand with two brushes and a pail of whitewash to clean off the spots.

"It's lucky you have nice neighbors," our neighbor Peshe said to my mother. "If you'd thrown your ink into Menashe the doctor's garden, you'd find out there's a God on earth."

"Well," my mother answered, "even in bad luck you still need some good luck."

What does that mean?

Three

"This time I'll be smarter," my brother Elye says to me. "We'll take the bottles to the river when night comes."

Of course, sure as I'm alive. What can be smarter than that? All kinds of junk is dumped into the river. They do laundry there and they water horses; pigs wallow. I'm a good friend of the river. I've already described how I catch fish there. You can now understand how I couldn't wait to get to the river.

With nightfall we packed baskets full of bottles and began carrying them to the river. We emptied the ink, carried the bottles back home, and filled them up again. We did this all night. I haven't had such an enjoyable night in a long time. Imagine: the town's asleep, the heavens are covered with stars, the moon shines down into the river. Gloriously still, the river comes alive. After Passover, when the ice melts, it really goes wild. It puffs up, spreads out, overflows. Later on it gets smaller, narrower, and shallower. By summer's end it's quiet altogether; it naps. Something on the riverbed makes noises like *"Bul, bul, bul."* A few frogs croak back from the other bank, *"Khwul, khwul."* This is a joke, not a river. I can get from one side to the other without taking off my pants.

The river rose somewhat from our ink—a thousand bottles can't be sneezed at. To empty a thousand bottles we had to work like oxen. We dropped off to sleep half-dead and were awakened by my mother's cry, "You've darkened my days! What did you do to the river?"

It turns out we've damaged the whole town. The washerwomen have nowhere to do laundry; the coachmen, no place to water their horses; the water carriers—they're all after us. That's what my mother says. We're not going to wait for them. We don't want to see how water carriers collect their debts. My brother Elye and I pick ourselves up and hurry over to his friend Pinye. "They'll look for us there if they need us," says my brother Elye as he takes my hand and we hurry downhill to Pinye's. When we see each other again I'll tell you about my brother's friend Pinye. It's worth knowing him; he has very interesting ideas.

A Street Sneezes

You want to hear the latest? Mice. A whole week my brother Elye has been studying the book that teaches how to make money, *For One Ruble A Hundred*. He's learned, he says, how to drive out mice, roaches, and other pests. Rats, also. Let him in with his powder and that's the end of the mice. They run away; lots of them die; no more mice. How he does this, I don't know. It's a secret, a secret only he and the book know—no one else. He keeps the book in his breast pocket and the powder in a paper. The powder is reddish and finely ground. It's called hellebore.

"What's hellebore?"

"Turkish pepper."

"What is Turkish pepper?"

"I'll give you a 'what is.' Soon I'll break open the door with your head."

That's what my brother Elye says to me. He hates to be asked questions in the middle of work. I look on and keep quiet. I notice that besides the red powder there's another ingredient, but you have to be very careful with that one. "Poison," says my brother maybe a hundred times, to my mother, Brokhe, and me. Mainly, me, so I won't go near it—it's poison.

The first test we made on our neighbor Peshe's mice. You couldn't count the mice over there. You know that Peshe's husband is a bookbinder. His name is Moishe. He always has a room full of books. Mice love books—not books so much, but the glue that holds them together. Because of the glue they eat the whole book. This causes a lot of damage. They've eaten holes through a holiday prayer book, a brand new one, just at the word "King" which is written in especially large letters. They've cut off the leg of the "K." "Let me in here for just one night," my brother Elye pleaded with the bookbinder.

The bookbinder didn't want him. "I'm afraid you'll ruin my books."

"How'll I ruin the books?"

"How do I know? I'm just afraid; the books aren't mine."

So. Try to talk to a bookbinder. We finally persuaded him to let us in there for the night.

Two

The first night was not a success. We didn't catch a single mouse. My brother Elye said that's a good sign; the mice smelled the powder and ran away. The binder shook his head and smiled with one lip; he didn't seem to believe. Nevertheless, the word has spread through town that we chase mice. The rumor started with our neighbor Peshe. She went very early to the market and proclaimed all over town that we "get rid of mice like no one else." She's made us a name. With the kvass she did the same thing. And again with the ink—ink that can't be beat. But what good did her talking do if nobody needs ink? Mice are not the same as ink. Mice are everywhere; almost everyone has them. Every house has a cat, but what's the good of one cat against so many mice? Especially rats. Rats are about as afraid of a cat as Haman is of a *grager*.

Some say the cat is afraid of the rat. Like Bere the shoemaker. He tells such horrible tales about rats. He tells tall tales but even if half of what he says is true, that's enough. He claims rats ate his new pair of boots. He swears oaths that would convince even an apostate. He says he saw two huge rats come out of their lair and eat up a pair of boots before his eyes. It happened at night. He was afraid to get near them, they were so huge—as big as calves. He tried to drive them off from a distance. He whistled, stamped his feet, and screamed, "Kish, kish, kish, kish, kish." Nothing helped. He threw a boot heel at them; they just looked at him and went about their business. He sent a cat after them and they ate it. Nobody wanted to believe him, but if a person swears . . .

"Let me in for a night," my brother Elye says, "and I'll get rid of all your rats."

"With pleasure," answers Bere the shoemaker. "I'll even say, 'thank you.' "

Three

We sat all night at Bere's. Bere sat up, too. The stories he told! He talked about the Russian-Turkish War in which he'd served. He was in a place called Plevne. They used cannon. Have you any idea how much a cannon holds? One cannonball is bigger than a house, and a cannon shoots a thousand balls a minute. Satisfied? The ball as it flies makes a noise so loud it makes you deaf. Once Bere was standing guard—that's what he says; suddenly he heard an explosion—and he was lifted into the air, up very high, over the clouds, and the ball split into a thousand pieces. He was lucky he fell on a soft spot; otherwise, he'd have broken his head. My brother Elye listened and his eyebrows smiled; not he—his eyebrows. A weird smile. Bere the shoemaker didn't notice; he went on with his stories, one stranger than the next. We sat that way until dawn. Rats? Not a one.

"You're a magician," said Bere the shoemaker to my brother Elye, and goes around town telling everyone how we drove out all the rats with a magic word in one evening. He swears he himself saw how my brother Elye whispered something and all the rats came out of their lairs and ran down to the river. They swam to the other side and never came back.

Four

"You get rid of mice here?" People keep coming to ask us if we'd please come to drive off their mice with our magic formula. My brother Elye, however, is an honest man; he hates lies. He says he chases mice not with magic but with powder. He has a powder that makes the mice run away when they smell it.

"A powder; a curse. Who cares just so long as you get rid of the mice. How much does it cost?"

My brother Elye hates to bargain. He says he wants so much for the powder, so much for labor. Usually he says more each time; every day he raises the price. Actually, it's not he who raises the price but my sister-in-law. "Make up your mind," she said, "if you're going to eat pig, let the juice run down your beard. If you drive away mice, at least make money."

"And what about justice? Where's God?" my mother interrupted.

"Justice? Here's justice," Brokhe answered, pointing to the stove. "God?" she said, slapping her pocket. "Here's God."

"Brokhe! What are you saying? God forgive you," my mother shouted as she wrung her hands.

"Why are you wasting your time with a fool?" my brother Elye said. He was walking around the room pulling at his beard. He already has quite a beard; it grows like the devil. He pulls at it and it grows. It looks funny: there's growth on the neck but the face is smooth. Have you ever seen such a beard?

Another time my sister-in-law Brokhe would have made him pay dearly for calling her a fool. Now she's quiet because he's bringing in money. When he earns money he becomes somebody special to her. I've also become dearer because I help my brother. Usually she calls me a pest, a wretch, a misfit. Now she has a new name for me, "Mottele."

"Mottele, pass me my shoes."

"Mottele, get me a quart of water."

"Mottele, take out the garbage."

When you make money, people talk differently.

Five

The trouble with my brother Elye is he does everything in bulk. Kvass—by the barrel. Ink—a thousand bottles. Mouse poison—a sackful. Our neighbor's husband asked him why he needs so much and my brother blasted him.

If only they'd locked up the sack on a shelf somewhere. They all went away and left me with the sack. So what if I sat down on it to ride? It was a good rocking horse. Should I know the sack would split and something yellow would shoot out of it? It was the powder my brother Elye used for catching mice. It has a smell so sharp you could faint. I bent over to pick up the spillage and fell into a sneezing fit. A whole box of snuff would not have made me sneeze so much. I sneezed so long I had to run outside; maybe I'd stop. Not a chance. I ran into my mother. She saw me sneezing and asked why. I could answer only, "Achoo! Achoo!" and more "Achoo!"

"What's wrong with you?" she asked, wringing her hands. "Where did you get such a cold?" I couldn't stop sneezing and pointed to the house. She went inside and came back sneezing worse than I. My brother Elye came by and saw us sneezing. He asked what's wrong. My mother pointed to the house. He went inside and ran back out excited.

"Who opened the—achoo! Achoo! Achoo!"

It was a long time since I'd seen my brother Elye so angry. He lunged at me. It's lucky he was sneezing, otherwise I'd have left his hands a cripple.

My sister-in-law Brokhe came by and saw us holding our sides, sneezing. "What's the matter with you people? Why the sneezing all of a sudden?"

What could we tell her? Could we talk? We pointed to the house. She went inside, ran back out red as a flame, and fell upon my brother Elye. "What did I tell—achoo! Achoo! Achoo!"

Fat Peshe our neighbor arrived. She spoke but no one could answer. We pointed to the house. She went inside, ran back out. "What have you—achoo! Achoo! Achoo!" She threw her hands about.

Her husband the binder came out. He looked at us and laughed. "Where did this sneezing fit come from?"

"Please go—achoo! Achoo! Achoo!" we said to him and pointed to the house.

The binder went inside and immediately reappeared, laughing. "I know what's going on. I took a sniff. It's hell—achoo! Achoo! Clutching his sides he sneezed heartily. After each sneeze he'd spring and land on his toes, where he remained until the next sneeze; a sneeze and a jump, sneeze and a jump, and so on. Within half an hour all our neighbors, their uncles, aunts, cousins, and friends—the whole street from beginning to end—was sneezing.

Why did my brother Elye become so frightened? He was afraid, I guess, they'd all let out their anger on him for their sneezing. He took me by the hand and still sneezing, we took off downhill to his friend Pinye. It was an hour and a half before we could talk like human beings. My brother Elye told his friend Pinye the whole story. His friend Pinye listened carefully the way a doctor listens to a patient. When my brother finished, Pinye said, "So, show me the book."

My brother Elye took the book out of his breast pocket and handed it to his friend Pinye. His friend Pinye read the title page, "For One Ruble A Hundred. How to make from scratch with your own hands one hundred rubles a month and more. . . ." He took hold of the book and threw it into the burning stove. My brother Elye thrust his hand toward the fire. Pinye held him back. "Slowly; take it easy," he said.

Within a few minutes my brother Elye's book was nothing but a pile of ash. One piece of page remained unburned. Barely legible, it read, "Hellebore."

Translated by Gershon Freidlin

BANDITS

"Is he still sleeping?"

"Dead to the world!"

"Wake him up! Wake him up!"

"Leyb-gizzard-fricassee!"

"Beautiful dreamer wake unto me—"

"Open your eyes and who do you see?"

The minute I open my eyes, lift my head, and look around, I see the whole gang of wise guys, my friends from *cheder*. The window is open. I can see the light in their eyes and the bright morning sunlight pouring into the room along with their joy and laughter. I look around.

"Look at him staring."

"Caught in the act."

"Don't you know who we are?"

"Don't you remember? It's Lag Baomer!"

Oh, my! Lag Baomer? The words go through me like a bolt of lightning. I shoot out of bed. In half a second I am on my feet, and a minute later dressed, washed, and ready to go. I look for my mother. She is distracted with breakfast and the little kids.

"Mama, today is Lag Baomer."

"Have a good holiday. What do you want?"

"Give me something to contribute for the meal."

"What should I contribute? My aggravation? Or my headaches?"

271

So Mama says, but she is ready to give me something anyhow. We bargain: I ask for more, she gives less. I want two eggs. She says, "Bellyaches is what you'll get." I get mad; she slaps me. I cry; she makes peace with an apple. I want an orange. She says, "Are you crazy? What are you going to dream up next?"

My friends outside are ready to explode.

"Are you coming or not?"

"Leyb-gizzard-fricassee!"

"Let's get going. We're wasting time!"

"Quick as a bunny—"

"Sonny!"

I finally manage to work it out with Mama, grab my breakfast and my contribution to the meal, and race out, fresh, frisky, happy, to my friends. In the bright warm sunlight, we rush downhill all together to *cheder*.

Two

Cheder is sheer noise. It's like a market day, a hollering unto the heavens. Twenty mouths all talking at once. The table is covered with treats. We've never yet had a Lag Baomer meal like this one. We even have brandy and wine, thanks to our friend Berl Yossel, the vintner's son. He brought a bottle of brandy, good brandy too, and two bottles of wine, the best, Yossel the vintner's own product. His father gave him the brandy. The bottles of wine he took on his own.

"What do you mean, on his own?"

"Don't you get it, dummy? He took it off the shelf when no one was looking."

"Well, that means he stole it, doesn't it?"

"Genius! So what?"

"What do you mean, so what? What about Thou shalt not steal?"

"For the holiday meal, turkey!"

"It's okay to steal?"

"Naturally. Look at this mastermind over here!"

"Where does it say so?"

"He wants us to tell him where it says so."

"Tell him in The Book of Pralnik."

"In the chapter on Taking."

"On page Lamed Bim-Bom."

"On the New Moon of Kremenitz."

"Ha, ha, ha!"

"Quiet everyone! Mazepa's coming."

Suddenly everyone gets as still as the silent standing prayer. We sit around the table like model pupils, innocents, quiet, well-behaved children, treasures, can't count to two, owe our souls to God.

Three

Mazepa is our *rebbe*. His name is really Boruch Moshe, but since he's come down recently from Mazepevka, the town calls him the Mazepevker, and we *cheder* boys have shortened it and turned it into Mazepa—"dark and ugly." Generally, when students crown their *rebbe* with a lovely name like that, he has earned it. Let me present him to you.

Short, shrivelled, and skinny—a creep. Without a trace of a beard, mustache, or eyebrows. Not, God forbid, because he shaves, but just because they don't care to grow. They talked themselves out of it. But to compensate, he has a pair of lips on him, and oh my! a nose! A braided loaf, a horn, a *shofar!* And a voice like a bell, a lion's roar. How did a creature like him get such a terrifying voice? And where did he get his strength? When he grabs your arm with his skinny, cold fingers, you can see the world to come. And when he slaps you, you feel it for the next three days. He hates lengthy discussions. For the least thing, guilty or not guilty, he has one law: Lie down!

"*Rebbe!* Yossel Yankev Yossel's hit me."

"Lie down!"

"Rebbe, it's a lie! He kicked me in the side first."

"Lie down!"

"Rebbe! Chaim Berl Lappes stuck his tongue out at me."

"Lie down!"

"Rebbe, lies and falsehood! It was just the opposite. He gave me the high sign."

"Lie down!"

And you have to lie down. Nothing helps. Even redheaded Eli, who is already *Bar Mitzvah* and betrothed and wears a silver pocketwatch—you think he isn't beaten? Oh my, isn't he! Eli says that he'll regret those beatings. He says he'll pay Mazepa back with interest; he says he'll give him something to remember him by until he has grandchildren. That's what Eli always says after a whipping, and we answer:

"Amen. Hope so. From your mouth to God's ears."

Four

When we've finished saying morning prayers—with the *rebbe,* as usual (he never lets us pray by ourselves; he knows that without him we would skip more than half of it), Mazepa announces to us in his lion's voice: "Well, children, wash up and sit down to the feast, and when we finish the grace after eating, I'll let you go out walking."

Actually we're used to having our Lag Baomer feast on the other side of town, in the fresh air, on the bare grass under God's heaven, throwing crumbs to the birds to let them know too that it's Lag Baomer in the world. But with Mazepa you don't start negotiating. When Mazepa says, "Sit down," you sit. Or he might order you to lie down.

"Blessed be all who are sitting at the table," the *rebbe* says after we've made the blessing over bread.

"Join us," we say, for form's sake.

"Eat in good health," he says. "I don't want to eat yet, but I think I wouldn't mind making a blessing over something to drink. What's in that bottle over there? Brandy?" he says, and puts out a dry hand with thin fingers for the bottle of brandy. He pours himself a little, tastes it, and makes such a face that we have to be strong as iron not to burst out laughing.

"This is strong stuff! Whose is it?" he asks and takes a little more. "It's not bad liquor, to tell you the truth." And he takes a little more and toasts us.

"*L'chayim,* children, may God grant we live to celebrate again next year, and . . . and . . . and isn't there something to eat with this? Well, I'll wash, and in honor of Lag Baomer, I'll have a bite to eat with you."

What's happening to our *rebbe?* This isn't our Mazepa at all. He's in a good mood, talkative, his cheeks red as beets, his nose red, his eyes shiny, chewing, talking, and pointing to the bottles of wine.

"What kind of wine do you have there? It looks like Passover wine." (He tastes and smacks his lips.) "One of a kind!" (Drinks.) "I'll tell you the truth, it's been a long time since I drank wine like this." (To Yossel the vintner's son, with a laugh.) "Devil take your father's cellar, hch, heh! I've seen the barrels at his place, countless barrels for wine and fruit of the vine, and made from pure raisins, too, heh, heh! *L'chayim,* children! May God make you honest, good Jews, and may you . . . may you . . . open the second bottle . . . Take a drop, why don't you take some? And drink *l'chayim.* May God grant . . . (he licks his lips and his eyes shut) . . . all . . . all good to all of Israel . . . "

Five

When he has finished eating and said grace, Mazepa's tongue gets tangled in his teeth. "So, we've observed the *mitzvah,* ha? The commandment of the Lag Baomer feast. Well, what next? Ha?"

"Now we're going for our walk."

"Ha? For your walk? Excellent. Where to?"

"To the Black Forest."

"Ha? To the Black Forest? That's excellent! I'm going with you. It's very good, very healthy, to go for a walk in the forest, because the forest . . . Ah, now I'm going to explain the nature of a forest to you."

And we set out all together, with the *rebbe* in our midst, for the other side of town. At the outset, we feel a bit uncomfortable having the *rebbe* with us. But M—, -um, Mum! And the *rebbe* walks along gesticulating and explaining the nature of the forest to us.

"The nature of a forest, you see, is that the One Above created it to be full of trees, and on them—the trees, that is—there would be branches, and the branches would be covered with leaves, green ones, and they would give off an aroma, a delightful smell, a wonderful mustardy scent . . ."

And meanwhile, the *rebbe* sniffs the wonderful mustardy scent, even though we are still far off from the forest and the odors aren't yet especially wonderful or mustardy.

"Ha? Why don't you say something?" the *rebbe* asks us. "Say something good, sing a song. Ha? I was once a boy, a wise guy like you, heh, heh. I also had a *rebbe,* like you, heh, heh."

That Mazepa was ever a wise guy like us, and had a *rebbe* like us, seems strange and weird to us, practically beyond belief. Mazepa—a wise guy? We look at each other and heh-heh silently, imagining Mazepa as a wise guy, and his *rebbe,* and how his *rebbe* used to . . . But we are afraid to think such things. . . . Only Eli dares to say it out loud, *"Rebbe,* did your *rebbe* beat you the way you beat us?"

"Ha? And how! Heh, heh . . ."

We look at the *rebbe* and at one another and understand each other. We help him laugh heh-heh until we are well on the other side of the town, in the wide open fields not far from the Black Forest.

Six

Out in the fields it is marvelous, a paradise. Sweet-smelling grass. White blossoms. Yellow motes. Wings light as air. The blue skullcap above, spreading without end. The forest before us dressed for a holiday. And in the trees the little birds hop from one branch to another and twitter. That's their way of welcoming us on our beloved holiday of Lag Baomer. We look for the shadow of a leafy tree, protection from the burning sun, and all sit down on the ground with our *rebbe* in the midst of us.

The *rebbe* is tired from the walk. He flings himself down on the ground and stretches out with his face up. His eyes close. His tongue gets tangled in his teeth, and he just about manages to say: "You are dear, golden chi-children . . . Jewish children . . . saints . . . I love you, and you love me . . . isn't that so? You l-love me?"

"Like a pain the eye," Eli answers.

"Ha? I know that you l-love me . . ." the *rebbe* says to him.

"May God love you as much," Eli says.

We get frightened and say, "For God's sake . . ."

"Dopes," Eli answers with a laugh. "What are you afraid of? Can't you see that he's drunk out of his mind?"

"Ha?" the *rebbe* says with one eye open (the other is already asleep). "What were you saying? Saints? All saints . . . on the other hand . . . it's all right . . . the Guardian of Israel chl- chl- chrrrrsss—"

And our *rebbe* falls fast asleep and his snoring resounds from his nose like the sound of a *shofar* far into the forest. And we sit around him feeling sad.

"This is our *rebbe* who makes us tremble at his look? This is Mazepa?"

Seven

"You guys!" Eli says to us. "Why are we sitting here like bumps on a log? Let's think up a punishment for Mazepa."

We suddenly feel afraid.

"What are you afraid of, fools?" Eli says again. "He's like a corpse now."

We grow even more frightened. Eli exhorts us, "We can do what we want with him now. He beat us all winter like sheep. Let's take revenge at least once."

"What do you want to do to him?"

"Nothing. Only to scare him."

"How are you going to scare him?"

"You'll see in a minute," Eli says. He gets up and goes over to the *rebbe* and takes off his sash and says: "You see this? We'll tie him to the tree with his own sash, so he can't get loose. And then one of us will go up close and yell in his ear, '*Rebbe*, bandits!' "

"What will that do?"

"Nothing. We'll run away and he'll yell *Shma Yisroel.*"

"How long will he yell?"

"Until he gets used to it."

And without further ado, Eli takes the sash and ties our *rebbe's* hands together and fastens both hands to the tree. We stand and watch. A shudder runs through us: "Is this our *rebbe*, whose looks made us tremble? This is Mazepa?"

"What are you standing there for? You're made of clay?" Eli says. "If God has made a miracle and delivered Mazepa into our hands, let's dance!"

And we take each other's hands and begin to circle around our *rebbe* like wild men, and dance and jump and sing like lunatics.

"So far so good!" says Eli. And we stop, and Eli goes over to the *rebbe,* leans down quite close to him, and yells into his ear loudly in a voice that could waken the dead: "Help, *Rebbe!* Bandits! Bandits! Bandits!!!"

Eight

Like a shot we all run off, afraid to stop even for a moment, afraid even to look back. We are all frightened, and so is Eli, even though he never stops yelling at us. "Fools, dopes, cattle! What are you running for?"

"Why are you running?"

"You're running, so I'm running, too."

We rush into town with all our might and with one cry: "Bandits! Bandits!"

People see us running and run after us. Other people see people running and run after them.

"What's the running about?"

"How should we know? Everyone's running so we're running, too."

Finally they stop one of us, and seeing this we all stop but keep on yelling, "Bandits! Bandits!"

"Where? Where? Where?"

"Over there in the Black Forest, we were attacked by bandits . . . tied the *rebbe* to a tree . . . God knows if he's still alive . . ."

Nine

If you are jealous of us because we're free now and aren't attending *cheder* (the *rebbe* is sick), don't bother. You can never feel the shoe pinch the other person's foot. No one, but no one, knows who the real bandits are. We hardly go to see one another. And when we meet, the first thing is, "How's the *rebbe?*" (It's no longer Mazepa.) And when we say prayers, we pray to

God for the *rebbe* and cry quietly: "Master of the
Universe! Master of the Universe!"

And Eli—don't ask about Eli. May his name be wiped
out. That Eli!

Epilogue

When the *rebbe* recovered (for six weeks he lay in a
fever and talked to bandits) and we returned to *cheder*
we could scarcely recognize Mazepa; he had changed
so much. Where was his lion's voice? He had tossed his
whip away somewhere. No more "Lie down!" No
more Mazepa. And a quiet, tender melancholy has
transformed his features. A feeling of regret steals into
us and Mazepa suddenly becomes dear to us, sealed in
our hearts. Ah! If only he would blame us, get angry at
us! It's just as if nothing had happened . . . But suddenly he breaks off in the midst of study and asks us to
tell him again the story of the Lag Baomer bandits. We
don't hold back; we tell him again and again the story
that we have by heart: how bandits suddenly came out
of the woods, flung themselves on him, tied him up, and
would have killed him with a knife if we hadn't rushed
into town with all our might and saved him with our
cries for help . . .

The *rebbe* hears us out with eyes closed. Afterward
he heaves a sigh and asks suddenly, "Are you sure they
were bandits?"

"What else could they be?"

"Maybe a band of imps?"

And the *rebbe's* eyes look off somewhere, and it
seems to us that a sly smile hovers on his incredibly
thick lips.

Translated by Seymour Levitan

THE GUEST

"I have a guest for you, Reb Yonah, for the Passover—a guest such as you've never had since you became a householder."

"You mean?"

"I mean, something special."

"What's 'something special'?"

"I mean, a really refined person, handsome and well-bred. He has only one failing, though. He doesn't understand our language."

"What language *does* he understand?"

"The holy tongue, Hebrew."

"From Jerusalem?"

"I don't know where he's from. All I know is that his speech is full of 'ahs.' "

Such was the conversation that took place between my father and our *shammes* Ezriel several days before Passover. I was bursting with curiosity to get a good look at this rare person who does not understand Yiddish and speaks Hebrew with "ahs" exclusively. In the synagogue I had already observed an odd-looking man in a traditional fur-edged hat and a Turkish robe of yellow, blue, and red stripes. We youngsters surrounded him and proceeded to inspect him from all angles. For this we were sternly reprimanded by Ezriel: "What a bad habit children have of sticking their noses into a stranger's face!"

After services the congregation shook hands warmly with the good-looking stranger, said "Sholem," and wished him a happy holiday, to which he responded with a charming smile, his red-cheeked face framed by a gray beard. His "Sha-lom, sha-lom!" in reply to each greeting elicited loud laughter in us boys. Infuriated, the *shammes* rushed toward us with an upraised hand, ready to deal out slaps, but we slipped out of his grasp and again edged up to the stranger, listening for his "Sha-lom, sha-lom" in order to explode once more into laughter and escape again from Ezriel's threatening hand.

Exultantly I walk behind my father and this personage to our home for the holiday, aware that my pals are envying me our extraordinary guest. Knowing that they are following us with their eyes from a distance, I turn around and stick my tongue out at them. The three of us walk silently all the way. When we enter the house, my father calls out to my mother, "Happy holiday!" Our guest nods, which makes his fur hat tremble, and says, "Sha-lom, sha-lom!" This makes me think of my pals and I turn my face aside so as not to burst into laughter.

I steal frequent glances at our guest and am pleased by what I see. I like his Turkish robe with the yellow, blue, and red stripes. I like his rosy cheeks inside the half-circle of gray beard. I like the shining black eyes which look out smilingly from under luxuriant eyebrows. I can see that my father, too, delights in him. My mother gazes at our guest as though at a divine creature. But no one speaks a word to him! With a respectful gesture my father requests that he be seated on the ceremonial chair bedecked with pillows. My mother goes into a frenzy of busyness, assisted by Rickel our maid. Only when the time comes to make the blessing does my father converse with his guest in the holy tongue. I am puffed up with pride because I understand practically everything that is being said. Here is their conversation in Hebrew, word for word:

Father: *"Nu?"* (Meaning in Yiddish, "Be so good as to say the *Kiddush* prayer.")

Guest: *"Nu, nu!"* (Meaning, "Go right ahead, *you* say it.")

Father: *"Nu, aw?"* ("How about you?")

Guest: *"Aw, nu?"* ("Why not you?")

Father: *"Ee-aw!"* ("Please, you first!")

Guest: *"Aw, ee!"* ("You first, please!")

Father: *"Eh, aw, ee!"* ("I beg of you, you say it first!")

Guest: *"Ee, aw, eh!"* ("You say it, I beg of you!")

Father: *"Ee, eh, aw, nu?"* ("Will it harm you to say it first?")

Guest: *"Ee, aw, eh, nu, nu!"* ("Well, since you insist, I'll say it!")

Our guest takes the cup from father's hand and recites the *Kiddush*. It is a benediction such as we have never heard before and do not expect to hear again. First, on account of the Hebrew with all the "ahs" in it; and second, on account of his voice which does not issue from his throat but from his Turkish robe with the gaily colored stripes. I think of my pals, of the laughter that would have pealed forth, of the slaps that would have flown about, had they been present at this *Kiddush*. But since I am alone, I restrain myself and ask my father the Four Questions in my usual tone of voice. All together we read the *Haggadah* and I am in a state of exaltation because this particular guest is *ours* and no one else's!

Two

Surely, the sage who advised that one should not speak during meals would pardon me for saying that he was ignorant of the exigencies of Jewish life. When, I ask you, does a Jew have time to converse if not at the dinner table? Especially at the Passover *seder* when there is such a great deal to narrate, during the meal and after it?

Rickel hands us the bowls of water for the washing of hands before saying the prayer at the breaking of the *matzo,* and my mother serves portions of the fish. It is only then that my father, rolling up his sleeves, begins a prolonged conversation with his guest in Hebrew. He starts with the first question that one Jew usually asks another: "What is your name?"

The reply is a mass of "ahs" in one breath, much as one reels off the names of Haman's sons when reading the Book of Esther. "Ack-Becker-Galush-Damat-Henoch-Yasam-Zen-Hafiff-Tatsik . . ."

My father remains sitting with an open mouth of food and gazes at him in astonishment, apparently because of the multitude of names, while I get an attack of coughing and stare down at my lap. My mother is alarmed and says, "Watch out when you eat fish. One can choke, God forbid, on a tiny bone."

She looks respectfully at our guest. Although she can make nothing of that string of names, she is awed by them. However, since my father does understand, he feels that an explanation is due her. "You see, 'Ack-Becker . . .'—it's the *aleph-beis,* and evidently, there, in that land, they have a custom of giving names in alphabetical order."

"Aleph-beis, aleph-beis." Our guest catches it up with the sweetest of smiles and looks at us with the utmost friendliness beaming from his enchanting black eyes—even at Rickel, our maid.

Having learned the guest's name to his satisfaction, my father is now interested to learn from which country he has come. I comprehend this from the names of towns and cities which ring out and which my father immediately translates for my mother. Each word, almost, is accompanied by an explanation, and my mother is impressed by each name separately. This is no small thing, after all! A man has journeyed ten thousand miles or so from a land which can be reached only by swimming seven seas and crossing a desert which takes forty days and forty nights to cross. But in order to reach the desert, one must first climb a mountain so high that its peak, covered by ice and swept by biting winds, reaches to the very clouds. An awesome spot! In the end, however, when one has scaled this mountain safely, there lies on the other side spread out before one an earthly paradise teeming with all sorts of good things: with spices, cloves, and rare herbs, and all kinds of fruit in abundance—apples, pears and oranges, grapes, dates and olives, nuts and figs. The houses there are built of pinewood only and covered with pure silver. The dishes are made of solid gold. (While saying this, our guest glances briefly at our silver goblets and silver spoons, knives, and forks.) Precious stones and pearls and diamonds lie strewn about on the streets but no one bothers to bend down and pick them up because they are valueless. (Here he peers at my mother's earrings and the yellowed pearl necklace about her milky-white throat.)

"Do you hear that?" My father motions to my mother with a radiant face.

"I hear," my mother replies, and wants to know, "Why don't they bring those treasures here? They'd make a fortune. Please, Yonah, ask him that."

My father relays the question and translates the reply to her in Yiddish. "You see, when you enter that land, you may gather as much as you wish, full pockets of the treasure, but when you leave, you must return everything. If they shake anything out of you, you're done for."

"What does that mean?" my mother asks fearfully.

"It means that they either hang you from a tree or stone you to death."

Three

The more our guest speaks, the more interesting become the stories he relates. We have finished the soup with *kneydlach* and are still taking small sips of wine when my father queries, "To whom does it all belong? Do they have a king ruling over them?"

To this he receives an immediate clear response which he transmits joyously to my mother. "He says that the entire wealth belongs to the inhabitants of the kingdom who are called *Sephardim;* and they have a king, he says, who is terribly pious and wears a fur-edged hat; and this king's name is Joseph ben Joseph. He serves as their high priest, he says, and rides in a golden carriage drawn by six fiery horses, and when he crosses the threshold of the synagogue, Levites come to greet him with song . . ."

"Levites sing in your *shul?*" my father asks in wonderment. Again he gets a swift reply which he promptly conveys to my mother, his face radiant as the sun.

"Wonder of wonders! He says they have a holy temple with priests and Levites and an organ . . . "

"An altar, too?" my father asks, and then tells my mother, "He says they have an altar with sacrifices and golden vessels, everything as it was in ancient times in Jerusalem, he says."

Concluding these words, my father sighs deeply, and watching him, my mother sighs too. I can't understand them. What is there to sigh about? Just the reverse: shouldn't they be proud and rejoice in the existence of such a land—a land ruled by a Jewish king who is also a high priest, a land where there is a holy temple and Levites and an organ and an altar and sacrifices . . .

Splendid, gleaming fantasies lift me up and transport me to that fortunate Jewish land where the houses are built of fragrant pinewood and covered with silver, where the dishes are made of gold and precious stones lie scattered about on the streets. Suddenly the thought comes to me that if I were there, *I'd* know what to do. *I'd* know how to conceal the treasure well. They would shake nothing out of me! I would bring back fine presents for my mother: sparkling earrings and more than one pearl necklace.

As I think this, I look at my mother's earrings and the pearls about her lovely throat, and I am seized by an overwhelming desire to visit that fabulous land. My mind is made up. After Passover I will go there with our guest. Secretly of course, so that not a soul will know of it. I will disclose my resolve to him only; I will pour out my heart to him and beg him to take me with him, even for the briefest time. Surely he will not have it in his heart to refuse me; surely he will do me this favor. He is such a good-hearted, amiable person. He looks at each one of us with such friendliness, even at Rickel the maid.

As I sit daydreaming and contemplate our guest, it seems to me that he has guessed my thoughts and is winking to me with his beautiful dark eyes, saying in his own language: "Be silent, little rogue. Not a word out of you. Be patient and wait until Passover is ended. You'll see, *then* the time will be ripe!"

Four

All night long I struggle with a tangle of dreams. I see a desert, a holy temple, a high priest. I scale a deep mountain on top of which grows precious stones, pearls, and diamonds. My playmates climb into trees and shake down jewels from the branches. Standing below, I pick them up and stuff them into my pockets. No matter how much I put into my pockets, there's room for more. Endlessly. I put my hand into my pocket and, instead of jewels, I pull out all sorts of fruit: apples, pears, oranges, olives, dates, nuts, and figs. I am terror-stricken and toss from side to side. The holy temple appears before me and I hear priests chanting and Levites singing. An organ plays. I want to enter the temple but can't because Rickel is holding me tight and will not let me go. I scream at her, I yell, I plead. In anguish I toss from side to side, and awake, and . . .

My parents are standing before me, disheveled and

half-dressed, both pale as death. My father's head is bowed, my mother wrings her hands, tears welling in her dear eyes. I sense that something wicked has happened, something so terribly wicked that my childish mind cannot conceive of it.

Our guest, the kind-hearted stranger from that magical faroff land where houses are made of pinewood and covered with silver and so forth, has disappeared. And with him much else has vanished, including our maid Rickel.

My heart is shattered. But not on account of the loss of our goblets and silverware or of my mother's scanty jewelry and the money. Not on account of Rickel the maid—the devil take her! But because now I will never see that happy, happy land where precious stones lie carelessly about in the streets, where there is a holy temple with priests, Levites, an organ, and an ancient altar with sacrifices. All these marvelous things cruelly, wantonly stolen from me . . .

I turn my face to the wall and weep silently.

Translated by Etta Blum

PART
FOUR

THE KRUSHNIKER DELEGATION

So we're at the point, aren't we, where my son Yekhiel was made mayor of Krushnik, and was running things, as they say, with an iron hand, and the Poles were scraping and digging, looking everywhere for lies to tell, spreading Haman's slanders against him and against all of us. Well, they kept at it, those Poles, may their names be blotted from memory, until finally the Germans began making "forays" into town. That is, they began searching and scavenging and shaking up people. And God helped them—they actually found something at Aba the *shochet*'s, some hidden circumcision knives, along with a packet of circumcision powder, which looks a bit like gunpowder. And then the fun began—God Almighty!

Translated here for the first time into English, the following sketch is taken from a longer narrative which Sholom Aleichem wrote toward the end of his life. It deals with the experiences of the East European Jews caught in the First World War between Germans and Poles. Some elements of the traditional Sholom Aleichem are still here, but the reader will quickly notice that the tone and substance have changed, as if the great humorist is giving way before the blows of modern history.

—Editors' Note

First off, they took the *schlimazel* (the *shochet,* I mean) and threw him into jail, solitary confinement, so that God forbid no evil should come near him, and no one disturb his rest. And the whole town became, what should I say, a very pit of desolation and bitter lament. And all at once they came running to me. "What's going on?" they said. "Yankel, why don't you speak up? Your son," they said, "is the mayor, isn't he? And you," they said, "you're such a big shot, if you said the word, that *schlimazel* (the *shochet,* that is) would be a free man."

Well, I tried to reason with them. "Get off my back," I said. "You're making a bad mistake, my dear friends. In the first place," I said, "I'm not the big shot you think me, and even if I am, let's say, that's no special advantage. On the contrary. Just because," I said, "my Yekhiel is mayor, and because I'm pretty important around here—a big shot, as you say—just because of this," I said, "I'd do more harm than good. Because if you knew the Germans," I said, "like I know them, you wouldn't talk that way. I'll tell you exactly what a German is," I said. "A German hates flattery as much as a kosher Jew hates pork. A German won't stand for empty words, and as for bribery," I said, "forget it. A German's not a Russian who'll watch your hand to see if you've got a bribe there for him. A German," I said, "needs delicate handling, if you see what I mean."

You'd think that that would do it, right? But you're dealing with Jews. You say salt, they say pepper. So you say pepper, they say garlic. And all the while the *shochet*'s wife and her children were standing off to one side, weeping and wailing, tearing their hair out. I don't know about you, Mr. Sholom Aleichem, but I have an odd habit—when I see tears, I'm struck dumb. I can't stand to see someone crying. I can't, that's all. I'm not bragging that I'm good-hearted; it's the power of tears, if you see what I mean. But in the long run all that made no difference anyway. As it turned out, I didn't have to be begged. The authorities ordered me to come. And not only me, but our rabbi too, and the *rabbiner* (the rabbi appointed by the government), along with all the other first citizens of Krushnik. Our hearts sank, I can tell you, but we gathered up our courage and got ready to go. That is, we dressed in our Sabbath best, with top hats—very elegant, very fitting and proper. It was as if we weren't being sent for, but had decided on our own to go as a delegation.

Meanwhile, my wife saw me all decked out on a Wednesday afternoon. "Yankel," she said, "where are you off to?"

Naturally I didn't tell her they'd sent for us. Does a woman have to know everything? So I made up a story that we were going as a delegation to the Germans, to the commandant I mean, in order to save a poor Jew from the gallows.

Well, she wrung her hands and started wailing, "Yankel, you mustn't do it!" There was a terrible pain in her heart, she said. Lightning, she said, had struck her. Evil days were coming upon the children of Israel. . . .

As you'd expect, a wife. What does a woman know anyway? Though to tell the truth, my wife (may she rest in peace) was not as foolish as other women. In fact, she wasn't foolish at all. You might even say the opposite. She was clever, quite clever; and sometimes she could talk like a wise woman, a wonderfully wise woman! I don't say it because she was my wife or because she's now in heaven. After death, as they say, you become a saint on earth, but that's not why I praise her. I'm not like other men. Here's an example—if you'd go to Krushnik and ask around about Yankel Yunever's wife, Miriam Mirel, you'd hear only praise and praise and more praise! First, she was pious, and not just "respectable," God forbid, like other women who won't move an inch from the letter of the law. Besides that, she was religious, very religious! But who's discussing religion? We're talking about kindness, about the meaning of character. This was a woman! A vessel of goodness! A person without a gall! Well, maybe not *without* gall. Everyone has a gall, naturally, and if you step on it, it's got to burst, because a human being can't be more than a human being, if you see what I mean.

But I don't want to mix things up, and as you know I hate to brag. So I'll get right to the point. We are going, I and the rabbi and the *rabbiner,* and the other good men of Krushnik, to the head authority, the commandant, to hear him out. And we went confidently. After all, we made quite a show, as they say, with the father himself of Krushnik's mayor there—you can't just dismiss something like that with a wave of your hand! And on our way we discussed what we'd say to the commandant. We decided that I would begin and address him in the words of Moses: "O Lord, you have begun to show your servants your greatness—that is to say, you have been gracious toward us, Herr German, from the day you set foot upon our land." And more of that kind of high talk. Why should we wait until he'd start? It would be best to get in a few words first, and then by the way, if you see what I mean, we could throw in something about the *shochet*—explain who the *schlimazel* was, why he'd hidden the ritual knives, just what that packet of circumcision powder meant—a regular lecture.

But as they say, if it's fated to be a disaster, you lose your tongue. That's where my real story begins. When I think of it even now, it makes my hair stand on end. . . .

In short then, we arrived at the commandant's headquarters, and there we found the *schlimazel,* Aba the *shochet* himself, tied up in the courtyard, and two soldiers with loaded rifles, one at each side of him. The *shochet* was trembling like a leaf and muttering something, probably his last confession. We were going to cheer him with a word or two, something like "Aba, God is with you!" But the soldiers gave us a nudge with their rifles—meaning one word to him, the *shochet,* and we'd be shot dead. And if a German says he'll shoot, trust him, especially when the whole world has gone crazy. At the slightest whim they'd shoot. Do you see what I mean or not? For example, someone comes by and says, "Got some tobacco, pal? If you do, all right. If not, I'll shoot." He doesn't give you time to think it over, let alone to defend yourself, to explain that you never use tobacco. Your life wasn't safe, that's the kind of world it was—try and do something about it.

To make a long story short, I don't have to tell you how we Krushniker Jews felt when we saw the *shochet* tied up and making his last confession. You can imagine it for yourself. I could only think, great God Almighty, what's going to happen to this Jew? And what will happen to his wife, the poor widow, and to his children, the orphans, if God forbid we can't get them to listen?

As we were standing around like that, thinking, out came not the commandant, but some other devil—a redhead, fat, well-fed, a cigar in his teeth. He'd just had a good supper and apparently more than a few drinks to wash it down. Along with him came two other officers. They looked at us; we looked at them. We examined each other, that is, without words for a while. No one knew what would happen. Now if it had been the commandant himself, and if he'd received us like human beings in his house, not outside there in the courtyard, then it would have been a different matter altogether, and quite a different sort of conversation. But this way, nothing. We stood and were silent—I and the rabbi and the *rabbiner* standing right up front, in the firing line, if you see what I mean. The other Krushniker dignitaries were standing behind us and pushing us from behind to say something. But how can you say something if you can't talk? Besides I was waiting for the rabbi to start—he was older. And the rabbi was waiting for the *rabbiner*—he'd been appointed by the government.

When they saw what they had there—a speechless delegation, a feast without food—the fat one yelled out to us, "Who are you?" So I stepped forward, let happen what may, and introduced him to the old man. "This is our rabbi," I said. "And the younger one, he's the *rabbiner,* the rabbi appointed by the government, and as for me," I said, "I'm Yankel Yunever, the father," I said, "of the lord mayor of Krushnik."

You'd think, wouldn't you, that he'd be impressed? Not at all. He didn't move a muscle. So seeing that reputation didn't work, I began to plead, putting first things first, as they say. "We, the foremost citizens of Krushnik," I said, "come before you as a delegation," I said, "with a request, to beg mercy for this Jew"—and I pointed to the *schlimazel,* to Aba the *shochet,* that is.

The fat German heard me out, then motioned to the soldiers to take us away. So they took us, if you see what I mean, and put us into prison like real criminals, each in a separate cell. It all happened in a minute, much less time than it's taken me to tell you about it. Did they let us send word at least to our wives and children? No, they shoved us in, locked the doors, and that's that. Should we have asked them why? Useless! First, a German won't answer. That's one reason. Another is it could make things worse, God forbid. Wartime's a powderkeg. You have to watch what you say, if you see what I mean, because who knows which side will win and what the result will be? It could be that the top dogs will be turned out into the cold, and the winners wind up six feet below.

In short, we were in a tight spot. Although if you look at it another way, what could they have against us? After all, we were dealing with Germans, with gentlemen. But then again, this was a time when Germans weren't really German, or Frenchmen French, or Englishmen English. They were wolves, not men—human beings acting like animals, like wild beasts, a plague on them! It was worse now than at the time of the flood; it was the end of the world. You probably think they fined us or beat us with whips. Well, think again. But you'd never guess, not if you'd live nine lives, so don't trouble yourself. Give me a minute or two to catch my breath, and I'll tell you a pretty story. Then be so good as to tell *me* what it was—a joke? the real thing? or a dream? . . .

Let's call it a story about the new moon—I mean, a story about how we Krushniker Jews prayed to the new moon. You remember, don't you, where we left off? They had kindly seated us in prison, me and the rabbi and the *rabbiner* and the other good men of Krushnik, the town's pride and joy, because of the crime we'd committed—we'd taken the part of Aba the *shochet*, pleaded on his behalf, if you see what I mean, and tried to save a Jew from the gallows. So there we sat, each one of us in his own cell, not studying Torah and not sitting at work for ten rubles a week, but just sitting, like common thieves and drunkards, in prison. What could we do? We'd been seated, as they say, so we sat . . . sat one hour, sat two hours, sat three hours. . . . Soon it would be night—what were we sitting there for, I ask you? At home they didn't even know where we were, that's where it hurt! And besides, everything has to end sometime, as they say, so let it come, I thought, one way or another!

I tell you, my head was ready to burst. I kept thinking and thinking, and only of evil things, and of worse to come. I imagined, first, that they'd condemn us as criminals and sentence us according to the laws of war. Next they'd politely line us up—the finest Krushniker citizens, including the rabbi and the *rabbiner*, all in a row, and twelve soldiers would stand ready, rifles loaded, waiting for the good word. And then the commandant enters in person, so I imagine, and asks us to say our last prayers—he's a German, after all, a gentleman! At this I get a bit hot under the collar and I think, "Yankel, the end's approaching. It's only a minute to death anyway; why not ease your conscience, as they say, and give him a piece of your mind?" And I begin in the language of our fathers, speaking as Abraham spoke before the gates of Sodom: "My Lord, harken to me, and hear me out. Do not take offense, O German, but let your servant's words find favor in the ears of his lord and master"—and so on, without putting the least emphasis on the fact that he's a German and a commandant and the conqueror of Krushnik.

And as I'm arguing with him (in my imagination, that is), the door opened and who do you think came in but a soldier with a loaded rifle. Once inside, he winked at me as if to say, "Be so kind as to follow me." Well, I could see there wasn't much choice, so I went. Outside it was pitch black. I looked around and saw the others were there, too—all of Krushnik's finest, the rabbi and the *rabbiner* included. Behind each of them stood a soldier, armed to the teeth.

Then the captain shouted "Forward!" and we went, the whole delegation, quietly, no words spoken, because talking wasn't allowed—strictly forbidden, as they say. Only sighs and groans that would break your heart, just like at Rosh Hashanah, during prayers before the *Shofar* is sounded. Did you ever hear the groaning then? My heart ached, especially for our rabbi, an old man seventy years old. What am I saying, seventy? He must have been then, according to my calculations, at least seventy-five, and if you really want to know, maybe even eighty, because I can still remember him at my wedding in Yunev. I was married in Yunev, you know. They brought him down from Krushnik, and by that time he was already an old man. I mean, not an *old* man, but gray-haired. And since then it's been . . . let's see, to be exact . . . no doubt as much as—actually, I don't remember; and anyway, I don't want to get off the track. That weakens the point of the story, if you see what I mean. I might forget where I'm at. Though as for my memory—God keep it always as clear as it is now. And to prove it, I'll tell you where I left off.

I was telling you about the old man, our rabbi, how he was walking out in front, and we Krushniker dignitaries were walking behind him, sighing and moaning and not allowed to speak a word. If only our families knew where we were—if only we ourselves knew where they were taking us! But nothing doing; like sheep to the slaughter, as they say. No sign they might be taking us to something good, because if so why wouldn't the Germans tell us where we were going? And certainly no one was waiting there to heap honors upon us, because then they wouldn't be pushing and shoving us— "Forward, march! Forward, march!" Before we could look around we found ourselves on Death Street, which leads to the new cemetery. I say the new one because in Krushnik we had two cemeteries, thank God, an old one and a new one. Of course, the new one was already old enough, and well populated, one grave set snugly beside the other. Pretty soon we'd have to find space for a third cemetery, if only God would let us live, and put an end to the war, and let Krushnik remain Krushnik and Jews, Jews.

Well, I won't drag this out. As we were going along the moon came out, and we could see that we were at the cemetery. What was I to think? Had someone in town died, some important person, or were they bringing some dead person here from another town, to be buried in a Jewish grave? But then why should *we* be here, and why, for that matter, a funeral with soldiers? But then again what other reason could there be for marching us suddenly, in the middle of the night, to the burial grounds?

As we were thinking this over, we looked up and saw—there he was, too, the *schlimazel,* Aba the *shochet,* I mean. He, and two soldiers with him! What was *he* doing here? Nothing much—just standing there with a shovel in his hands, digging a grave, and weeping, tears streaming down his face. Well, we didn't like the looks of it. In the first place, who was he digging a grave for? Second, what sort of a gravedigger was Aba the *shochet?* And besides that, what was he weeping about? Any way you looked at it, it was a puzzle, if you see what I mean, a mystery of mysteries, incomprehensible.

But it didn't take long—maybe as long as it's taking to tell you this, maybe even less—and all questions were answered. The captain gave an order and there emerged from out of nowhere a group of soldiers carrying shovels, and they took us, if you see what I mean, and stood us several steps apart from each other. Then they handed each of us a shovel and asked us to be so good as to dig graves, every one on his own private plot, since in two hours at most, so they gave us to understand, we'd be shot.

You want to know how we felt when they told us the good news? I can't speak for the others; that's their business. But for myself I can say absolutely, and give you my oath, that I felt—nothing. Simply and truly nothing. What do I mean *nothing?* Take a healthy person, strong and able, with wife and children and suddenly put a shovel in his hand and order him to dig his own grave since he's about to be shot! I ask you, Mr. Sholom Aleichem, think it over carefully—do you have any idea of what that means? No, you have to go through it yourself. It's a waste of time to explain. Though actually it wasn't so complicated. If a person had brains and was level-headed and could think around and about, he could see it all plainly for himself and stop worrying himself so much. "After all," I said to myself, "what's so special here? It's the old story. As they say, if God wants you to die, don't be a smart aleck; you've got to die. You're not the only one. People are dying in the thousands, tens of thousands, falling like flies, like straws in the wind. So just imagine, Yankel Yunever, that you're a soldier and in the heat of battle. Fool! Who thinks of death in the heat of battle? Or rather who thinks of anything *but* death? Because if you get right down to it, what's war if not the angel of death? And what's the point of telling the angel of death, if you see what I mean, to fear death?'' Think it over, Mr. Sholom Aleichem. You'll soon see how deep that is!

Still, what's the good of philosophy? You want to get to the point, right? Well, I can tell you this much—I know as much about what happened next as you do. Suddenly confusion broke out, a clamor from heaven, a drumming of drums, a chaos of soldiers running and horses galloping. Great God Almighty, I thought, what's going on? A revolution? The earth opening under Sodom and Gomorrah? The end of the world? In an instant the soldiers vanished, and we Krushniker Jews remained all alone on the new burial grounds, shovels in hand, and—silence.

It was then we understood—not that we *understood* anything (why should I lie to you?), but we felt with all our five senses, if you see what I mean, that something extraordinary had happened, a true and genuine miracle from heaven, and we'd been saved from disaster. But for all that, we just couldn't say a word to each other, not a word! We'd lost our tongues, and that was that. And like one man, as if we'd decided on it beforehand, we threw down the shovels, pulled ourselves together, and hit the road, as they say—slowly at first, then a little faster, and then we ran, but really *ran,* if you see what I mean, like you run from a blazing fire.

Where did we get the courage? And especially the old rabbi, where did he get the strength to run like that? But he didn't last long, poor thing, and when he couldn't go any further he stopped short, with his hand on his chest, barely breathing. So we stopped too—it's not decent to leave a rabbi by himself in the middle of nowhere. We still couldn't say a word, and we still didn't know what was happening. But we could hear the drumming and the galloping and the shooting. Something was going on, God only knows what, but as it's written, "God will provide, so keep quiet." Quiet we were—we couldn't speak.

The first to say something was the old rabbi. "Children," he called to us, looking up toward the bright moon. "I can tell you that it's the Almighty," he said, "the Creator of heaven and earth who has done these things. God Himself," he said, "has taken pity on our wives and children and saved us from disaster. And so we owe it to God," he said, "to give thanks to His moon; it's the right time of the month." And without another word, he turned his face to the new moon—the rabbi, I mean—right there in the middle of town, and we stood around him. And the rabbi started chanting, "Hallelujah," cheerfully, and we all followed him, growing livelier as we went along, chanting, clapping, and leaping. By the time he got to "Let us dance in praise of His name," we were really dancing! Such a prayer to the new moon, believe me, Krushnik had never heard of since Krushnik was Krushnik. Never had and never will again. It was, as they say, a once-in-a-lifetime prayer to the new moon.

You can imagine we didn't know where we were, whether in this world or the next, when it came to the *"Sholem aleichem's."* I heard someone blubbering, right into my ear, *"Sholem aleichem."* I answered, *"Aleichem sholem!"* and looked around. It was him, the *schlimazel,* Aba the *shochet,* I mean. How did *he* get here? Had he also been with us there at the burial grounds? A curse on it all! I'd completely forgotten— he'd been the first one! We must have been out of our minds, if you see what I mean. I only wanted to hug and kiss that *schlimazel,* and at the same time I wanted to hug the rabbi (may his memory stay with us always— he's now in another world, a better one). And the way he died! God Almighty! May it happen to all our enemies! You'll hear about it, don't worry; I won't leave out the details. That was a Jew! Where can you find Jews like him today?

But just think what a rabbi can do. Once we'd finished our prayer to the new moon, he wanted to say a few more words. He decided, if you see what I mean, to explain a passage from the Song of Songs. "The voice of my beloved," he began. . . . I hope he'll forgive me for saying this, but he had one fault, our rabbi: he loved to hold forth, to give lectures. So we took counsel and decided nothing doing. A prayer to the new moon was one thing, but a commentary on the Song of Songs, with interpretations and illustrations and exhortations, in the middle of town, late at night, after such horrors and such miracles and wonders—*that*, brother, we could leave for another occasion. So we tucked in our coattails, as they say, and ran for home, each one of us. And there we met with another happy scene, I mean a real celebration. By comparison, everything we'd been through was mere child's play. You'll say that yourself when you hear the story. . . .

You know, Mr. Sholom Aleichem, Jews brag about the town of Kishinev. Kishinev, they say, was world-famous for its pogroms and its hooligans. Ha! I'd laugh at them if there were any Jews left there to laugh at. Kishinev! You call *that* a town? Kishinev was a dog compared to Krushnik. Do you hear me? Kishinev wasn't worthy of washing Krushnik's feet. Concerning the treatment of Jews, the Kishinever hooligans could have learned a lesson or two (if they don't mind me saying so) from our Russian Cossacks. To begin with, they didn't even have the right weapons. In Kishinev, if they felt like smashing a house, they'd have to gather up a hundred people, along with sticks and rocks and pebbles. But what good are such weapons?—if you can call them weapons. By the time you get something going, smash up a house or two, all the excitement's gone out of it and the party's over. Now in our town in Krushnik, there were dozens of good guns, or if you preferred there was a fine cannon. A few blasts of that cannon, and you've shot up the whole area, wiped out the marketplace with all its stores and stalls and the houses all around to boot. Do you see what I mean, or don't you? With one blow they wiped out all of Krushnik, didn't leave a shred behind, not a trace! They rooted us out from the bottom up, demolished everything Jewish, just as if it wasn't their own country they were in but the enemy's. As if Krushnik was some kind of fortress, another Paris, or a Warsaw! Though I must tell you that Krushnik was always, what should I say, a helter-skelter town, a town thrown open to the wind and the rain, without courtyards, without orchards, without gardens, without fences or walls—only houses and shacks, naked, bare Jewish homes; and these they smashed up, cut down, hacked apart, split in pieces, ground up, wiped out. Finished, no more Krushnik!

And was it only Krushnik, you think? The way it was with Krushnik, that's how it was with Rakhev, too, and with Mazel-Bozhetz, and with Bilgoray, and with every other Jewish town all around as far as Lublin. But not Lublin, of course—that was the provincial capital, and Poles lived there as well as Jews; and it was they, the Poles, who unleashed the furies. If not for them, if they hadn't poured oil on the fire with their lies, then maybe nothing would have happened.

The first to show up was the Honorable Mr. Pshepetsky, head of the administrative council. The morning after our prayer to the new moon, he ran to tell the Russian officials, personally, that we Krushniker Jews were hand in glove with the Germans. Proof was, he said, that no one wanted the job of mayor; only my Yekhiel, he said, would take it on.

Well, the Russians didn't have to hear more. They were furious, beside themselves with rage against all Jews, and especially against the mayor himself, against my Yekhiel. A summons was issued from headquarters that he should be taken—my Yekhiel, that is—dead or alive! And not only him. They were to take all of us, if you see what I mean, all the first citizens of Krushnik, along with the rabbi and the *rabbiner,* and bring us to Ivan, dead or alive—he desired to see us.

Don't you think I knew beforehand it would turn out that way? I knew! My word as a Jew I knew, and the proof is that I warned everyone. "Jews," I said, "as you love God, let's get out of here!" I told them in good time, too, that night, just as soon as we heard the Germans running and Ivan coming on with his Cossacks. Because I knew that where Ivan set foot no grass would grow. So I told them, "Let's get out of here, wherever our feet will carry us. Anywhere in the world," I said, "but not here."

Well, I almost convinced them—all but one. That was the old man, the rabbi. He just dug in his heels and refused to budge. He didn't want, he said, to run for the sake of running. "If the God of Israel wants to preserve us," he said, "He'll preserve us, as He has up until now; and if not, God forbid, then it's a sure sign," he said, "that that's our fate. And if so," he said, "then let it at least be as it's written, 'I shall sleep with my ancestors.' " In short, all he wanted was to be buried like a Jew and remain forever in his own Krushnik. The world's full of evil temptations. But he couldn't have even that satisfaction. Man thinks and God winks, as they say. He forgot to reckon, our rabbi, with those two-legged beasts.

If you remember, the whole business began during the night of the new moon. Ivan and his Cossacks set out to ransack our homes on the pretense of looking for runaway Germans, and in the course of things they did what they always do—what they did, for example, in Kishinev, in Bialystok, in Balta, in Kateri-Neshov, and in other Jewish towns. The only difference was that there they beat people and robbed them, while here they very methodically emptied our pockets, inquiring of each one of us, *"Tschari? tschari?"* ("watches? any watches here?"), not meaning watches in particular:

watchchains, rings, earrings, and money-purses would also do. Then when they'd taken it all, everything finished and done with—as the text has it, "emptied out Egypt," carried off all its treasures of wealth—then they proceeded to the people: bound them, beat them, stabbed them, shot them, and hung them. Especially hung them. They hung so many of us there weren't any trees left for hangings. They had to place logs over the rooftops, and there on the logs they continued hanging the Jews of Krushnik, one by one.

Their first victim was our rabbi, the old man, blessed be his memory. The Cossacks broke into his house early, just at daybreak. He'd already put on his prayer shawl and phylacteries and was starting to pray, when they tore in like a flood. "Vodka!" they shouted—meaning they wanted whiskey. Why whiskey at daybreak? Simply out of hunger, if you see what I mean; they were faint and famished, poor men, and so they needed a drop of whiskey. But how would an old rabbi come by whiskey, especially at a time when it was, as they say, strictly forbidden? So he gestured with his hands (not wanting to interrupt his prayers) that he had no vodka to offer them. For that he received a healthy curse, along with a slap for good measure, so that his prayer book fell from his hands. When he bent to pick it up he received another blow to the head from behind. Then the Cossacks lifted him, unconscious, from the floor, wrapped him neatly in his prayer shawl and phylacteries, tied him to a horse (to the horse's tail, I mean), and dragged him through town into the marketplace. There they hung him from a tree and set guard over him, with orders that he must hang like that for three days and three nights. No one should dare take him down.

So he hung there, the old rabbi, wrapped in his prayer shawl, beaten and bloodied, in the middle of the marketplace, swaying back and forth in the wind, as though in prayer. Whoever passed by stopped to look, then ran off shuddering to tell his neighbor, and the neighbor told *his* neighbor, and soon people all over town were whispering the news to each other, and then the crowd came running to see. Cows! Cattle! Why were they running? What was so special here? Hadn't they seen a hanged man before? And for that matter, what about me, old fool that I was—why did *I* run to see it? Don't ask how much health it cost me, how many sleepless nights. To this day I see him when I close my eyes—wrapped in his prayer shawl, his face petrified, blue and streaked with blood, swaying back and forth as he stood there saying his prayers. What am I saying? He wasn't standing, he was hanging, if you see what I mean, hanging in prayer!

But let's not talk about it anymore. Silence is best, as they say. Let's talk of happier things. Wasn't there a pogrom in your town? Didn't they hang Jews there? And by the way, what country are *you* running from, Mr. Sholom Aleichem?

Translated by Sacvan Bercovitch

ONE IN A MILLION

I could swear it's him from head to toe. His slightly hooked nose, his warm, dark, smiling eyes, that one bucktooth that juts out when he starts to laugh. He's no youngster now. He must be my age. And I'm past forty.

Should I approach him? He seems very well dressed—a white vest over his belly, a heavy gold chain, a splendid tie, and from what I've heard, he's living the good life, "in the chips" as they say, a real wheeler-dealer.

I am afraid to say hello. Will he think I'm after something? You should know, I've always considered myself a little proud. Not vain, mind you, just proud.

A proud man scorns the world. Well, it's not that he scorns the world but that the world scorns him—especially if he happens to be poor. There's nothing wrong

---

This monologue takes place in Odessa, the major port of Russia on the Black Sea. In the late nineteenth century it was a flourishing city that attracted a large multinational population—not the least being Jews seeking their fortune.

The magic of Odessa entered the Yiddish language in the popular expression, *Er lebt vi Got in Odes* (literally, he lives like God in Odessa), which translates: he is living the good life. In all probability, Sholom Aleichem had this well-known expression in mind when he wrote this story. —Translator's Note

with poverty—it's no sin, so they say. And knock on wood, I'm no millionaire—far from it. Let's understand each other, I belong to that rich class of the well-disguised poor who cloak their poverty at home behind a mirror and a grand piano and in public with a showy coat and a new felt hat. But when you really come down to it, they don't even have a crumb to eat or a penny in their pockets.

To be frank, I'm not in the best of straits. Things could be better. I've tried my hand time and again at every kind of hard work and run after enough bad tips—but nothing helps. It's reached such a point I can't stand myself—and neither can others.

Maybe he doesn't give a hoot about me, couldn't care less. The few people who do notice me think, "Watch out, here comes trouble. He wants to wheedle a loan out of me. I won't give him anything." Over my dead body would I ask him for one red cent.

"And how are you?" he asks and looks me straight in the eye.

"How am I?" I say and stare right back.

"How are things going? Pretty well?"

"Not bad."

"Good to hear, thank God," he says and shakes my hand.

"Some people have all the luck," I say to myself and shake his hand.

And so we go our separate ways.

But the person whose story I'm telling didn't look at me like that when we met on the boulevard in Odessa. His look was entirely different. I could read straight into his warm, dark, smiling eyes.

And with those smiling eyes he draws me to him and I feel myself at ease. From afar he stretches out his hand to me. He opens his mouth to laugh and his bucktooth protrudes. "Is it?"

"Could it be?"

We tightly grip each other's hand. I must confess that

ever since things have not gone well for me, I can't stand rich people. I can't put up with their healthy, happy, fat faces; I can't bear a face that looks content with itself and the world. But this charmer bends over to me somehow so warmly that we embrace each other.

I don't know how to address him. If I am too familiar, am I taking advantage of our past closeness and reminding him of how time flies? But how can I be formal with him? Didn't we pore over the same texts together for so many years in the same schoolroom?

This very thought must have run through his mind too, for as we start talking, we both use language in such a way that during the entire time we rack our brains to avoid being either too intimate or too formal.

He: I keep looking and looking, maybe it's him, maybe not? How goes it?

I: And I kept thinking the whole time, can it really be him? It looks like him. Maybe it's not? Where is he from?

He: From where? I'm already a native. I've lived in Odessa for who knows how long.

I: And I arrived not too long ago . . . to look for a business.

He: A business? Looking for a business? For me it's just the other way around. I have too much business. If only I had as many good employees! It's bad without good help. And what it costs me each year! ["A braggart," I think to myself.] I don't have any luck with them. How many times have I thought to myself: if I had even one reliable man whom I could trust, it would add ten years to my life. What did I say? Ten? Twenty years for sure! I've already tried to keep all kinds of help—cheap help, expensive help, even very high-priced help—they're all the same, there's not a loyal one among them. I once had so many friends. When one of them came to me seeking help, I would shower him with money from head to foot. ["What a liar!" goes through my mind.] And as if for spite, I never meet anyone from the old days. I can really say that this is the first time I've had such a meeting since I settled here. It seems to me we once were really close friends, right?

I: Friends? Anything passes for friendship today! We studied together, we boarded together at a rabbi's, we slept on the same bed together.

He: I can even remember at which rabbi's, at Reb Zorah's on top of the Russian stove throughout the whole winter.

I: And summer in the open air on the ground.

He: Like pigs in the muck, with all the frogs.

I: And Tevye the neighbor standing by his broken window screaming at whoever had thrown stones and scaring the entire household half to death.

He: And at Pironditshke's, who swiped the apples right out of the basket with a spiked pole?

I: And the watermelons? Lifted straight off old Gedaliah's wagon at Succos!

And so on.

It isn't easy to stop talking about the good old days. Our memories flow like water from a tap. But he doesn't get down to brass tacks until we come bit by bit to the present and we tell each other about the good and bad in our lives, the happy and the sad.

Things are going well for one of us, very well. With the other, things are going poorly, really badly. One is rich, a millionaire; the other barely ekes out a living. One spares no expense for his children's upbringing: his oldest daughter is happily married off; the sons are all in the finest schools. The other eats his heart out about his children: his eldest daughter wants to give private lessons and has no students, and his son can't get into the first-rate school. You need "pull" and it costs a lot. One has his own house in Odessa with a garden, all sorts of antiques—in short, a paradise. The other has been wandering a good number of years from one hole to the next. Not too long ago they "took inventory of him" from head to foot, sold his bedding, and threw him out on the street. Steeling himself—"what will be, will be"—he moved to another city! They say it's an answer: "Move away and your luck will change!"

With no one else have I ever opened my heart so fully as now with my friend. And no one else listens with such interest to the bitter end. I feel a load off my chest, a weight off my mind. And I notice how his warm, dark, smiling eyes are moist, and he says to me: "That's enough. Things will be better, I swear it. 'Move away and your luck will change.' I know from my own experience; once things did not turn out well for me either. From now on we will be together again."

"What do you mean," I ask, "by 'together'?"

"What 'by together' means?" he says in a singsong, and his warm, dark eyes are laughing. " 'By together' means, when someone has a business and needs help desperately and looks for someone—an honest man, a loyal man, no matter what he costs he's worth twice as much—and with God's help he meets a friend of his whom he hasn't seen for such a long time and learns that unfortunately time hasn't treated his friend well and he's looking for a business, it means simply, they need each other. And what could be better than that today?"

And in order to make this bit of luck seem more real, he draws out his wallet, opens it, and wants to show me a telegram. But my eyes don't fix on the telegram but fall on the wad of bills in his wallet—a nice thick wad of crisp bills in hundreds and five hundreds. And my eyes apparently are wide open, and his eyes meet mine and he guesses why I'm staring and says again in the same singsong: "The business, thank God, can bear it all. And when a new person enters the firm, he needs I'm sure a little extra cash. And there's enough money so why should he not take as much as he needs? What is there to be ashamed of? We all understand what it means to move to a new place with children. I know from experience. I was once in no better shape. I dreamt about greenbacks, too."

And my friend sits down on a bench with me and tells his whole life's story, full of extraordinary events, like tales from the *Thousand and One Nights*. My own life—even with my present troubles—is a bowl of cherries compared to his. I look at him and wonder, "What one man can endure!" And if God could help him after so many troubles, perhaps there's hope for me, too.

And my friend pulls out his wallet again and puts it right under my nose. "Why should one feel embarrassed?" he says to me. "One should take as much as one needs to tide one over."

I ask myself if this isn't a dream and look into the open wallet, and the hundred and five-hundred bills smile at me as do my friend's eyes, and I extend my hand and say: "Two will be enough."

I don't know what I should say: two one-hundreds or two five-hundreds? And to make it easier for me, he says, "Two thousand, I think, won't go very far."

And he counts out six five-hundred bills and says, "Is three thousand enough on the first go-round?"

"Ah . . ." I couldn't say one word more and fold the wad of bills and stuff them into my breast pocket and feel a strange warmth from them, a soothing feeling.

And so I won't be embarrassed, he adds, "And I should really like to take a look at my old friend's children, may they be well!"

But I don't answer him immediately. My thoughts are elsewhere—there in the breast pocket with a wad of five-hundreds which warm and caress me and will not leave me alone. And my thoughts lead to my wife and children. I imagine the happy scene when they suddenly will see so much money and hear of this good luck.

"Well," I say, "we can go straight to my place. I live a few doors away. The children must be home. Shall we go?"

"Why not?" he says, and I can see in his eyes that he knows my thoughts are on the money in my breast pocket because I automatically pat it and sigh with pleasure. And he, that dog, completely understands, and drags the conversation back to those old, foolish, happy days of our childhood and recalls long-forgotten moments as we make our way to my place.

And then I start thinking about my place, my furniture . . . and I am embarrassed for my rich friend and begin to make excuses: "A new apartment . . . recently moved in . . . summertime . . . not yet settled in."

He understands at once what I mean, and before I can go on he says: "Oh, my . . . the usual . . . it's the same thing all over! No better at my place. Come summer and everything's upside down."

And at the same moment I remember the money flat against my chest and it warms and heats and ignites my thoughts. What shall I do first? . . . And quickly I add up in my mind: rent, the butcher bill, the child's tuition, my wife's shoes, my daughter's hat, a coat for myself, some furniture . . . today's debts, yesterday's debts, debts, debts!

Before I know it, the door is opened and one of my children comes toward me looking very sad. My poor children, I'm afraid, know we can't make ends meet. They know what it is to be poor. Not to be able to buy milk or meat at the market. In the morning the rent collector is coming, along with the woman who supplies us with tea, and the wood man, a brazen youth with a short beard who jeers from far off: "For the wood, you could have paid three times over already."

"Where's mother?" I ask.

"In the kitchen," the child answers.

"We have no maid now. The maid just went off yesterday," I explain to my rich friend and almost die from shame. And I wonder how my wife will enter, Heaven forbid with greasy hands and God-knows-what clothes.

"It's the same at my place," he says. "They come and go; we have a new maid every week."

I don't know what to do. Shall I let my friend remain

seated while I go myself into the kitchen and announce the good news to my wife? That miracles do happen? Or would it be better to remain here with my friend in the parlor?

I say "in the parlor" as if there really were a parlor. A large room, yes, but empty, bare—that is, a few tables, a rug, an old piano, a mirror, plus a lamp (a real ugly one), and a bed smack in the middle of the parlor! And still not made so late in the day! I would give a crisp one-hundred right away just to have someone remove the bed from there. My face turns red.

My friend guesses why I'm acting so strangely and calls out: "A nice apartment—airy, roomy, and not a bad idea to have someone sleep in the parlor. At my place, too, the children sleep in the parlor during the summertime."

"Here comes my only son," and I introduce him to my son who decides, just then, to take off his boots and walk around barefoot. My friend, seeing that this little scene bothers me, thinks up a white lie: "In summertime all my children go barefoot, too."

And then my daughter enters, the second oldest. I present her to my old friend. She turns red as a beet, not because she is shy, but because she is so plainly, even poorly dressed. And the proof is in the shoes—everyday shoes but with patches, without heels, bent out of shape and torn.

And just for spite she sits down in such a way that he sees the shoes, and she notices where he's looking, and I notice how they both are staring at her shoes and I'm ready to die. Give me a hole in the ground, I would jump in alive.

"A lovely child," he whispers in my ear, "pretty as a picture."

I want to say something in reply when my eldest daughter, a real beauty, enters. At least she is wearing a decent pair of shoes, but she has put on a jacket made of thin muslin worn out at the elbows. She's not aware that there is a hole at the elbow and she sinks into her chair a little too deeply so that the elbow juts out straight at him. He looks at the elbow, and I look at him. I wink at her. She doesn't understand, becomes red as a beet, gets up and turns her back to go. Don't look, what a mess: her whole jacket is in shreds.

"One's more beautiful than the other," whispers my friend. "With such fine-looking children one must begin saving for the dowry immediately."

"The hell with this guy and his modern stove, his fancy house and courtyard, and all courtyards. They can all go to hell with Odessa itself for all I care."

By now you must have guessed: it's my grumbling wife who enters from the kitchen, bathed in sweat and burning up, the poor thing, without a maid. She must cook the food all by herself—something she has never been used to. The coal stove is smoking, the butcher will no longer give meat on credit, the milkmaid keeps demanding her money and won't leave the kitchen; in the market everything's overpriced; and the children carry on—they want new potatoes for lunch with sweet butter, no less!

I want to stop her, to call her away, first to announce the good news and second to have her change her clothes. But my friend doesn't let me, he holds me back and says: "I'd prefer introducing myself."

And he goes up to her, presents himself, and a dialogue ensues:

He: I knew your husband, madam, way before you.

She: A rare piece of luck!

He: We've been friends from childhood on.

She: Tell me who your friends are and I'll tell you who you are.

He: We studied together, ate together, slept together, and even stole apples from a basket together.

She: That speaks well for both of you.

He: Not only apples alone, but watermelons, too.

She: That's enough. I already know who you are.

My wife pronounces the last few words with so much venom that my friend can't say a word. I wink to her, I give her a high sign with my eyes to stop her sharp needling talk. But she's wound up and answers me: "What are you winking for? I know this type, this friend of yours."

"Madam!" says my friend with the voice of a man who feels himself somewhat insulted. "Madam, from what I see, you don't hold your husband in high esteem. May I remind you that I know him better than you."

"May I remind you," answers my wife in the same words, "that no one asked your opinion. He can stand on his own two feet and doesn't need your help."

I see my friend's face change. His cheeks turn flaming red. The warm, dark, smiling eyes have stopped sparkling and he is sweating as if his life were at stake. What shall I do? I'm finished. I may as well end it all. My surprise has turned sour, ruined. I've forgotten about the money in my breast pocket, I've forgotten about everything. Only one thing remains in my head: How can I take my wife aside? How do I let her know what he has done for us? I plead with my eyes: "Keep quiet! Stop talking!" And just for spite, she speaks up.

"I know all about his good friends and old school-mates!" she says. "Nothing good will come of it. They're either good-for-nothing bums, or big shots dropping by with a story. Just last week a friend of his showed up from his home town, such a close friend, and from so far away—may he go to hell—and sold my husband such a bill of goods that our heads swirled: he's a real millionaire, a big philanthropist, a soft touch, only one of his kind in the world. And when it came time for my husband to ask for . . . What are you getting all embarrassed for? He's a good friend of yours, isn't he, with whom you once stole apples. And when it came time for my husband to tell him that . . ."

I cannot stand it anymore. I'm losing my temper. I

can barely see straight. I must stop this talk at once.
And I shout to my wife with a voice that's not mine:
"That's eeeeee—nough!!!!!!!"

"What's the matter? Why are you screaming? Wake
up!" blurts my wife, frightened to death, and shakes me
out of sleep.

I sit up, rub my eyes, and look around. "Where can
he be?"

"Who? Whom are you looking for?"

"My blood brother, that friend of mine."

"What blood brother? What friend? You were
dreaming. Spit three times to ward off the evil eye! You
went to bed late. How many times have I told you that
you should stop writing late at night?"

I reach for my pocket and feel for the money. God, it
was just there, just as I left it. A wad of crisp five-hundreds! I can still hear the crackle and feel the fresh bills
in my hand.

And I remember that tomorrow at ten in the morning
the tax collector is coming to draw up a list and auction
off my chairs, and the landlord is throwing me out of the
apartment, and the butcher wants his money and the
milkmaid wants hers, and the woodcutter won't stop
either—he comes by all the time and repeats, "Can't
pay yet?" . . . And my son has an announcement: he's
ready for his exams. Good luck to you, son, you should
live to give better news. . . .

I'm bathing in sweat and trembling with chills.

Translated by Seth Wolitz

ONCE THERE WERE FOUR

CHARACTERS
Mendele Mocher-Sforim, a fine old man with a gentle
   voice; referred to as "grandfather"
Bialik, a young poet; contemplative
Ben-Ami, a person prone to excitability
Sholom Aleichem, an old acquaintance, who listens
   and writes down everything in a notebook

Everyone says mountains are immovable. But I disagree. Mountains move, and how! They run! I discovered this when we four Jewish writers, one of us a poet,
took our first walking trip in the famous, eternally
snow-covered Alps.

A few miles out of the city—and the mountains
seemed almost upon us. Just stretch out a hand and bid
them hello. But the closer we came, the farther they
moved. Indeed, ran away. We began to walk faster and
faster. They outran us.

"Are they teasing us?" I called to the others.

"Who?"

"The mountains."

"I don't understand it," exclaimed my hot-tempered
colleague who knew his way in the Alps like a Jew
knows his prayer book. "They were never so far before. If you want my advice, we should walk a bit
faster."

319

Urging us on, each time with greater force, he tired even more quickly than the rest of us, grew irritable and angry, and let out his bile in an invective against the "Russian hoodlum with his revolution and his constitution."

"Wait! I want to ask you something," Reb Mendele called out. We all paused for a while. "I want each of you to tell me how you feel at this moment."

It seems my choleric companion was the first to understand the question. He hastened to answer, wiping the sweat from his forehead with the corner of his jacket. "I feel so light I could fly like an eagle, without once looking back."

"As for me," said the young poet, staring at me as he spoke, "I don't feel badly, but I doubt that I could fly."

It was my turn to answer: "I would feel wonderful," I said, "if we could sit down for a while, right here on the grass."

This irritated my excitable colleague who declared that if we continued at this pace, we would spend Sabbath at the foot of the mountain. Turning on me, he asked how I could have undertaken such a hike when I knew that I could hardly walk? Nevertheless, he did fold his umbrella, tuck under his jacket, and throw himself with the rest of us on the fragrant green grass to enjoy a taste of Paradise under God's sky and to beg "grandfather" Mendele for a story. . . .

Have you ever wanted to be someone you're not? I, for example, once wanted *not* to be a Jew—not permanently, God forbid!—but for a short time only, so that I might look with non-Jewish eyes at a group of Jews walking and talking, shouting and arguing and gesticulating. It must be an engrossing sight. An ordinary conversation must look like a quarrel, and a disagreement over a matter of importance—as, for example, the exact time of sunset or the cost of a certain building—like an impending fistfight.

Such were my thoughts as we walked in the Alps. Almost all those we met on the way—Frenchmen, Germans, Englishmen, and others—stopped to gaze in wonder at these odd creatures in strange garments. Perhaps this was because we spoke too loudly and all at once. Speaking all together is an art that only we Jews have mastered. Our assemblies, adjudications, celebrations, and councils are famous the world over. Parliamentary procedure, meaning that every person is required to speak singly, is an innovation for which we have Zionism to thank, and Dr. Herzl in particular. It is surely a fine thing, but not always and not everywhere. How would parliamentary procedure work for four Jewish writers, one of them a poet, climbing together in the famed, eternally snow-covered Alps, and discussing such matters as literature, *Talmud,* history, politics, poetry, and revolution?

The people we meet of other nationalities walk the same mountains, but their progress is dull. They walk in silence or talk so softly one can barely hear a word. Each is aware only of himself and his own stomach. You may consider this a rule: when several people walk together in silence, they are surely engrossed in their stomachs. But Jews are far from such matters. For us the stomach is one of nature's contraptions, an internal pouch and a source of vexation, as our "grandfather" Mendele has so often described it.

In any event, the passersby stared at us in amazement. Some even stopped to listen, waiting for the fight to begin. Dunces! They don't begin to understand that friends as close as we are cannot be found the world over. We may not flatter one another, play cards together, or engage in other such worldly pleasures; but when the Jewish exile occasionally brings us together in one place, our greatest joy is pouring out to one another our bitter hearts. Sometimes, over a nip of brandy, we grow so merry, the tears flow from our eyes. . . .

The sun, strolling across the bright blue Swiss sky,

spilled golden sheaves that scattered like stalks of light over the eternal rocks and down the mountainside, falling at last with the serpentine streams into the restless Rhone . . .

We were still at the foot of the mountain which was growing taller, broader, and more beautiful before our eyes. It seemed no longer on the run from us, but to the contrary, it came out to greet us in friendly fashion, though with a touch of hauteur, too. If we four Jewish writers would kindly take the trouble to approach a little higher toward the Throne of God, there we would be exposed to vast marvels, recited to from the Book of Creation, and told of God's mighty powers. From its peak the mountain would show us the foolish little world below where children built tiny houses and called them cities, put tiny carts on wheels and called them trains, played at royalty and politics, at war and at slavery—quite as if they were grown up.

Each of us has a different name for the mountain: "The Sage," "Celebrity," "Reb Begging Your Pardon." Grandfather Mendele, in full flight of fancy, summons forth the greatest of giants, Og King of Bashan, who hoists the mountain on his shoulder and runs with it hundreds of miles in a single breath to hurl it upon the Jews. Suddenly God performs a miracle, and the murderous giant stops short with two enormous teeth growing from his mouth, one up, the other down. Unable to move, neither here nor there, he stands fixed in a singular tragi-comic pose! . . .

"What's its name, this magnificent mountain?"

All eyes turn to our hot-tempered friend, the acknowledged expert on all the mountains, rivers, and streams of the region. Instead of replying, he hesitates, flushes, rubs his forehead, stares up at the mountain's peak, and cries out, as if someone had stamped on his toe: "Tfoo! I've forgotten. Just a second ago I knew it—and now I forget! Can you imagine!"

"Forget?" says Reb Mendele. "If you want to know

about forgetting, just ask me. There's no worse punishment on earth than forgetting. To have something fly from your head, like a bird from a cage, just when you need it most! It's an illness, a plague, a tragedy! Why, I could tell you a story—not a fiction either, but a true story—that happened to me in Odessa a few years ago, a story of a hotel . . ."

"I'll tell you a better one, that happened to *me* in Odessa! It's worth hearing!" cried my impulsive colleague.

He was on the point of beginning when he was interrupted by the poet: "My story is even better, though it happened not in Odessa but in Zhitomir!"

"And what about me?" protested the fourth, me myself. "I can tell you a story that took place in three cities at once, and you'll split your sides laughing!"

"Three cities at once? In that case, the honor is yours!" called Grandfather Mendele with a ringing laugh and a wave of his hand as if to say, "You bid for it? The bargain's yours!"

All four of us burst out laughing, and I felt quite the fool. It had been tactless of us to barge in on Grandfather with our stories, and we were now eager to make amends. For some time we pleaded with him to tell us what had happened in Odessa, and Grandfather, if you coax him long enough, always relents. He rolled up his sleeves, as was his habit, and pushed his glasses high up on his high, clever forehead, under the shock of wavy white hair. His small eyes, sharp and piercing, closed somewhat, and his face opened into that radiant, childlike smile that takes fifty years off his age and adds so much charm that you want to sit beside him forever, listening on and on.

Grandfather's Story

This happened, as I told you, some years ago in Odessa—that is, not in Odessa proper, but a couple of train stations away. I was on my way home. It was autumn. The outdoors was cloaked in a mantle of rain. The sky poured tears, the wind howled, the earth mourned for its lost mate, the warm dear sun. From time to time the rain lashed in anger at the sweaty windows of our railway compartment where we sat quite comfortably in the warmth—a companionable group, chatting amiably about the issues of the day.

The passenger opposite me was an educated and well-read man, a Christian as it happened, and a singular friend of the Jews. Now you know that I dislike fawning Jews even more than converts, and I don't fall all over myself with gratitude to every Gentile who has a good word for us either. But for this gentleman I felt a deep affection and an instinctive attraction that goes beyond rational understanding. What can I tell you? I felt so comfortable with him that I would readily have traveled in his company another three days. I was eager to be of some service to him, even in a small way, and happily the opportunity came immediately to hand. Since he was traveling for the first time to *my* city, Odessa, he wanted to know of a good place to stay, a decent hotel. As a longtime resident of the city, could I recommend to him the best hotel in the city?

A hotel? Why, of course!

I grabbed with both hands at this chance to be of help to him, and proceeded to describe in the most glowing colors a well-known hotel, the largest and most beautiful in the city. First, the view: the building was so artfully designed that all its windows faced the sea. Then the spacious, high-ceilinged, bright rooms; the splendid winter garden; the hothouses, reading rooms, the service, the excellent help. There was also the restaurant, the music—in short, I got carried away, as if I were describing Paradise, not a hotel.

With such a dreary outdoors, the prospect of a warm, cheerful oasis in a strange city was ten times more welcome than at any other time. My traveling companion heard me out with grateful shining eyes and a happy expression. I watched him take out his notebook, unclasp a tiny gold pencil, and wait patiently for me to finish so that he could jot down the name of the hotel. So absorbed was I that I failed to notice we were almost in Odessa. Only when people began to rise from their seats and collect their packages did my companion tactfully and with a friendly smile turn to me and ask the name of the hotel.

"Oh, of course! The name? Right away, I'll tell you . . ."

I thought for a moment. My God! What was its name? I knew it a second ago. . . . Damn! It slipped my mind! . . . Uselessly I rubbed my forehead, searched my memory. I simply couldn't remember! You probably think the name was unusual, complicated, hard to remember? Not at all. There is no easier name in the world—in fact, as you'll see, it's impossible to forget! The name was on the tip of my tongue, I had only to pronounce it—but it eluded me. If only the ground could have opened to swallow me!

Seeing my predicament, my companion wanted to effect a rescue, to drag me from the swamp. He applied all his skill and began to recite the names of hotels all over the world: *"Grand Hotel, Belleview, Terminus, Metropole, National, International, Bristol, Paris, Madrid, St. Petersburg, Chicago, San Remo, London, Hamburg, Constantinople . . ."*

No, no, and no again!

Seeing that these were of no use, he turned to national names: *"Hotel France? Montenegro? England? Hotel Russia? Austria-Hungary? Belgium? The Holland? The Brazil? Argentina?"*

Not a hope. We were getting nowhere!

"How about *Hotel Post? Hotel Royale? Hotel Europa? Hotel Louvre? Hotel Imperial?"*

To make it short, I watched him put away his notebook, reattach the tiny gold pencil to his watch fob, courteously bid me good-bye, thank me, and urge me to trouble myself no longer. He would surely, somehow, find his way to that best of hotels.

And as for me, had a grave opened up before me, I would gladly have leapt in. What an embarrassment! What humiliation! I was nothing but a useless old man. There I was each day, repeating my own version of the *Midrash:* better to be wicked all one's life than foolish for a single hour—and to commit such a folly! Who asked you to become such a do-gooder and to recommend an Odessa hotel to a complete stranger? What do you know about hotels anyway, and how can you forget a name that you *know,* that you see every day of your life? . . .

Well, I won't go on. I came home in a state of agitation. I paced the house, rubbing my forehead, in the hope that here, at least, the name would come to me.

"Maybe you know," I asked my wife, "the name of the hotel?"

"Which hotel?"

"She wants *me* to tell *her* which hotel! But I'm asking *you!*"

"Just tell me the name," she says.

Well, go talk to a woman! I would simply have to make my own way to the hotel to see for myself. But when you have just returned from a journey there are eighteen-hundred chores to be taken care of, all kinds of correspondence and business details to get through. So I grow even more nervous and annoyed, and because I am angry with myself and at the world I let it out on the innocent.

Finally night falls. It's hours since we've eaten, time to go to bed, and I'm still struggling with the name of the hotel. Have you ever heard such a story? . . . It was agreed that the next day, at dawn, I would go to the hotel without fail! But I couldn't fall asleep! There I lay, waiting for morning when I could dress and get over to the hotel to look at the sign.

Suddenly I jump out of bed and begin dressing.

"God be with you!" says my wife, frightened almost to death. "Where are you going?"

"I can't stand it any longer," I cry. "I must go and look!"

"Where? At what?"

"Take a lantern, and just come with me!"

I will spare you the description of my wife's plight. You can imagine for yourselves the feelings of a woman whose husband set out on a journey in good health and spirits, and returns home angry, sullen, pacing the house and rubbing his forehead like a madman. Then he suddenly leaps from his bed at night, tells her to light a lamp, and says, "Come on!" And she goes!

What won't a poor wife do for her husband? I say, "Come on!" and she follows. I walk through the mud, and she follows. With God's help we reach the hotel. I raise the lantern and look at the sign. Go ahead, see if you can guess the name! If you had eighteen heads it wouldn't help. The hotel's name is . . . *Odessa!*

The Poet and His Bride

"Well now, tell your story. You said you had a better one."

With these words Mendele addressed himself to our irascible colleague who began to protest that, first of all, he had not said his story was "better"—that had been the poet's claim. And if he had said it, it was not what he had meant to say. To prove his good will, let the poet tell his story first and he would wait his turn.

So it was decided. The poet cleared his throat and spoke as follows:

Each of you, naturally, was once a bridegroom and you had a betrothed. You're all older than I, so perhaps you've already forgotten. But I remember it as though it were yesterday. I was in a state of bliss, the whole world belonged to me! I am engaged to a lovely girl with six hundred rubles for dowry. I have two years free board, and a golden watch in my pocket. Not least, I am in the great city of Zhitomir! It is springtime, the sun is showering diamonds of light, the sky is mirror smooth, the birds sing, and in my heart, a holiday reigns. I want to embrace the world, to kiss everyone! The word *stranger* no longer has meaning. How can anyone be a stranger! If you love someone he is no stranger, and I love everyone: Zimel the tailor who scurries about with his work; Chaim-Hersh the wagoner who reeks of tar; Lazer-Ber the water carrier with his swollen ankles and peeling face; even Ivan the *Goy* who swears whenever he gets drunk that he will kill all the Jews. I could even embrace Ivan and kiss his charming, prickly puss!

If that's how it is with Ivan, you can imagine my feelings for an old friend with whom I grew up and with whom I went to the *yeshiva* at Volozhin. We hungered and grew ragged together. I ran into him the very first day I went walking with my beloved in town! I need hardly explain how eager I was for my betrothed to become acquainted with my friend, and my friend with my betrothed, so that they too might become friends and learn to love one another as I love them, and they me, and all of us the great wide world!

I fell on my friend's neck and kissed him, and drawing my beloved to my side, I introduced them to one another. "This is Miss . . . Miss . . . eh, my fiancée. . . . Her name . . . her name is . . . Oh, yes! And this is . . . this is Mr. . . . Mr. . . . my best and dearest friend. Surely I have told you all about him, my dearest. . . . His name . . . his name is. . . . Well, what is your name? You know what your name is, don't you? Why don't you say something? . . ."

Well you can understand why my friend remained silent. He probably thought that from an excess of happiness I had altogether lost my senses. As for my bride, to this day I don't know what she was thinking.

We've been married now, praise God, for several years, but we have never referred to the incident. Neither of us would find it pleasant. There are moments you want to forget, to blot out from memory—but it is impossible. We forget what should be remembered and remember what should be forgotten. That, in a nutshell, is the moral of the story. Now it's someone else's turn.

What Is My Name?

The young poet concluded, and our choleric companion began his account with a curse, as was his wont when speaking of matters he found unpleasant.

When all the uprisings began in our Odessa over the battleship *Potemkin*—with the bombs whizzing over our heads, and the fires and the slaughters—I said, "Let it sink for all I care! I don't want to be here! I'd rather go to the ends of the world, may the devil take them!" And I began preparing for my departure. But it's easy to say *leave!* You think it's just a matter of letting kvass flow from a barrel. You first need a pass! Don't blame me if *kvass* rhymes with *pass* and *mishegass!* . . . Where was I? Oh, yes. You have to work at getting a pass, contact all sorts of people (may their names and memories be erased!), and meet all the petty officials (may the cholera take them this very day!).

"Now that you've exhausted the chapter of curses, perhaps you could stop swearing and get on with your story," Grandfather Mendele suggested.

Am I cursing anyone? To hell with them! It's just a passing comment: may they burn in hell! In short, I started arranging for a passport—and you well know what that means! Get friendly with all the parasites and hand out the money—just like Yom Kippur eve (to distinguish between sacred and profane), when the beggars line up in front of the synagogue. Every face is an open maw waiting to be filled. Well, I looked into plenty of open maws before I reached the Chief himself.

Having passed through all the circles of hell, I entered his office and found the Chief in the thick of work—scraping with the pen. You know very well that to interrupt an official in the act of scribbling is to put your life on the line. The world may be going under, but you must wait patiently until he finishes. But since I am not so good at standing politely, I decide to cough lightly, sending a herald, as it were, to announce that someone has arrived.

The Chief doesn't pause in his scribbling, so I cough a little louder. This time he raises his head, fixes me with a pair of bloodshot eyes, and hollers in Russian, "What do you want?"

At this reception, of course, I flare up like a match. What is this "What do you want?" Why should he shout at me? And when I get angry, I forget where I am. I see red. I want to break, tear, destroy everything in sight. I remember when I was a child, an orphan, I hated pity more than anything in the world. Once a neighbor made me a wonderful new pair of pants—pants that you see once in a hundred years. She felt sorry for me, you see. She called together the whole neighborhood, showed off every feature of the new pants, and not content with that, called me over to try them on so that everyone could admire their fit. That was the final straw. I ran over, grabbed the pants, and tore into them with my nails and teeth until there was nothing left but shreds and tatters. . . . Where was I? Oh, yes, the Chief has just showered me with his "What do you want?" and I am so angry that I want to make a scene he will never forget. But then I may find myself without a pass. So I control myself this once, approach the table, and hand him my papers. He glances at them and asks, "What is your name?" I remain silent. Seeing that I am silent, he raises his voice several notches and tries again: "What is your name? What are you called?"

My name? As you see me here alive, at that very moment I forgot that in addition to my pen name, I also

had my own name. When I say forgot, I mean *forgot!*
But completely! All the names of my relatives, friends,
and acquaintances parade before me, but one name, my
own, has disappeared to where the Holy Sabbath vanishes . . . *Lord of the Universe, tell me: what is my
name? What do they call me?* If you'd chopped off my
head, I couldn't remember. Meantime, the Chief stares
at me as if I were a criminal. Any moment now—I am
thinking—he will call me up for a proper sentence, send
for two angels of hell to carry me off, and I will be back
in exile again. Well, enough! I've had my taste of it, and
I don't need any more.

But there is, after all, a great compassionate God
above who guides the just, and He inspires me to main-
tain my composure—*like iron.* These people, if you
treat them offhandedly and raise your voice just a little,
will melt like putty. And so it was.

The Chief: What is your name?
I: Who? Me?
He: Who else? Me?
I: Exactly as it says in my papers.
He: What does it say in your papers?
I: Can't you read?
He: Who? Me?
I: Who else? Me?
He: (loudly) Wha-a-t! How dare you talk to me like
that? Do you know to whom you're speaking?
I: (also loudly) And do you know to whom *you* are
speaking?

Hearing me speak in a tone of voice such as he has
never in his life heard from a Jew, he looks into the
papers and reads my name aloud. And that was all I
needed!

What happened subsequently is of little interest. I got
out of my predicament safely, and I praise and thank the
good Lord every day and every hour for having saved
me from exile. May He never have to extricate me from
such a dilemma again. . . .

"Amen," we three responded in chorus, and Grandfather Mendele winked to let me know it was now my turn.

A Story of Three Cities

This happened a few years before the "Constitution." I was then making tours to cities and towns on behalf of various organizations throughout Lithuania. Once, around Chanukah time, I received invitations simultaneously from three neighboring cities—Mogilev, Vitebsk, and Smolensk—all three on the same railroad line. The requests came from three separate organizations: the "pure" Zionists, the Labor Zionists, and the Bundists. Naturally these organizations coexisted amicably, like cats and mice. Careful not to speak evil on their friends, the "pure" Zionists let it be known that the *false* Zionists were bringing me to the above-named cities in order to exploit me for their work which bore no relation to Zionism. The Labor Zionists were similarly restrained in their remarks about the "pure" Zionists: they merely regretted the agitation of these Sabbatian heretics, these false Messiahs, for a cause long since dead. . . . The Bundists, however, poured out their wrath on both Zionist groups, and assured me that a tour under the Zionists' auspices would be a guaranteed failure.

In short, I wasn't overjoyed by the prospect before me. What could be done? Finally I conceived of a Jewish plan: unite and divide. I said, "Children, I will come to you on the condition that all three organizations unite for the evenings in all three cities." My proposal was accepted, and there followed a flurry of letters and telegrams regarding the schedule and itinerary.

To which city should I go first? This became the point most difficult to resolve. Each day my route was changed. At first it was decided that I should begin in Mogilev, go from Mogilev to Vitebsk, from Vitebsk to Smolensk, then back to Mogilev—and home. Next it was agreed that I had best start in Smolensk, from Smolensk to Mogilev, from Mogilev to Vitebsk, from Vitebsk back past Mogilev—and home. Then that plan was scratched, and it remained that I should go to Vitebsk, Mogilev, Smolensk, and then back home via Mogilev. Finally they drew up another route "for my convenience": I was to stop first in Smolensk, then proceed to Vitebsk via Mogilev, go from Vitebsk back to Mogilev, and from Mogilev (immediately after the evening's lecture) straight home. The schedule was as follows, and please pay attention: *on the 18th, Smolensk; the 19th, Vitebsk; the 20th, Mogilev.*

On the evening of the 17th I set out, telegraphing ahead to all three cities that I would be there on the specified dates. In the meantime, they prepared all that was necessary—posters, tickets, programs, and so on. While driving to the station, I went over my itinerary again and again, and because of the many changes, naturally enough, I lost track. It seemed to me that I was to be in Vitebsk on the 18th; in Smolensk on the 19th; and in Mogilev on the 20th.

And I acted accordingly. I bought my train ticket and rode calmly to Vitebsk. When I got there, I walked about the depot for half an hour—an hour—two hours—on the chance of spotting one of the Zionists or Bundists. Has no one come to meet me, to welcome me? They may be Zionists and Bundists, but it still isn't right!

So I hired a carriage and asked the driver to take me to the best hotel. I ordered a room, washed and changed quite serenely, and thought to myself: "If that's the kind of jokers you are, you can take the trouble to search for me in the hotels. Sholom Aleichem is not a needle in a haystack, after all—search long enough and you'll find him."

When I went down to the dining room for lunch, I caught sight of two large posters:

VISITING OUR CITY!!!
SHOLOM ALEICHEM, THE GREATEST JEWISH HUMORIST!
THE 19TH . . .

The19th? Why the 19th? I call over the waiter, a young Litvak with coarse red hands, a black muzzle, and a white serviette under the arm of his soiled jacket.

"Please tell me, my good man, what's today?"

The waiter blows his nose into the white serviette and says: "Today? Today we have beetroot borscht with cabbage, farfel pudding, and duck, if you like . . ."

"No, that's not what I mean. I mean what day is it today?"

He thinks a while. "What day is it today? Tuesday, the 18th."

"And what is the name of this city?"

"Which city?"

"*This* city. *Your* city. What is it called?"

He stands motionless, stares at me and says: "What do you mean, what's it called? It's called Vitebsk, that's what it's called."

"You're lying!" I retort, "You're dreaming, my friend. The name of your city is Smolensk, not Vitebsk."

"Ha, ha, ha! Ha, ha, ha!"

Apparently the greatest Jewish humorist has impressed the waiter as the greatest fool in the world, for he turns aside and buries his snout in the serviette so that I shouldn't see him choking with laughter. I turn back for another look at the posters. There it is in huge letters:

SHOLOM ALEICHEM IN VITEBSK!

In Vitebsk? All-Merciful God, how can I be in Vitebsk when I'm supposed to be in Smolensk? I don't know what to do with myself. Who needs borscht? Who can think of duck? I must leave for Smolensk. But in order to know my "right place in the liturgy" I decide first to check with my wife. She can telegraph me immediately to tell me where I am to be the first evening. In all matters concerning dates and itineraries, my wife is the expert. And in order to speed things up, I knock out an urgent message: "WHERE AM I TODAY? TELEGRAPH REPLY."

The telegram sent, I feel more relaxed and return to the beetroot borscht, the farfel pudding, and the duck. Then I lie down for a snooze and, as the custom is, fall asleep. In my sleep I am beset by dreams of blonde women and black cats. A bad sign: whenever I dream of blonde women and black cats I can expect the worst. And so it was. Suddenly, as I woke, I realized it was late. If I don't hurry, I'll miss Smolensk. I run to the train, climb aboard, and sitting comfortably in the compartment, I ask the conductor, "When do we arrive in Smolensk?" He pauses, fixes his eyes on the points of his boots, and informs me that we will be in Smolensk at six o'clock the following morning.

"What do you mean, six o'clock tomorrow morning? I must be in Smolensk no later than seven this evening!"

The conductor listens to me patiently and shows me on his watch that from here to Smolensk it takes even the express train no less than twelve hours and some minutes—and since it is already some minutes past four, how can we possibly reach Smolensk today? As it happens he is correct, but what good is that to me? I have lost Smolensk! What am I to do now? Return to Vitebsk? The devil take it! Let me at least figure out where I stand with Mogilev. And no one knows this as well as my wife. At this point I recall that I asked her to wire me in Vitebsk. Now I am enroute to Smolensk.

How will the cat cross the stream? A learned Jew, as they say, finds a way. So I get busy and write another telegram to my wife and I give it to the conductor at the next station: "TELEGRAPH SMOLENSK. WHEN AM I IN MOGILEV?"

Now, let us take a moment for a bit of language analysis, Tractate Philology, and translate literally two telegrams from the language in which they were written, Russian, into our own Yiddish. In the first I seem to be asking my wife, "Where am I?" *(Srotchi, gdie ya sevodnia?)* In the second, I seem to ask her to telegraph Smolensk while I am still in Mogilev *(Telegraphiroi Smolensk, kogda ya Mogiliovie?)* If you, for example, were to receive two such wires, you could only conclude that the sender has gone mad. And let's not forget that Smolensk is no possum and did not play dead either. At Smolensk they waited for me at the station on the 18th from 1 p.m. till 12 midnight. The audience stormed through the hall and accused the Zionists of having perpetrated a swindle, of having dreamed up a Sholom Aleichem and then run off with the cash. There was nothing for it but to open the money box and refund the tickets. In great dismay, the Zionists and Bundists got together after midnight and sent off a telegram to my home: "WHAT HAPPENED TO SHOLOM ALEICHEM?"

Now let us turn our attention from the prince to the princess. My wife, may she live and be well, when she received these three jolly telegrams, wasted no time and started out immediately to Mogilev. Now this may seem absurd. Why Mogilev? Well, if you'll hear me out, you will see for yourself that she is a sage.

In the first place, she knows me well—we weren't married yesterday. She knows that if I telegraph her from Vitebsk to wire me at Smolensk, I must be in Mogilev. You see, she remembers a previous occasion. I was once in Warsaw on my way home to Kiev for Passover. Suddenly, on the first day of Passover, she gets a wire from me that I am spending the holiday in Holendre, not far from Wapniarke. How did I get to

Wapniarke, of all places, which is on the way between Szmerinke and Odessa? Don't ask. I meant no evil, God forbid; my intentions were good. As I was in a terrible hurry to get home, I changed from one express train to another until I found myself on the Odessa line, stranded at the Holendre station. Still, it could have been worse. At least I didn't go as far as Riga! That's what comes of hurrying. No wonder people say, "Haste makes waste." Well, that was in the first place.

In the second place, my wife figured that according to my telegrams the misfortune had occurred not in Vitebsk, nor in Smolensk, but somewhere in between. Accordingly, she could choose no better central point than Mogilev. She was certain that even in the best of circumstances there must have been a collision between two locomotives: the one from Smolensk to Vitebsk with the one from Vitebsk to Smolensk. In such a crash, she assumed, all the cars must have been crushed into splinters—no fewer than two hundred passengers killed, several hundred badly wounded, and among the rest, many deranged, including (it stands to reason) myself.

Generally my wife has a habit, whenever I leave home, of imagining the very worst disasters in the world. Wherever there may be a flood, a collision, a collapsed bridge, a thunderstorm, an earthquake, a conflagration, a sudden epidemic, an ambush of armed guerillas, a snake bite (which occurs once every five hundred years)—she imagines these disasters lurking for me, waiting for me to set out. And when I return home in one piece she can't believe her eyes, staring at me incredulously as though I'd been snatched from the very jaws of death.

This time, too, when she saw me hale and strong, she burst into tears like a child. "Why are you crying, my little fool?" I ask her.

"He wants to know why I'm crying!" she replies. "For him this is another Rovno!"

What has Rovno to do with it, you ask. That's another episode from my travels. If you really want to hear it, I'll tell you what happened in Rovno. A few years ago, I was languishing in Petersburg, trying to get a permit for a Yiddish newspaper, and I decided to go home by way of Vilna. I had told my wife that I was leaving Petersburg on such and such a day; that if I were required to be in Vilna, I would stay there for a day or two, and if not I would come home right from Petersburg. So it was. It turned out that the stopover in Vilna was unnecessary, and knowing how agreeable this news would be to my wife, I sent her a night telegram en route. As sleepy as I was, I translated the words "coming directly" somewhat carelessly; instead of *Yedu priamo,* I wrote *Yedu Rovno.* And since I hadn't seen the children for some time, I added two more words, *Vstretshay dietmi,* meaning "Meet me with the children." Short and sweet. I reach home that evening and rush around the depot like a lunatic. Where is my wife? Where are the children? Not a soul! I ride home—the house is dark as a cemetery. I ring and ring, tear at the bell, pound at the door. At last the cook appears, like a sleepy cat. I grab the swarthy Litvak. "Where is the Mistress? Where are the children?"

"The Mistress?" she says, wiping her nose. "She's not here."

"What do you mean, *she's* not here?" I ask her in Litvakese.

"They all went away."

"What do you mean, went away? Where did they go?"

"How should I know? To Rovno."

"Why on earth to Rovno?"

"You're asking *me?* You told them to join you in Rovno."

"*I* told them to join me in Rovno? *Me?*"

"Who then, *me?*" answers the cook, and it seems to me that she is laughing.

You understand? My blood is running out, and she is laughing! I swear to you in all honesty—I'm ashamed to say it, to no one else would I confess this—that never before have I even lifted a finger against another human being! But this sleepy Litvak with her silly laughter so enraged me that I forgot where I was in the world! . . . And how do you think it ended? I had a lawsuit on my hands . . . The word, *Rovno,* cost me plenty, and I had to beg the cook's pardon besides.

In any event, after hearing the good news that my wife and children are in Rovno, I hoist my feet on my shoulders and fly to Rovno. I arrive, but where? What? I can find no one. I make inquiries about a woman with several children. And I am told, "They were here and left." It seems there is nothing left for me to do but to return home. When I get back I find the doctor. What happened? My wife has fallen ill from all her troubles. . . .

"Well, now, let me ask you," I say to my wife after we have both calmed down a little, "why did you fly off with the children to Rovno, and what were you thinking?"

"Don't ask!" she replies. "When I got your telegram telling me to meet you in Rovno with the children, I almost went out of my mind. All kinds of thoughts flew into my head. I thought you had fallen sick somewhere, somewhere around Rovno, with typhus, God forbid, or smallpox."

"What on earth put the idea of smallpox into your head?" I asked, controlling myself.

"That same day I read in the papers that there was smallpox . . . in India."

At this point I can no longer restrain myself and leap up from the chair. "I don't understand! Where is India and where is Petersburg?"

She gazes at me tenderly, like a mother at her child, and says, "Where you're concerned, who knows?"

Now tell me, how much is such a wife worth?

Translated by Etta Blum

GLOSSARY

Aguna—deserted wife who, according to Jewish law, cannot remarry unless her husband's death is certified

bris—ceremony of circumcision for a male child

Chanukah—Jewish holiday commemorating the re-dedication of the Temple in Jerusalem by Judah Maccabee in 165 B.C.

cheder—school

Chelm stories—legendary comic stories told about Jews from the town of Chelm

Gemara—a section of the *Talmud;* sometimes refers to the *Talmud* as a whole

Gevalt!—Help!

golem—a human creature without a soul; a Frankenstein

goyisher kop—literally, in Yiddish, a "Gentile head"; used to suggest something less than brilliance of mind

grager—a noisemaker used in celebrating the Jewish holiday of Purim

Haggadah—set form of comments, prayers, and songs recited on the first two nights of the Passover holiday

haroses—paste made of fruit and wine used in the Passover ritual to symbolize the mortar Jews made as slaves in Egypt

Hasidic—refers to Hasidism, a movement of pietistic enthusiasm among East European Jews that flourished in the late eighteenth and early nineteenth centuries and continues to exist even today

341

havdoleh candle—braided candle used at the ritual that marks the conclusion of the Sabbath

Hershel Ostropolier stories—comic stories about a Jewish scamp named Hershel Ostropolier

Kaddish—mourner's prayer, usually said by the son

khale—Sabbath bread loaf

Kiddish—blessing said over a cup of wine to celebrate the Sabbath or a holiday

kneydlach—dumplings

knishes—pastries usually filled with potatoes, meat, or buckwheat

Kol Nidre—introductory prayer at Yom Kippur

Lag Baomer—spring holiday commemorating spiritual and armed resistance to the Romans

L'chayim!—a toast to life

mazel tov—congratulations

Megillah—scroll; usually refers to the Scroll of Esther, read on Purim

Midrash—a homily or homiletic interpretation

Purim—holiday commemorating the defeat of Haman by Esther

Rambam—Rabbi Moses ben Maimon, Maimonides, 1135-1204, a great rabbinic authority and philosopher

Rashi—most authoritative commentator on the Bible and *Talmud;* lived 1040-1105

reb—mister

rebbe—rabbi, learned man, teacher

rebbetsen—wife of a rabbi

Rosh Hashanah—Jewish New Year

schlemiel—a loser, sometimes used interchangeably with *schlimazel*

schlimazel—a luckless creature of infinite misfortune

seder—ceremonial meal held during the first two nights of Passover

Sephardim—descendents of Spanish and Portuguese Jews

shammes—sexton

Shavuos—Feast of the Pentecost; holiday celebrating the giving of the Torah to Moses *shimenesre*—the eighteen blessings said in three daily sets of prayers

Shma Yisroel!—the Jewish creed or cry: "Hear, O Israel!"

shochet—ritual slaughterer

shofar—ram's horn blown on the High Holidays

Sholem aleichem—a greeting: "Peace be unto you"

shprakh—language

shtetl—small town in East Europe inhabited mostly by Jews

shul—synagogue

Simkhas-Torah—holiday after Succos celebrating the completion of a year's reading of the Torah

sliches—penitential prayers recited the week before Rosh Hashanah

Succos—autumn holiday of the harvest, celebrated by meals in the *suke* (or booth), commemorating the desert life of the Jews after the Exodus

tallis—prayer shawl

Talmud—collection of writings constituting traditional Jewish civil and religious law

tefillin—phylacteries

Tisha Bov—the ninth day of the Jewish month of Av; a day of fasting and mourning to commemorate the destruction of the Temple in Jerusalem and other disasters

Torah—Pentateuch, the Five Books of Moses; also a term for Jewish learning in general

treyf—unclean; ritually impure

Vilna Gaon—outstanding Jewish scholar and religious authority, Elijah ben Solomon Zalman (1720-1797), known as the sage of Vilna

yarmulke—skullcap

yeshiva—school of advanced Talmudic and rabbinic studies

Yom Kippur—Day of Atonement

BIOGRAPHICAL NOTES

SHOLOM ALEICHEM is the pseudonym of Sholom Rabinovitch, born in 1859 in the small Ukrainian town of Pereyeslav. There and in the neighboring *shtetl* (or Jewish town) of Voronkov he spent his youth. He was educated first at a traditional Jewish *cheder* and then at the local government high school; at seventeen he became resident tutor to the daughter of a wealthy Jewish landowner. The predictable romance between tutor and student flourished into a lifelong marriage.

Rabinovitch worked briefly as a government rabbi *(rabbiner)*, a clerk, and a businessman-speculator, but his writing soon eclipsed all other occupations. After publishing several works in Hebrew, he turned to writing Yiddish fiction in 1883, initiating a prolific and varied literary career. Under the jovial pen name of Sholom Aleichem, the most common term of greeting among Jews, he wrote hundreds of short stories, dramas, novels, feuilletons, and poems. His career coincided with the rapid expansion of the Yiddish press, of which he was one of the major and most popular contributors.

Sholom Aleichem lived with his growing family in Kiev and briefly in Odessa until the pogroms of 1905. Following those disturbances the family left Russia for almost a decade of wandering. In 1906 Sholom Aleichem made his first trip to New York, but was unsuccessful in his attempt to establish himself as a playwright of the flourishing American Yiddish Theatre. He returned to Europe and in 1907 undertook a reading tour through Poland and Russia. He collapsed midway through what had been a triumphant series of personal appearances and spent the following six years recuperating in Southern Italy and Switzerland. In 1914 the family settled in New York, where Sholom Aleichem died on May 13, 1916.

SAUL BELLOW is the distinguished American novelist, author of *Herzog, Humboldt's Gift,* and *Seize the Day,* among other works, and recent winner of the Nobel Prize for Literature.

REUBEN BERCOVITCH has written two novels, *Hasen* and *Odette,* and translated the work of David Bergelson, I. L. Peretz, I. D. Berkowitz, Rachel Weprinsky, and Chaim Grade.

SACVAN BERCOVITCH, Professor of English at Columbia University, is the author of *The Puritan Origins of the American Self,* among other works.

ETTA BLUM has published two books of poetry as well as translations of short stories by Eliezer Blum-Alquit, and poems by Jacob Glatstein.

FRANCES AND JULIUS BUTWIN are pioneering translators of Yiddish literature, and Mrs. Butwin is also the coauthor, with her son Joseph, of a critical study of Sholom Aleichem.

GERSHON FREIDLIN has translated works by Ber Mark, Jacob Celemenski, Y. L. Dashevsky, Isaac Raboy, and Raphael Mahler.

HILLEL HALKIN, an American-born writer now living in Israel, is the author of *Letters to an American Jewish Friend.*

NATHAN HALPER was born in New York City, where he attended the Natzionale Radicale Shule and Columbia University; he now lives in Provincetown, Massachusetts.

IRVING HOWE is Distinguished Professor of English at the City University of New York; his most recent books include *World of Our Fathers,* which won the 1977 National Book Award, *Leon Trotsky,* and *Celebrations and Attacks*.

SEYMOUR LEVITAN is currently translating a collection of Rochl Korn's poems and stories.

The late ISAAC ROSENFELD was the author of the novel *Passage from Home;* his essays have been collected as *An Age of Enormity*.

MIRIAM WADDINGTON, professor of English at York University in Toronto, is the author of twelve books of poetry and the editor of *The Collected Poems of A. M. Klein*.

RUTH R. WISSE, Chairman of the Jewish Studies Program at McGill University in Montreal, is the author of *The Schlemiel as Modern Hero, The Shtetl and Other Modern Yiddish Novellas*.

LEONARD WOLF has written, among other books, *The Passion of Israel, A Dream of Dracula, The Annotated Dracula,* and *The Annotated Frankenstein*.

SETH WOLITZ was 1978-1979 fellow at the National Humanities Institute at the University of Chicago and professor of French and Comparative Literature at the University of Texas.

LAUGH and LEARN

Sam Levenson—everyone's favorite comic. He pokes good-natured fun at everything while offering insights that really hit home.

His invaluable words of wit and wisdom never cease to amuse and entertain.

So if you want to laugh—and learn—read Sam Levenson in paperback from Pocket Books today.

_____44744 IN ONE ERA AND OUT THE OTHER $2.75

> *"A higher laugh quotient than any other book I have read in months. Sam Levenson is worth his wit in gold."*
> —John Barkham

> *"Superb Levenson...there is nothing superber."*—P. G. Wodehouse

_____44743 EVERYTHING BUT MONEY $2.75

> *"Sometimes rollicking, often tender. Most readers savoring this witty memoir of a family rich in everything but money will find it as tasty as a bagel plastered with cream cheese."*—TIME Magazine

---

POCKET BOOKS
Department SL
1230 Avenue of the Americas
New York, N.Y. 10020

POCKET BOOKS

Please send me the books I have checked above. I am enclosing $_____ (please add 50¢ to cover postage and handling for each order, N.Y.S. and N.Y.C. residents please add appropriate sales tax). Send check or money order—no cash or C.O.D.s please. Allow up to six weeks for delivery.

NAME_____

ADDRESS_____

CITY_____STATE/ZIP_____